Wilder
Ashburn

Evangeline
Sullivan

A PERFECT SONG

copyright

ISBN: 979-8-9922707-4-7

Cover design by Laura Halloran. No generative AI.

Editing by *Lawrence Editing*

lmhalloran.com

author's note

Your mental health matters, so please review the following content warning. If you have no triggers, skip this to avoid spoilers.

This duet contains the following mature themes: heavy emotional angst, anxiety disorder rep, depression rep, neurodivergence rep, other woman drama (no cheating/open relationship), explicit MF sex, degradation/praise kink, nyctophobia (fear of the dark), insomnia, on-page drug use (pills/opioids), active addiction including denial, relapse, and suicidal ideation, narcissistic abuse (not by MC), references to the grooming and abuse of a teenage girl, reference to the miscarriage of a side character, and complex PTSD.

Buckle up, lovely. You're in for a wild ride.

FIRST
VERSE

"It is by going down into the abyss that we recover the treasure of life. Where you stumble, there lies your treasure."

JOSEPH CAMPBELL

intro

intro : *the opening piece of a song that establishes key, tempo, and rhythm*

prologue

LATE AFTERNOON SUNLIGHT dances among leaves in the giant sycamore tree, polka-dotting Wilder's dark, messy hair and broad shoulders with flares of gold. His face is downturned, his focus on the open notebook in his lap. As I watch, he pulls a pencil from between his teeth, scratches a few words onto a page, then tucks it back in his mouth.

This has been going on for ten minutes. Write-chew-write-chew. The anxiety of not knowing what he's writing, coupled with the fact I can't seem to look away, makes me feel like I'm being sunburned in the shade.

I can't take it anymore.

"Stop chewing on my pencil. What are you, five?"

"Better than chewing my nails," he mutters without looking up.

I tuck my hands discreetly under my crossed legs. "Whatever. Are you done yet?"

Speckled green eyes lift from the notebook. He pulls the pencil from between his teeth, the wet eraser briefly depressing his lower lip. My breath catches and my thoughts turn hazy.

"Why do you care what I do with my mouth, Evangeline?" he asks teasingly.

Snapped out of my trance, I glower at him. "I care about my pencil, dumbass."

He wipes it off on his chest, then offers it to me.

I make a face. "Forget it. It's yours now."

His grin is a sunrise that begins in his eyes and spreads across his face, so bright it scorches my cheeks.

"I'm done," he says lightly, tossing the notebook into my lap.

Seizing the distraction, I flip to the page of lyrics we're working on. He left most of them untouched but rewrote the chorus. When I read his messy words in the margin, my stomach flips.

I look up to find him smirking, his eyes narrowed as he waits for my reaction.

"No way. I'm not singing this."

His brows lift. "Why not? Besides, we'd sing it together."

A breeze skips around us, rustling leaves and shifting the paths of sunbeams. My gaze bounces between the words and him. He's not looking at me anymore, his face upturned to the lush, arterial beauty above us.

"It's…" *Incredible,* I think. But what comes out instead is, "Cheesy."

His eyes cut to me sharply. "You think it's cheesy?"

Instant regret fills me. I clear my throat, shaking my head. "No," I say softly. "I don't know why I said that."

But I do.

The words are unlike any he's written before. I don't know

how to feel about them—or maybe they make me feel too much. I'm surprised. Flustered. Curious. My heart is racing. There's a knot in stomach I can't explain.

I read the lyrics again.

BABY, THIS IS DESTINY
I'LL FOLLOW YOU INTO THE SEA
I'LL COME FOR YOU, YOU'LL SEE
SET US FREE — YOU AND ME
DEAD OR ALIVE

Someone definitely inspired this. Does he have a crush on a girl at his school? Is he going to ask her out? Has he already? Is that why he canceled last weekend?

Normally, the fact we go to different high schools is annoying, but I'm suddenly grateful for the distance between our houses and everyday lives. I don't want to see his sunrise smile aimed at someone else.

I refuse to analyze why.

Swallowing the questions clogging my throat, I remind myself that Wilder and I aren't the kind of friends who share every little detail of our lives. Our bond is music, and it transcends the trivial and mundane.

After reading his words a few more times, I close the notebook and drop it to the grass.

"I still like my chorus better."

He scoffs, his gaze drifting past me. Around me. Never landing directly. Silence falls between us, vibrating with words in a language neither of us knows.

I stretch out my legs, then recross them. Chew on a hangnail. Rip out my ponytail and redo it. Pick up my guitar, tune it halfheartedly for a minute, then lay it back in its case. I look at my phone to check the time and am bummed to see my parents aren't picking me up for another half-hour. I can't even text them to come sooner because they're probably already on their way.

Wilder's exaggerated sigh snaps my head up. Frowning, he studies my face. "Are you going to tell me what's wrong?"

I blurt, "Who are the lyrics about?"

His eyes widen. "*That's* why you're being weird?"

My body boils with embarrassment, but I shrug like I don't care about his answer.

Wilder shakes his head slowly. Then he laughs, a burst of disbelief. "I was thinking about *you*, Evangeline."

My ears ring. "W-what?"

He drags a hand through his hair, shoulders twitching in agitation. "Why is that a big deal? You know you're my muse. It's always been this way. It will always *be* this way."

When I don't say anything—I can't even breathe—he huffs and glares at me.

"It doesn't mean I want to see you naked, so stop freaking out."

"I'm not freaking out."

I'm definitely freaking out.

A cloud eclipses the sun, dimming the world. Darkening his eyes from a sunlit glade to a shadowed forest. Despite the warmth of the air, the next gust of wind lifts goose bumps on my arms.

"We aren't a love story." His voice is low. I feel it beneath my skin. In my bones.

"I know," I whisper.

His head tilts. "Do you? Girlfriends and boyfriends are temporary. Background noise. We're neither. We're *more*."

I nod, but it's a reflex, my mind disconnected from the

action. The ground suddenly doesn't feel solid under my hands. My *hands* don't feel solid.

Wilder leans forward, one finger connecting with the cover of the notebook. His eyes are maelstroms sucking me into depths unknown.

"Tell me you understand. Swear to me that no matter what happens, we'll stay the same. You and me—forever, Evangeline."

After a second that lasts a lifetime, I echo, "Forever."

That afternoon, in the dappled shade beneath the sycamore, I swore to wilder we'd always stay the same.

That background noise would never come between us. Never infect our art.

We both lied that day.

It wasn't the first time. Or the last.

Maybe the lies started earlier that summer, when we accidentally brushed against each other in the pool, then jerked away like we'd been electrocuted.

Or maybe they started six years before, when he held my hand as my dad dug a grave in our backyard for our family cat, Pickle. As I'd soaked wilder's shoulder with my tears, I'd asked him to swear he'd never leave me.

Maybe it's my fault for setting the precedent for impossible promises.

Or his fault for believing we could fight gravity by pretending it didn't exist.

Wilder was right about one thing, though — we weren't a love story.

We were something better and immeasurably worse...

we were a perfect song.

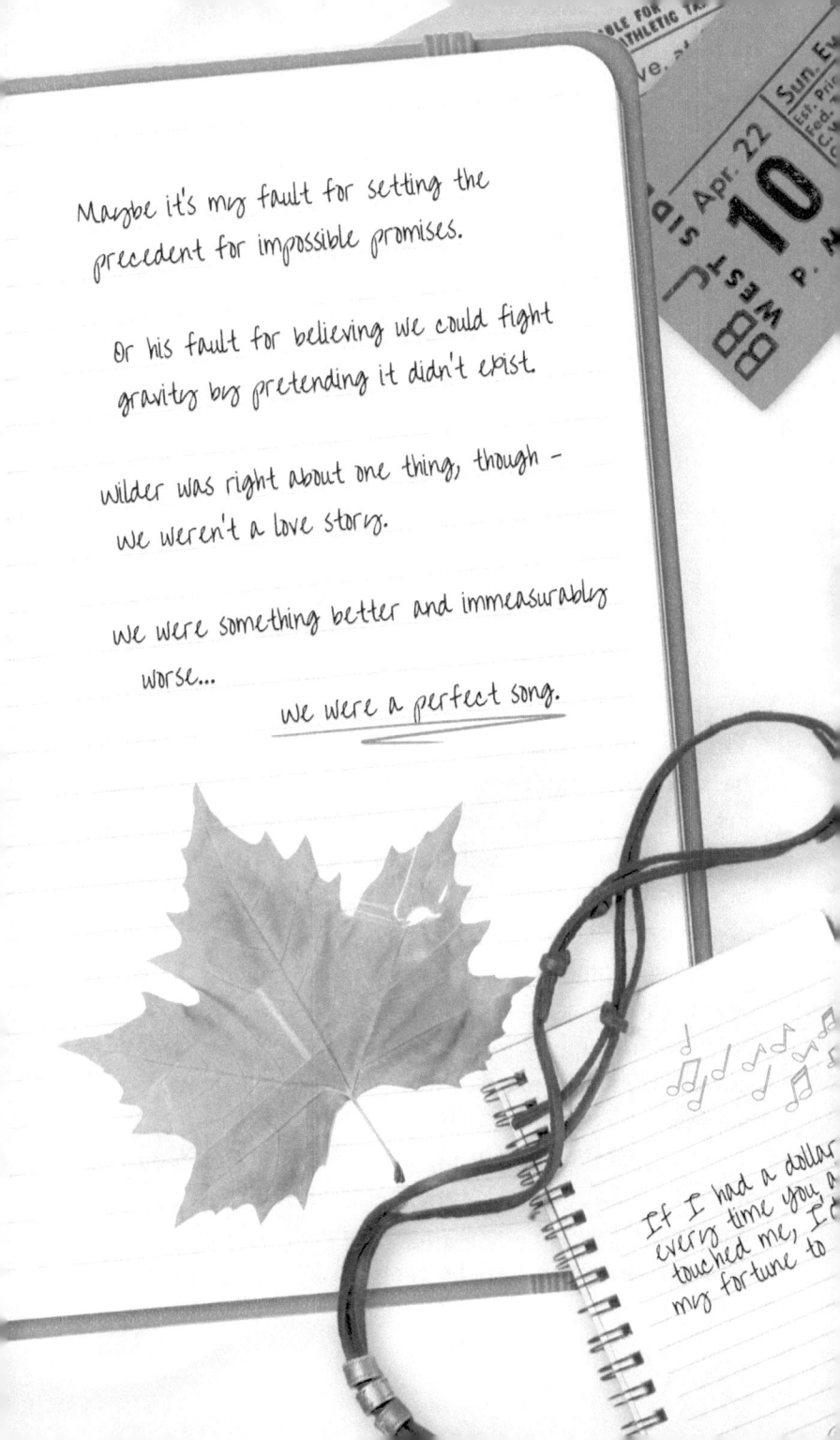

♪ ♪ ♪ ♪ ♪

If I had a dollar
every time you a
touched me, I'd
my fortune to

CHAPTER ONE

evangeline

EVA 20 | WILDER 22

THE VOICES around me melt together, pooling into a backdrop of discordant static. Words drift like debris through my exhausted mind, knocking together, drifting apart. Shapes and sounds. Rhythms and melodies. I can't hold any of them for more than a second before they, too, fade into obscurity.

I don't want to be here. I should be in my backyard, relaxing in my hot tub. Cocooned by silence and reveling in solitude. Instead, the very people I'm most sick of surround me: musicians, the people who work with them, make money off them, and drool over them.

A familiar laugh pulls my gaze across the crowded living room to Wilder, who towers over a cluster of sycophants. Four out of five are displaying too much cleavage; the one man in the bunch has the same look on his face as the women, though. They all want a shot at being the lucky one tonight.

The giant potted plant I'm tucked behind partially obscures Wilder's face, but I can see half of his smile. Straight white teeth. A dimple made more pronounced by the scruff on his face. Dark hair that's too long after the last leg of our tour—so long it skims his broad shoulders and frames his poster-worthy face with haphazard waves.

Eddie offered to buzz it for him a few weeks ago, but Wilder declined and instead started using one of my hair ties to make a ridiculous, tiny topknot to keep it out of his eyes onstage. His flippant excuse was he didn't trust our drummer not to make him bleed. An obvious lie; no one has steadier hands than Eddie.

The real reason is that our fanbase is obsessed with his hair. It has its own hashtag: #wildmane. And after the explosion of concert photos on Instagram in the last few weeks, his topknot has a hashtag, too: #knotmewilder.

Cue eye roll.

"What or who are we hiding from?" asks Rye, sidling up beside me. My best friend's blue eyes sparkle at me from his handsome, freckled face, and for the first time in weeks, my smile is genuine.

"The blob mind," I whisper.

He laughs, clinking his half-empty beer bottle to my full one. We're both underage, but no one here cares. I don't even know whose house this is, only that it belongs to someone from our record label.

"It's good to have you guys home," Rye says, hooking a muscled arm around my neck and smacking a loud kiss on the top of my head. "Life is boring without you."

"It's good to be home, Riley Piley."

He pretends to gag. "You don't call Wilder Why-Why

15

anymore. Stop torturing me. It's not my fault my parents gave me a girl's name."

I smirk. "It was your grandfather's name."

"That was like a hundred years ago."

I concede with a laugh. "Fine. I'll give it a rest."

"Thank fuck."

He rubs his bearded cheek over the top of my head. He may only be nineteen, but he's built like a tank and has been growing beards since puberty. Probably why no one has blinked an eye at the fact he's drinking.

"Did you stop by your parents'?" he asks.

"Not yet." I wince, remembering the disappointment Mom tried and failed to conceal when I told her I needed to decompress for a day. "I'll see them at the barbecue tomorrow. I wouldn't even be here if it weren't for..." I trail off, my gaze moving across the room at the exact moment a woman strokes her hand suggestively down Wilder's chest. He smiles indulgently at her.

Rye sighs heavily. "He guilt tripped you, huh?"

I tear my gaze from Wilder and shrug at Rye. "He had a point. It would have been weird if I didn't show up at our tour wrap party."

He hums. "It's okay to say no to him sometimes, Eva."

I don't bother responding; the argument is ancient and I agree with him. Closing my eyes, I relax into my best friend's solid frame, his wintergreen and moss scent as familiar to me as hugs from my parents.

Looking at us from the outside, we're a mismatched pair. A redheaded behemoth and his lanky blond sidekick. But the bond between Rye and me began when we were in diapers and solidified into something unbreakable over the years.

We've known Wilder just as long, but he's always been a few steps outside our circle. And not because he's two years older than me and three years older than Rye, or because we never invited him in. It's just who he is. No one gets too close to Wilder. Not even me, despite my reputation in our families as being the only one he listens to.

If only they knew.

It surprised no one when the three of us formed our first band at ages ten, eleven, and thirteen respectively. We have music in our blood. Our dads are legends, members of the insanely popular indie rock band, Breaking Giants. Wilder's dad, Julian Ashburn, is the lead singer and songwriter. Rye's dad, Nick Henderson, plays drums. And my dad, Matt Sullivan, handles lead guitar and backup vocals. Suffice to say, our families have been enmeshed since before our births.

Nine years later, Wilder and I are still making music—music being about the only thing we agree on. Rye caught the bug, too, but realized early on he preferred to be behind the scenes. He found his niche in mixing and production, and his talents scored him an internship right out of high school at Icon Studios, one of Seattle's oldest and most revered recording studios. He even submitted his application with a fake name to ensure he was granted an interview on his own merits and not the power of his father's fame.

"Have you figured out what you're going to do?" he asks softly, gaze roaming the spacious living room and the throngs of people before snapping back to me.

A lump forms in my throat. "I think so."

Hearing what I'm not saying, he gives me a sympathetic squeeze. "No one is going to judge you." He pauses, wincing. "Except maybe You Know Who. But he'll get over it."

I doubt that.

My gaze slides across the room right as Wilder looks our way. He smiles when he sees Rye—his real smile, not the one he uses on the public—but it freezes when he sees me tucked

17

under his arm. Our eyes meet. His glisten with an apology I don't want to hear again.

"Whoa," Rye whispers. "Why is he looking at you like he thinks you hate him? What happened?"

My mouth opens, then closes. There's no polite way to say a girl my age almost OD'd in Wilder's hotel room last week while he was screwing her friend a few feet away.

He finally realized what was happening and called our manager, Mack Martinez, who called me. The two of us cleaned up the mess like we always do, and afterward, I hung back like an idiot to ask Wilder if he was okay. Still wasted, he invited me to give him a blowjob—like he was doing *me* a favor—because he hadn't finished earlier.

Shoving the memory away, I lie to my best friend's face. "Nothing. He just knows I don't want to be here." I hand him my unfinished beer. "On that note, I've done my time. We'll catch up tomorrow, okay? Don't let Wilder suck you into any craziness tonight."

Rye's eyes scan mine before he nods. "See you tomorrow. Love you."

"Love you, too."

I make it halfway to the front door before a familiar figure intercepts me. Eddie's eyes have a telltale glaze as he grins at me.

"Don't tell me you're leaving!"

I force a chuckle. "I have an overdue date with my mattress. We've missed each other very much."

He laughs, then clears his throat and runs a hand over his short blond hair. "Well, I'm glad I caught you. I was wondering... now that we're home, do you want to go on a date? With me?"

For the twenty-millionth time, I regret the night a month into our tour when I found myself drunkenly making out

18

with Eddie in a hotel hallway. The shittiest part is I hadn't even known it was him at first—even though he and our bassist, Jax, are a year apart in age, the brothers look like twins. They have similar haircuts and both had been wearing black T-shirts and jeans that night.

As embarrassing as Wilder's interruption was, I'm grateful he showed up. I wasn't in my right mind.

I *should* say yes to a date with Eddie. He's objectively attractive, talented, and kind. Despite the fact I essentially threw myself at him that night—I might have also begged him to take my virginity—he's never made me feel uncomfortable or brought it up since.

In a perfect world, I'd be smitten with him. But my world is chaos.

"Sorry, Eddie. I don't think it's a good idea to mess with our working dynamic."

To my relief, he lives up to my opinion of him when I see disappointment but no anger in his eyes. "I figured. No hard feelings, Eva. See you next week?"

Probably not.

I nod and give him a hug, aware that the next time he and Jax hear my name, they'll probably curse it.

Over Eddie's shoulder, I spot Wilder and Rye chatting. The groupies have been dismissed, which shouldn't please me but does.

Like he can feel my gaze, Wilder turns his head. Before our stares can connect, I jerk away from Eddie and make a beeline for the door.

CHAPTER TWO

evangeline

If I had a dollar for every time
you almost touched me
I'd give my fortune to the wind
cause unlike me she can move
Move against your skin

CURLS OF STEAM lift from the glowing surface of the hot tub. Water ripples decadently around my bare shoulders. Above me, strands of string lights bisect a sky framed by evergreens. The neighborhood is quiet at 2:00 a.m., so quiet that if I close my eyes, I can almost believe I'm in a peaceful, remote forest.

My peace shatters as the back slider on my two-bedroom bungalow slams open and Wilder storms onto my deck.

I sit up fast, my stomach somersaulting as I quickly cross my arms over my naked chest. "What the hell! What are you doing here? I gave you a key for emergencies only!"

"This is a fucking emergency," he growls. Both hands

clenched in his hair, he paces back and forth across the deck, each footstep a resounding *thud*. "Tell me it's bullshit. Tell me you're not thinking about quitting."

My breath stills, a near-crushing weight settling on my chest. *Goddammit, Rye.* I shouldn't have left him at the party unsupervised, not with Wilder there. Rye is shit at keeping secrets, and Wilder is a master at spotting and extracting them.

I open my mouth with no idea what I'm going to say, but Wilder continues, "Is this about what happened in Vegas? I already said I was sorry. I was drunk, okay? It's not an excuse, just an explanation. I fucked up. Simple as that. You said you forgave me."

He stops suddenly, his chest heaving. Two steps bring him to the edge of the sunken hot tub. "What do I have to do? Do you want me to beg?"

My jaw drops as he lowers to his knees and clasps his hands over his chest.

"Wilder—stop. Get up."

His eyes veer downward, then widen and jerk back up. "You're naked."

"No shit," I snap. "I thought I was home alone."

Sagging backward so his weight rests on his feet, he whispers, "Please don't do this."

None of this is going how I wanted it to, but on the heels of that thought is the realization that it was never going to happen according to any plan I made—nothing with this man ever does.

"Grab my robe," I tell him. "Behind you on the chair."

He drags himself to his feet and fetches my robe, then holds it open and averts his eyes from my body. Bitterness makes my teeth grind as I step out of the water and snatch it from him, then slip into it. Once the belt is tied, I push past him and walk into the house.

He follows me inside, yanking the slider behind him. The frame is a little warped, and he mutters obscenities under his breath as he wrestles the door closed.

"I'll never understand why you live here."

I flop onto my second-hand couch in my tiny living room, ignoring the barb. Wilder, despite being obsessed with making a name for himself separate from his father's, has zero problems using his family's wealth to erase every inconvenience from his life.

He thinks Rye and I are idiots for not taking advantage of our parents' money; we think he's a hypocrite and a snob. If he was only that, maybe this would be easier. But he's also the most complex, beautiful, insanely talented person I know.

Dropping onto the couch beside me, he cradles his head in his hands. I steel my heart against the dejected curve of his shoulders. The sad fact is I can't be certain if it's an act or not.

At least he doesn't seem to be drunk or high.

"I *have* forgiven you for what happened in Vegas," I say hesitantly. "But forgiving isn't the same as forgetting. I can't do it anymore. I'm tired of being your babysitter, of making sure you don't run out of condoms, disappear for hours at a time, or choke on vomit—"

"I get it," he interrupts, hands falling as he straightens and faces me. "I got caught up in the bullshit. I'll slow down. I promise."

My heart pounds so hard my mouth tastes like pennies. I want to believe him—so, so badly—but it's too late. If all we did was write songs and perform together, it might be another story. But that's only a small part of the life we've chosen, and the insanity of the last two years has sucked the joy from it. From me.

Now that the rollercoaster of signing to a label, recording our debut album, and our first official tour has finally slowed, I want off the ride. Even if it means blowing up the most intimate, maddening, ecstatic partnership I've ever known and probably ever will. Even if I'm passing up a once-in-a-lifetime opportunity to have my music in millions of ears. Those are risks I'm willing to take—that I *have* to take.

It's a simple matter of survival. Thanks to the magic we make in the studio, the line between my head and heart is already blurred where he's concerned. I have to get away from him before I cross the point of no return.

Falling in love with Wilder Ashburn will destroy me.

"I hope you do slow down," I say carefully, "but I can't be your conscience anymore. I want a life that's mine, not one that's an extension of yours. You and I both know the label will bend over backward to find you another keyboardist and backup vocalist. The album is taking off, and the tour created a ton of buzz. Besides, Night Theory is your baby, not mine. You'll be fine without me."

Desperation twists his features. The hand closest to me twitches like he wants to reach for me. But he won't. He never does—sober, at least.

"Is this about the attention I'm getting? The spotlight? I wanted you to do lead vocals on half the album, but you refused! Fuck it—let's rerecord. Take my guitar, take my mic. You can have whatever you want!"

"No." Pain claws at my chest, propelled by the real agony on his face. "They don't want me, Wilder. They never have. The label, the fans, they want you. Your voice, your presence. They need you."

"But I need *you*," he grinds out, his unique, spotted irises flashing with fury. "You're my fucking muse, and you know damn well I'm yours. Nothing will ever compare to us, to

23

what we make together. You and me—we're musical destiny. So you can't leave me. You can't. We're endgame, Evangeline. We're forever. You *promised*."

I suck in a breath, heat blooming in my chest and face. Tears prick my eyes, my heart breaking and overflowing at the same time.

Those words... they're weapons and he knows it. He knows all about my confusing feelings and he's using them against me. There's no mercy in his eyes. No remorse. Only anger and calculation.

"Fuck you," I choke out.

His gaze sharpens and darkens. "If that's what it takes, then let's go." He reaches for the hem of his shirt, lifting it enough for me to see a swath of taut, golden skin and a trail of dark hair.

"You're unbelievable," I snarl, leaping off the couch and knocking my shin against the coffee table in my effort to put space between us. I stalk to the front door and pull it open, ignoring the throb in my leg, the throb in my chest.

"I'm leaving the band. I'd really hoped we could handle this like adults, but I should have known better."

He rises and moves around the couch, his eyes tracking me like a predator. I stand my ground even when he veers toward me instead of the door. Even when he towers over me and his intoxicating scent surrounds me. It's not bodywash. Not cologne. Just *him*, like he was born with a midnight rainstorm in his cells.

The heat from his body breaches my robe, sinking into my still-drying skin. His gaze drops to my mouth and my breath hitches. Ribbons of heat curl and twist in my belly and lower.

I hate that after everything I've seen, everything I know about him, my body still betrays me like it's done for the last

24

four years. Ever since I walked in on him getting a blowjob from Christine Buchanan, a girl he went to high school with. Until that moment, I'd been able to *mostly* separate his physical allure from my attraction to his mind, his soul. But when he'd looked at me standing frozen in his bedroom doorway, Christine's head bobbing in his lap, and his eyes flared with something I'd never seen directed at me before, that boundary was erased.

I've been fighting a losing battle since.

"I hate you," I whisper.

"No, you don't," he says huskily. "And that's the problem, isn't it? You want me so fucking bad and you can't handle the fact I haven't taken you."

He steps even closer, his chest grazing my robe as his other hand pushes the front door closed. The soft click makes me flinch.

I scream at myself to move, but I can't. Right now, I hate us both. Hate what we've become. But most of all, I hate that he's right. I want him, and I can't handle that he doesn't want me back.

I'm powerless to protest when he grabs ahold of my messy bun and jerks it so that my head falls back. He doesn't touch my skin—his unspoken rule—but he doesn't have to. He's all around me, his nearness caressing every inch of my body. A hot, prickling sensation shoots from my scalp, pulsing down my back to settle between my legs. I squeeze my thighs together, but it only makes the ache worse.

All I can do is stare up at him, silent tears of anger and misery pooling in my eyes as he lowers his mouth toward mine.

"We made a pact," he murmurs, his breath tickling my lips. "Are you asking me to break it?"

I swallow hard, remembering the night we swore to never

cross the physical line. It wasn't long after I caught him with Christine. We were sitting on his bedroom floor with our guitars. We'd just written our best song to date—the same song that would eventually get us noticed by a scout from Indigo Records. We hadn't known it then, of course, but we still had that feeling of achieving something impossible. Capturing lightning in a bottle.

We were grinning at each other. I don't know who kissed who first, but I do remember him jerking away seconds after our lips touched. I remember the panic in his face as he jumped to his feet and started pacing, his voice shredding all the joy of the last moments.

"We can't. No. That didn't happen. We're not going out like that, Evangeline. How many incredible bands have broken up because they couldn't keep sex separate from the art? Too many. We can't risk it."

Reeling from his tirade, I hadn't protested when he made me swear we'd never kiss again. Never touch. Never, ever fall in love.

One more promise made.

One more nail in our coffin.

Now, I summon the fraying threads of my dignity and snap, "I don't want anything to do with you. You disgust me."

His lips curl mockingly. "Oh yeah? That's not what your pupils are telling me, or that pulse in your pretty neck." His gaze drops over my chest, dragging along the sliver of skin between the robe's lapels. When his eyes lift back to mine, they're blazing with derision. "If you're so horny, why didn't you go home with Eddie? Or did he not pop that sweet little cherry yet?"

A flash of shock gives way to rage. "He did," I lie. "My first time was perfect."

His nostrils flare, his jaw flexing, eyebrows drawing together.

Lost in the chaos of us, I laugh bitterly. "What—you thought I was going to stay a virgin forever while you screwed every groupie over eighteen?"

His fingers tighten in my hair, sending more fiery bolts across my scalp. "He doesn't deserve you," he growls. "I don't, either. But if you need me to fuck you, Evangeline, I will—if that's what it takes to prevent you from throwing away our future. But I'll never be your boyfriend. I'm more than that stupid label, and you're more than that, too. *We* are more than meaningless physical release."

Something inside me breaks—the final piece of me that was holding onto impossible hope. A fresh swell of tears makes tracks on my face as I look up into eyes that no longer feel like a safe haven.

"Get out," I whisper, my voice thin but unyielding.

His lips part as he sucks in a breath. His fingers spasm, releasing my hair, and I take a swift step back.

"Evangeline." My name trembles in the air. "Please. I'm sorry. Just tell me what you want."

"Get out of my house, Wilder. And leave the key." My voice is strong now, as cold and hard as my newly fossilized heart. "Whatever we were is done. We broke it. It's time to move on."

With sluggish movements, he dips a hand in his back pocket and holds up a silver key. I snatch it from his fingers, then wrench open the front door. He walks past me, stalling on the threshold.

Not looking back, he says softly, "Maybe you're right—

maybe we're broken. But we'll never be done, Evangeline. Never."

The second his foot is out of the way, I close and lock the door, then throw the key into a nearby bowl. Then I walk to the kitchen where my phone is charging on the counter. Adrenaline makes my fingers shake as I type a text and send it.

> Fuck you Rye. I can't believe you told him

My phone rings in my hand, a picture of Rye on the screen that normally makes me smile. His eyes are crossed, his tongue out. I jab the red X to decline the call. Seconds later, the device buzzes with a series of texts.

> I'm so fucking sorry

> Did you talk to him? What did he say?

> Are you okay?

> I suck. I'm sorry

After an internal war that lasts close to a minute, I sigh and text him back.

> I'm fine. It's done. I'll see you at the barbecue tomorrow

I throw my phone back on the counter and drag myself to the couch, where I collapse and finally, finally let the last two years pour out of me in sobs.

CHAPTER THREE

FROM BEHIND DARK SUNGLASSES, I watch Evangeline and Rye chatting on the other side of my parents' backyard. They're standing not ten feet from the sycamore tree.

Our tree.

My fingers squeeze the neck of the bottle in my hand, my knuckles cracking from the force. If it weren't for the bruises beneath Evangeline's eyes and the furtive glances she's been sending me since she got here, I'd think she was unaffected by blowing up our lives last night.

> *"Whatever we were is done. We broke it. It's time to move on."*

She didn't break it, though. I did. And like an absolute asshole, last night I took what was broken, lit it on fire, and kicked the ashes into our eyes.

But it wouldn't have mattered if I'd been a saint. From the second Rye told me she was leaving the band, I knew there was nothing I could do to stop her. Once Evangeline makes up her mind about something—from a lyric to what she wants for dinner—there's no arguing with her. No changing her mind.

And she's done with me.

Distracted by the heaviness in my chest and the way the sunlight glints off her pale hair, I startle when someone sits in the Adirondack chair beside mine. My dad stretches his tattooed legs over the grass, crossing his ankles. I don't look at him, instead letting my gaze wander over the backyard and the dozen or so people I've known most or all my life.

My dad's bandmates—Nick Henderson, Matt Sullivan, and Jackson Everett—are playing some weirdly complicated frisbee game. For dudes in their fifties, they're pretty fit. I hope I'm half as active as they are when I'm their age. Their wives, including my mom, are sprawled on lounge chairs near the giant pool where six kids between the ages of eleven and seventeen are currently competing for the biggest cannonball.

The younger kids periodically call for Eva and Rye to join them in the water. They won't ask me, though. Even if I wasn't basically hiding on the far side of the yard, everyone knows I'm not much for group activities. Sometimes—today, as a prime example—I wonder why I still come to these things.

"You've been avoiding me all day."

My dad's voice is mellow, but I feel the pressure of his stare on the side of my face. I take a sip of lukewarm root beer, wishing it were alcohol, then look at him—at the famous, handsome face that still gets photographed and drooled over, the dark hair without a single gray, and the bronze eyes that are currently filled with concern.

"Don't take it personally. I avoid most people." I tip the bottle his way. "I am, after all, the son of Julian Ashburn."

I hate the worry creasing his brow. Right now, I hate

pretty much everything, including the fact I look so much like him. My hair is curlier and my eyes are my mom's, but the tabloids aren't wrong—I'm basically my father's clone.

He opens his mouth, but I speak first.

"Please don't spout some AA slogan about how we're only as sick as our secrets. I told Mom what happened when she cornered me right as I walked in the door, and I know she told you."

"Fair enough." His gaze veers away as he settles deeper in the chair. Thinking he's done grilling me, I relax a little. Then he says, "There are times I wish you weren't, you know."

I frown. "Weren't what?"

"So much like me."

Yeah, same.

Only my reasons are different than his. I detest the constant comparisons between my music and his, but he's talking about the similarities in our temperaments. My moodiness and isolation, especially when I'm working on songs. My tendency to horde my private thoughts and mask myself with a false persona in public. All of which makes him and my mom worry that in addition to following in his musical footsteps, I'll walk his darker roads, too.

I'm not stupid; the concern is valid. Addiction and music are intertwined in our family tree. Mom was spared the genetic bullet that took her own mother when she was a kid, but Dad was a crazy alcoholic during his teens. Thankfully, he straightened his life out when he was twenty and has been sober longer than I've been alive. He's told me enough stories over the years to make me both appreciate the fact I've never seen him drink and have a healthy wariness of my own habits.

But he's wrong—they're wrong. I'm not him. I can handle my shit.

Memories of that night in Vegas arise, but I shove them down. I know I made mistakes on tour. I overindulged. We all did, even Evangeline. I'd never seen her as drunk as she was the night I found her and Eddie in a hotel hallway dry humping each other.

The thought of them sneaking away on a different night, of him taking her virginity, makes me want to kill someone.

Preferably Eddie.

My eyes find Evangeline again, but I look away before she can feel me watching her.

"I know you're angry at her, Wild," murmurs my dad, "but I'm sure she has good reasons for stepping away. Give it a little time. Don't let this end your friendship."

I bite my tongue.

Evangeline and I aren't *friends*. We never have been. Most of our childhood, she was my unwanted shadow, following me around and poking her nose into my business. I could never escape her and by extension Rye, who trailed in her wake.

It all changed when I was thirteen and she was eleven and she handed me a sheet of lined paper covered in short verses. As I read them, I heard a melody. Halting and imperfect but still shockingly clear. I grabbed my guitar and a pencil. We spent three hours perfecting our first song, and it didn't matter that the song itself was crap.

Those hours changed us. We traded parts of our souls, and since that day, when she writes, I hear, and when I write, she hears.

We're not friends. We're *entangled*. She's inside me just like I'm inside her.

And now she wants the pieces of her soul back? *My* pieces?

Never fucking happening.

32

"Anyway, I'm here if you want to talk."

I nod. "Thanks, Dad."

He squeezes my shoulder and walks toward the pool where the kids are now waging war on each other with foam noodles. My eleven-year-old twin sisters, Olive and Ivy, are currently trying to drown Eva's fifteen-year-old brother, Hunter. Normally their antics would make me smile, or at least take the edge off my bad mood.

Not today.

My mood sours even further as Eva and Rye approach the pool. They're still talking. Always fucking talking. Rye's mouth moves nonstop as he peels off his T-shirt, leaving him in black swim trunks. He winds up the fabric and whips it at Eva, who dodges and laughs. A forced laugh, but still a laugh. I'm sure she's pissed at Rye for spilling her secret to me last night. But him, she'll forgive. Even though I didn't say a damn thing to prompt Rye's confession, I have no doubt I've been cast in the role of the villain.

Eva pulls her tank top over her head and steps out of her shorts, revealing a blue bikini. My stomach tightens at the sight of her full breasts in the tiny top. Her long, lean legs. Small waist. Subtly flaring hips.

The house could explode right now and I wouldn't even notice.

My parents' biggest worry is that I'll become an addict. They don't know I already am one, that I've been heroically abstaining from my drug of choice for years, fighting its hold over me with everything I am.

Like an alcoholic with booze, one sip of Evangeline will be too many and a million not enough. It's why I don't touch her. Ever. Last night was the closest I've been to succumbing. Even contact between my fingers and the silky strands of her hair was a risk, one I'm paying for now as I watch her wind

33

the heavy, white-gold mass into a bun on the top of her head and remember the way her pupils dilated as I yanked that hair last night.

Given the pointedness of my stare, I'm unsurprised when her head turns in my direction. I've long chalked up our weird awareness of each other's regard as a symptom of our souls' entanglement. I know she can't see my eyes through my sunglasses, and she's too far away for me to see her mismatched irises—one hazel, one pale blue-gray—but it doesn't matter. For five long seconds, we're alone in the universe.

Then Rye picks her up and throws her into the pool. I hate that he can touch her without consequence. I hate that she lets him.

Dropping my head back, I close my eyes and take long, slow breaths until my balls stop aching and my dick deflates. The discomfort eventually fades—at least the physical one. Mentally I'm still a fucking wreck.

An indeterminable length of time later, a shadow falls over me. I blink up at my mom. Her dark curls are haloed by sunlight, her expressive face wearing a soft smile.

She holds out a small black notebook and a pencil.

"No," I rasp.

"Yes."

If anyone on Earth can come close to understanding me, it's my mom. Maybe because she understands my dad so well. Or maybe because everyone's wrong and I'm actually more like her than him. At least on the inside.

"I can't," I whisper, but I still take her offering.

She clasps my face in her graceful hands and stares at me with eyes I see in the mirror every day.

"We don't back away from pain," she says gently but firmly. "We seek out the cracks in our hearts and dive inside.

34

It's okay to be afraid of the unknown, but we have to take the dive. It's the only way to keep the darkness at bay. Scoop it out with words, Wild. With music. Don't let it rise over your head."

My voice cracks as I confess, "I don't know if I can do it without her."

Her eyes burn with understanding and compassion. "You can, and you will."

CHAPTER FOUR

evangeline

THE PALATIAL HOME Wilder grew up in is shadowed
and quiet as I walk up carpeted stairs and down a hallway.

Sounds from the backyard drift through open windows:
squeals from the kids still in the pool, laughter and shouts
from adults. My stomach grumbles at the scent of smoking
wood chips. I should be outside helping my dad with the grill
—it's been a Sullivan tradition since I was a kid. But when he
started prepping burgers, I decided to avoid the questions in
his laser-like blue eyes and hid in a chair on the outskirts of
the women.

Unfortunately, where I sat put me in Rose's direct line of
sight, and her concerned glances made my skin itch with
guilt. Or maybe the itching was due to all the sun and chlo-
rine in combination with my lack of sleep last night. Either
way, when Wilder's brother, River, walked over to ask Rose
where he went and she said he was taking a nap, I slipped
away with a mumbled excuse of needing the bathroom.

I just want to make sure he's okay.

In the light of a new day, the certainty and conviction I
felt last night are murky, clouded by a jumbled mix of anxi-

ety, longing, and sadness. We both said hurtful things; it wasn't the first time and likely won't be the last. All I really feel right now is the pain of the distance between us. I don't want to accept that a lifetime of friendship could be over, that the boy I grew up with has changed so much he's now a stranger.

At the door of his old bedroom, I press my ear to the wood and hear soft music. My heart kicks against my ribs as I knock.

"Wilder?"

When seconds pass with no response, I turn the knob and push the door open a crack. He's on the bed facing the window, his old gray comforter tangled around his jean-clad legs. From his deep, even breathing, he's fast asleep.

I slip into the room and close the door behind me. Approaching the bed, I step out of my sandals and crawl onto the mattress, then lie down and press myself to his warm back. I want to put my arms around him. Hold him. But that would be breaking the rules. I'm already bending them by touching him through his clothes.

I don't know how long I lie there, my cheek against his spine, but it's long enough for my tears to darken his soft gray T-shirt.

"Are you crying on me, Fairy?"

His gravelly words throw my heart into my stomach. It takes me several tries to find my voice. "You haven't called me that in years."

When I was five, a kid in my class called me a freak because of my heterochromia. I developed an immediate and overwhelming insecurity about my eyes. I begged my parents to buy me an eyepatch and when they wouldn't, I made one myself by gluing yarn to a piece of cardboard I'd cut from a cereal box. Then I refused to take it off my gray eye, even hiding it at night so they wouldn't find it and throw it away.

My mom told Rose what was going on, and Wilder overheard the phone call. When our families gathered that weekend, he pulled me aside. With all the solemn authority in his seven-year-old self, he told me that my pale gray iris didn't make me a freak. It made me a descendant of powerful fairies and meant I could see beyond the veil of the physical world to realities invisible to everyone else. Then he pulled off my homemade eyepatch and threw it away. I didn't make another one, and I never felt self-conscious about my eyes again. He called me Fairy until I was ten and told him to stop.

Wilder shifts on the bed, rolling over until we face each other. Three electrified inches separate us. Afraid to see his eyes, I stare at the base of his throat where his pulse flutters close to his skin.

"I'm sorry about last night," he whispers.

I close my eyes. "Me too. I don't..." I swallow back the urge to sob. "I don't want to lose you. I love making music with you —I do—but I can't ignore what I'm feeling anymore. I'm not happy."

"I know." His tone is low and agonized. "I've been such a dick to you. Getting away from me is the right choice."

"Why?" My voice aches like my heart. "Why do you say the things you do? Why can't you stop?"

My eyes fly open at a touch on my jaw. He stares at his fingers like he isn't sure they belong to him, but he doesn't move them. Long, dark lashes flicker as his gaze lifts to mine.

The world around us blurs; we're static figures in a shaken snow globe.

"I wish..." His throat bobs. "I wish I wasn't so afraid."

My brows draw together. "Of what?"

His thumb coasts across my cheek. Blood races to the

gentle pressure as if my very essence wants to catch and trap his touch.

"Everything," he whispers. "But mostly you."

My whole body turns hot and prickly. "What? Why?"

The barest of smiles curves his lips. "Silly Fairy who sees so much and so little at the same time."

His lips press to my forehead. Silky soft, dry, and warm. I freeze in shock, tingles radiating from the illicit contact and spreading down my limbs. My stomach swoops as his fingertips slide over my jaw. His hand forms a hot band around the side of my throat.

"I can't be what you want me to be," he murmurs as he draws away, "but not for the reason you think. Look at me, Fairy."

I lift my gaze. The brown speckles in his green eyes are black as pitch around giant pupils. His cheekbones are flushed, his brow furrowed like he's in pain. I've never seen this look on his face—abject hunger, spiraling torment.

"I'm poison." His gaze locks onto my mouth. "Sometimes I think you're the antidote, but at the end of the day, I won't risk infecting you. That's why I push you away. Not because I don't want you. As much as I need you, I have to save you from me."

Emotions punch me, one after the other: surprise, elation, sadness, confusion, anger. "What the fuck? That's such bullshit."

His eyes flare. "Oh yeah? You think your pussy will banish all my demons?"

To my horror, my eyes begin to sting. "I've never asked you to have sex with me or be my boyfriend. The only thing I wanted was your respect."

I push backward, but he moves faster. One of his hands sears my bare thigh while the other whips up to reclaim my hair. He surges against me, bringing our bodies flush. I gasp at the unmistakable feel of his erection at the juncture of my thighs. That painful ache only he incites unfolds in my center, and a small, helpless sound escapes me.

"This happens every time you walk in a room," he grinds out. "Every time you open that pouty mouth or give me those glistening 'fuck me' eyes. You make me insane. Don't you get it? The problem is I *do* respect you. I respect your mind and talent more than anyone else on this planet does. You're *sacred* to me, Evangeline. But your body? That, I want to disrespect in the worst fucking ways."

Fear and uncertainty shiver through me, amplifying the sensation between my legs. I want him to kiss me. Take me. *Ruin me.*

I want to run as fast and far as I can.

His piercing stare tells me he knows exactly what I'm feeling. He always knows—he stole the book of my unspoken language years ago and memorized every word.

The fingers on my thigh clench and unclench, and he makes a sound in his throat that arrows between my legs. My hips twitch forward, primal need overruling reason. His nostrils flare, lips thinning, but he stays unmoving. A pillar of rigid heat and tensed muscle.

"You're wet for me, aren't you?" His voice purrs beneath my skin. "I bet you're always wet for me, just like I'm always hard for you."

Beyond reason, I nod, my gaze falling to his lips. Full and flushed, glistening from frustrated bites and swipes of his tongue. Two inches separate our mouths—two inches to freedom or catastrophe. I don't know which awaits us, and I'm starting not to care.

His frown deepens, his eyes narrowing to glittering slits.

More fear pours through me, equaled only by my body's rising demand.

I say his name—a plea for him to stop this. Or finish it.

"You have no idea the depraved shit I want to do to you," he whispers harshly. "What if how I treat your body disgusts you? Would you get over it? Would we go back to partners while I use other girls as substitutes? Could you handle that? I don't think you could."

I can't breathe. Can't think. My greatest fantasy and worst nightmare are colliding, stripping me of denial. He's right—I couldn't handle that. And I was right last night—this is toxic.

But I don't move as he releases my hair. I don't stop him when he lifts my leg over his hip and nestles his hardness against my center. And when his hips swivel against mine, the friction makes me moan. He does it again and again. A tease and a threat I want him to make good on.

I want it all. I want him to fill me with his body like he fills me with his art.

"Open those fairy eyes," he demands.

My lashes part but immediately want to shutter again when I see his face. *Too much. He's too much.* Beautiful and savage. A provoked god of destruction.

His grip on my thigh tightens to the point of pain. "Did Eddie make you come when you fucked?"

"I..." Words fail me as his thrusts push me inexorably toward a sensory cliff's edge. Only this feeling is a thousand times more powerful than anything I've felt with my fingers.

"Answer me."

"We didn't have sex," I gasp out.

I must imagine it, but it feels like he grows even thicker, harder. He makes a noise between a gasp and a groan, and my legs begin to shake.

"Goddammit, Evangeline," he hisses.

He stills and releases my thigh. Before I feel the loss, his fingers dive between my legs from behind, yanking aside my cotton shorts and the gusset of my bikini bottoms, exposing me completely. I whimper as calloused fingertips graze my slit before confidently delving deeper. A finger pushes inside me, the invasion not deep but still shocking. My body tenses in resistance as he pulls it out and sinks it back in. His hand begins to move as well. Back and forth. Circling. Slowly at first, then faster. Discomfort shifts to a sparkling, consuming pleasure.

The sound of my wetness brings a mortified flush to my face. I duck my head against his chest.

"Fuck, fuck, fuck," he chants against my hair. "Tell me to stop."

He doesn't wait for an answer; I can't speak, anyway. His forearm flexes rhythmically against my ass, marrying the movements of his hand to the sinuous, purposeful drives of his hips. His jean-trapped cock grinds against my exposed clit, sending confusing signals of pain through the haze of euphoria. I clutch his shirt, small, animalistic sounds riding each of my panting breaths.

Another finger sinks inside me. It hurts, too. And feels better than anything I've ever felt before.

"Eyes on me," he demands.

My head weighs a thousand pounds as I lift it. His gaze flickers between my eyes, then drops to my lips.

"So beautiful," he whispers.

Prickling sensation eats my fingers and toes. Between my legs, the pain fades, replaced by languorous, spreading heat. I feel loose, unfolded, *possessed*, as my hips jerk erratically against his.

Wilder licks his lips. "Fuck yes. Chase it, Fairy."

My fingers dig into his chest. "Oh God—"

"I'm your god right now, and I want this virgin cunt spasming around my fingers and gushing all over my hand. Give it to me."

My mind recoils at his crass words, my head rearing back. His smile is slight, cruel, and knowing, his eyes hard on mine. I search his face frantically for anything familiar—any tenderness at all—but I can't find it, and it's too late to stop what my body has already claimed.

The orgasm sweeps through me. Devastating. Ecstatic. Humiliating. I smother my cries against his chest as I tremble and jerk, soaking his hand like he told me to.

I'm still pulsing, my senses floating, when he slips his fingers from my body and holds them between our faces. His skin glistens with my release. Eyes holding mine, he licks a line up his wet palm to the tip of one finger.

He groans. "You taste like sin."

Opening my jaw with his other hand, he shoves the same two fingers that were inside me against my tongue. Startled, I pull back. Not from the flavor—unexpected but not bad—but from the invasiveness. He pushes them in more, hitting the back of my tongue and making me gag.

This time when I shove him away, he doesn't resist. We stare at each other with a foot of space between us, both of us panting.

"Why?" My voice cracks.

His face remains marble, his eyes cold. "Go, Evangeline. Right now. Unless you want me to break you in half and make you choke on my cum."

Horrified, I scramble off the bed, yanking my bikini bottoms and shorts back into place. I snatch my sandals off the floor and back away.

Wilder watches me with narrowed, frigid eyes.

"What's wrong with you?" I whisper.

His brows lift mockingly. "According to a lot of women, absolutely nothing."

My fingers tighten on my shoes as my eyes burn with unshed tears. "You know I'm not experienced. You were trying to shock me. You hurt me on purpose. Why would you do that?"

For a second, the mask over his eyes cracks. What I see makes my stomach bottom out—horror, self-loathing—before ice numbs everything. He sits up fast, feet thudding to the floor. I tense, ready to run, but he only grips the edge of the mattress, the tendons in his arms pronounced.

"You came to *my* room. Pressed your soft tits against *my* back. I got you off and you never once said no." His lip curls in a sneer. "Not everything you hoped it would be? Well, I'm sorry to disappoint, but I did warn you."

My mouth opens and closes. He rolls his eyes, then snatches his phone off the nightstand and swipes a few times. Ringing fills the room.

The line connects and a woman's voice croons, "Hey you. What's up?"

His eyes stay on my face as he says, "I need some relief. You free?"

"For you? Always."

"My place in twenty."

She giggles. "On my way."

He disconnects.

"I hate you," I tell him.

And this time, I mean it.

CHAPTER FIVE

wilder

YOU STOLE SEEDS OF ME
AND REPLACED THEM
WITH SEEDS OF YOU
BUT YOU DIDN'T KNOW
WE'LL NEVER GROW
BECAUSE I'M POISON

EVANGELINE WRENCHES OPEN my bedroom door and flees at a run. Every muscle in my body tightens with the urge to go after her, but I curl forward instead and fist my hands in my hair.

"Eva? Whoa—what's wrong?"

She must ignore Rye, because seconds later his frame fills my open doorway. He scowls at me. "What did you do this time?"

The low laugh that comes out of me sounds batshit crazy. "Made sure she'll never come back to me."

His eyes widen. "On purpose?"

"You hurt me on purpose."

I didn't mean to. Fuck, I didn't mean to hurt her. I was barely hanging on to sanity, every shred of my self-control focused on not kissing her soft pink mouth. Not stripping off her clothes and feasting on every inch of her skin. Not freeing my dick and shoving inside her, stretching and claiming what no other man has.

I almost lost it a few times, overwhelmed by the way she looked at me, lust drunk and needy, and the texture and scent of her. Her blushing face, her supple thigh, her pussy... She was so wet. Drenched for me. So fucking soft. So hot and tight around my fingers.

My dick pulses angrily. I have no idea why I didn't blow my load in my pants, the fly of which is currently wet from her. Probably because I was so focused on every breath she took that—for the first time ever—I wasn't thinking about myself.

But I still fucked it up. I hurt her. Again.

Shame slithers around my shoulders, tightening around my neck.

"No," I say hoarsely, "not on purpose."

"What the hell, man?" Rye's voice is low and concerned. "I know whatever happened on tour made things more complicated for you guys, but why can't you apologize? Make it right?"

I shake my head, another unhinged laugh leaving me. "It's not that simple." Before he can say anything, I lift a hand and aim my glare. "Look, I get that you want to help, but leave it. Besides, you should be thanking me."

He frowns. "For what?"

I stand, grabbing my car keys. "Come on, dude. It's

obvious you're in love with her." Ignoring the pound of trepidation in my chest, I force more poison out. "She's all yours now. Virginity intact. Maybe give her a few hours to recover from how hard she just came on my fingers, though."

The blood drains from Rye's face, making his freckles stand out even more. He takes a step into the room, his big hands clenched into fists.

I hope he comes at me. I won't even fight it.

I hope he breaks my fucking jaw.

"You're a piece of shit, Wild. I love Eva like a sister. She's my best friend in the whole world. I thought you were my friend, too. I thought you were *her* friend."

When I don't say anything, he shakes his head slowly. His anger drains away, replaced by pity. My skin crawls.

"You've always been a moody fuck, but the last year has been off the scale. Get some help, man. None of us want to see you crash and burn." He spins on his heel and stalks into the hallway, yelling back at me, "Burgers are ready, asshole."

Tossing my keys to the floor, I flop back onto the bed and press the heels of my hands into my eyes. A mistake I realize too late as Eva's delicious scent invades my nose. I hold my fingers to my face, breathing her in until I can't stand it anymore. Then I sit up and grab my phone, shooting a text to Christine to cancel.

Maybe I didn't mean to hurt Eva physically, but I definitely meant to shock and hurt her emotionally when I said that vulgar shit and called Christine right in front of her.

Rye's right.

I'm a piece of shit.

Muted footsteps in the hallway bring my head up. Twisted anticipation dies suddenly when Matt Sullivan appears. One look at his face tells me I'm about to get my ass

47

handed to me. While I'm not worried that Eva ran downstairs and told her dad I fingered her, she *was* on the verge of tears when she left my room. Matt knows I'm the reason his daughter was crying.

I open my mouth.

"Don't bother, kid," he says, leaning against the doorjamb and crossing muscular, tattooed arms. "Shut up and listen. I came here to thank you."

My jaw drops. "What?"

A mirthless smile curves his lips. "Eva's been thinking about leaving the band since before you signed to Indigo. She stayed for you, to support your dream. You know something else? The music she makes alone sounds nothing like Night Theory. It's fucking good, though. Got this dark, electro-pop vibe."

She makes music without me?

"Anyway," Matt continues like he didn't just shatter a fundamental pillar of my reality. "I don't know what you did to make her finally cut the co-dependent cord between you guys, but regardless of your motives, it was the right thing to do. You feel me?"

I nod numbly.

"Also—and this is important, so open your punk-ass ears—I'm not happy Eva's hurting, but in the long run, it's a good thing. Because you and I both know you're not it." I'm confused until he adds, "She deserves more than you're capable of giving. On every. Fucking. Level. Wanna know how I know?"

My stomach churns at the implication he's aware that whatever Eva and I are, it's more than friends. Unable to hold his stare, I lower my head. Knowing it's futile, I still quip, "No, thanks."

"Tough shit," Matt says lightly. "I know because looking at

48

you is like staring into the past. But unlike all the idiots on the outside, I'm not implying you're Julian 2.0."

I look up, stupidly hopeful.

His blue eyes spear me. "You're ten times worse. Stay the fuck away from my daughter, Wilder."

"Jesus Christ," I hiss, rubbing my face—again, a mistake, because all I smell is his daughter's pussy. At least my windows are all open, and my jeans are black, so he can't see the wet spot she made.

Matt knocks his knuckles against the doorframe. He turns to leave, then pauses. "Final piece of advice?"

"Sure, why not," I say bitterly.

"You're a helluva songwriter and musician. Maybe even better than your dad, though I'll deny it if you tell anyone I said that. But if you keep treating the people who love you like currency, you're gonna go bankrupt. And when that happens, all the fame in the world won't be worth a damn thing."

With a final nod, he disappears.

"Whatever," I mutter to myself. "That makes no fucking sense."

Except the longer I sit here thinking about the fact Evangeline makes her own music just fine without me, the more sense it makes.

I've been using her for years, since the first song we made together. Sucking away at the bond between us, treating her like a commodity to be consumed. All for my benefit. To make my dreams come true. Not hers—never hers. I don't even know what her dreams are, having always assumed they aligned with mine.

When was the last time I asked her anything about herself? Does she want to pursue a solo music career? Go to

49

college? Why does she rent that crumbling house and never buy shit for herself when she has a giant trust fund?

A shaky feeling overtakes my body as I realize the one person I thought I knew better than anyone might actually be a stranger. What I thought was solid ground is crumbling under my feet.

Until yesterday, I had no idea she wanted to leave Night Theory. No idea she wasn't fully invested in our future as giants in the industry. Because our nine-year musical partnership was about me, not her. Not us.

She *does* deserve more than I can give her. Even if I don't know how to think of her as anything but mine. Even if I want to kill Eddie for kissing her, and the thought of some other man touching her body, of her wanting him to, makes me see red.

Maybe I don't know Evangeline like I thought I did, but she knows me in a way no one else does—not even my mom. I've already given her more of myself than anyone else; giving her the rest terrifies me. Maybe that means I'm a coward. Or maybe I'm simply obeying instinct, a cellular wisdom that transcends logic. It would explain why I've kept her at arm's length all these years. Why I haven't let myself know her. Really, really know her.

Because falling in love with Evangeline Sullivan will destroy me.

Sitting up, I look around at the poster-strewn walls that have heard hundreds of our songs and harmonies. Arguments, shouts of excitement, and belly-aching laughs. Tears sting my eyes, which finally drop to the nightstand and the black notebook my mom gave me.

My breath stills as a new emotion rises, faint but growing more defined every second.

Despite the betrayal still burning inside me at Evangeline's choice, despite feeling abandoned and fractured and bereft at the thought of her leaving the band—leaving *me*—I suddenly feel something else, too.

Something a lot like hope. A lot like freedom.

She doesn't need me.

Which means maybe I was wrong.

Maybe I don't need her, either.

verse

verse : lyrical or instrumental section
of a song used to advance the plot

CHAPTER SIX

evangeline

EVA 23 | WILDER 25

MY FRONT DOOR OPENS, letting in a draft of cold, damp air before it closes again. Anna's voice filters to my ears along with Rye's deeper tones. I can't hear what they're whispering over the sounds of Slow Pulp from my Bluetooth speaker, but I have a pretty good idea.

"Hey, guys," I call over my shoulder. I catch a glimpse of Anna's wide eyes and Rye's grimace before I turn back to the counter and focus on chopping cucumbers for a salad.

They finally make it to the kitchen. Rye drops a kiss on my head before heading to the fridge for a beer. Anna gives me a side hug, enveloping me in a cloud of perfume and stale marijuana smoke.

"Smells good in here," Rye says with forced cheer. "I love your lasagna almost as much as my mom's."

"Thanks. I made enough for you to take home and freeze."

"Hell yeah. You're a goddess."

"She is," Anna agrees. She grabs a cucumber slice off my cutting board and takes a bite, then grins at me. "An immortal goddess now."

"Anna," warns Rye.

She waves a dismissive hand in his direction, still grinning at me with manic, glazed eyes. "So, Eva? Have you listened to the song?"

I lower my knife before I stab her with it. "Yes, I've heard it."

Fifteen different people have sent it to me since it dropped online this morning, and that's not including family members. The only person to not contact me about it is Wilder himself. Probably because he knows as well as I do that the song doesn't mean anything. Maybe I inspired the lyrics, but I'm not naive enough to think they're about me specifically. That would be ridiculous.

Plus, his number is blocked in my phone.

Behind her, Rye mouths, "I'm sorry."

Still firmly in the bubble of my personal space, Anna bounces on her heels and screeches. The high-pitched sound makes me wince.

"And? Do you love it? You have to love it. It's unreal. So freaking good." She spins around, almost slapping me in the face with her hair-sprayed beach waves. "Where's your phone? Let's put it on."

I share another look with Rye. This time I let him see exactly how much I like his newest girlfriend, which is not at all.

"Anna, give it a rest," he says in a tired voice that tells me their four-month relationship is on its last legs.

She pretends she doesn't hear him—or she can't be bothered to read the room—because she grabs my phone off the counter.

"What's your passcode? Oh wait, I remember it." Her fingers fly over the screen, and I drown in regret for letting her borrow my phone last week to call hers when she couldn't find it in her purse.

The Slow Pulp song ends abruptly, and a second later, a dreamy, piano-driven intro begins. Moody and airy with a fuzzy bassline, it makes me think of salty ocean spray and moonlight.

Just like it's supposed to.

Sea glass and churning foam
Her eyes call me home
Now I'm trapped in her snare
But she isn't here
She's nowhere

Heterochromia
Heterochromia

Wilder's voice has changed in the last three years. I can tell he's worked on it with a professional. His range has expanded; his pitch is perfect. Now his baritone is so smooth it melts in my ears, with a raspy edge he uses to a spine-tingling effect on certain notes.

The track itself is arranged beautifully. The piano, the synth, the guitar and drums that build and culminate in the bridge, where they pound like a furious heartbeat.

There's a second chance
To be what you said you'd be
Come home to me

Another lovely transition leads to the last chorus and a fading outro. The final note of piano hangs delicately in the air until Anna shatters it with another screech. She throws herself dramatically against the kitchen table, rattling plates.

"I'm literally dead. Can you believe how beautiful that was? You're so lucky. I'd shit myself if someone as fuck-hot as Wilder Ashburn wrote a song about me."

Rye drops his head to his chest.

I pick up my knife and massacre more cucumbers.

♪

RYE AND I EAT ALONE.

We talk about our families, our jobs, and my show at a local venue tomorrow night. Rye is a natural chatterbox and carries us from one topic to the next with barely a pause. But the skin around his eyes is tight, his smile not its usual wattage.

A cord of tension hangs in the air, poised to choke us with all the topics we're avoiding. Like how after Anna made me listen to the song, Rye discreetly ordered her an Uber, then took her outside and dumped her.

And we definitely don't talk about the fact the song, "Waves," has racked up over a hundred thousand streams already, its instant popularity due to a two-month-long social media strategy. The kind that points to deep pockets, with professional behind the scenes videos of the four-man band, aesthetic track teases, and photoshoots with famous photographers.

After dinner, Rye does the dishes, then rejoins me at the table, where I'm slouched and picking at my cuticles.

"You okay?" he asks softly.

I nod and offer a smile that makes him grimace—which makes me laugh, albeit weakly. "I'm okay. Really. I'm happy for them. For him." Clearing my throat, I look away from the gentle understanding in his eyes. "You did good work on the track."

"Thanks, Eva. That means a lot coming from you. I'm still in shock that my name will be on the list of producers for the LP." He hesitates, his voice lowering. "It's good. Beyond good."

I nod a few times. "I look forward to hearing it."

"You don't have to wait. You can listen to the masters whenever you—"

"No," I say sharply, then blow out a breath as his face falls. "Sorry. I just mean I'll wait like everyone else. When's the release again?"

"Late April. Two more singles will land before then."

I whistle softly. "I take it the label is backing a full-scale release campaign? The whole nine yards?"

His smile is wry. "What is nepotism for five hundred."

I laugh.

Despite a nearly three-year delay in laying tracks for their sophomore album, Night Theory still has a recording contract with Indigo Records—the same company that signed Breaking Giants back in the day and has since become one of the most coveted pop and rock labels in the business.

"Good for them."

Rye grins. "You almost sound like you mean that."

"I do mean it." I pause, then concede, "It's bittersweet, I guess."

Mostly bitter.

As much as I don't regret leaving the band, and as much as I believe in Wilder's music and think his talent deserves the biggest platform possible, I still mourn the loss of what we shared. The loss of *him*. My childhood friend. My song-writing partner. The temperamental, driven, passionate person who made my world brighter. Sharper. More colorful. Who challenged me, inspired me, and ultimately betrayed everything I thought we were.

What we are now is... nothing.

I haven't seen Wilder in over six months, since our families' joint, end-of-summer barbecue last year. Our brief interaction followed a three-year pattern of avoiding and ignoring each other at gatherings.

The only difference last time was that Wilder brought a guest. A pretty brunette named Kendra, who ended up awkwardly introducing herself to me after Wilder walked past me with a muttered, "Hey."

According to my mom, Kendra is still around. Wilder's parents are happy for him. Everyone is happy for him.

Sensing my withdrawal, Rye scoots his chair back and stands.

"I'm gonna head out and let you get a good night's sleep. Excited about the show tomorrow?"

My smile is almost genuine. "Definitely."

After what happened with Wilder, I didn't write music for close to a year. I drifted for a while, living off my savings and the modest royalty payments from Night Theory's first album. Eventually, a tough love conversation with my dad snapped me out of my fugue. I found a part-time job at a music academy teaching piano and guitar to kids and enrolled at a local college.

I met Lily Aoki in my second semester during a music theory course. Our personalities are as different as night and day, but creatively we're a perfect match. We've been making music for a couple years, but in the last year we've gotten serious. Our talents are a marriage of mediums: I'm analog—

notepads, keyboard, guitar—and she's digital, mixing and producing each song in ways I never imagined. We don't need anyone else with us onstage, either, because she does it all with her fancy laptop and DJ equipment.

We've performed a few dozen times at open mics around the city, but tomorrow night is our first legitimate show. We got a call last week from a booking agent at a small but respected venue in Fremont. He'd heard us at an open mic the weekend before and grabbed our flyer. When the original openers for tomorrow canceled, our flyer happened to be sitting at the top of the pile on his desk. He decided that despite our relatively unknown status, we were the right sound and worth the risk.

And the best part of it is he has absolutely no idea who I am—or rather, who my father is.

"It's going to be epic," Rye says, squeezing my shoulder before grabbing the container of leftovers.

I follow him to the front door, where I wrap my arms around his middle and take a deep breath of his comforting, mossy scent.

"Like hugging a tree trunk," I mumble into his flannel.

He chuckles and gives me a squeeze that forces the air from my lungs. "Like hugging a fairy—" We both freeze. "Fuck. Sorry, Ev."

"All good," I say brightly, stepping back and opening the door for him. "I'm sorry about Anna. You really didn't have to... you know."

"Trust me, it was about to happen anyway." Winking, he adds, "You know I won't suffer alone for long."

I groan and shove him. "Get out of here."

Laughing manically, he saunters down the brick path to the curb. I wait until he's in his car before closing and locking my door. After cleaning the kitchen, I retreat to my bedroom, strip off my clothes, and pull on my heavy terry robe. Then I grab my phone and head for my hot tub.

The night is cold and clear. I don't bother turning on the string lights, the glow from the living room bright enough to buffer me from the dark. With a grunt, I pull up half of the cover and let it flop onto the other side. My robe hits the deck and two seconds later, I'm submerged in steaming, liquid bliss.

Dropping my head back, I watch the fog from my breath merge with the steam rising from the water. The urge to cry comes and goes like a tide, like the melody that trickles in and out of my mind.

There's a second chance to be what you said you'd be. Come home to me, come home to me.

When I realize I'm humming the words, I sit up and rub my face roughly. "Stop it," I admonish myself.

Ejecting the song from my thoughts, I focus on what's important: the show tomorrow. I mentally run through the timeline of the day—everything from when I'll wake up to my usual voice-prep routine to what time we need to be at the venue and what I'm wearing—then review the song list Lily and I decided on.

Like she can hear me thinking, my nearby phone lights up with a text from her.

> Just got off work. Do you want company?
> We can make fake accounts and spam Night
> Theory's posts

A begrudging smile tugs my mouth to one side. She knows enough details about my complicated history with Wilder to loathe him on my behalf.

> Nah, I'm good. Thx tho.

Here's an idea

Unblock Wimpy's number and tell him the
song sucks

My laugh is small but genuine.

Not happening. I'm soaking now and going
to sleep in a few. See you tomorrow. Get
some sleep!

Will do. Love you girl. Nite

I start to put my phone down, but a sudden impulse makes me swipe to my contacts and scroll to the bottom. To his name. I press it. Another swipe brings me to two little words.

Unblock Caller.

My thumb hovers, then descends. Before I can stop myself, I text him.

Congrats, Wilder. It's a great song

It shows as delivered. I stare at the screen far too long before deciding I'm the biggest fool to ever live.

"Stupid," I whisper.

I step out of the hot tub, so angry with myself I don't even feel the cold. I towel off my legs and pull on my robe, then haul the cover back over the water and head inside. When the slider sticks a bit, I have the insane urge to smash my fist into the glass. Finally, it closes. I lock it and stalk toward the kitchen, where I chug a glass of water.

Wilder isn't going to text me back. I've given him the cold shoulder for years. He's given it right back. Whatever bond we had is gone. It's also close to eleven on a Friday night. He's probably partying with friends. With his super awesome girlfriend.

My phone rings in the pocket of my robe, startling a yelp out of me. It takes three tries to pull it out, my fingers fumbling and numb.

Staring at the name on the screen, I read it over and over, seeing but not believing. Right before it goes to voicemail, I answer with a weak, "Hello?"

"You hate the song, don't you?"

His voice is warm and deep and dark. Both achingly familiar and shocking. An uncomfortable, spinning feeling consumes me—a blurring carousel of longing, resentment, and nostalgia.

"No." I clear my throat. "No, not at all. It's phenomenal."

"Liar," he whispers.

Against all common sense, my lips quirk. How many times have we spoken this script? Hundreds.

"Finished art is arrested progress," I tell him. "Time to let it go."

He says his line. "I don't know how."

And I finish it. "Write another song."

He's silent for one second. Two.

"Do you hate me, Fairy?"

My heart races. My face tingles. I drag my knuckles over my cheek, finding it hot to the touch.

"Yes."

"Good," he says, then hangs up.

CHAPTER SEVEN

wilder

CROSSING THE SIDEWALK, I yank open the passenger door of Rye's SUV and hop inside. When he just sits there, gripping the steering wheel so hard it looks like he's trying to shape it into a square, I slap the dash. He jolts and turns to me with panicked eyes.

"What's wrong with you?"

"She's going to kill me."

I scoff and finish buckling my seatbelt. "Come on. She won't even know I'm there."

"What about your parents? My parents? *Her parents?* Half the crowd is going to be people we're related to or friends of people we're related to. Plus, have you seen your Instagram account today? You have ninety thousand followers. Oh, and one of your videos went viral last night. God only knows why —you're eating a fucking burrito. But you seriously think no one will recognize you?"

I grimace at the potential truth of what he's saying. "I'll keep my hood up and stick to the back of the club."

"It's not a big club!"

Rye tugs at his earlobe, a lifelong tell that he's perilously close to a meltdown. They were epic when he was a toddler. I have no interest in seeing one from a two-hundred-and-twenty-pound former high school linebacker.

I make my voice calm and even—not difficult given the pill I took thirty minutes ago. "Like I already told you, I'm not trying to fuck up her night. I know she doesn't want me there. If I have to listen from the freaking bathroom, I will."

Rye nods a few times, relaxing marginally. Reaching into the backseat, he produces a beanie and tosses it in my lap. "Wear this. And don't look directly at her. I know it's been a while, but I doubt her Wilder-radar is broken."

Warmth spreads through me at the words, but I shake it off. Probably the Oxy kicking in, which I'm now regretting swallowing. I'll need to be careful to avoid my dad, who will take one look at my pinned pupils and lose his shit. But I wasn't thinking about seeing him—I was thinking about staying calm in a crowded room. Mostly, though, I was thinking about seeing Evangeline and dulling my reaction to her.

"Thanks for doing this," I murmur as I put on the beanie, pulling my sweatshirt hood over it.

Rye grunts and finally puts the car in gear. "I used to tell Eva all the time she needed to learn how to say no to you. I should take my own advice."

There's a pinch in my chest, but I ignore it and punch his bicep. It's like hitting a brick. "It's going to be fine, man. Trust me."

"I trust you as much as gas station sushi," he mutters.

I bark a laugh, then settle back for the short drive to Fremont.

I'm not unsympathetic toward Rye's dilemma. He's the center of Eva's and my Venn diagram, the only place we overlap these days. This is the first time he's felt the pressure of his position, the first time I've tested our bond against his loyalty to Eva.

Neither Rye nor I expected that sitting in the studio for months would spark a friendship completely separate from the drama of the past. His talents are incredible, and I would have been a fool to pass up having his input on the album over some beef that wasn't even with him. I'm doubly glad I didn't—not only is he as much of a perfectionist as I am when it comes to arranging music, I actually like the guy now.

Ten minutes later, Rye finds parking a block away from Side Stage, a black building covered in colorful, graffitied murals. It sits snugly against Tullamore Café, the beloved neighborhood landmark formerly owned by my mom and her cousin and now owned by my mom's longtime friend, Allison Montgomery, and her wife. About four years ago, they bought the lot next door and tore down the ancient fabric store. They renovated the café and built the attached venue.

Welcoming light pours out of the cafe's glass front, high-lighting the short line in front of Side Stage's box office.

Rye turns off the car, then shoots me an unreadable look. "I don't even want to ask, but you didn't have anything to do with this, right?"

I frown in confusion. "With what?"

"Getting her the gig."

My brows jump. "Are you for real?"

"I know your parents are tight with the owners."

"So are her parents." When his suspicious expression doesn't change, I groan. "No, dumbass. I had nothing to do with it. You think I want Evangeline to hate me more than she already does?"

He sighs. "She doesn't hate you."

67

"She does," I say decisively.

He stares at me another moment, then shakes his head and exits the car. I follow, tugging the beanie down over my forehead.

Rye doesn't understand what happened between Evangeline and me. Hell, I barely understand it myself. All I know is that she hates me. She *needs* to hate me.

Three years of almost-silence, of seeing her from a distance at family functions, hearing her laugh, her voice, watching as the final vestiges of girlishness dissolved to reveal exactly how fucking gorgeous she's always been... all of it has proven one immutable fact.

I'm still an addict.

Believing she hates me makes it easier to abstain. It works for me. Or it worked until last night, when I made the impulsive mistake of calling her after realizing she'd unblocked my number.

When I heard her voice, when we played that old game, my craving was triggered.

Now I'm fiending for her.

"You all right?" asks Rye.

I realize I've stopped walking and am staring blankly at the ground.

"I, uh..." I glance to the side to see we've stopped in front of Tullamore's front doors. "I'm gonna get something to drink."

Rye frowns and glances at his watch. "She goes on in five."

I nod. "I'll catch up in a minute."

"You mean creep inside, keep to the shadows, and pretend you don't know me?"

I roll my eyes. "Yes. I'll leave before the set ends and Uber home."

His frown deepens, but his love for Eva trumps his concern for my moody ass. "'Kay. See ya."

He strolls toward the box office.

I pivot and walk into the bustling café, making it five steps before my name, wrapped in surprise, is called from behind gleaming espresso machines.

Allison hustles around the counter, her familiar smile bringing one to my face.

"Hey, Auntie A," I say as she wraps her arms around my waist. She earned honorary aunt status when I was three and I've never considered calling her anything else.

"It's so good to see you, Wild," she says, grinning up at me. "It's been way too long. I don't remember you being this tall."

My smile turns smug. "Officially taller than my old man now, much to his annoyance."

She laughs. "I bet. Congrats on the single, by the way. Katie told me she heard it on the radio six times at work yesterday. Well deserved—it's incredible." Her smile softens, as does her voice as she leans closer. "Are you ready for what's coming your way?"

She looks meaningfully to the side, and I follow her gaze to a group of teenage girls at a nearby table who are staring at me and whispering. A quick glance around the café shows me they aren't the only ones.

I stomp my first instinct—which is to throw up in my mouth and run out the door—and instead give the table of girls a cocky grin. They turn bright red and dissolve into hysterical giggles.

When I look back at Allison, she squints at me like I've been body-snatched. "That was disturbing."

I agree with her. I'm disturbed every time I have to act like Wilder Ashburn, lead singer of Night Theory, instead of

Wilder Ashburn, an introvert who'd rather stab himself than socialize.

From the corner of my eye, I see the girls stand, phones in hand.

Oh, fuck.

A steel band cranks tight around my chest. Soft ringing fills my ears.

I should have taken two pills.

"Come on," says Allison, grabbing my arm and tugging me past tables, most of the occupants of which follow me with their eyes.

I'm naked beneath the piercing stares of strangers. My jaw aches with how hard my teeth are clenched. Every sound is too loud, every light too bright. I'm freezing and burning up, my stomach churning, sweat popping from my pores.

Allison squeezes my arm harder. "Hang on, almost there."

I keep my gaze pinned on her curly hair, peppered throughout with glistening silver strands. We enter a back hallway, passing a few people in Tullamore-branded shirts, who give me probing looks. Finally, she opens a door and pulls me into what looks like a staff lounge. Thankfully, it's empty and quiet.

"Sit," she says, pointing to a padded bench beside the door.

I drop onto the bench and hang my head. Slowly, my stomach settles and the ringing in my ears fades.

"Just like your dad," Allison murmurs.

I force myself to straighten. "I'm fine."

Her eyes narrow as she hands me a sealed water bottle. "Sure you are. Drink that, then I'll walk you next door through the staff entrance. You'll come out backstage."

I swallow half the bottle before shaking my head. "I have to go in the front."

The shrewd look in her eyes makes me feel like I'm five years old again and trying to convince her there's no mud in the mud pies I just made.

"Eva's onstage by now. As long as you don't make your presence known, she won't see you." She pauses, head tilting. "Have you heard her music?"

"A little," I admit. "A shitty recording."

Rye played the sample a few months ago for Eddie—who has no problem occasionally pumping him for information about Eva—and I happened to be in the same room. I've wanted to hear more since that first taste, the urge masochistic but undeniable.

"Then you're in for a treat." Allison glances at the clock on the wall. "All right, kiddo, let's go."

I haul myself to my feet and take an experimental inhale, relaxing when my lungs fill without pain. "Thanks for saving my ass back there, Auntie."

"Anytime." She scans my face. "Anxiety isn't something to be ashamed of, but it does need to be managed. Especially with the trajectory you're on."

Hearing her unspoken warnings and concerns—the same ones I get from my parents—I offer a disarming smile. I know better than to ask her to keep this from my mom, so I give her something else to tell her.

"Thanks, but this was a one-off. I don't usually venture out solo like this. And I have solid support from my bandmates."

"And Kendra, right?" she asks mildly.

My nod comes a second too late. I wince internally as Allison's gaze sharpens.

"Yep. She's great. Super supportive."

It's true. Sort of.

The door opens and a guy in a Tullamore shirt walks in,

halting at the sight of me. His eyes widen and veer to Allison. "Oh, sorry—"

"It's fine," Allison says. "We were just leaving. Have a good break."

I give the man a nod, avoiding eye contact, and follow Allison out of the room. She leads me farther down the main hallway, around a corner, and through another door. This hallway is dimmed, the distinctive sound of live music apparent from the behind the door at the end. The popping bass makes the walls vibrate.

I can't hear her voice. But I feel it.

"Head up the stairs and turn left."

"Thanks," I say distractedly.

"Good luck, Wilder."

By the time I turn to ask her what she means, she's gone.

When I walk through the door, though, and Evangeline's voice wraps around me like thick silk, dancing with immaculate control atop a wicked beat, I begin to understand.

Then I see her and suddenly know exactly what Allison meant.

But it's too late for luck.

I'm fucked.

LOCAL MUSIC CORNER

At Side Stage last Friday, Eva Marie and Lily Aoki of Glow walked onstage with little fanfare. When they walked off thirty minutes later, they took my old, jaded heart with them.

Glow is a breath of fresh air. So fresh that for the first time in years, I'm scratching my head trying to apply genre conventions. Are they Electropop? Indie? New or Dark Wave? Post-punk? They're all of the above and so much more, and they deliver it with the kind of symbiosis and crowd responsiveness I rarely see live anymore. Just who are these young women?

Eva Marie is the daughter of Matt Sullivan of Breaking Giants, and you may also remember her as a former founding member of local Alt-Rock favorites, Night Theory. She met Tacoma native Lily Aoki two years ago in PacNorth's Interdisciplinary Music Arts program. The rest is history... or rather, the beginning of Glow.

Frontwoman and lead songwriter Eva brings a stunning trifecta of lyrical prowess, electrifying stage presence, and a voice so rich and versatile it'll make you believe in miracles. If that's not enough, she's also a multi-instrumentalist. Over the course of eight songs, she transitioned effortlessly between electric guitar and keyboard and even brought the club to a standstill with a

73

violin solo. And she wasn't the only talent on stage making this old man gasp.

Lily Aoki is an alchemist of a DJ, her style reminiscent of early trip-hop greats and yet categorically her own. Her complex arrangements are disarmingly direct, with the unmistakable, shiver-inducing instincts of an orchestral conductor on a new music frontier. Paired with Eva Marie? It's a match made in music heaven.

I know what you're thinking. If Glow is so great, why haven't we heard of them? Well, despite support from famous faces in the crowd during their set, the duo has been climbing the ladder of success the hard way and not skipping any rungs. They've been on the open mic circuit for over a year, getting comfortable and earning their stripes.

In the opinion of this humble critic, we won't see them as an opening act much longer. Catching their set was the happiest accident in the last decade of my career.

Take note—Glow is here and they're about to light up the city.

ALEX ILOKA

CHAPTER EIGHT

evangeline

IN THE PASSENGER seat of my car, Lily lowers her phone to her lap after reading the article for the five hundredth time since it landed online yesterday. I'm pretty sure she has it memorized at this point.

Her royal blue hair sways in my peripheral vision as she shakes her head in lingering disbelief. "*The* Alex Iloka. I can't get over it."

"It's pretty surreal," I agree, throwing a quick smile her way and an even quicker glance at the navigation screen on my dash. There are three more miles before I have to change lanes for a left-hand turn, but I put on my blinker anyway and merge over while no one is beside me.

I've freaked out over the article plenty myself, but right now navigating the dark, wet roads takes precedence. I'm hyper focused and ultra-defensive, my eyes swiveling between mirrors and the windshield, my palms damp on the wheel.

According to Rye, my aversion to driving at night is merely another trait in a long list proving I'm an old woman in a twenty-three-year-old's body. I tried explaining astigmatism once but got nowhere, probably because it was a flimsy excuse and he knew it. My astigmatism—if I even have one—is minor and nowhere close to the real reason, which is so embarrassing I've never told my best friend.

I'm afraid of the dark and have been since I was a little kid and got lost in the woods during a camping trip. Unfortunately, the phobia didn't fade as I grew up. It matured right along with me.

I almost wish darkness were still synonymous with monsters under the bed. It seems simpler, somehow. Now the threat is both bigger and more nebulous. The danger of the unknown and its hidden potential for shock and pain. Plus spiders.

Most days, I manage okay. The fear is easier to ignore when I'm with others, and when I'm onstage it doesn't bother me at all. I generally feel safe at home, too. As long as I take precautions, I'm even fine using my hot tub at night—although I still freak out occasionally and sprint soaking wet into my house.

But no matter where I am or who I'm with, I can't sleep without multiple nightlights. I won't check the mailbox at the end of my driveway if it's close to sunset. And I absolutely hate driving at night.

The only reason I'm behind the wheel right now is because I don't trust a stranger to drive us. That, and I volunteered to be the designated driver so Lily can unwind. Between her full-time job and classes, she deserves a night to let loose and celebrate.

Her sudden, giddy laugh makes my lips twitch. "You know what I can't get over? How we had no idea he was there. Just did our thing, totally oblivious."

"Same."

Especially since my first thought after reading the article

was a cynical one—that someone had pulled strings on our behalf. Despite knowing Alex's reputation as strictly unbiased, I'd immediately called my dad and grilled him. He swore he had nothing to do with the critic's presence in the audience and even called the Ashburns to confirm they didn't overstep, either. I've since accepted that it was dumb luck. He'd been there to see the headliners, The Remnants, and happened to show up early.

"If we *had* known," I say dryly, "would we have made it onstage?"

"Definitely not. We would have been too busy puking." Lily groans, palming her stomach. "Actually, even thinking about it in hindsight makes me want to hurl."

I smirk. "That's from the shots you did before we left. Told you they were a bad idea."

"I know," she whines. "I'm just really nervous."

"You're gorgeous and fierce as hell. Now eat the granola bar I hid in your purse."

She grabs it with a laugh. "Thanks, Mom."

I roll my eyes, then glance at the navigation screen. Seven more minutes until we arrive at the party The Remnants invited us to. Lily's nervous because she has a crush on their drummer, Tyler, after chatting with him last weekend and texting with him all week. I know she's anxious, too, about the party itself. It's not at a club, bar, or in someone's cramped apartment like we're used to, but in a private home in a nice neighborhood.

The Remnants and their ilk definitely aren't our usual social circle. To use Alex Iloka's metaphor, they're at least a dozen rungs ahead of us on the success ladder. While only a few years older than us, the men are full-time musicians with a label, four albums, and two international tours under their belts. Their sound is a little too niche for music charts or consistent radio play, but they have a rabid fanbase who think they're the second coming of Depeche Mode.

I'm nervous, too, but for different reasons. I haven't been to a party like this in three years and never without Wilder, Eddie, and Jax. It's a weird feeling. An almost vulnerable one. I won't have a clear purpose like I did before—Lily isn't Wilder. I won't need to babysit her so she doesn't do anything crazy or downright dangerous.

The thought should bring relief but instead leaves me unsettled, a feeling that intensifies as I turn onto a darker, residential street.

Lily finishes the granola bar and tucks the wrapper back in my purse. "Are you excited to see Michael again? That man looked at you with boners in his eyes after our set."

My stomach flutters at the mention of The Remnants' lead singer. "First off, ew. Second, I guess? Maybe? I don't know. He may not even talk to me."

"You're delusional. I think you should go for it. He's hot. Those dark eyes? The smile?" She fans herself.

I side-eye her. "You sure you're interested in Tyler and not Michael?"

She grins. "I can appreciate a good-looking guy, but you know I prefer the teddy-bear types. Perfect example: Rye Henderson. Now there's a bear I wouldn't mind pawing my underwear off."

I almost miss a stop sign, slamming on the brakes at the last second. Thankfully, there are no other cars around us.

"Dude," I moan.

Lily giggles. "Sorry."

"I'll never understand your obsession with Rye," I grumble as I slowly accelerate.

"That's because he's basically your brother and incest is

gross," she says flippantly, then peers out the passenger window. "Whoa, take a look at these houses."

Stately homes line the curbs, two- and three-story facades gleaming from the rain. Custom exteriors and manicured front yards glow beneath artfully placed lighting—and not the kind you buy from a hardware store and shove in a ground, either, like the ones all over my tiny front yard.

Lily's next laugh is shrill. "I had no idea we were headed to *rich*-rich territory. How close are we to the water?"

I swallow another surge of uneasiness. "A few blocks."

"I think I see the party," she murmurs, leaning forward in her seat. "Dang, that's a lot of people."

We're still a block from our destination, but the street ahead of us is lined with cars on both sides. To avoid having to circle around—or worse, attempt parallel parking in the dark in front of spectators—I pull against the nearest empty curb and park.

As I turn off the car, Lily says in a small voice, "I've changed my mind. Let's go back to your place. Hot tub and movies and bad tequila."

"Aw, honey."

My own nerves forgotten, I unbuckle my seatbelt and grab her cold hands. I'm one of the only people she allows to see beneath her tough exterior, and it doesn't happen often. On the rare occasion it does, there's only one way I know to help her—summoning the version of myself who grew up in a house like these, who walked the red carpet at the Grammys when I was eleven, and who isn't easily intimidated.

"We can leave, sure. Or we can walk in there like we belong, *which we do*, and give it twenty minutes. If no one impresses us, we'll bail. Just because we were invited doesn't mean we owe anyone our presence."

She cracks a smile. "I love it when you do the diva voice. I'm sorry, Ev. I know you don't even want to be here. You'd be in pajamas by now."

I nod. "Truth."

She laughs. "Fine, fine. If you can do it, so can I." With a sharp inhalation, she straightens and unbuckles her seatbelt. "You're right. We belong here. I'm an alchemist on a new-music frontier, and you're a powerhouse frontwoman. We're basically famous now."

After tucking my purse in the trunk, I lock the car, slip my keys and phone into my jacket pocket, and join Lily on the sidewalk. Worries forgotten, she links her arm with mine and propels us swiftly toward the split-level mansion.

We pass a few small groups loitering outside and approach the oversized front door. A massive deck facing the water sits a level above us to our right, packed with people talking, smoking, and laughing. Beat-heavy music punches into the damp air through open glass doors behind the crowd.

Inside is the same story—people, people everywhere. Even with Lily's arm against me, I feel exposed. Off-kilter. A few smiles and nods are aimed our way, but I don't recognize anyone.

"This place is insane," Lily whispers, and I nod.

I hate to admit it, but I'm impressed. The style of the home is a classic for the area, but it's been fully remodeled into a contemporary-modern masterpiece. I can't imagine the mortgage payment this close to the Sound. No doubt there are mountain views, too.

We walk up a short rise of stairs into the crowded living space that leads onto the deck. The first thing I see—besides more people—is the massive wall opposite us. My jaw drops as I take in the colorful, graffitied mural that spans the entire space from the baseboards to the high, beamed ceiling. Within the mostly abstract design are whorls of distorted musical notes and skewed instruments.

I instantly recognize the style of the artist who did the murals at Side Stage.

An artist I personally know.

"Whoa," Lily says with quiet awe. "That's a Riv original. Do you have any idea how much that probably cost?"

"A lot more than we can afford."

Unless they did it for free.

My stomach does a slow, downward roll, my skin prickling as I turn my head sharply to look around the room. I scan the crowded couches, deck, and nearby kitchen. When I don't see who I'm looking for, I release a slow breath.

I'm being paranoid. This isn't Wilder's house. It's simply a weird coincidence that his nineteen-year-old brother, River, graffitied an entire wall when I know for a fact he rarely takes commissions for private homes.

"Lily! You made it!"

The shout turns us toward the deck, where Tyler breaks away from a group of guys. He weaves his way toward us, a huge smile on his face. As Lily's body relaxes against mine, I have a sudden suspicion I'll be leaving alone.

She confirms it with a whisper in my ear. "I'll text you when I get home?"

I smother a pang of disappointment and smile. "Sounds good."

"You're the best." She hugs me before hurrying to meet Tyler halfway. He waves at me; I lift a hand, then watch them until Lily gives me a thumbs-up behind her back, signaling that I'm officially dismissed.

I normally love her independence. I'm a lone wolf as well, so it works for us. But right now I wish I'd had the courage to be as honest with her in the car as she was with me. I could have told her I'm not as confident as I pretend to be. That it's been so long since I was a part of this scene, I'm not sure how to act.

With a mental sigh, I decide to give myself a tour of the house. Maybe I'll run into Michael or someone I know, or maybe I'll cut out early and head home to work on songs. Despite the prospect of driving alone in the dark, I'd actually prefer the latter.

Plan in place, I turn and take a step... right into a tall, broad-shouldered body. My face hits the middle of a hard chest, which rises on a swift inhale. I jerk back, but it's too late to prevent his midnight storm scent from invading my nose.

Steeling myself, I look up into narrowed, freckled green eyes.

"What are you doing here, Evangeline?"

CHAPTER NINE

evangeline

you used to be my lullaby
your smile my favorite lie
I would have given you the sky
But all you wanted was goodbye

I YANK my arm from Wilder's hold the second the door closes behind us. My skin hums from shoulder to wrist, like the contact sank through my leather jacket and top and is spreading like a toxin. I instinctively move away from him, deeper into the small room. A few seconds of disorientation later, my eyes finally partner with my brain to tell me where we are.

"Really? A bathroom?"

"It was the closest option."

His voice is calm. Unnervingly so. Despite that, the rich tone causes an immediate physical reaction. *Panic.* The walls of the arguably spacious bathroom seem to pulse closer, spiking my blood pressure. Not helping is the fact he's blocking the door, one shoulder resting on a brick wall painted as black as his heart.

I can't seem to make myself look at his face, so I focus instead on the fingers he's currently rubbing against his denim-clad thigh like they're tainted. The same fingers that were around my arm.

His hand stills, then he shoves up his long sleeves and crosses his arms over his chest. I stare at his muscled, veiny forearms, the golden skin now covered liberally with ink. My roaming gaze snags on a hyper-realistic lighthouse, the artistry as distinctive and familiar as that on the wall in the living room.

For a second, I forget the last three years—forget that he's a stranger. My mom's brother, Josh Marshall, is a world-renowned tattoo artist, and Wilder has been begging him to work on his skin since he was eighteen.

A smile quirks my lips. "My uncle finally agreed to tattoo you?"

He shifts against the wall. I risk a glance up to find his gaze fixed on the floor near my feet.

"Yes," he says shortly. "You didn't answer my question. What are you doing in my house?"

My smile dies, its echo reverberating in my chest. "I didn't know it was your house."

"Who invited you?"

"Michael Dresden."

He stiffens even more. "Stay away from him."

I suck in a breath, then release it slowly through my nose. There's a pinch in my chest, its source the same old wound: my inability to reconcile who he used to be with who he's become.

84

"Move. I'm leaving."

His eyes finally lift to mine. In the soft glow of the vanity's lights, their green is so dark I can't see the brown flecks. I'm grateful for the anger in my blood diluting the effect of him actually focusing on me, but I also can't stop my eyes from roaming, absorbing, *seeing* him in a way I haven't allowed myself to for so long.

His body is a man's now. Broad shoulders, narrow hips, long lines, and lean muscle. His face, too, has lost all vestiges of childhood. He's haughty and chiseled, almost ethereally beautiful.

I hate that he takes my breath away.

When one of his brows arches up, amusement flaring in his eyes, I wrench my gaze from his annoyingly perfect face.

"Whatever," I mutter. "You're pretty but your personality sucks."

He makes a small sound. Almost a laugh. Then he says, "Michael doesn't date. He fucks and ghosts."

Inwardly, I flinch. Outwardly, I scowl. "Don't pretend you care. Maybe I want to fuck and ghost *him*."

His lips curl, a challenge more than a smile. "Do you?"

I throw my hands up in exasperation. "What are we even doing right now? The first conversation we have in three years and we're already arguing? Clearly we need another three. Or better yet, ten."

"I don't want to argue with you."

He drags a hand through his hair—shorter than when I saw him last but still unruly—and makes a soft sound of frustration. When he looks at me again, my knees go weak.

It's *him*.

My friend.

"I saw the show last Friday." This time when his lips

curve, it's a real smile. "Snuck in the back so you wouldn't see me."

Every muscle in my body locks.

"You were amazing, Evangeline. I'm in awe of you."

I stand in mute shock, my face burning and my mouth open. Wilder pushes off the wall. Two steps bring him to me. I have to crane my neck to maintain eye contact.

"What are you doing?" I whisper.

His gaze roams my face. "I don't know," he answers as softly. "I miss you. So fucking much. Do you really hate me?"

I swallow hard. My body burns; my scalp feels like mist. I have a sudden, visceral memory of the last time we were this close. In his childhood bed. His hand on my thigh. Between my legs.

Before I can do something stupid, I force the memory to play to its disastrous end.

"Yes."

I want to mean it, but I can hear my uncertainty and so can he. His teeth catch his lips, arresting a smile. Slowly, so slowly, he bends forward, caging me against the counter with his hands to either side of me. His head drops beside mine, warm breath cascading over my neck.

I stiffen, paralyzed between an urge to push him away and savor this dangerous moment. My toes and fingers tingle, and I can't stop myself from sucking in his scent.

"I wish that were true," he murmurs, my body vibrating with the low words. "God, I wish you hated me."

"I do," I choke out.

"Liar." His mouth grazes my skin above the collar of my jacket. Not a kiss. Worse, almost. He breathes me in, and with every breath, he sucks out more of my sanity.

You drank me dry so slow

86

The words shoot through my mind like comets, fiery tails dissolving my mental haze. I plant my palms on his chest to shove him back but freeze when I feel him shaking. The world shifts and presents itself from a new angle, one in which he isn't intentionally provoking me but collapsing against me.

"Please." His voice cracks. "Don't push me away. Just for a minute, let me come home."

My heart pumps painfully against my ribs. There's something in his voice I've never heard before. Sharp barbs and fathomless shadows. Coupled with the trembling of his body, it scares the shit out of me.

My arms automatically wind around him, anchoring tightly and pulling us flush. With a choked groan, he wraps his arms around me in return. His heart thunders against my ear. Every quake in his frame spikes my worry further.

The fact that this is our first hug registers only dimly as I rub his back and massage the tight muscles of his shoulders. Slowly, his trembling abates.

"Fuck, that feels good," he whispers.

"Wilder," I say against his chest, "what's going on?"

His hold relaxes a fraction. "Nothing."

I try to lean back but he doesn't release me. "Please talk to me. Tell me you're okay."

He sighs, a hand shifting to cradle the back of my head. "I'm okay. A cockroach, remember? Ugly and indestructible."

I fight the urge to smile. "Grudge much? I was eight when I called you that. Right after you told me I was a toothpick with a cotton ball for a head."

This time when he shakes, it's with laughter. His fingers dive into my hair, spreading across my scalp. When he begins to lightly massage me, my knees melt. His other arm tightens, holding me up.

"Does that feel good?" he whispers.

It feels really fucking good. So does his big, hard body, still curled around me like a heated, muscly blanket. I haven't been held in close to a year and never by someone built like Wilder.

Never by *Wilder*.

All the things I should be feeling—alarm being the foremost—are nowhere to be found. I feel fuzzy and warm. Oddly safe. A tapestry of colorful patchwork memories surrounds me. Lying in the shade of the sycamore in his parents' backyard, scribbling in our journals and playing guitar. Arguing about whether *place* rhymed with *decay*. Comparing calluses on our hands.

Our first sold out show as Night Theory, the screams of the crowd in our ears as we looked at each other and realized we'd done it. Built something special, something *magical*, together.

My voice wavers with emotion. "I'm really confused by what's happening right now. We're hugging. Is this an alternate dimension?"

I can't see his smile, but I feel it.

"Never hugging you is now on the list of my biggest mistakes."

A warm hand encompasses the back of my neck. I shiver as he nuzzles his face into my neck and drags in a deep breath. "You smell the same," he whispers, a gravelly note in his voice that makes my stomach drop.

The arm around my back flexes, canting our hips together, and the world tilts again. My body wakes up apocalypse-style—boiling seas and giant plumes of fire.

That is *not* his belt buckle growing harder and bigger against my stomach.

"Wilder," I squeak.

This time when his lips find my neck, there's no mistaking his intent. A small, involuntary moan escapes me as he presses a soft, open-mouthed kiss beneath my ear. His hands float down my spine and seize my hips. He lifts me onto the counter, immediately pressing forward between my legs. My fingers dig into his waist as his tongue touches my pulse. I moan again because logic has clearly left the room and *it's been so damn long* and *holy shit I forgot how enormous his dick is.*

The last time his hands were on me, I wasn't ready for it. My heart was too invested; we were both hurting. I was a virgin and his experience was daunting. He shocked me on purpose to push me away.

I may not be that much more experienced now, but I'm three years older. No longer a virgin. I'm not afraid anymore. My body screams for what he can give me and my head suddenly doesn't care about the consequences.

"Fuck, I want you so bad." He nips at my earlobe as one hand dives between our bodies. His thumb circles, manipulating the seam of my jeans against my clit. "Tell me to stop."

"No." I gasp. "Don't st—"

My voice chokes off as a fist pounds on the bathroom door.

His head whips up and he snarls, "Go away!"

"Wild?" asks a concerned female voice. "It's me. Are you sick? I'm coming in."

The doorknob rattles. Wilder leaps backward so fast he collides with the brick wall. Our eyes meet for one second—a second that stretches for years—before he jerks into action, grabbing the door before it can swing open all the way. I glimpse Kendra's pretty, worried face before he slips out and closes the door behind him.

Over the pounding of my heartbeat, I hear the rumble of his voice.

"I'm fine... She followed me in... Yeah, just some girl..."

My eyes close.

Just some girl.

CHAPTER TEN

wilder

THE HANDS that were on Evangeline's luscious body are now on Kendra's shoulders, steering her away from the bathroom. Halfway down the hallway, she digs her heels in and spins to face me. Brown eyes full of a familiar blend of cunning and curiosity narrow.

"The bathroom? Really?"

My eyelids twitch as she echoes the same words Evangeline used but with an entirely different meaning. I glance back to see the door still closed. All I want is to go back inside. Be inside *her*. I want it so badly I can barely breathe.

I force my focus back to Kendra. "It's not what you think."

She glances below my waist, then lifts a sculpted eyebrow. "You know I don't care. Why all the secrecy?" She takes a sultry step toward me, pressing herself to my chest. "We usually share."

"Not this one." The rough words slip out. Kendra's eyes instantly shimmer with suspicion.

"Why not?"

Her gaze veers past my shoulder, narrowing on some-thing. *Someone.* My spine stiffens, prickling under the scrutiny of mismatched eyes. When the sensation fades, I glance back to see Evangeline walking away from us, back toward the party. Hips swinging. Blond hair waterfalling over a cropped leather jacket.

She's probably going to find Michael Dresden.

Fuck that guy.

"No. Not her."

My head swivels back to Kendra. Despite the Botox keeping her forehead smooth, it's easy to see she's furious. I'm not surprised. She doesn't know much about Evangeline's and my history, but she possesses the same instincts as all women. She recognizes a great white shark in our waters.

I want to laugh in her face. Laugh at our fucked-up excuse for a relationship. We barely tolerate each other unless we're high, and we both sleep with other people. Sometimes together, sometimes separately.

Rye hates her and thinks she's using me. I know she is. But I'm using her, too.

"She'll never accept your life, your needs," continues Kendra, misinterpreting my silence. Her voice is smooth now. Cajoling. "I know you don't want to lose what we have."

She lifts a hand to my face, cool fingertips on my jaw.

Evangeline's fingers were warm.

Irritation flares inside me. Pulling Kendra's hand from my face, I frown. "You think I can't find someone else? There are at least ten people in my living room right now who would happily set me up."

Her lips compress, nostrils flaring. Just as fast, her expression clears and a soft smile forms. The same smile that sucked me in when we met. When I thought she was a nice, normal girl. Someone I could tolerate and have a good time with. Introduce to my parents so they'd get off my back and stop thinking I was hung up on Evangeline.

By the time I found out Kendra's smile was as fake as mine most days, I lacked the motivation to cut her loose—due in large part to the pills she sells to me.

"Wild." My name is wrapped in syrupy superiority. "Think about what you're saying. You can't trust any of these people. You think they want you to succeed?" She shakes her head, eyes pitying. "You and I both know they'd love nothing more than to bring you down. You don't want to risk that, do you?"

Unfortunately, she has a point. Outside of Rye and the guys in the band, the list of people I trust starts and ends with my family. But even that trust only goes so far. None of my friends or family know about the rigid control I maintain day in and day out. How I self-medicate in order to show up as the frontman my band needs. They don't know that once every few months, I cut myself off and spend a week in the misery of withdrawals.

They all think my weird, periodic ritual of locking myself in my room for days is a part of my songwriting process. It's not entirely a lie—I wrote the bulk of our next album while my skin felt like it was melting off my bones. But it's not the whole truth. I do it so I won't become a true addict, upping my doses over and over until I can't function without the drugs.

There's only one person who actually knows my secret and that's the woman in front of me... who just *oh so subtly* threatened to sell me out if I dump her.

I wish I could hate her, but thanks to a night last year when she poured out all the details of her twisted childhood to me, I have a damned soft spot for her. I understand why she is the way she is, and if she doesn't quite understand why I am the way I am, then she accepts it. Accepts me.

Would Evangeline accept me as I am? The narrow line I

walk? The method I use to manage my demons? *Definitely not.* And the kicker? If she did, I'd lose respect for her. She'd cease to be the woman I've put above all others in my mind and heart.

My muse. My Fairy.

Kendra slips her arms around me. I don't pull away, but I don't embrace her, either.

"I'm sorry, Wild. I had a knee-jerk reaction, and that's not fair to you." She exhales noisily against my chest. "You know what? If you need to sleep with her once to get her out of your system, then go for it. I trust you. You won't break what we have."

My heart stutters, adrenaline shooting through my veins. "You don't mean that."

Kendra gazes up at me. Her face is impossible to read, but the look in her eyes is sly. "I do. In fact, the more I think about it, the more I think it will be a good thing."

I frown. "That's an abrupt shift. Me sleeping with Evangeline will be a *good* thing? Why?"

She draws away from me and shrugs. "I've heard rumors about her."

My eyebrows shoot up. "From who?"

She inspects her manicure. "An old friend of mine dated her for a while last year. You don't know him."

I swipe a hand over my face, exhausted with this conversation. "Enough with the manipulation tactics. Spit it out."

She gives me a satisfied smirk. "He said she's a bad lay. Boring. He wasn't her first, but he said it was like fucking a virgin."

For a few seconds I just stare at her, stunned by her audacity and an overwhelming need to rip this random guy's head off.

Then I replay what happened in the bathroom. The way

Evangeline arched against me, rubbing herself against my hand. Her breathy moans and clutching fingers, panting breaths and flushed cheeks. How her body fit against mine like a puzzle piece I've been searching for my entire life.

I think about how she came apart on my fingers three years ago even though she fought it. How she initially fought her reaction to me tonight, too. How she gave me the fucking green light, and if it weren't for Kendra's interruption, I'd be balls deep inside her right now.

Sex with Evangeline will be explosive. Call it masculine instinct or learned experience, or maybe I'm finally realizing how bored *I've* been. Kendra knows all the tricks—so do the women she brings into bed with us—but something has been missing for a while. Authenticity. True abandon. I'm sick of performative sex with women who are more concerned with moaning at appropriate times than actually enjoying themselves.

There's never been anything artificial about Evangeline's response to me or mine to her. Not mentally, emotionally, or physically. Time apart didn't dilute our alchemy. I'm starting to wonder if anything ever will.

"Wild? What are you thinking?"

My eyes narrow on Kendra. "Talking shit about another woman's sexual history is low."

She flushes, decent enough to be embarrassed. "I only repeated what he said."

"Uh-huh." I pause, eyeing her like she's a scorpion about to strike. "Do you really mean it?"

She doesn't bother pretending confusion, though her nod lacks confidence. "Sure. *Once.* And don't bring her here."

I can't completely smother my reaction. Excitement. Anticipation. Relief. Kendra sees it all. She doesn't say anything. Neither do I. But in our silence is an acknowledgment that on some deep level we know this is a mistake. It's in the pinched skin around her eyes. The layer of disquiet that sits atop my elation like oil.

But I can't stop myself.

"Tonight?" Kendra asks softly.

I nod shortly. I can't wait anymore. I've waited so long already.

She looks past me toward the party. Toward the dozens of people, most of them superficial friends and hangers-on, who show up whenever I want. When she turns back to me, she wears a bright, false smile.

"In that case, I think I'll have some fun, too."

She wants a reaction. My jealousy. Possessiveness. Sometimes I pretend I feel them for her sake because while I don't love her, I'm not a complete dick. But I can't pretend tonight. I can't feel anything but my need.

Bending forward, I brush a chaste kiss on her cheek. "Be safe," I tell her.

"You too," she whispers.

She walks away, her head held high, off to find an unsuspecting man or couple to keep her entertained. I wait thirty seconds, then follow, weaving through the throngs of people in search of a white-blond head. When I don't see Evangeline in the living room or on the deck, I swallow a surge of trepidation. Has she left? Did she leave *alone*?

When I see Michael Dresden chatting up a brunette on a couch, I breathe a sigh of relief and pull out my phone to text her. My fingers hover over the screen.

What the fuck am I supposed to say? *My girlfriend says I can fuck you, so are you down?*

I rub my forehead.

"Wild! Did you see Eva?"

I turn to find Eddie and Jax approaching me from the

deck, matching grins on their faces. The brothers look so similar they're often mistaken for twins—or they were until Eddie adopted his signature neon-green mullet last year.

"I did," I say, my fingers curling around my phone.

"It was so good to see her, right?" asks Jax. "She said she's already getting calls from venues after that writeup from Illoka."

Eddie nods rapidly. "She's killing it. We have to catch her next show."

I like Eddie and Jax. They're great musicians, low-drama roommates, and all-around decent guys. I've even forgiven Eddie for kissing Evangeline before me.

But right now I want to strangle them both.

"I'm actually looking for her. Any idea where she is?"

Jax's expression falls. "Sorry, man. She just left. Said she was tired."

Eddie laughs. "She still hates parties."

A knot of tension inside me releases.

I slip my phone in my pocket, then clap my hands to their shoulders. "Can you hold shit down here? Kick these fuckers out before dawn?"

Eddie blinks in confusion, but he's thankfully too buzzed to put two and two together. Jax, on the other hand, raises a knowing eyebrow.

"Sure," he says dryly.

Eddie lifts his beer in a salute, turning away from us to shout, "The Thompson brothers are in charge, assholes!"

There's a chorus of laughter and cheers. Jax rolls his eyes. Someone cranks the music higher, and under Eddie's encouragement, the entire living room turns into an impromptu dance floor.

I nod at Jax, then slip away in the chaos.

CHAPTER ELEVEN

evangeline

WITHIN TWENTY MINUTES of arriving home, I'm curled on my couch in pajamas, a cup of steaming tea on the coffee table, my Kindle in my hands. Everything is exactly as it should be. I'm relaxed. Alone. My peace restored.

No one will ever know that when I got home, I ran around like a crazy person turning on every light, opening every closet and door, until there were no more shadows.

What happened tonight—*what almost happened*—has gone the way of all my other memories of Wilder. Locked in a box, chained closed, and thrown into the Mariana Trench of my mind.

I refuse to go back to the dark place I was in after I left the band, when dwelling on the loss of him and everything we'd shared felt like slow suffocation.

Never again.

I'm so engrossed in my book, my ears dismiss the first knock as a part of the music playing on my nearby speaker. It isn't until the song ends that I register the sound of a fist pounding on my front door.

Then his voice. "Evangeline!"

I rocket to my feet. My stomach doesn't come with me, clinging to the couch cushions, most of the blood in my head racing to join it. For ten frenzied seconds, my body is a statue while my mind erupts like Vesuvius.

He's here.

Why is he here?

Oh God, he's here.

Another song starts. Wilder's voice pushes into my ears over the intro. "Open the door, Fairy!"

The nickname is what propels me into motion—what breaks chains and locks and releases what I've been trying to forget. I stalk to the front door, unlock the deadbolt, and yank it open. Wilder's head whips up, relief etched on his features.

I look around pointedly. "Sorry, no Fairy here. Just *some girl*."

He catches his lower lip in his teeth, wincing. "I panicked. Can I come in?"

It's ridiculously hard to ignore the puppy eyes he's giving me, but I manage to scoff. "Absolutely not. What happened in the bathroom was a mistake. Momentary insanity. Go back to your girlfriend. Or, wait—did she dump you? Good for her!"

His lips twist as he smothers a smile. "Kendra and I have an open relationship. She knows I'm here."

I blink a few times, hoping the words will become less presumptuous. Nope. They don't.

"You think I'm going to sleep with you?" My voice rises with every syllable. "You're out of your mind. I don't even like you!"

He steps closer, hands lifting to grab the top of the door-frame. Ducking his head, he pins me with a heated stare. "You may not like me anymore, Evangeline, but you still want me. You told me not to stop."

I used to love that he was one of the few people who

called me by my full name. Now it feels aberrant. An unwanted intimacy.

Wilder's gaze travels down my body, lingering on my braless breasts. I cross my arms over my white T-shirt.

"It's cold out," I snap.

Leaning toward me even further, he murmurs darkly, "Don't lie to me." He licks his lips, a quick flick of his tongue that echoes as a pulse between my thighs. "We've been dancing around this for years. There's no pact anymore. Let's get it out of our systems. Tomorrow we can go back to strangers."

"Get fucked," I snarl.

His brows twitch up. "Trying to, actually."

With a growl, I swing the door closed. His boot catches the wood, then he's pushing into my house. He slams the door behind him, locks it, and faces me. My heart gallops, my darting gaze capturing him in ecstatic bursts like furious notes on a piano. Flushed cheekbones. Heaving chest. Twitching fingers. Eyes full of naked longing.

He's a siren song of chaos and desire, so beautiful my conviction disperses like sea foam. I'm swept away.

"Evangeline," he whispers.

We reach for each other at the same time. It happens fast but feels like slow motion. I'm waiting forever—*I've waited forever*—for his hands on my waist. They clench and lift me, slamming our chests together. My legs wind around his hips, my arms locking around his neck. Planting one hand on my ass, he sinks the other into my hair. With a sharp tug, he angles my head and brings my mouth to his. So close I can feel the condensation of his breath.

"Kiss me, Fairy."

It's a plea. A prayer.

I can't resist.

His lips are exactly how I remember them from our brief kiss when I was sixteen. Silky soft and warm, firm and full. They part slightly but he doesn't kiss me back. Doubt surges, but when I start to pull away, the hand in my hair tightens to hold me still.

"No," he whispers.

His thumb finds my chin and presses down, opening me to him. He breathes into my mouth. Hot, heavy, slow. Sucking me in, filling me up. Shivers wrack my body. My fingers and toes vibrate.

His groan expands my lungs, and then he's kissing me like I've never been kissed before. Like he's pouring the entirety of our lives into my mouth. Our tongues tangle like our verses used to: seamlessly, effortlessly.

I had no idea a kiss could feel like this. Like arriving somewhere I've never been but where I've always belonged.

I don't notice we're moving until we're falling onto my bed, until the weight of him reminds me I have a body instead of only lips and tongue. I gasp when he breaks the kiss, instantly bereft without his lips on mine.

He rises above me and tugs my shirt up my chest. Hot, rough hands slide over my bare stomach to encompass my breasts. He squeezes them gently, his expression rapt in the too-bright room.

"I've thought about touching these for so long. Fucking them. Giving you a pretty pearl necklace."

A choked moan leaves me as he circles my nipples with his thumbs. Lightly at first, then with more pressure until my breasts ache and my nipples are flushed and tingling. With a satisfied hum, he lowers his head. When his mouth covers one peak at the same time he pinches the other, I gasp his name.

"You like that, huh?" He punctuates the low words with

flicks of his tongue and finger. His teeth scrape over hypersensitive flesh—I whimper. My hips lift, searching for him, but he shifts out of reach.

"I know you can be louder," he says, dark amusement in his voice. "Let me hear you sing."

He devotes himself to making me lose it, suckling my breasts, blowing onto wet skin, biting and massaging and *feasting* until I'm giving him what he wants. Making sounds I've never made before. Feeling sensations I've never felt, like my breasts have a direct line to my clit.

Suddenly there's pressure right where I need it, a heavy hand rubbing roughly. Fireworks explode in my head and I explode with them. He swallows my cries, kissing me with feverish intensity until I melt, boneless and twitching in the aftermath.

I open my eyes to find Wilder smiling down at me. His real smile. A little lopsided, one dimple deeper than the other. I haven't seen the expression in so long, my heart tugs in my chest, aching and overfull. I touch his face, my fingertips dancing over his cheekbone where a single, small mole rests.

His smile falls. "Don't," he whispers. "This doesn't end like one of your romance books. I'm no hero."

Another tug in my chest, this one a scythe slicing through old, stale hopes. The *maybes* and *could have beens*. Silly wishes of a girl for her perfect love story, her perfect prince.

The pain fades fast, though, more nostalgia than anything else. I grieved that girl and her foolish dreams three years ago. I grieved the idea of *him*. Right now I'm not interested in a pretty, boring prince.

I want the villain.

I swallow, finding my voice. "Trust me, I know. You're an asshole, and I'm ghosting you tomorrow."

His lips twitch even as darkness flickers in his eyes. Tension ripples down his body. To break the unbearable moment, I arch into him. His gaze lowers to where I'm rubbing myself shamelessly against his erection.

"What are you waiting for? An invitation?" I angle my hands between us, coasting my palm over his cock before grabbing his belt buckle. "Fuck me like you hate me, Wilder."

"Jesus Christ," he hisses.

The next seconds are a blur as we tear off our clothes. His hands and mouth are everywhere. My stomach. Neck. My ankles, knees. Thighs. He shoves a foil packet between my teeth, his hand transferring to my throat and staying there as he slides down my body. One of my legs is yanked up, my knee shoved outward and held to the mattress. I spit out the condom foil, which slides off my chest.

He bites my inner thigh, then covers me with his mouth.

I gasp, arching. "Yes."

He eats me out like it's his calling. No hesitation, no tender exploration or reading my cues. He takes my pleasure like he owns it, and before I know it, I'm bucking against his mouth and crying out his name through another orgasm.

I'm still twitching with aftershocks as the hand on my throat releases, calloused fingertips floating over my chest and stomach and lifting goosebumps. He rises from between my legs like a fallen angel, all chaotic hair and straining muscles and inked skin. The lower half of his face glistens with my release, speckled green eyes catlike with smugness.

He licks his lips. "You still taste like sin."

I'm useless, panting and drugged by back-to-back orgasms, and can only watch as he straddles my hips. His hard cock juts out over my stomach, and of course it's as pretty as the rest of him. He strokes himself slowly, his grip loose over the long, thick shaft and a broad, flared head that shines wetly at the tip. Something else shines, too—silver balls that disappear and reappear as his hand passes over them.

My eyes widen.

"Apadravya piercing," he says with a smirk. "Consider those orgasms appetizers to the main course. I'm about to blow your mind."

I squirm, an uncomfortable emptiness taking up residence between my legs. His other hand plays with my breasts lazily, but I can't focus on his touch because I'm fixated on his cock. I wish his hand were my mouth. I want to roll my tongue over the silver balls and taste them. Taste *him*.

But when I try to rise, to reach for him, his hand plants on my chest. "That's not on the menu."

"You don't want a blowjob? Who are you?"

He doesn't answer. Doesn't look at me as he begins to tease my nipples again until my breaths turn to pants and I'm making small, needy sounds. His too-perceptive eyes lift to mine.

Shaking his head, he *tsks* softly. "How many men have tried and failed to read your music? How many have left you unsatisfied?"

The words rattle me, but they anger me, too. If he thinks I'm the same girl he shocked in his childhood bedroom, he's about to find out that I abandoned her on the floor where we used to write songs.

Stretching my arms over my head, I fake a yawn. "Sorry to break it to you, but you're not special. I'm one of those lucky girls who gets off easily." I nod at his hand, still working over his shaft. "Are you going to do something with that or just wave it in my face?"

For two absolutely perfect seconds, he stares at me in

shock. Then he laughs. It's not a nice sound, though, but a sinister chuckle.

"You're such a fucking liar."

I glare at him, but he only smiles slightly and reaches for the condom. He tears it open and rolls it on with brisk efficiency.

Don't think about how many women have watched him do this. Don't think about it...

Too late.

I grimace, my eyes closing.

Hands grab my face. My eyes snap open as he covers me with his body, blanketing me with heat. The tip of his nose touches mine, his eyes so close I can count the freckles like stars in an alien sky. I grab his forearms for stability because it suddenly feels like I'm plummeting down from space.

"No," he whispers, pressing a soft kiss to my mouth. "You stay right here. It's just us. You and me. Like it's supposed to be."

My body goes rigid. "You can't have it both ways. And you're not a hero, remember? So stop acting like one. Either fuck me or get the fuck out."

An emotion crosses his face too swiftly for me to name, but it bounces in my chest like I'm an empty chamber. Heavy and hard.

His jaw clenches. "You want me to treat you like them? Fuck you like I don't give a shit about you?"

No.

"Yes."

He bares his teeth. "Fine."

I yelp in surprise as he flips me onto my stomach. My hips are wrenched into the air. His knees bump mine apart. My hair is gathered, spiraled into a chord, and yanked until my spine bows. He shoves two fingers inside me and pumps hard.

"Fucking dripping."

He says it like it's a curse, like he's angry my body likes his aggressive handling. I'm a little confused myself, but there's no time to think about it because the head of his cock drags over my center. Up and down, up and down.

"If it's too much, tap my thigh," he growls.

"Wh—"

The rest of my question is lost—*I'm lost*—as he slams inside me with one brutal thrust.

CHAPTER TWELVE

evangeline

I spent years describing love
using too many words
specifically verbs
before finally realizing
you weren't really listening
only nodding along

EVERY TIME I shift in my chair, phantom fullness pulses between my legs. Two days after Wilder broke my vagina, I still feel him. Every time I wipe. Sneeze. Bend over. Muscles that have no business interfering with my life are sore and cramping. Yesterday I was convinced I was starting my period. But no—just another consequence of the most intense, depraved, earthshaking sex of my life.

"Not hungry, Eva?" asks my dad, his eyes lifting from my untouched waffle and narrowing with concern.

I summon a smile. "Not really. Filled up on fruit."

"I'll take that," Hunter says, snatching my plate. At eighteen and still growing, he's perpetually starving. He's already finished off two servings of waffles, bacon, and scrambled eggs.

Mom shakes her head with a fond smile while my uncle Josh chuckles. "I remember that age well."

The conversation veers in a safe direction—namely, away from me—as they reminisce about keeping my uncle Patrick fed when he was a teenager. I devote myself to my cup of coffee, pretending to listen while trying not to think about how sore I am and ignoring my dad's periodic, searching glances.

He's always been the worrier in the family, especially when it comes to me. His overprotectiveness used to piss me off when I was a teenager. Now I'm grateful for it. *Mostly.* Right now it's knives sawing on my already frayed nerves.

Unfortunately, Sunday brunch at my parents' requires an excuse to skip. A worthy one in the realm of sudden hospitalization or amnesia. My mom is militant about the tradition. In the early years, it was chaos with both sets of grandparents and four aunts and uncles every weekend. Now most of my parents' siblings have families of their own. Uncle Josh and his wife don't have kids, and since she works most weekends as a trauma nurse, he still comes more often than not. My grandparents are usually fixtures as well, but they travel a lot during the colder months. This month all four of them are on a cruise to Panama.

"Eva."

My mom's gentle voice jolts me. I look up, blinking in surprise when I see that Hunter's gone and Dad and Uncle Josh are clearing the table.

"Sorry. Spaced out."

My dad opens his mouth, that familiar frown of concern on his face, but my mom gives him a *look*. He closes his mouth fast. He and my uncle trade a humored glance and head for the kitchen with plates.

Mom rounds the table and smiles down at me. "Come on. I have something for you."

Whereas my dad is all about frontal assault, Sophie Sullivan is the master of sneak attacks. With her gentle spirit and angelic beauty, she's a Trojan Horse of life lessons I'm never ready for.

Sighing, I push back from the table and follow her down the hall. She veers into her art studio, a bright, colorful space that's one of my favorite places on the planet.

Growing up, I spent countless hours curled in the armchair by the window, watching her draw. Sometimes I fell asleep, but mostly I read books, listened to music, and later, played guitar. Most of our difficult conversations have also happened in this room. The Sex talk. The Red Flags and Safety talk. The Why-Your-Best-Friend-Isn't-Your-Best-Friend-If-She-Kisses-Your-Boyfriend talk.

Leaning against the doorjamb, I cross my arms and school my expression.

"What's up?" My voice is unconcerned, masking my unhinged inner dialogue.

You're fine. Everything's fine. You did not have life-altering, semi-hate sex with Wilder. And he definitely didn't shred your G-spot with his pierced dick.

A vivid flashback hits me—the tender, fierce expression on his face when he ripped off the condom and came all over my chest, then rubbed his cum into my breasts.

My whole body flushes. Between my legs, a painful pulse makes me wince.

Thankfully, Mom has her back to me as she rummages through a small closet. I take slow, deep breaths until I feel calm again.

"Ah, here it is! I found this in the attic last week and thought you might like to have it."

She turns around, offering me a small black box, the kind you buy in a craft store for keeping mementos. It's covered in band stickers.

My face goes numb. "I don't want that."

There's nothing remotely normal about my voice this time.

"Oh, honey." She sets the box down on a drafting table. "Come sit."

With no reasonable excuse not to, I drag myself to the armchair and collapse into it. Mom pulls over her rolling stool and settles in front of me. Grabbing my hands in hers, she leans forward until we're eye to eye.

"It's the new song, isn't it? I'm sure it brought up a lot of complex feelings."

"Um, yeah."

She leans back an inch, her brows lifting.

I screw my eyes shut. "Don't look at me like that."

"You just lied to my face." There's amusement in her voice. "You haven't done that since you were four and tried to convince me the cat covered *himself* in pink marker."

Slipping my hands from hers, I rub my face. "I'm sorry. I... I didn't really lie. The song did throw me for a loop." *And started this mess.*

When she doesn't say anything, I make the mistake of looking at her calm, compassionate face. My defenses crumble.

Cheeks burning, I whisper, "He came over Friday night."

Her eyes widen and flicker to the left side of my neck. Specifically to the spot where I piled concealer over a hickey. My skin crawls. I'm hoping it's a prelude to spontaneous combustion.

"Oh," she whispers, then sits back, blinking fast. "*Oh.*"

I groan, dropping my head back to stare at the ceiling. "It was a mistake, Mom. It was—" I choke, my eyes stinging. *Perfect. Mind-blowing.* "I hate him so much."

There's a long pause. "You don't hate him, sweetie."

"It's just us. You and me. Like it's supposed to be."

As his words whisper through my mind, I finally allow myself to feel them. My gut clenches, my heart pounding in thick misery. Tears push against my closed eyelids, forcing their way through my lashes.

"You're right," I concede, angrily swiping wetness from my cheeks. "What I hate is that he changed. I wish I knew what happened my senior year. One day he was the Wilder I'd always known, and the next day he was different. Like he had a... a poison inside him that spread so slowly I didn't notice until it was everywhere. I think that's the worst part—the guilt. I feel like he needed me to help him, but I didn't even know something was wrong until it was too late. I lost him before I knew he was slipping away."

My mom makes a soft, sad sound. She grabs my hands again, squeezing hard.

"Listen to me very carefully, Eva. You're not responsible for anyone else's mental health. The road Wilder is on is his to walk. We all worry about him, Rose and Julian especially. But they know there's nothing they can do but provide support, set boundaries, and be there for him if he decides he's ready for a change."

My lungs atrophy, turning my voice brittle. "What are you saying?"

She sighs, her head briefly bowing. When it lifts, determination and sorrow shine in her eyes. "What changed back

111

then was Wilder started having debilitating panic attacks. He refused to see a therapist or consider medication. Rose thinks he started using drugs to manage his anxiety and that over the years his using has progressed."

Shock erupts from me in a breathless laugh. "What? No. I mean, sure, he smoked a lot of weed back then." *We both did.* "And I'm sure he drinks and stuff now, but he's always been super careful because of his family history..." I trail off at the unchanging expression on her face. My spine stiffens further. "He's not an addict, Mom. He wasn't loaded on Friday. I would have known."

"Maybe not," she says softly, but I can tell she thinks I'm being naive.

Maybe I am.

Was he on drugs?

The idea nauseates me.

I jerk to my feet, forcing her to push back the stool. "I have to go."

"Eva, please—"

"No! He's not a fucking addict!"

Buzzing silence follows. I've never yelled at her like that. Shaking my head in dismay, I whisper, "I'm sorry."

"It's okay, honey. It's okay."

She reaches for me, but I back away.

"I can't do this right now."

Movement in the doorway makes me flinch. My gaze flies to my dad. His expression is neutral, but his voice emerges hard. "Julian says it's opiates. Probably pills. He's careful around his family, but he's not fooling his parents. He's always high these days." He pauses. "Stay away from him, Eva."

"I haven't seen him since the barbecue last year," I blurt.

My dad's eyes narrow. "You think after years of watching

him toy with you that I didn't recognize the look on your face the second you walked in this morning?" His gaze drops to my neck. "Please tell me that's not from him."

Mortified, I slap a hand over the spot.

His shoulders bunch, then relax. He shakes his head slowly, blue eyes filled with such disappointment that shame spreads like ink through my chest. My chin wobbles. He's *never* looked at me this way.

My mom takes a few steps toward him. "Let's take a breather," she says softly.

He stays laser focused on me. "Deep down, I knew it was only a matter of time before he came after you, but I really, really hoped you'd be smarter than this."

"Matthew," hisses my mom.

He ignores her again. "I know you guys were close growing up. You had a bond anyone could see. Hell—Julian, Rose, your mom, and I used to joke that the two of you were a done deal. *Soulmates.*" His lips twist over the word. "We were wrong. What Wilder feels for you isn't love. Maybe it could have been, but the second he decided to take the coward's way out, he became incapable of the feeling. If you let yourself believe the bullshit he's telling you, he'll drag you down with him. He's an addict. He's *using* you. Did he tell you he was single now? He's not. His girlfriend moved in with him two months ago."

"Enough!" snaps my mom. "Take a walk, Matt."

He looks at her, but it's like he doesn't even see her. His jaw ticks, then he spins on his heel and disappears into the hallway. I stare after him, silent tears spilling over my cheeks.

My mom wraps her arms around me; I barely feel the embrace. "He shouldn't have said all that. It was coming from a place of pain that has nothing to do with you."

"His dad?" I ask weakly.

She nods against my shoulder. "And Julian. There was a rough period in the early days before he got sober. It almost broke up the band. But it's not an excuse. He went too far." She leans back, framing my face in her hands and smoothing away my tears. "Expect him to be groveling tomorrow."

Preternatural calm descends on my shoulders, numbing and welcome. My tears slow and stop.

"You agree with him, though. Don't you?"

Her gaze flickers away from mine, her hands falling. "I won't lie and say I don't have some of the same fears." She looks like she wants to say more, but instead presses her palm to my chest over my heart. "Be careful with this, okay?"

I manage a small smile. "Don't worry. I have no intention of seeing Wilder again, at least not on purpose." I pause. "He told me he was in an open relationship. Do you know if that's true?"

She frowns. "I don't, sorry. Do you want me to ask Rose? I can be discreet."

I shake my head, regretting letting the question slip out. "No, that's okay."

I know exactly who to ask.

♫

ONCE AT HOME, I make myself tea and take it onto my back porch. The sky is a pale, crystal blue, the air cold enough that I have a blanket wrapped around my shoulders and my tea has doubled its steam.

Despite the still-bare branches of the maple above me, green stalks are pushing through the soil along my fence. In a few weeks, white and yellow daffodils will bloom. I've always loved this time of year—the first yawn of spring—but for the first time, I can't connect to the symbolic beauty of new beginnings. All I see is barrenness.

Dropping into a chair, I take a few sips of chamomile.

Then I make the call.

Rye answers on the second ring. "Yo! Good timing. Just got in the car to head home from Casey's. I can't wait for you to meet this girl, Eva. She's super cool. No crazy vibes at all."

"Is this a different Casey from the one you dated before Anna?"

There's a telling silence, then a deep groan. "Shit. Oh, fuck me. Her name is Kelsey. I totally called her Casey this morning. No wonder she gave me that weird look."

I try not to laugh, but it's impossible.

"What am I going to do?" he whines.

"I'd start with an apology. Was it a first date?"

He makes an affirmative sound. "I was going to be a gentleman and drop her off at home, but then she dragged me in—"

"Got it," I say quickly. "If it was a first date, she might accept an apology. No promises, though. Getting her name wrong after spending the night gives major fuckboy energy."

He laughs, unoffended. "Anyway, what's up? How was the party on Friday?"

I lean back to stare at the bare branches above me. "It was at Wilder's house. Is that why you suddenly had last-minute plans?"

"Uh, maybe?"

I sigh. "You don't have to pretend you're not friends with him, Rye. I don't care about that. I'm calling because I have a question. After you answer it, we're going back to never talking about him. Cool?"

"Cool." He clears his throat. "I'm sorry, Eva. We were in the studio for months—"

"It's fine," I interject. "My question is about Wilder and his girlfriend. Do they have an open relationship?"

This time the pause is so long that if it wasn't for the background hum coming from moving tires, I'd think he'd hung up.

When his answer comes, his voice is uncharacteristically serious. "They both sleep with other people. But I wouldn't even call it a relationship. It's super fucked up. They don't even like each other. Why are you asking? What happened?"

I open my mouth, but before I can speak, he explodes.

"Oh, *shit*! He seduced you, didn't he? That motherfucker. Were you drunk? Do I need to beat his ass? I knew I should have gone with—"

"Rye, chill!"

He falls silent, but his breathing is harsh through the line.

"I wasn't drunk, okay? I went home early and he showed up at my house. We slept together. It was consensual. He left. The end."

Memory seizes me.

Wilder buttons his jeans and buckles his belt, bare chest and arms flexing with the movements. I know I have to get up to lock my door behind him, but I need another minute. I'm not sure my legs can hold me yet.

"You really have no idea," he murmurs, heavy-lidded gaze dancing down my body.

I sit up, dragging the sheet with me. "About what?"

Avoiding my eyes, he grabs his shirt and pulls it on, then slips his feet into unlaced boots. His socks are tucked into a pocket.

Finally, he looks at me. "Be stronger than me. Block my number. Don't open the door if I knock."

I swallow so hard I hear it. "Obviously."

His smile is tender. Sad in a way I don't understand. "I mean it. Someday you're going to realize the way it is between us isn't the norm. But when that happens—when you're tempted—remember that I'm not worth it."

Before my shock can transition to anger, he stalks to the bed and grabs my throat, then presses his lips to mine in a short, hard kiss.

"Goodbye, Fairy."

Then he's gone, striding from the bedroom. He doesn't look back.

"Eva?" asks Rye in a tone that tells me he's been talking but I haven't heard a word he's said.

"Sorry. I'm here."

"Are you sure you're okay?"

I force confidence into my voice. "Yep."

He hesitates. "Are you guys talking now? Is this going to happen again?"

A sudden gust of wind throws my hair across my face and whistles through high branches. I shiver, then grab my tea and stand.

"No. It was a one-time thing."

Rye says nothing.

He doesn't have to.

I'm not sure I believe me, either.

CHAPTER THIRTEEN

wilder

YOU GAVE ME WHAT I ASKED FOR
THEN TOOK IT WITH YOU
OUT THE FRONT DOOR
NOW I'M BROKEN OPEN
EVERYTHING UNSPOKEN
POURING OUT OF ME

SO I SPIN... SPIN
ON THIS CAROUSEL OF SIN... SIN
A GAME I'LL NEVER WIN... WIN
WITHOUT YOU

SIX LONG WEEKS have passed since Evangeline's gasps and moans became my favorite soundtrack. I've replayed our night together so many times the vinyl is worn out. Muffled and muddy, the melody distorted.

Sometimes I'm not sure it really happened.

The only time it feels real is when I'm asleep. In my dreams, I experience it all again. The silky slopes of her hips under my hands. Her arching neck. Sweat-slick spine against my chest, her hair in my mouth, in my fist. The graceful, serpentine waves of her moving body as she matched me note for note. Bright, lust-drunk eyes and her voice sobbing my name.

Evangeline is a perfect song, but she's stuck in my head like a bad one.

Kendra is *not* happy.

I've successfully avoided having sex with her, but I'm running out of excuses. Thus far, she hasn't confronted me. As much as I need her, she needs me, too. The threat goes both ways. She's not willing to risk losing all the perks of being my girlfriend, so she's pretending everything's fine while I pretend I'm not revolted by the idea of touching anyone but Evangeline. And that, of course, is off the table.

Evangeline did what I told her to and blocked my number. I may not be a good person, but I'm not enough of an asshole to push her or show up at her house uninvited again. Even if I fantasize about knocking down her door a hundred times a day.

I'm in a constant state of hunger, but the only sustenance that will sate me is one I can't have.

The band is my saving grace. Our second single released and the response was even more insane than the first. Whatever anonymity we enjoyed before is gone, at least with the under-forty crowd in the city we call home. I wasn't a fan of social outings before, but now I can't even hit up my favorite record store or local coffee shop without being forced into conversation with strangers.

Not that I have much free time.

Between multiple daily rehearsals, the guys and I have been running ourselves ragged. Every day there's somewhere we have to be or something we have to do. Interviews. Photoshoots. Music videos. Our social media accounts have ballooned so much we've hired an agency to handle them. A team of people now generates our content, one of whom is currently recording us while we watch a basketball game in our basement.

Our keyboardist, Zander, shoves his glasses up his nose, his eyes darting from the TV to Eddie. "Are we supposed to be talking?" he hisses.

"Just act natural," chirps the woman behind a tripod holding her phone.

The first two replacements for Evangeline only lasted months before being fired. Zander has been with us for over a year. He's normal. Kind of quiet. So far, he seems to be handling all the attention pretty well, but he's definitely more freaked out than the rest of us. We, at least, remember our first tour. Although that brief flare of fame was nothing compared to what's happening now.

"This is so weird," Zander mutters.

Next to me, Jax chuckles. "If you think this is weird, wait until we hit the road."

Eddie throws a piece of popcorn at him from the other end of the L-shaped couch. "Stop scaring the newbie."

Ignoring his brother, Jax leans toward me and lowers his voice. "How are you holding up?"

"I'm fine."

His eyes fall to my hands. I curl my fingers, subduing their spastic drumming.

I'm on day ten free of pills. Normally by now, I'd have taken a quarter of a pill, my usual starter dose for reentry into my life. But after I cut the tablet, I couldn't bring myself to swallow it.

This detox was more brutal than any I've gone through before. The withdrawals more painful, the cravings so intense I almost broke a dozen times. It scared the shit out of me. My skin still feels raw, like I'm recovering from a sunburn. My head is a mess, my thoughts a fireworks show—blinding, loud, chaotic. At least my stomach settled today and I can swallow without gagging.

"Dude," Jax whispers. "You've gotta stop."

Five days ago—my worst day—Jax heard a crash in my room. When I didn't answer the door, he busted in and found me on the floor, moaning, sweating, and shaking. My mumblings about having the flu went down like a lead balloon.

I ended up telling him the truth minus where I get my pills. He yelled a lot. I puked on his shoes. It was a fucking mess.

"I told you," I whisper back, "it's under control."

Jax frowns. "When the tour starts—"

"Did you guys see this?" Eddie interrupts as he jumps to his feet. He veers around the coffee table and shoves his phone in our faces. "Glow is headlining tonight at the Cathedral!"

Jax whistles. "Damn, go Eva. Main stage?"

"Side stage," I murmur, having already seen the post on the band's Instagram. Cathedral's main stage has a capacity of six hundred, but the attached hall for lesser known acts is nothing to sneeze at with a cap of three hundred.

Eddie bounces on the balls of his feet. "We have to go!"

"Sounds good to me," says Jax with a shrug.

Zander stands fast, his relief obvious. "I'm down."

Eddie and Zander head for the stairs, Eddie rambling about how awesome Evangeline is and how he's going to text everyone he knows to come to the show in case ticket sales are lackluster. They're not. I checked fifteen minutes ago and the show is nearly sold out.

I wonder if Eddie would be as supportive of Evangeline if he knew I fucked her into a coma last month.

121

Sighing heavily, I press the heels of my hands to my aching eyes.

"Can we have the room?" Jax asks the woman whose name I can't remember.

She smiles brightly and removes her phone from the tripod. "Sure thing. Are you going to the show, Wilder?"

I start to shake my head but pause. If everyone leaves, I'll be here alone with nothing to distract me from the craving beating in my blood. I have no idea where Kendra is—she stays away during my detox—but she's the last person I can talk to about this, anyway. The last person who would tell me *not* to take a pill... or three. Much more likely, she'd crush them up and snort a line, then offer me the straw.

"Yes," Jax answers with a quick glance at me. "He's coming."

I cock an eyebrow in his direction but don't object. Do I want to see Evangeline? More than I want my next breath. But that doesn't mean seeing her is a good idea, especially not in my current state. My impulse control is hanging by a thread. If I see her fingers on a guitar, hear her sing, I'm probably going to do something stupid like weasel my way backstage and use my effect on her to get under her clothes.

Blood flows south at the thought, and I suddenly can't remember why that's a bad idea.

The social media woman claps her hands in excitement, shattering my daydream about Evangeline's tits in my mouth.

"Awesome! I've been wanting to see Glow, so this is perfect!" Leaving the tripod, she runs up the basement stairs.

Jax sighs. "Mae is a lot."

"That's her name?"

He snorts, then grabs the remote to turn off the TV. Sensing that I'm about to get lectured, I sigh and face him.

"Look, Jax, I'm sorry I worried you—"

"Let's do a dry-thirty. You and me. No booze, no drugs for a month. Gym, vitamins, the whole nine."

I stare at him, floored, as the words cycle through me and incite an uncomfortable blend of fear and yearning.

The last time I was sober for that long was after Evangeline left the band. I don't even remember why I did it, though it probably had something to do with the shame of all the fucked-up shit I did on tour and what happened after. I'm sure some part of me also thought if I could show her I was changing, she'd come back.

She blocked my number instead, and I got blackout drunk the night I realized it.

"It'll be good," Jax continues. "We'll reset our systems before the tour."

Without thinking, I say, "I don't know if I can go that long," then immediately wish I could take the words back. They make it sound like I'm admitting...

I can't even finish the thought.

Jax grabs my shoulder, his expression determined. "It's going to suck for me, too. I don't think I've gone more than a few days without weed for—shit, probably two years. Point is, we'll be miserable together. But then we'll be jacked from all the gym time and so healthy our piss smells like lettuce."

A reluctant smile pulls at my lips.

"Is that a yes?" he asks, grinning.

Yearning briefly eclipses fear, and my chin jerks down.

He squeezes my shoulder, then stands. "Come on. We have time to clear out our stashes and tell Eddie and Zander to lock their shit up."

Just as fast, fear rises again, this time a monster with fangs dripping venom. Panic curls through me, accelerating my pulse. I stand, locking my knees when they wobble. The urge to take a pill hits me so hard my vision tunnels.

"Jax." My voice is strangled.

He turns at the base of the stairs, his expression swiftly shifting from questioning to concerned.

I open my mouth, close it, and finally force out the words that don't want to come. "I need your help getting rid of the pills. Like you're going to have to do it because I don't... I don't think I can."

His expression softens in understanding. "You got it."

I swallow the lump in my throat, pushing back against the pressure inside me. "One more thing. The Oxy... Kendra gets it for me."

He stares at me for several seconds, processing, then blows out a heavy breath. "A lot of shit about your relationship suddenly makes sense." He pauses. "Do you love her?"

I shake my head.

He nods decisively. "Kick her to the curb tonight, then crash at your parents' for a few days. Eddie and I will move her shit out and get the locks changed. Okay?"

A frenetic energy sizzles through me. Not fear or panic. Something far more dangerous.

Hope.

I nod. "Okay."

♩

AS DESPERATE AS I am to see Evangeline, I know she isn't the answer to my problems. She can't change the way my brain works, can't protect me from the feeling I've had since I was a kid that I was different from my peers.

For as long as I can remember, I've thought of it as the Shadow.

There are three manifestations. Sometimes it's subdued

or muted, usually when I'm hyper-focused on music. For minutes or hours, I'm able to forget about it.

Other times, the Shadow overtakes me like a fog, becoming a veil between me and the world. It's a haze that numbs me. Separates me. Those are the times I withdraw because I'm afraid that when people look at me, they'll see it. My *wrongness*. They'll recognize I'm not like them and everything I've worked for will vanish.

The third manifestation is the worst. When the Shadow isn't distracted or numbing me, it hovers around me as a constant threat. When triggered, it snaps closed like a medieval Iron Maiden, piercing me with dozens of sharp spikes. I'm hypersensitive. Raw, exposed nerves and emotions. The world and all its madness and loudness invade me, overwhelm me. I lose perception of time. Lose control of my breath and senses.

I panic.

When I was six, I drew a picture of the Shadow. A crayon kid surrounded by a cloud of swirling black and purple with needles sinking into the small body and making it bleed. My mom found the drawing and showed my dad. They put me in therapy. I don't remember the therapist's name, but her voice was soft and I liked her smile. We played with sand trays and drew pictures more than we talked.

I stopped going after a year. My parents and the therapist seemed excited about me not coming back. It was a celebration to them, but I was sad. I'd liked the one hour a week I spent in her office full of toys and no expectations.

More than that, though, I liked that my parents were happy. So when the Shadow next appeared, I didn't say anything. Didn't draw any pictures. I kept my weird thoughts to myself and started watching how other kids acted. Classmates at school,

Rye and Evangeline on the weekends. I learned to mimic them, how they interacted with each other and adults. I was still a quiet kid, but I learned to smile more. Say the right things.

Pretend there was no Shadow.

When the topic came up again, I was eleven. My parents were worried because one of my teachers expressed concern that I didn't have friends at school. But by then I'd become adept at faking normalcy. I convinced them I was fine by making friends I didn't really want. A lot of friends. I joined after-school activities: drama, musical theater, and even soccer for a couple of years. I went to birthday parties and hangouts. Spent my free time at home entertaining my younger siblings, playing guitar with my dad, and learning piano from my mom.

I distracted myself, which distracted the Shadow. During the day, at least. Almost every night, I'd wake up gasping and shaking beneath an enormous pressure on my chest. When the numbness invariably came, it was a relief because for however long it lasted, I could sleep.

Then Evangeline and I wrote a song.

It was the first time in my life the Shadow actually disappeared. Almost like it had been waiting for that moment. Waiting for her and our music.

For years afterward, I went through each week knowing that relief was coming in the form of Evangeline every weekend. Being around her, making music with her... she made me feel both normal and extraordinary.

I overheard my mom once referring to Evangeline as an old soul. I didn't understand it then, but I do now. She was a calm kid. Slow to anger. Perceptive and compassionate beyond her years. She always smiled with her eyes. She always knew what she wanted. Said what she thought. She was brave. Real. Those traits only grew as we did.

Unlike me, her insides have always matched her outsides. She's never been a fraud pretending to be someone she wasn't.

With her influence, I stayed in control of the Shadow until I was almost twenty. And when I lost it, it was also because of her. Because my mom showed me a picture of her at her senior prom. A grinning boy had his arm around her waist. She was smiling up at him. I asked who he was, and my mom told me he was Evangeline's new boyfriend.

That night, the jaws of the Shadow snapped closed with more force than ever before. It wasn't my first panic attack, but it was by far the worst. There were moments when I thought I'd die from it, alone and unable to call out.

The next day, shaky and weak from the worst night of my life, I texted a friend who I knew stole Xanax from his mom. I'd tried them before. They didn't make the Shadow disappear, but they dimmed its effects.

He offered me Vicodin instead.

Relief.

I KNOW Evangeline can't fix me.

But she's still my favorite high.

CHAPTER FOURTEEN

evangeline

BOTH LILY and I are breathing hard and dripping sweat when we collapse onto a worn leather couch in the small dressing room attached to Cathedral's side stage. We sit in giddy silence, listening to the cheers and whistles slowly tapering off outside the walls.

The last six weeks have been a whirlwind. In addition to coursework and our jobs, we've played shows around the city every weekend. Each one bigger than the last.

Thanks to Rye pulling some strings to get us studio time and his skills as a producer, we also recorded fifteen songs: all the crowd favorites and a few newer ones we've barely debuted. As of yesterday, we have eight thousand monthly listeners on Spotify, and CDs and merch Rye's been peddling for us at shows are dwindling fast.

"Did you see the first rows?" asks Lily in a dreamy voice. "They knew the words of almost every song. Every beat drop. Fucking nuts. What is this life?"

A smile stretches my aching cheeks as I roll my head toward her. There are tears in her eyes.

"It's really happening, isn't it?" she whispers.

"I told you it would."

She laughs, sniffing. "You did. I believe you now."

There's a knock on the door.

Lily sits up and wipes her face, then stands and quickly checks her reflection in the mirror. I don't move except to reach over to the mini fridge and grab a bottle of water. I have a feeling I know who's outside—and it's not Rye like she thinks. I saw a familiar man offstage with Cathedral's general manager, and I'm fairly certain Lily's about to have her mind blown.

I'm content to watch. She deserves this moment, one I experienced at eighteen.

She swings the door open, her smile huge. When she sees the man waiting outside, her jaw drops and her complexion pales noticeably. I grin behind my water bottle.

"H-hello," she squeaks. "How can we help you?"

"Ms. Aoki," comes a warm, masculine voice. "My name is Cory Donovan. I'm here on behalf of Indigo Records. Do you and Eva have a minute to chat?"

Lily blinks at him a few more times before her brain restarts. "Yes, absolutely." She shifts back into the room, throwing me an *I'm-freaking-the-fuck-out* look before sitting on the arm of the couch beside me.

The sandy-haired vice president of Indigo Records walks into the room. His eyes find me and he grins. "It's about damned time."

I push to my feet, smiling as I shake the hand of my father's longtime friend.

"Good to see you, Cory. I take it you got the demo?"

From the corner of my eye, I see Lily's head whip toward me. I didn't tell her I gave my dad a USB last week to pass on to Cory. Maybe because I wasn't a hundred percent sure this moment would come, but more likely because I'm still

129

reasoning through why I finally felt okay using my family connections.

Now that the moment is upon us, I have no regrets. It doesn't feel like we skipped any rungs on the ladder; we're already being courted by two small labels. Both have solid reputations, but they can't launch us like Indigo can. And for Lily—for myself—I want the best of the best behind us.

Indigo would never screw us over, and not only because of who my father is. They're a well-oiled machine. While their roster isn't enormous, their acts routinely go platinum, sell out tours, and bring home industry awards.

Cory chuckles. "I sure did. You were already on my mind after that Illoka article, but when I listened to your demo..." He shakes his head, his gaze turning speculative. "Any chance you'll tell me why you haven't reached out before? You've clearly been ready for the next step for a while."

I glance at Lily, who watches me with ecstatic hope in her eyes, then shrug at Cory. "We were earning our stripes the old-fashioned way."

His smile grows. "Well, it shows. I heard you were booked to headline at McClane Concert Hall next month?"

Lily and I exchange a grin. "We were."

McClane beats Cathedral's main stage in size and capacity, and their booking process is strictly *Don't Call Us, We'll Call You*. When that call came two days ago, Lily and I barely kept it together for the duration, then lost our fucking minds.

Cory grabs a nearby chair for himself and gestures for me to sit back down. Unbuttoning his suit jacket, he settles and props elbows on his knees. "All right, ladies. Let's get down to business. I've been informed there are other offers on the table. What's it going to take?"

From the hallway, a low, familiar voice says, "Don't fuck

around, Cory. They get the same contract Night Theory has or better."

A wave of shock ripples down my body, followed by a surge of crackling heat as Wilder steps into view. He leans against the doorjamb, arms crossed over his chest, his gaze steady on Cory.

Six weeks of forcibly compartmentalizing our night together peel away one by one. My eyes drink in the dark hair held to his cheek by the side of his sweatshirt's hood. Full lips currently compressed. Sharp, unshaven jaw. Lowered brows. Eyes like shadowed emeralds against black lashes, the golden skin beneath them smudged by stress or sleeplessness.

I want to touch him so badly I can't breathe.

Lily's hand clamps hard on my shoulder. I suck air into my oxygen-starved lungs.

"I should have known you'd be lurking around here, Ashburn," Cory says with a boisterous laugh. He stands and shakes Wilder's hand. "You don't have to worry. You know I'll do right by Eva."

Wilder nods. "Good." His eyes flash to me for an instant. "Great show tonight."

He slips back into the hallway.

I'm on my feet before I process moving. "I'll, uh, be right back."

Ignoring the surprise from Cory and panic from Lily, I race into the hallway right as Wilder turns a corner.

"Wait!"

He jerks to a stop but doesn't turn as I catch up to him. I stare at his back, every part of me buzzing. My skin, blood, and bones.

Words slip past the knotted mess of my thoughts. "I thought I felt you."

He shifts, giving me his profile. "Felt me?" he asks softly.

My stomach spirals downward. "In the audience. You know, the infamous Wilder-Eva radar?"

His head bows, then lifts as he turns to face me. Soft, sad eyes fix on mine. "I shouldn't have come back here."

Feeling like a passenger in my own body, I take a step toward him. "Why did you?"

His chest expands on a swift inhale. "The guys are here, too. They're helping Rye pack your gear. I saw Cory walk back and wanted to make sure—" He shakes his head, glancing over his shoulder. "I should—"

"Wilder." I take another step toward him, frowning as he stiffens.

My mind is quite static now.

This isn't the man who pounded on my door and gave me the best sex of my life. But I remember this version of him, one I haven't seen in years.

Uncertain, vibrating, awkward.

I grab his hand, wrapping my warm fingers around his cold ones. "Hey. It's me."

"That's the problem," he murmurs, his fingers spasming in mine. "I want to be wherever you are. I don't know how to let go. Tell me to leave you alone."

My lips part and the truth ejects. "I can't."

His eyes find mine. For endless seconds, we stare at each other.

Then he says, "Fuck it," and yanks me forward.

Our mouths collide and I open for him instantly, a starving flower finally feeling the sun. The low, rough noise he makes tells me he feels this, too. How our mingled taste fills up parts of us that are otherwise empty.

I forget where I am.

Who I am.

Until Lily says loudly, "Ahem!"

I break the kiss with a gasp.

Behind us, Cory says, "Great to meet you, Lily. I'll see you and Eva Monday afternoon," then a bit louder, with clear amusement, "Have fun, kids!"

Mortified, I jerk backward but barely move, belatedly realizing Wilder's arms are locked tight around me.

"Let go," I hiss.

His hold only tightens, pulling me against the bulge in his pants. He stares down at me, cheeks flushed, lips glistening, eyes feral and hopeful and bewitching.

"I broke up with Kendra," he whispers fervently. "I haven't touched anyone since you. I'm yours if you want me. Only yours. Say yes, Fairy. Say yes to us."

The world drains away. We're alone in space. Just us. Like it's supposed to be.

I nod, and his smile is a sunrise.

CHAPTER FIFTEEN

evangeline

AFTER A FINAL, searing kiss and a promise to meet me at my house in an hour, Wilder retreats to the stage to help load our gear into Rye's SUV. Lily drags me back to the dressing room, closes and locks the door, then spins on me.

"What the ever-loving fuck? What did he say to you? You look like he knocked your brain out."

I swallow, my tongue moving over my teeth, tasting him. Mint and storms. "He dumped his girlfriend," I tell her, lingering shock in my voice. "He said he wants to be with me."

She blinks fast, then frowns. "That's a complete one-eighty from what he told you last month, what he's been telling you since you guys were teenagers. What changed?"

"No clue. I guess sleeping together made him reevaluate? It was... super intense."

"No shit. You limped for three days." She pauses, her voice lowering. "What happens if he wigs out again? This is the same dude who knew you had feelings for him but still paraded groupies into his bed right in front of you. Who gave you just enough attention to keep you tethered to him and starving for more." She shakes her head. "We've talked about this, Ev. Tortured bad boys with magic dicks are only acceptable in fiction."

I wince. "I know. But I couldn't say no, Lil. I've wondered for so long, wanted him for so long. I've never felt anything like what I feel when I'm with him."

She drags me to the couch and pulls me down, threading our fingers together. Her eyes brim with worry.

"I know we're not the type of women who share every little feeling with each other, but you're still my best friend in the whole world. If I could grow a wiener, I'd put a ring on your finger right now and fuck Wilder out of your system."

I laugh weakly. "Thanks."

She grins, but it fades fast. "This is coming from my love for you and your giant, beautiful heart: this is a bad idea. You've told me a thousand different times how toxic your friendship—or whatever you'd call it—was toward the end. Think of what happened when you left the band. All the shit he's said to you over the years."

You're my muse.

I'm poison.

Nothing will ever compare to us.

I need you.

We're musical destiny.

This isn't a love story.

I hear her words and remember his. I even remember my father's warning. *He's an addict. He's using you.* But nothing penetrates the golden haze of Wilder's declaration. I can't feel doubt or fear.

All I feel is a lifetime of us.

His haughty, little-prince voice telling me to stop following him around and me never listening. Wearing him down until he played with Rye and me—but mostly me. Endless games of hide-and-seek and him begrudgingly pushing me on the swings in my backyard. Piggyback rides and popsicle-stick crafts and sneaking into the kitchen before dinner to swipe frosting off cupcakes. Backyard barbecues and pool days and camping trips. Sharing a blanket under the stars as one of our dads played guitar. Singing together, our small voices harmonizing in a way that made our parents trade surprised looks over our heads.

Sunlight shifting around sycamore leaves. His frowning face as he scribbled in one of our journals. Falling asleep on his bedroom floor while he puzzled through melodies on his guitar. Rare, throaty laughter. Freckled, mood-ring eyes. The expression on his face whenever I sang, like I was the only person who mattered in the world.

Stage lights and cheers and that perfect, glowing space of our creation. Our eyes and hands and voices and lyrics. The connection between us burning like a star, infinite explosions drowning out all background noise. Everything beyond us reduced to colorless ash.

His flexing hips and supple, ink-littered skin. His tongue licking sweat from between my breasts. Eyes holding mine as he drove me toward oblivion and then commanded me to jump like it was the most natural thing in the world. Like he was and will always be the architect and master of my body's secret codes.

"Shit," whispers Lily.

Her face comes back into focus, as does her apprehensive expression. I quickly press my hand to her bouncing knee.

"Whatever happens with Wilder, my number one focus right now is our future. If he wants to be a part of my life, that's up to him. But I'm not going to sacrifice everything we've worked toward for him. I can promise you that."

As I say the words, I hear the truth in them. So does Lily.

Her shoulders relax, but she still asks, "And if he pulverizes your heart again?"

I force a smile. "What's that Grace Cunningham quote you were obsessed with last year after that asshole dumped you?"

"'Love is good for music, but heartbreak is good for art.'" She makes a face. "To clarify, I liked that quote before I knew Wilder's grandmother said it."

I laugh. "Fair enough."

A knock on the door is followed by Rye's voice. "All loaded up and ready to go!"

Lily smirks and calls back, "The gear or your dick, Henderson?"

"Date me and find out, Aoki!"

I roll my eyes and stand to gather my things from around the dressing room. Lily lets Rye inside, and they trade flirtatious comments as she does the same.

In the last month and a half—with Rye acting as our roadie, merch-man, and producer—I've grown used to their glaring chemistry. And ever since Lily ended her fling with Tyler from The Remnants, their banter has taken on an increasingly sexual charge.

My best friends' private parts are on a collision course, but I've come to terms with it. In fact, I have a feeling when they finally give in, they'll discover they're actually perfect for each other.

Ten minutes later, I give Lily a hug goodbye and she hops into Rye's passenger seat. He lingers beside my car with me, flipping his keys around his fingers.

"Thanks for taking her home, Rye. Don't knock her up, okay?"

He almost drops the keys. "What? I wouldn't. I mean—

Lily's not like that. Or I'm not like that. With her. *Fuck.* Shutting up now."

Laughing, I open my car door and drop into the seat. Rye bends down to make eye contact, his solemn face wiping the smile from mine.

I swallow hard. "You don't have to say it—I know. I can't tell you this isn't a huge mistake. But I have to find out. I hope you understand."

He nods. "I do understand. I think it's true for both of you. It's time to find out." He looks like he wants to say more, but instead smacks the hood of my car and grins. "You good to drive, grandma? It's pretty dark out there."

I roll my eyes. "Goodnight."

He winks. "Night, Eva."

He jogs toward his car and Lily. I start my car and drive home. To Wilder. To *us*.

I don't notice the darkness.

CHAPTER SIXTEEN

wilder

BELLS WERE RINGING
AT THE END OF TIME
THE SKY WAS ON FIRE
BUT YOU WERE MINE

SITTING against Evangeline's front door, I wage a mental war on the doubts and fears assailing me. Do I regret what I said to her? Not even a little bit. I want her—want *us*—more than anything. More than the drugs my body and brain still crave. More than success or recognition or acclaim. I'd burn everything down for her. Give up everything I think I want and need.

And therein lies my greatest fear: the complete lack of control I have over my feelings for her. I don't know how to stop needing her. Craving her. Suffering when we're apart.

At eleven years old, she stole pieces of my soul. The best

pieces. I'm not whole without them, without her, and I never will be.

Three years ago, I thought I could learn to live and thrive and make music without her. And I tried. God, I fucking tried. But it wasn't until I gave up and started writing down all my memories of her that my music came back.

Every damn song on the new album is about her in one way or another. Even with a chasm between us, she shaped every note and word.

Now, sitting here in the shadows on her small porch, my skin twitchy from nerves and the aftershocks of withdrawals, I finally admit to myself a truth I've known all along.

I love her.

I've loved her all my life and have been in love with her since I was seventeen.

The epiphany ricochets, punching me with the same truth upside down. There's something wrong with my love. Wrong with me.

My love has hurt her.

Will it be different this time? Or will I hurt her again?

My phone lights up with a text, pulling me from my bleak thoughts. It's Kendra again. I don't read it. I'm sure it's more of the same—anger, denial, threats. She's called me eight times and sent a dozen messages in response to the text I sent her on the way to the show.

I'll have to deal with her at some point. Do the right thing and have a face-to-face conversation. I owe her that much. I should probably be worried about her threats, too, but the freedom I feel right now drowns out potential consequences. If anything comes of it... that's what lawyers and PR teams are for.

Headlights momentarily blind me as a car pulls into the narrow, weed-choked driveway beside her bungalow. My pulse jumps. I stand fast, gritting my teeth at a punishing wave of dizziness, then quickly turn off my phone and tuck it in my back pocket.

As Evangeline exits the car and walks toward me, my various physical discomforts fade. *Background noise.* My eyes suck in her angles and curves, her colors and textures. Neon pink fishnet tights and calf-high boots. An electric blue halter dress that would be sleazy on anyone else but on her looks edgy and cute. The crown of braids on her head a wispy mess after the high-energy show.

She steps up to me, chin lifted and lips lightly pursed. I can't read the look in her mismatched eyes.

My heartbeats are bruising.

I clear my throat, bracing myself. "Regrets already?"

She hesitates. "No. I just didn't expect you so soon." She glances down at herself. "I was hoping to shower before you got here."

Tension drains from me so swiftly I almost sag against the front door. "I could use a shower, too."

"Is that so?" She fights a smile, her gaze flitting down my body. My cock jerks in my pants, and I have to bite my tongue to keep from groaning.

She adds, "I need to eat, too."

I nod quickly. "Shower, food. What else? How do you wind down after a show these days?"

She shrugs. "A book. Tea. Sometimes a movie or a soak in the hot tub. I usually eat and pass out, though."

I grin. "Same as always, then."

Her soft laugh is silk on my raw skin. "Pretty much. Right this second, though, all I want is for you to move so I can open my front door."

I smirk and make space for her, stooping to grab my backpack.

"Think you're spending the night, huh?" she asks cheekily.

I shrug, feigning indifference when there's nothing I want more. "I don't have to, but I'm staying away from the house for a few days. Kendra's moving out."

Her eyes narrow. "Wait—when did you break up with her?"

I wince. "Uh... today."

To my surprise, she laughs and rises to her toes to give me a soft kiss. "You can stay."

This must be what winning the lottery feels like. My heart can't decide if it wants to stop or race.

As soon as she turns toward the door, I step into her. My chest against her shoulders, my erection above the swell of her ass. Keys rattle as she misses the lock.

"I'm gross, Wilder. No touching until I shower."

"Not happening."

Lowering my face to her hair, still damp from sweat, I suck in her scent. Then I bend further, my mouth finding the soft, warm skin beneath her ear. I gather her essence in my nose, on my tongue. Salt and musk and the natural fragrance of her skin that comforts me as much as it drives me wild.

"You smell and taste like heaven. Someday I'm going to eat you out the second you step offstage."

She chokes. "That's nasty."

Sliding my free hand around her hip and under her dress, I cup her between the legs. Heat bathes my palm. She shivers, her thighs clenching.

"You want me nasty," I whisper against her ear. "Don't you?"

Her breathing speeds up. "Maybe."

"Open the door," I say hoarsely. "I'll give you a sixty-second head start. Shower or bed—your choice. But when a minute is up, my mouth is devouring this pussy."

She squeaks and finally gets the door unlocked, then runs across the house to her bedroom, flipping on lights as she goes. I lock the door behind me, smiling to myself when I hear the shower turn on. I knew it would. Despite her body's response to my suggestion, she's not mentally ready for my filthy appetite.

I don't even know if *I'm* ready for it. The shit I want to do and say to her... it shocks even me. No woman has ever incited such unhinged sexual need in me. With Evangeline, all my self-control is stripped away. For better or worse, I'm fully myself with her.

When I make it to the bathroom doorway and see her already in the shower, suds and water dripping over her head and down her gorgeous body, I jerk to a stop and squeeze the head of my dick so I don't fucking erupt.

I'd almost forgotten how much Oxy dulls physical sensation. I didn't *feel* high the first time we had sex, but the drugs were still in my system. If she's hoping for a marathon like last time, she's going to be disappointed.

I'll make it up to her.

Sparkling eyes rise to my face. "Problem?"

I exhale a laugh. "Nope. It's just been six weeks."

Those eyes widen. "You haven't even... you know?"

"Rubbed one out imagining your cunt spasming around me?"

She rolls her eyes even as her cheeks flush scarlet at my crude words. "Obviously."

"Oh, I definitely have." Keeping a firm hold on myself, I allow my gaze to wander down her body. My eyes linger on her pink nipples and the trimmed, fair hair between her legs.

Breath shudders out of me as I drag my gaze back up. "Memory doesn't compare to the real thing, though."

She smiles tentatively. "Aren't you coming in?"

I shake my head. "Changed my mind."

Taking two steps into the bathroom, I lower to my knees on a thick bathmat. The flash of disappointment in her eyes shifts to curiosity.

"What are you doing?"

I point at my mouth. "Waiting to be fed."

Her blush spreads down her chest as her eyes roam over my face. "You're serious."

"Deadly. Finish up and get out here before I starve."

I've never seen anyone wash so fast; she's out of the shower less than a minute later. To my surprise, she doesn't bother reaching for a towel before walking right up to me. Her wet hands sink into my hair, guiding my face upward. She bends down until her lips hover over mine, hair dripping all over my face.

"Time to eat, Wilder."

I blink in surprise. Then I laugh in sheer joy.

She's perfect.

So fucking perfect.

My eyes on hers, I back her up until her ass hits the counter. I lick a line up her stomach, making her spasm before yanking one long leg over my shoulder and spreading her open for me.

"Goddamn," I whisper as I drag my index finger lightly around her silky, rose-colored center. "So pretty."

I blow on her and she jerks.

"Quit teasing."

Looking up, I take in her heaving breasts and quivering stomach. Her parted lips and dilated eyes. Water droplets

144

slide down her body. Drip onto the floor and me. She shivers, goosebumps blooming all over.

"Cold?"

She nods.

I spread her with my fingers and press a kiss to her clit. Her legs shake. "Lean into it. Feel that chill as you feel this." I lick her heavy and deep. Her breathy moan makes me feel like a starving god whose chains have broken.

I devour my feast.

It doesn't take long for her to fall apart. She cries out softly, pulsing against my mouth.

"More," I demand.

I push two fingers inside her. She flutters around me, tight and scalding. I give her no quarter, sucking and flicking her clit with my tongue as I curl my fingers and pulse them. My other hand dives around her thigh and up. I hook my pinky inside her and apply counter tension to my still-moving fingers, then press my index finger to her asshole and massage the tense surface.

She jerks. "Wilder!"

My mouth is too full to respond, but I lift my eyes to her startled face. It takes a few seconds, but with a trembling breath, she nods.

Fuck yes.

She's so wet, it takes barely any pressure for my finger to sink into her ass. Her beautiful voice fills the steamy room as I work. Gasps and cries and pleas. My balls tighten in warning but I hardly notice.

She whimpers my name as she unravels, her pussy and ass clamping hard on my fingers. It's too much sensory perfection—I groan against her as my cock jumps and I nut in my pants like a preteen.

CHAPTER SEVENTEEN

evangeline

WILDER SITS BACK on his heels and wipes his face on his sleeve. His cheekbones are flushed, a grin teasing his lips as he peers up at me.

"I think I'll take a shower, after all."

I'm so wrecked from that second orgasm, it takes a few beats for me to register the wet spot near the fly of his jeans. I bite my lips but it's no use—a giggle slips free.

He climbs to his feet, his grin lighting up his eyes. Warm hands slip around my back, tugging me against his front. His nose nuzzles mine.

"Go ahead and laugh. We both know you'd be just as big of a mess if I hadn't licked it all up."

My already flushed skin burns. He chuckles and gives me a brief, wicked kiss, then moves to the shower and turns it back on. His shoes come off. Then his socks and shirt. A belt buckle clanks. Jeans and boxer briefs hit the floor. I ogle his perfect ass and muscled back as he steps into the tub and pulls the glass door closed.

His head tilts back. Water cascades over his face, misting

above his open mouth, running down his chest and rippling abs to his half-hard cock.

"If you're going to stare, you might as well do it from in here."

My eyes flash up to his playful smile.

Am I dreaming?

I almost say it out loud. Maybe Wilder senses the words because he says, "This is really happening, Evangeline. You and me. Come on."

He opens the shower door. Steam billows out, stirring air and making me shiver.

My feet carry me toward him.

Like they always do.

♫

THE REMAINS of a pizza sit on my kitchen table, half-eaten. We each managed a slice and a half before gravity forced a collision of our mouths.

We're on the couch now. I rock in his lap, the position both torturous and exquisite, his cock so deep inside me it passes the line of intimacy into possession.

Making the moment even more intense is the fact he won't let me break eye contact. His hands frame my face, fingers in my hair, gentle pressure holding me still or adjusting my head when I try to look away. Between consuming kisses, his freckled eyes stay on mine, penetrating me as deeply as his body.

I've never felt so safe and threatened at the same time. He's familiar and new. A fantasy I'm not completely convinced has become real. Our history melts around us, viscous and powerful as it reshapes everything I know about my own heart.

There are no clothes between us. No condom, either. He didn't bring any and Lily stole the last of mine a few weeks ago. When Wilder and I surfaced from lust long enough to realize what was missing, it was already too late. At least for me. He tried to stop me from sliding down his length, but my rational brain was offline. The second my body took an inch of him, his brain likewise ejected reason.

I shift from grinding to lifting slowly and dropping back down. Every time his piercing hits a spot inside me, scorching heat flashes through my entire body.

"Holy fuck," he groans, neck arching and eyes closing. "Slow down, baby, or I'm not going to last."

My heart thuds at the endearment. I don't slow down. The sight of him beneath me, all flushed skin and clenched muscles, his abs flexing as he struggles not to take control, makes me feel like a goddess.

"Does it feel good?" I ask breathlessly.

"Better than anything."

His hands sink further into my drying hair. Calluses snag on strands, igniting pinpricks of sensation that make me pant harder. He pulls my head back, bowing my spine, and his tongue laves my nipples.

I whimper and move even faster.

"You're so wet. Hot. Soft." He yanks my face back down, his tongue diving between my lips. "I'm so fucking glad you're the first person I've felt without a rubber. Worth. The. Wait." He punctures the words with bites on my lips.

"Same," I whisper. "This first is yours."

His cock throbs inside me, turning to steel. A hiss whistles through his clenched teeth. "I'm super close." He tries to lift me off him, but I sit fast and clamp my knees on his hips.

His eyes widen with panic. "Evangeline—"

"I'm on the pill. Fill me up, Wilder."

His eyes darken, features tightening. Releasing my hair, one arm snakes around my back. He presses his other thumb to my clit.

"You're coming with me," is all the warning I have before he takes over from below, rolling his hips into mine with deep, devastating precision. Those flashes of heat from his piercing build and compound until they become an inferno that swallows me whole.

"I'm—" The rest of my words are a stuttering cry.

He groans. "Oh, fuck yes." His hips lose their rhythm, jerking hard against me as his body goes taut. The sound he makes—the feel of him pulsing inside me—heightens my orgasm to catastrophic levels. The feeling is so intense reality slips away.

"Hey," he whispers, "it's okay. I've got you."

My senses return and provide context for his low, tender tone. I'm cradled in his arms and sobbing into his neck.

Shit.

I sit up fast and wipe my face, sucking back the next sob before it can release. "Sorry. I, uh... Need to pee."

Avoiding his searching eyes, I shift my legs to climb off him.

"Not so fast." His arms flex and I fall back against his chest. "Tell me what's going through your head."

This is a dream.

A huge mistake.

You'll hurt me.

Turn on me.

Leave me broken again.

"Nothing," I mumble.

A quick twitch of his hips makes me gasp. He's still inside me, hard enough that his thrust triggers an aftershock. I screw my eyes shut, fighting the instant rise of desire.

"Let me see those fairy eyes."

The words trigger a three-year-old memory. A frisson of old hurt follows, tumbling fast into anger. When I look at him, his eyes widen, shoulders stiffening.

"What's wrong?"

"We need to talk," I say with forced calm. "But I can't have this conversation with your dick in me. And I actually do need to pee. I don't want a UTI."

He studies my face another moment, then closes his eyes. When they open, they're full of resignation. "I'll get dressed and make us tea."

He lets me go. I scramble off him, wincing as he slips out of me, and escape to my bathroom. After peeing, I use a washcloth to clean my wet thighs, then splash cold water on my face and study the woman in the mirror. I barely recognize her beneath a glowing complexion, swollen lips, love-marked skin, and tangled hair.

"What are you doing?" I whisper to her.

Her eyes hold no answers, only naive hopes. *She* wants nothing more than to fall back into the fantasy, the pretend world where Wilder has never hurt me, where his offer backstage at Cathedral came with no strings, no history, no fears.

The woman in the mirror has been in control the last few hours, but the real me is back in the driver's seat. Ironically, I have that brain-melting orgasm to thank. It broke my delusional bubble, reminding me of the many tears I've spilled over him.

I reach for my robe, then decide I need more terrycloth between us for this conversation. A minute later, I'm armored in leggings, a sports bra, and a sweatshirt I stole from Rye that covers me to mid-thigh.

I find Wilder in the kitchen, sweatpants riding low on his hips. To my relief, he also pulled on a T-shirt. When he hears the creak of my footsteps on old floorboards, he glances over his shoulder.

His jaw clenches, nostrils flaring. "Please tell me that's Rye's sweatshirt."

I love his jealousy.

I hate that I love it.

"It is."

He blows out a breath, turning back to the counter. "Go have a seat. I'll bring your tea. Two spoonfuls of honey still?"

"Yes," I say weakly, then retreat to the living room.

My steps slow and stop when I see the couch, specifically the lack of cushion where we'd been sitting. The cushion itself sits near the slider, stripped of its casing. I'm still staring at the empty space when Wilder comes up behind me.

"I put the cover in the washer. The cushion should be fine."

There's something in his voice that brings my head around. Amusement mingled with... *pride*? I squint at him, growing more confused by the second. We couldn't have made that big of a mess. Could we have?

"Thanks," I say uncertainly.

He hands me a mug. I wrap my hands around the warm ceramic as he takes a sip of his tea to hide a smile.

"What are you not telling me?"

Twinkling eyes snap to mine. "Have you ever squirted before?"

I almost drop my tea. "*What*?"

He grins. "I didn't notice until I stood up, probably because that was the most intense orgasm of my life." His smile turns smug. "Apparently it was good for you, too."

Closing my eyes, I will the heat crawling up my neck to recede. It doesn't work. Warmth eclipses my entire face. How

151

did I not notice? My thighs had been excessively wet, but I'd thought it was sweat.

"That's definitely never happened before."

"Hey." His thumb stokes my jaw and my eyes pop open. "It was a first for me, too, and I'm not even remotely weirded out. There's nothing your body could ever do that would make me not want to worship it." He pauses, then smiles slightly. "Remember that night on tour when you did too many tequila shots and spent an hour puking in the hotel parking lot and I held your hair back for you?"

I grimace. "Yes. Why?"

His smile widens. "I still wanted to fuck you."

A startled laugh escapes me. "Ew."

He chuckles and heads for the other end of the couch, then flops onto one of the two remaining cushions. I follow slowly, my thoughts bouncing between gratitude for how fast he normalized what happened and trepidation for the conversation we need to have.

A few steps from the couch, I realize that sitting next to him will be too much of a distraction. And if he touches me, I'll forget everything I need to say. So I veer to an adjacent armchair and sit, tucking my feet under me.

Wilder sips his tea and watches me with a cocked eyebrow. "What's on your mind?" he asks, a note of wryness in his tone.

I swallow the sudden lump in my throat. "I'm not sure how to start."

He puts his mug on the coffee table, sinking back into the couch and crossing his arms over his chest. While the position is defensive, his expression remains easy to read. Resigned. A little wary.

"I bet I can guess at least one thought banging around in that beautiful head." When I don't say anything, he continues, "Since you're close with your parents and hate keeping anything from them, you told them we hooked up last month and your dad flipped out. He probably reminded you what a piece of shit I am. And now that the orgasm endorphins are wearing off, you're remembering I'm a piece of shit, too."

I stare at him, my vocal cords paralyzed. I shouldn't be surprised by how well he can read me, but I am.

Wilder's smile is a sardonic twist of lips. "We may not know all the boring little details about each other's lives these days, but don't forget I've known you since before you could walk." The smile dies. "I know I've hurt you. I wish I could undo the past, but I can't."

I find my voice. "I don't think you're a piece of shit. I think you've made mistakes. We both have."

Dark eyebrows lift. "But?"

My stomach clenches with unease as words rush to the tip of my tongue. Words that might send him out the door—words that still need to be said.

"If this is going to work, if you really want a..." My throat closes.

"Relationship with you," he supplies, eyes steady on mine. "Yes, I want it. I've been obsessed with you for years, but I was a fucking coward. I'm not saying I deserve your forgiveness or even that I want you to forget what a shithead I was. But I hope you'll give me a chance to be the man I know some part of you believes I can be."

My chest tightens; my eyes sting. Fear and hope seesaw.

"What is it?" he asks softly. "I'm a big boy. Just say it."

The words finally pour out of me. "You were pretty close —about my dad's reaction. But he also said you're an addict. And my mom said your parents suspect you've been using opiates since you started having panic attacks at nineteen. Is it true?"

His body stills, expression going eerily blank. My heart pounds like a drum. Tea sloshes in my mug as a tremor moves through my body. It's warm in the house, but I'm suddenly freezing.

"Were you high two months ago, Wilder? When we had sex the first time? Are you... are you on drugs right now?"

A bit of life, of *hurt*, returns to his face. "You really can't tell if I'm high?"

I study his clear eyes. "I don't think you are," I begin hesitantly, "but honestly? I don't trust my own ability to tell. I also know my dad wouldn't have said that without reason. And your parents..." I shake my head helplessly.

He makes a rough noise, his gaze falling to his lap. "No wonder you're freaked out." He sighs heavily. "It's my fault. I don't return their calls enough and ignore most invites to the house. It makes sense that they'd think I'm fucked up. I've been so focused on the band for the last two years, I didn't realize they were so worried."

His gaze lifts to me. "It's not an excuse, but I don't have the kind of relationship with my parents that you have with yours. You know it's always been hard for me to open up to people. Even them. You're the only—" He cuts himself off with a grimace. "To answer your question: no, I wasn't high when we hooked up last month. I'm not high right now. Have I used drugs? Obviously you know the answer to that. But I'm not a fucking junkie."

The beginnings of relief tingle in my body. "And the panic attacks?"

His eyelashes flicker; discomfort radiates from the tense line of his shoulders. "I get them. Have since I was little. They became intense in my late teens. I don't have them too often anymore, but I still get anxious. Usually in social situations or

154

around strangers. The only place I'm truly comfortable is onstage." He pauses. "And with you."

More hope rises in me, carried on a wave of sympathy and affection. He's being honest. Opening up to me. It feels precious, like a new beginning.

My voice softens. "Do the guys know?"

He shrugs a shoulder. "They know I have limits on how long I can handle fan meets and press stuff. They're used to my weirdness by now."

"I don't think it's weird to have boundaries to protect your peace."

His lips quirk. "You're giving me too much credit. Most days, I'm winging it and hoping for the best."

Flashes of memory pass through my mind, years and years' worth, building a picture of Wilder I never fully saw until this moment. How he always stayed on the edges of gatherings, outside the raucous mingling of our families. Disappearing often to sit alone with headphones on. His dislike of casual touch. Shadows under haunted eyes. How he did shots right when we stepped offstage before we were swarmed. His lyrics, which have always shown a mind that experiences the world differently than me—than most.

My heart fractures at the thought of his long, silent struggle.

I shake my head slowly. "I wish I'd known. I wish you'd told me. I could have supported you better. Maybe what happened three years ago—"

"No," he interjects gently. "Nothing that went down is on you. You were right to cut me out of your life."

I almost contradict him but pause and acknowledge that who he was—the things he did and said—still hurt. Not like they once did, but regardless, even if I understand him better now, how he treated me back then wasn't my fault.

Wilder leans forward, resting his elbows on his knees. His head hangs down for a few moments. When he looks up, the raw, glassy-eyed expression on his face steals the air from my chest.

"Can I be real with you?"

"Of course."

He holds up his hands; the strong, graceful fingers visibly tremble. "My heart is going a mile a minute right now. I'm fighting the urge to bolt. It's not you—I don't *want* to feel like this. But talking about this, letting you finally see how fucked up my head was, still is..." His voice drops to a whisper. "Please, please don't regret me."

My mug meets the coffee table and then I'm climbing into his lap and wrapping my arms around him. A shuddering breath leaves him before his arms squeeze me in return. His head drops to my shoulder, warm breath showering my collarbone.

My heart is a furnace inside me, its fiery glare dissolving the stains of our past.

There is only now and a future so bright it stings.

"Never," I swear.

CHAPTER EIGHTEEN

evangeline

I WAKE in the morning to sparkling sunlight. The bed is empty, the space where Wilder slept cold. Before the thought that he left fully forms, I smell freshly brewed coffee and hear a soft melody being plucked on my acoustic guitar. A familiar melody: "Waves." It sounds different, though—lighter and more hopeful.

He's here. He stayed.

After our talk, we were both so wiped we stumbled to bed and passed out. I remember little of the following hours, save for the pervasive warmth of his body wrapped around mine and a feeling of deep contentment.

The need to see him infuses my limbs with energy. Scrambling out of bed, I dart into the bathroom to pee and brush my teeth, then yank on yesterday's leggings and force myself to walk at a reasonable pace into the living room.

Wilder looks up from the guitar in his lap, his fingers flattening against the strings. My stomach flutters as his gaze caresses me, a small smile deepening one dimple.

"You're so beautiful."

The sincerity in his voice makes my face warm. A deliriously happy smile spreads across my face.

"Good morning to you, too."

Rising to his feet, he sets my guitar back on its stand. "Come here."

Despite willingly obeying the command, he meets me halfway. Warm palms cup my face.

"Good morning," he whispers before giving me a kiss so sweet and tender that I sigh. "I ordered bagels. Do you still like bagels?"

I don't normally eat breakfast right when I wake up, but I'm so touched by the gesture that I nod eagerly. He releases me to stride into the kitchen, asking over his shoulder, "Everything with cream cheese?"

"Sounds good. Thanks."

I follow and pour myself a cup of coffee, watching him askance as I do. He cuts a bagel and pops it in the toaster, then braces his hands on the counter and stares at the glowing grates like his focus will speed time. His fingers tap rhythmically on the tile, making the tendons on his tattooed forearms pulse. A wavy chunk of dark hair obscures one eye.

The longer I watch him—the longer he stares at the toaster, ignoring my focus—the more surreal this all becomes. Despite last night's emotional closeness and the euphoria of mere seconds ago, I'm once again engulfed by the disquieting feeling of not really knowing him.

Can you know someone's soul—their deepest, truest self —without knowing anything about their actual life? He thinks so. He believes he knows me. But do I know *him*?

I thought I knew him once. I thought the bond we shared was unbreakable, and it wasn't.

Who are you, Wilder?

Unable to stomach the silence or my spinning thoughts any longer, I clear my throat. "Did you sleep okay?"

His gaze snaps from the toaster to me. The stark relief in his eyes tells me this is as surreal for him as it is for me, which in turn calms my erratic pulse.

His lips curve. "I finally know why you always talked about missing your mattress. Best night's sleep I've had in weeks."

I laugh. "I'm glad."

His smile fades from his face but stays in his eyes. When he continues staring at me, I shift on my feet.

"What?"

He shakes his head. "Nothing."

The toaster pops, burnt bagel slices leaping. We both jump, then share a short, awkward laugh. With a little plastic knife, Wilder slathers cream cheese on each side. I bite my tongue when he uses far more than I normally like, then snort at the thought.

He gives me a questioning look.

"Sorry, I just—" I wave aimlessly, struggling to keep nervous laughter at bay. "You're making me a bagel. It's weird, right? This is weird."

His lips quirk before he gives in to a wry smile. "Yeah. But I like it. I like this. Us."

"Me too."

His smile heats, making my toes curl. "Come eat." He brings the plate to the table and pulls out two chairs. I sit and look at the bagel—more cream cheese than bread—and take a gulp of coffee.

"Will you eat half?" I ask as he settles next to me.

There must be something in my voice because Wilder glances at the bagel and grimaces. "Hold on." He jumps up, grabs the knife, and starts scraping off the pillowy excess. Some plops onto the table. The remaining bagel is black with a thin white glaze.

His shoulders tense. "Shit. I'm sorry. I can make another one."

Before he can move away, I grab his hand. He freezes, the fingers beneath mine vibrating. My ribs contract, pinching my heart.

Growing up, he might have shown me more of himself than he did others, but he never showed me *this*. The man beneath the mask. I wonder if he was ashamed of this part of himself. Or maybe he was afraid I wouldn't accept him, that it would change us, and that fear became a self-fulfilling prophecy.

Oh, Wilder...

"Please sit," I say softly.

He drops into the chair with none of his usual grace, gaze flickering but avoiding my face.

"The bagel was a really sweet thought, but I'm more of a coffee-only person first thing in the morning."

His eyes find mine, glittering with what I now recognize as anxiety. The desire to help him—to fix this for him—overwhelms me. Questions rise: is this an all-day, every-day battle, or is this a side effect of our conversation last night? Does he really believe therapy can't help? Are there supplements that would benefit him? Is he eating right?

Then my mom's voice jumps into my mind. *"You're not responsible for anyone else's mental health."*

The reminder halts the questions but doesn't alleviate the spiky, weighted feeling inside me. The same one I lived with constantly from that fateful summer when he changed until I left the band. An intuition that no matter how hard I try to reach for him, he'll always orbit just outside my reach.

One day, I tell myself, *you've had less than one day with him.*

"I'm sorry," he mumbles. "I'm already fucking this up."

The tangled threads of my thoughts unwind. He's *trying*, and that means more to me than he'll ever know.

"The only thing you fucked up is the bagel and my vagina last night."

His eyes widen, a startled, raspy laugh tickling my ears. When his shoulders and expression relax, warm satisfaction spreads through me.

He grabs a strand of my hair, curling it around his fingers. "Can I ask you something, Fairy?"

"Of course."

He gives the strand a gentle tug, the sensation echoing between my legs. Only the serious expression on his face keeps me from squirming.

"Will you tell me about yourself? About your life the last three years? Everything I know is second-hand from Rye or my parents."

The warmth inside me intensifies. "What do you want to know?"

"Everything. You're working, right? At a music academy?"

"Yep. Weekday afternoons. I teach guitar and piano to kids."

He grins. "I bet they love you."

I laugh and shake my head. "I'm actually one of the tougher teachers. Most new students don't last more than a few months, but I do have a few who've been with me for a couple of years. Amalie and Jordan are pianists and already composing, and Micah is my guitar prodigy. You should hear him shred. It'll blow your mind."

"I'd love to hear him." The look Wilder gives me makes my heart stutter. He tugs my hair again. "And you're in school, too?"

"Yes. Mostly online." I take a hurried gulp of cooling coffee, then voice a thought I haven't even told Lily. "I'm not sure I'll keep going after this semester, though. We have the meeting with Indigo on Monday and if we sign—"

"*When* you sign."

"When we sign," I amend with a smile, "so much will change. I guess it all depends on the contract, the size of the advance, timeline for an album, how fast they want us on tour..." I trail off.

"The advance is going to be a lot." His voice is soft and careful. "Based on the fact Donovan himself showed up last night and salivated all over you two, I'm guessing mid six-figures."

My jaw drops. "What? No way. We're unknowns."

"You're not, though," he says with another tug on my hair. "Before you think I'm talking about who you're related to, let me put it to you this way—no matter how close Donovan and your dad are, he's a businessman first. He wouldn't sign you at all if he didn't think you'd make him truckloads of money."

"Yeah," I say vacantly. "Logically, I know that."

I don't realize I'm chewing on my thumbnail until he gently pulls my hand from my face.

"Come back, baby."

My eyes jerk to his. He holds my gaze in a way only he can, with a magic that makes the world stop. "You can't change who your parents are or that some people will automatically attribute your success to nepotism. It's a shadow we can't escape. You have to learn to ignore the negative noise."

"Is that what you do? Ignore it?"

He smirks. "My music speaks for itself. Anyone who says I don't deserve what I've earned is just jealous."

My laugh blends with a groan. "Still an egomaniac, I see."

He chuckles, then sobers. "I know it's going to be hard for

you to hear this, but you and Lily aren't run-of-the-mill talent. You're the Holy Grail—young and attractive, with a unique and commercially viable sound. I'm confident in Night Theory's staying power in the industry, but in a hundred years we'll be forgotten. Glow, on the other hand, has the potential for immortality. Your sound might very well shape a new generation of artists."

At my horrified expression, Wilder laughs and kisses my forehead. "So cute. I can't wait to remind you of this moment twenty years from now when I'm putting up yet *another* shelf for your awards."

Before I can even begin to process either of his predictions—my success, our longevity—he continues, "Back to what to expect after Monday. You're right to think your life will change fast. The pressure will be on immediately and it'll be intense as fuck. The landscape has changed even in the last few years, too. There's so much more to do now. Social media is probably the most demanding and time-consuming, at least when you're starting out. Then there's a million small networking events, random shows, last-minute festival slots they maybe give you twenty-four hours' notice for... and in the midst of it, recording an album, writing the next one, rehearsals, tour planning—" He stops suddenly, misinterpreting my blank expression. "Sorry. You already know all this."

"I don't, actually." My skin prickles as I drain my mug, then slip off my chair to refill it. With my back to him, the next words are easier. "After leaving the band, I sort of disconnected from everything music and industry-related. I didn't write songs for a year. Barely touched a guitar outside of giving lessons. For a while, I even thought I'd never go down this road again. Then I met Lily and it just... happened. My passion came back. I'm excited again. But I'm also freaked out because it feels overwhelming in a way it didn't before."

When he doesn't say anything, I turn to find him staring at his lap with an expression I can't read. Sensing my attention, he looks up.

"I'm glad you found Lily," he says softly.

I study him, reading the tension around his eyes, and make myself address the elephant that has stomped into the room. "Are you? Glad that I'm making music with someone else?"

His chest rises sharply. "Yes. It would have been a tragedy if you gave up music." He smiles, but a veil of sadness lingers in his eyes. "I guess everything happens for a reason."

"Maybe," I say mutedly. "It's scary, though."

"What is?"

A lump rises in my throat. I swallow it and avoid his eyes. "Doing it without you."

His chair scrapes over the floor as he rises and comes to me. My mug is pulled gently from my hand and set on the counter. His arms enfold me, warm and solid. *Midnight rainstorms.* I lean against him, clinging shamelessly.

"You won't have to do it without me," he says into my hair. "I'm right here, and I'm not going anywhere. I'm sorry if I overwhelmed you. Next time tell me to shut up."

I shake my head but don't speak, afraid if I open my mouth all my fears will spill out. About the future. About *him.* About the darkness I can't see but worry hovers outside the light of this moment.

Wilder lifts my face in his hands. Sunlight streaks through a nearby window, turning his eyes into my favorite kaleidoscope of green, gold, and brown.

"I couldn't write, either," he murmurs. "That's why the album took so long. Eventually I stopped fighting myself and

164

wrote for you again. You may not have been next to me, but you were inside me. Every note, every word. You're still my muse, Fairy."

Lightning streaks down my centerline. My breath hitches.

His eyes darken. "I'm going to kiss you now," he rumbles, "and I'm not going to stop until we need another shower."

I kiss him first.

CHAPTER NINETEEN

I WANTED TO GIVE YOU ALL MY
GLASS-HOUSE TRUTHS
BUT I LOVED YOU TOO MUCH
TO SHATTER ON YOU

THREE HOURS LATER, the temporary catharsis of worshipping Evangeline's body has worn off. I'm anxious and twitchy again, this time due to the front door looming in front of me.

My parents' front door.

While I would have preferred staying naked in bed with Evangeline all day, she had lunch plans with Lily. Inviting myself would have exposed what a needy bastard I am, so I kept my mouth shut and my insecurities to myself. Instead, I gave her a goodbye kiss that left her flushed and told her I had somewhere I needed to be, too, and would text her later. Playing it cool when I felt anything but.

Unfortunately for me, my first plan of heading home for the distraction of a grueling workout was quashed after a call to Jax. Kendra and three of her friends descended like a pack of hyenas this morning and are causing a ruckus as they pack her stuff. Jax and Zander are supervising so they don't fuck anything up, but he did me a solid and sent Eddie to meet me a few blocks away with my car.

At least I have wheels now. And, after a deep dive into my text threads, a place to be. Not that I actually want to be here. The alternative, though, is sitting in Evangeline's house, crawling out of my skin as I wait for her to come home.

My pulse ping-pongs around my throat as I finally ring the doorbell. A handful of seconds later, the door swings open.

"Hey, Mom."

She stares at me in shock. Right when I'm on the verge of expiring from how fucking uncomfortable I feel, she snaps out of it. Launching at me, she slams against my chest and squeezes the air from my lungs.

"Can't breathe," I huff, patting the curls on her head.

Her arms tighten even more. "Hug me back or I'll cry," she mumbles into my shirt.

The smile that was forming on my face dies as I realize she's probably not joking. I haven't seen her since Christmas and not for lack of trying on her part. I think the last time I answered her call was two or three weeks ago. All I gave her was five minutes before making an excuse to get off the phone. I didn't even answer her text that invited me over today.

If her hug wasn't restricting my oxygen, toxic guilt would surely suffocate me. My arms weigh a thousand pounds as I lift them around her, and the sound she makes nails my heart to my spine.

Fuck. She's crying.

Movement in the doorway brings my head up. My gaze connects with River's. A small, humorless smile on his face, he drawls, "The prodigal son returns." Lifting his wrist, he checks the time on an invisible watch. "Thirty seconds to make Mom cry. A new record."

My molars grind, but I keep my mouth shut. I deserve worse. I haven't just shut out my parents for the last two years but my siblings, too.

"Give him a break, Riv," Mom says, sniffing as she finally releases me. She grabs my hand. "Come on. Katherine will be so happy to see you. Can you believe she's turning seventy-five? I can't. I have more gray hair than she does."

River steps to the side as she tugs me into the house. His eyes, the same golden-brown as our dad's, follow me with a mixture of skepticism and resignation.

I'm braced for my mom to drag me to the living room at the back of the house where I can hear the rest of the family, but halfway there she veers into the empty kitchen. River pauses outside, then shakes his head and continues down the hall.

Releasing my hand, she moves around the island to grab two glasses from a cabinet, then opens the refrigerator to pull out a pitcher of iced tea. In spite of the almost frenetic energy buzzing in her movements, watching her is soothing. Like listening to an old, familiar song.

It suddenly hits me how much I've missed her, the emotion so visceral my stomach clenches hard.

"Have a seat," she says gently, glancing my way as she pours our drinks.

I drop onto a stool at the island. She sits beside me and slides a glass my way. Cradling it, I swipe my thumbs across the cool surface. The prickling under my skin slowly fades.

Calm descends deeper with every inhale of my mom's perfume and the intangible aura of my childhood home. Citrus, herbs, and safety.

My sisters' voices carry down the hallway, along with Katherine's raspy laugh and my father's lower tones. Nostalgia and comfort filter through me.

My mom clears her throat lightly. "How's Eva?"

My head whips gracelessly in her direction. Her eyes shine with mirth. "You're tagged in a bunch of photos from her show last night, including a few of you walking backstage. Speculation online is you broke up with your girlfriend and are pursuing her." She waggles her eyebrows, her smile teasing.

Despite her effort at levity, my head bows in embarrassment. My own mother scours the internet for news on my life. Fucking pathetic.

Steeling myself, I meet her gaze. "The last couple of years..." My tongue tangles. Eventually I mutter, "I've been a self-centered ass."

"You're forgiven," she says, blinking away a glassy sheen from her eyes. "Is it true, though? You broke up with Kendra?"

I confirm with a nod. Though she tries to hide it, her relief is obvious. "That's too bad."

I laugh shortly. "Nice try. I know you never liked her."

She winces. "True. I have no idea what it was—she was a nice girl—but something about her rubbed me the wrong way." Her eyes narrow. "Maybe because once she came into the picture, my firstborn son stopped answering my calls."

It's my turn to wince. Thankfully, she continues before I have to decide how to respond.

"So... Eva?"

I shift in my seat. "It's new. Like last night, new."

She lays a hand on my forearm, squeezing lightly. "It's not new, though, is it? The two of you have always been..." she trails off, and another voice finishes.

"*Fated* might be the word you're looking for."

Our heads swivel to the smiling woman standing in the kitchen doorway. Katherine is technically my great-aunt—the twin of my maternal grandmother—but she raised my mom after her parents' deaths and is the only grandparent I've ever known. And my mom's right: despite signs of time on her face, she doesn't look anywhere near seventy-five. Long, dark hair spirals to her waist. As usual, her lips are curled as though holding back secrets. Her clothes have always been eccentric, and today she's wearing a floor-length, crushed velvet dress that could easily pass for a Halloween witch's costume.

Dad believes she's psychic. Mom refuses to admit it, but her denial is more habit than conviction. As for myself, I've witnessed enough of Katherine's eerily accurate predictions over the years that I'm a believer. I don't know if she has actual psychic powers or if she's simply a thousand times more observant than the average person, but either way, there's something undeniably supernatural about her.

Katherine meets me halfway for a hug, and it's only then I'm confronted with the passage of time. Her body is more frail than I remember, her incense and rosewater musk pronounced. I feel like if I squeeze too hard, she'll disperse into smoke.

Releasing her, I kiss her soft cheek. "Hi, Granny. Happy birthday."

She lays a cool, soft palm on my cheek. From the way her eyes pierce mine, sparkling dark and eerily calm, I know what she's going to say before she says it. My fingers and toes tingle in fearful anticipation.

"I have a message for you, my boy."

I barely hear my mom's groan over the ringing in my ears. I've been waiting six years for those words. For an answer to the question I asked the first time I felt like I was losing everything.

Losing Evangeline.

"Can't you read your cards or talk to your spirits or something?"

At my irreverent demand, humor crinkles the skin around her eyes. "I'm sorry, Wilder. I don't have a message."

I stop pacing and face her. "What if she falls in love with this douchebag? Am I supposed to watch it happen? You said—"

"I remember what I said," she interjects softly, something like regret briefly eclipsing her expression before it smooths.

"No message?" I ask in a final, desperate plea.

She shakes her head, then sighs. "How about a word of advice from an old lady with two eyes and a lifetime of experience?"

"Please," I whisper.

"A flower needs water, sunlight, and space to grow."

The memory tumbles into others from the following years. They all clash before merging into a glaring epiphany. Back then, I'd decided she meant I shouldn't pursue anything romantic with Eva. That conviction worked for me, complementing my fears. But hindsight is clear—Katherine was warning me not to suffocate her. Which I ended up doing anyway by putting her in a box built of my selfish needs.

Cold radiates down my spine.

Is that what I'm still doing?

My heart races, my muscles tensing. All I see are Katherine's ageless eyes. I'm suddenly not sure I want her message.

Pounding footsteps and squeals in the hallway drag my attention from Katherine. She steps aside right as Olive and

171

Ivy careen around the corner. They gape at me for two seconds before darting forward and almost knocking me over with their double-strength hug. Their voices fill the room, words overlapping and creating a familiar, beautiful chaos in my ears.

"I can't believe you're here!"

"Freaking finally."

"Your hair is so short!"

"And you have a thousand more tattoos."

"Ohh, he has to listen to our new song."

"No way, Liv! It's not done."

"Fine, fine. Selfies!"

Over their heads, I meet my dad's amused gaze. He mouths, "Welcome home."

CHAPTER TWENTY

wilder

AFTER HELPING River clean the kitchen and put away leftovers, I step onto the back patio and take a deep, cleansing breath.

The sun sits low in the sky, its golden light filtered by giant pines. A dog barks somewhere in the neighborhood, the sound muted and echoey. Closing my eyes, I focus on the familiar susurration of evergreen leaves and bare branches. The wind is cool, damp, and earthy in my nose.

I can't remember the last time I felt this mentally exhausted, but it's not the frazzled fatigue I'm used to. I feel calm. Almost peaceful.

"Beautiful evening, isn't it?" asks Katherine.

I open my eyes and turn, finding her on a bench angled toward the sunset. Her eyes are closed, that familiar, enigmatic smile on her lips.

"It is," I agree, making my way to her. She pats the bench and I settle beside her.

I'm still wary of whatever she has to tell me, but my initial apprehension has faded. Evangeline texted an hour ago to ask if I wanted to hang out and watch a movie tonight. I said yes, obviously, though all I plan to watch is her face when she comes.

No matter what Katherine says, it won't change the fact Evangeline is finally mine. That she's waiting for me right now. I can almost taste her. Smell her. My skin aches for the pinch of her nails, my ears for her strangled moans.

"I'm glad you and River were able to reconnect."

Shifting in my seat, I glance at Katherine. Her eyes are still closed. It's probably my imagination, but her smile looks different. Knowing. My neck heats. *No way she knows what I was thinking about. Right?*

I cough over my embarrassment. "Me too."

River was smarmy and passive-aggressive toward me most of the afternoon, but at some point between hauling plates to the kitchen and loading the dishwasher, the friction smoothed. We had a long, animosity-free conversation about graffiti, tattoos, and music.

"He's going to need you," Katherine murmurs.

I stiffen, thoughts of Eva vanishing. "What does that mean? Is he okay?"

Her eyes find mine. "Right now, yes, but there will come a time when he isn't. You're not as dissimilar as you think you are. He has his own shadows."

My chest burns. I suck in air, the reflex alone alerting me that I was holding my breath. A tremendous weight descends on my shoulders, like giant hands pressing me down. Making me smaller. Reminding me how powerless I am.

"Don't worry," Katherine continues, her gaze shifting to the tree line. "When the time comes, you'll be ready."

The vague reassurance doesn't help, the spectral hands on my shoulders moving to my lungs and squeezing, *squeezing*. I can't hear the wind in the trees anymore. I can't hear anything but my heart pounding on my eardrums.

A soft hand covers the fingers clamped on my knee. "We need to talk about Evangeline."

Shaking my head like the movement will dislodge the demon using my chest as a stress ball—it doesn't—I force my eyes to Katherine. My mouth opens to say, *Stop. No. Don't tell me,* but nothing emerges save for a harsh exhale.

I shouldn't have come outside.

Katherine's face sags slightly, her eyes losing focus. Tiny fires ignite all over my body as she begins to speak.

"Force and effort. One destroys harmony, one maintains it. What you cannot hold gently will be destroyed. To become who you're meant to be, let go of who you think you are."

She sucks in a breath, her eyes closing. Beneath fragile lids, her gaze darts back and forth. Whatever she sees brings a lattice of wrinkles to her forehead and makes her fingers twitch around mine.

"Ah, I understand now," she murmurs. Her eyes open and look at me—no, look *through* me. Every hair on my body stands up. "If you're both afraid of the dark, there will never be light. One cannot exist without the other. There must be balance. Be brave again. Dive into the dark and find the light inside you. For yourself and for her."

An old memory rises and pops like a bubble, splashing me with sights and sounds from a multi-family camping trip when I was seven. Thin, cool air. A crackling fire. Itchy mosquito bites and sunburns. The sun falling fast over jagged mountain peaks. Adults panicking because no one could find Evangeline. An hour's long search with flashlights.

My legs carrying me in a direction opposite everyone else. Crunching pine needles. Scratching brambles. My shaking hand on a cold metal tube, the glowing orb bouncing with my steps, my too-fast breaths.

A small body curled in a depression at the mossy base of a tree. Pale hair like a beacon.

"Fairy," I whisper now, as I did then.

"She cannot survive in your dark," Katherine murmurs.

Goose bumps roll up and down my body like sound waves on a loop. "Am I going to lose her?"

Not again. Not again.

Her mind back from whatever strange place it went, Katherine pats my hand. Wrinkles deepen around her eyes as she smiles softly. *Sadly.*

"She's a woman, Wilder. Not an object to find, keep, or lose."

"I know that."

"You don't. Not yet. But you will."

CHAPTER TWENTY-ONE

wilder

BY THE TIME I let myself into Evangeline's with the key she gave me, it's past midnight. I almost didn't come, and it took hours of driving aimlessly for me to get here.

The house is quiet and dark—or as dark as she can stand it, with nightlights plugged into multiple outlets in every room. At the threshold of her bedroom, the sight of her sleeping face almost takes my knees out. I grab ahold of the doorframe to steady myself.

She's curled on her side, a nightlight glowing on a flushed cheek, pale hair rioting across the pillow and around her shoulders. She looks ageless. Both young and ancient. Her thick, dark blond eyelashes flicker with dreams; from her furrowed brow, unpleasant ones. Probably about me.

She cannot survive in your dark.

Katherine's words whisper through me for the thousandth time since I left my parents' house hours ago.

The need to protect Evangeline from harm bucks against another need, just as potent and driven by selfishness. I *want* her. It consumes me. Owns me.

How can I protect her from me when I can't even protect myself?

"Wilder?" She rubs her face sleepily and sits up. The comforter slips down her torso, giving me a glimpse of her breasts outlined by a silky camisole before she shivers and yanks it back over her shoulders. "Are you okay? I was worried. You weren't answering your phone."

She's too sleepy to be as annoyed as she should be. Her gray eye shines silver in the light from the bathroom, her darker one shadowed. That single, otherworldly gaze spears me like nothing else can. I'm a naked, quivering fool beneath it.

I'll never be worthy of her. She's a goddess of truth and goodness, and I'm a formless, slithering shadow.

Find the light inside you.

How am I supposed to find my light when all I see is hers?

I have no idea what expression I wear, but when Evangeline reaches a hand toward me, the ache in my chest increases a hundredfold. The pressure of regret and longing and fear presses down so fast and hard I gasp.

Then she says, "Come to bed," and desire ignites like a flash fire inside me. My fingers curl with the impulse to take, consume, *feed*. Warp her and mark her. Brand her with my body so deeply she'll never want another. Only me. Only us.

"Are you sure?" My voice is a dangerous rasp, the crackling death of my good intentions. Her eyes flare, pupils expanding, chest lifting on a swift inhale.

"Yes." Her consent is both a demand and a plea.

My feet carry me across the room. I shed my clothes as I go, already hard for her, leaking in anticipation. She lifts the covers and I slip beneath, my hands finding purchase on soft skin. I yank her against me. She's music and light and warmth. Infinite sunrises in my black world.

178

I press my face to her neck and breathe. Just breathe.

Her fingers weave into my hair, short nails grazing gently over my scalp, sending tingles down my spine. She's soothing me even though my grip is punishing enough to leave bruises, a thought that makes me even harder—makes me hate myself even more.

I'm afraid to move my hands. Afraid of not being able to stop myself from hurting her. *Using her.* I'd rather die.

I've never felt this out of control.

"It's okay," she murmurs. Like she can hear my thoughts. Like she *knows* me.

A full-body tremor rattles my bones and tightens my skin. I open my mouth against her neck, the tip of my tongue finding her racing pulse. A new urge rises and eclipses all others.

I want to taste her pulse and swallow it.

Swallow *her*.

Evangeline squeaks as I suddenly lift her, rolling onto my back and dropping her knees to either side of my head. My hold keeps her upright as I press my nose to the soaked cotton between her legs, then gently bite the swollen folds beneath.

She gasps. "Oh God."

I bite harder, making her jerk. Her head drops forward, our gazes clashing. "That's not my name."

Her pupils blow out, black swallowing gray and hazel. She licks her lips. "Wilder." So soft, barely audible, then louder and ragged with need. "*Wilder.*"

"That's my girl."

Releasing one of her thighs, I drag her camisole up and grunt at the sight of her breasts rising and falling as she pants. Pebbled nipples framed by spun-gold hair. Gorgeous, heart-shaped face and half-lidded eyes hazy with lust.

Mine.

Flattening my tongue, I lick the fabric between me and what I crave. She whimpers and rocks forward in search of friction, but I don't give her what she wants. The next sound she makes is an angry one, causing my dick to jerk and my lips to curve.

"You want to suffocate me with this perfect cunt so badly, don't you?"

Her lips part on a silent gasp. My tongue finds her clit, flicking it through the cotton. This time her gasp has tone, a pure note of desperation. Her body pulses against my hold, thighs flexing beneath my hands.

"I need to hear it, baby," I murmur into her heat, my eyes never leaving hers. "Tell me what you want and I'll give it to you. I'll never say no."

The look in her eyes darkens until all I see is the pieces of me inside her reflecting the pieces of her inside me. Two jagged halves locking together seamlessly.

She licks her lips. "I want to be your perfect little slut."

Shock and a dagger-like stab of arousal vacuums the air from my lungs. My arms weaken, depositing her on my chest, while every other muscle group in my body stiffens with the same resistance I felt the first time we slept together. When she asked me to fuck her like I hated her. Like she didn't mean anything to me.

Denial tangles in my throat with an equal truth: I want what she's offering with every depraved inch of me.

Her fingers dip into my hair and tug gently until I look up. I'm flayed open by her gaze, which I'm terrified sees too much. *Everything.* All my sick desires, my compulsion to break her apart so I can steal more pieces of her soul for myself. Tarnish her perfection with my shadows. Imprint myself into her every cell so she can never be rid of me.

She's offering me exactly what I crave, and it feels both unbelievably right and unbearably wrong.

"Eva, I—" Her palm presses gently against my lips, quieting my weak protest.

"Before you say no, listen." She moves her fingertips to my jaw, painting a line of heat up to my ear. Her gaze flickers away from mine, her cheeks turning deep rose. "You were right when you said no one has been able to read my music. I've never been able to climax with anyone but you." Her eyes return to me, flashing with determination. "I feel safe exploring this with you. I know you respect me, Wilder. I'm asking you to safely, consensually *disrespect* me. I want this. I've wanted it for years, since that day in your bedroom. And I know you want it, too."

Blood surges to my cock, making it pulse in time with my heart. Her words have the opposite effect on my thoughts, which shift from whitewater rapids to a placid lake. My skin stops feeling like it's stretched too tight. The burning in my spine dissipates.

She feels safe. She wants this. *Me.*

"You mean that?" I ask unnecessarily. If there's one thing I trust in this world, it's that Evangeline says exactly what she means.

Confirming it, she rolls her eyes. "Obviously."

I swallow once, twice, my fingers tensing on her waist. "Then yes, of course I'll explore this with you. But if I say or do something you don't like, you'll tell me immediately. Promise me."

Triumph shines in her eyes as she nods. "I promise."

The last of my doubts float away.

"In that case..." Lifting her back to her knees so she hovers above my face, I yank her underwear to the side. She's wet as fuck, as aroused as I am, and the knowledge turns my next words guttural. "Grab the headboard and sit on my face."

She doesn't hesitate and neither do I. The second her weight comes down, I'm lost in her flavor and scent. The music of her moans, gasps, and cries. When she stiffens, her hips jerking, pussy fluttering on my tongue, I throw her to the mattress and follow her down.

Her chest heaves against mine, her eyes wide. "I wasn't done." She sounds so irked, I fall in love with her again. Deeper. Even harder.

I wrap a hand around her throat, squeezing lightly. Angling her face up, I drag my teeth over her chin, then kiss her hard and deep, forcing her to taste her release. She writhes beneath me, legs tightening around my waist.

"More," she whines.

I find her ear and bite the lobe, whispering, "You're a greedy little slut, aren't you?" And when she moans breathlessly and grabs my cock with both hands, I briefly wonder if I died on my drive here and accidentally wound up in heaven.

My vision blurs as she feeds the first inch of me into her hot, tight body. Every instinct demands I thrust all the way in, but the erotic euphoria of her wiggling as she tries to impale herself is too fucking perfect to miss.

"That's right, baby, stuff yourself full. Take every inch you can. God, I love stretching this pussy. I love how soaked you are. How you drip all over my cock."

My rough words make her even wetter. More desperate. When I'm seventy percent inside her and she can't get me any deeper because of the hovering position of my hips, she growls in frustration. It's the cutest sound I've ever heard.

"Wilder, I swear—"

I give her throat a gentle squeeze. "Shut your mouth unless my tongue is in it."

I don't give her time to think about what I said, punching my hips forward with every ounce of my pent-up hunger. She cries my name, her spine bowing and her eyes closing. I fuck her hard and fast, the slap of our bodies as rhythmic as a metronome.

"Look at me," I snarl. Her lashes flutter, parting on hazy, victorious eyes. "This is what you wanted, huh? Me off the leash? Fucking your cunt like it's mine?"

She nods.

"Good. You *are* mine. Do you understand? My dirty, needy girl. My little toy. No one else's. This pussy only comes on *my* cock, *my* mouth, *my* fingers."

"Y-yes," she pants. "Only yours."

"Right answer. I think you deserve a reward."

Scooping a hand beneath her ass, I hold her against me as I shift to a tight, rolling grind that stimulates both her clit and G-spot. She starts to shake and gasp.

"Such a perfect toy," I whisper, inhaling puffs of air from her parted lips, "telling me what I want to hear, stretching for me and clenching me so tightly. I can't wait to find out how many inches I can fit down your throat. See your pretty tears as you gag for me. I bet you want my cum dripping from every hole in your body, don't you?"

The hot gush and constriction around my cock tells me the answer even before her eyes roll back in her head. "I'm—oh—"

Another orgasm crashes through her, her body clamping down and throbbing hard. I watch her face, enthralled, my own release taking a back seat. Knowing she's never experienced this with anyone but me feels better than a stadium full of screaming fans, better than any high.

As she relaxes, I kiss her languidly. "Say 'thank you, Wilder.'"

"Thank you, Wilder." She smiles up at me, soft and open, all her defensive walls abolished. She's never been more beautiful. "Was I good?"

My breath stalls in my lungs. My heart turns to fiery goo. I'm one thousand percent here for all her kinks, but something about her wanting praise does me in. My cock agrees, jumping with renewed vigor, begging for friction.

I press my forehead to hers. "So good, baby. So, so good. But it's my turn now. You're going to take everything I give you, aren't you?"

She moans. "Give me everything. I want it all."

Holy fuck.

I yank her legs from my waist, bending them so her knees are pressed to her armpits, then drop my weight. My hands seize fistfuls of her hair, close to the scalp so I don't actually hurt her as I pull her into me with every thrust. Slow at first, then faster and harder as I chase my release.

I'm already close to the edge, acute physical pleasure compounded by the visual perfection beneath me: her gorgeous face slack with ecstasy, her eyes a doorway to the secret world that exists solely for us.

My tongue finds the succor and sanctuary of her mouth. On my next and final thrust—as my orgasm explodes like a nuclear blast in my body and she clutches me to her, holding me with all her strength—I understand how foolish I was to think I could steal more pieces of her.

Evangeline Sullivan is a law unto herself: impossible to subvert, immune to external force.

She'll never need me like I need her.

As more fragments of my soul break free, flying into her keeping, I decide it doesn't matter. She can have them. Every last piece of me.

I'd rather be lost in her than found anywhere else.

evangeline

How fast does a heart beat
when it can't tell time?
And how long must I wait
for you to be mine?

"MS. SULLIVAN? DID YOU HEAR ME?"

I jerk on my stool, blinking at my student, Micah. He's frowning so hard his eyebrows are almost touching. Annoyance shines in his big brown eyes.

"Yes," I say on reflex, then sigh and shake my head. "No. I'm sorry, Micah. What did you say?"

He squints at me like I've been possessed by a stranger. Fair point as this is the first time I've ever been less than fully immersed in a lesson with him in the two years we've been working together.

"I asked if you were okay," he says, each word enunciated with the singular condescension of a twelve-year-old. I

185

almost smile, until he adds, "You don't look so good. Mom's gonna be pissed if you get me sick."

"I'm not sick," I assure him. "I just..." I trail off, my gaze bouncing around the familiar, cluttered room. Over assorted instruments, amps and mics, bookshelves of sheet music, bundled cords and the ancient whiteboard.

A soft pain spreads through my chest. When I look back at Micah, I see he feels it, too. And he knows.

"You're leaving?" he asks in a cracked whisper, all traces of bravado gone.

I nod and clear my tight throat. "I am."

His thoughts play clearly across his face—panicked reasoning, then relief—so I'm not surprised when he asks, "Where are you going? My mom will totally drive me. Or if you're, like, moving to another state, we can do online lessons, right?"

My smile hurts, not because it's forced but because it feels like the rest of me: happiness eddying against the cliff of unavoidable loss.

"Actually, I signed a recording contract with Indigo Records yesterday. After next week, I'll be taking a hiatus from teaching."

His jaw drops. "Indigo Records? Holy shit! That's amazing."

I laugh even as I wag a finger at him. "No cussing. And thank you." I glance at the clock over the door. "We have twenty minutes left, so let's use them. We can talk more about it when your mom gets here."

Unsurprisingly, my words fly in one ear and out the other. "This is so freaking cool. I'll know someone famous. Will you hook me up when I'm older? Introduce me to people? I can't wait to tell my friends at school. They're gonna flip."

Biting back a smile, I say as sternly as I can, "Let's focus,

Micah," but a sudden knock on the door undermines my effort. Micah grins at me as I sigh and call out, "Come in."

The owners' daughter, Molly, pokes her head inside. A student at the nearby University of Washington, she works the front desk occasionally. Her cheeks are flushed, eyes shining with a manic light as they veer from Micah to me.

"You have a visitor," she stage-whispers.

I frown. "I'm in the middle of a lesson. They can wait or leave a message."

She expels a breathy giggle and glances at Micah again. "Actually, he said he's here specifically to sit in on your lesson. And I *really* think Micah would like him to."

Understanding hits, knocking my stomach down an elevator shaft.

Wilder.

I haven't seen him since Sunday morning. He was still sleeping when I left for brunch at my parents' and was gone when I got home. He later texted to tell me he would be rehearsing late. We've exchanged sporadic texts for the last two days, a fact I've shoved in a mental box along with the nagging fear that something changed Saturday night. That what we shared—which made me feel closer to him than ever before—had the opposite effect on him.

Even if I'd *wanted* to confront him about the sudden distance between us, there's been no time to do so. Yesterday was a whirlwind. Lily and I spent the morning with my dad and his lawyer, prepping for the meeting at Indigo. After the meeting—which went exactly like Wilder said it would—we met my family, Rye, and Lily's dad for a celebratory dinner that lasted several hours. By the time I got home, all I had the energy to do was shower and pass out.

Wilder did call me this morning, but I was listening to an online lecture for one of my classes. And even though I had time before work, I didn't call him back. I'm not entirely sure why.

Now that he's physically here, suppressed emotions roar through me. Uncertainty. Anxiousness. Yearning. I want to see him almost as much as I want to hide in the nearby supply closet.

"So? Can I show him back?" asks Molly.

I look at Micah, his confused but curious face making the decision for me. I nod at Molly and she disappears.

"What's going on, Ms. Sullivan? Who's here?"

Instead of answering, I reach over and switch on the amp his guitar is plugged into. A soft, crackling hum fills the air as the door opens again.

Wilder walks inside with his battered guitar case, looking like dirty sex from the toes of his boots to his inked arms, faded Misfits T-shirt, and jeans that fit so well they should be outlawed for the sanity of humankind.

I can't control the wave of heat that spreads from my chest, pooling and pounding in my head and between my legs.

He flashes me a look so carnal I have to fight not to squirm on my stool. Thankfully he glances away just as fast, approaching Micah with an easy grin.

"Hey, man," he says to the boy whose face has gone slack with shock. "I was wondering if I could join you for a bit?"

evangeline

AFTER SAYING goodbye to Micah's tearful mom—doubly overwhelmed by news of my leaving and a rock star's surprise appearance in her son's lesson—I head back to the room where I left Wilder.

Outside the door, I pause to listen to him playing. He unplugged his guitar so the sound isn't as rich, but there's no question of his innate talent. Or the song, which is one of ours.

"I see your shadow on the glass, Fairy."

I press a hand against my tumbling stomach. *Get your shit together.* Steeling myself, I walk inside. The latch clicks behind me, the tiny sound making me flinch.

Wilder's fingers flatten over the chords, his smile falling, brow furrowing. "Hey, what's wr—"

"Thank you," I blurt. "I can't tell you how much that meant to Micah. And me. How did you even know when—" I pause when I realize the answer is obvious. "Rye."

He nods, still frowning. "I want to say 'you're welcome,' but from the look on your face, I'm not sure you actually meant that." He lays his guitar in its case and stands. Dragging a hand through his hair, his gaze bounces around the room. "I, uh—I wanted to see you. I'm sorry if I crossed a boundary I shouldn't have."

"Why haven't you come over the last two nights?" The words burst out of me without permission, expelling from the tender place inside me I've been studiously avoiding.

He looks startled, then relieved, then ravenous as he takes a step toward me. I suck in a breath and he stops, scanning my face.

"The truth?" he asks.

"Always."

"After rehearsal on Sunday, I was going to come back over, but when I was getting ready to leave, the guys laid into me. They said I was giving off needy, codependent vibes. So I've spent the last two and a half days freaking out about it while missing you and trying not to call you a thousand times or show up at your house."

I blink in surprise, then laugh as the underlying emotional strain of the last days drains away.

Wilder takes another step toward me, his shoulders losing some of their coiled tension. "Tell me why you're laughing."

I shrug, my grin slowly fading. "Next time, can you talk to me about what you're feeling? I've been low-key wondering if I scared you off Saturday night."

Long legs eat the space between us until we're chest to chest, his hands cradling my head as I stare up at him.

"Nothing would *ever* scare me away from you." The low, fervent words hum in my marrow. "Saturday night was perfect. *You're* perfect." He sighs. "The guys did have a point, though. I'm needy as fuck when it comes to you. I could barely sleep the last two nights without you, so we might as well check the box next to codependent as well. Shit, if you wanted to put a collar on me and drag me around by a leash, I'd let you."

"Okay," I whisper.

His brows rise, lips twitching. "Okay, what? Okay you like the idea of a collar on me, or okay you forgive me for not knowing what the fuck I'm doing when it comes to you?"

"The second one." I tilt my head. "Maybe the first one, too."

He drops his forehead to mine. "I don't deserve you."

Lifting onto my toes, I kiss him softly. "I don't know what I'm doing either. Case in point, instead of asking you what the hell was going on—"

"You got all up in your head about it, then shoved everything in a little box at the back of your brain."

My mouth drops. "What?"

He kisses my forehead. "You're my favorite song. I know every note. Plus, you're a Taurus. Overthinking and compartmentalizing are your thing."

My scowl of annoyance makes him laugh. Releasing me, he walks back to his guitar and closes the case. Over his shoulder, he asks lightly, "How was Sunday brunch?"

The shift in topic startles me. Then I understand what he's getting at—*he knows me*—and I cover my cheeks to hide their quick flush.

"I, uh…"

Wilder chuckles as he stands, case in hand, and approaches me. He sets the case beside us, then tugs my fingers away from my face.

"I promise I'm not trying to make you feel bad. I know why you haven't told your parents about us—for the same reason that when I told my parents, I asked them not to mention it to yours."

Sadness tinged with guilt swiftly eclipses the surprise that

191

he told his parents about us. Brunch on Sunday was exhausting, and not just because of Wilder's welcome interruption of my sleep the night before.

I hate lying to my parents, even if it's lying by omission. I hate even more that it's becoming easier by the day. But I can't handle the alternative, which is telling them Wilder and I are officially together. The look on my dad's face weeks ago is a thorn in my memory. I never want to be on the receiving end of that expression again.

"They don't hate you or anything," I say quickly. "It's... complicated."

"I get it. It's going to take time to prove to them that I'm not a fuckup anymore. But we have time. Right?"

My mouth goes dry at the careful words, the suggestion of a deeper question beneath them.

"What are you asking me?"

He takes one more step, and I tilt my face up to maintain eye contact.

"Will you be my girlfriend, Evangeline?"

My pulse trips over itself. "Aren't I already?"

His eyes simmer. "Answer the question."

"Yes," I say breathlessly. "I'd love to be your girlfriend."

His smile expands, deepening dimples and filling my head with sparkling fog. "Good. What are you doing tonight?"

You, I think, and his eyes flash like he heard the thought.

"Why? You want to take me on a date?" The skin around his eyes tightens, his smile freezing. Realizing my mistake, I add quickly, "Not in public or anything. I don't expect that. Especially since, you know, my parents... and people with cameras, and crowds, all that stuff." I laugh, the sound a tad shrill. "Do you even read the comments on your socials?

192

They're wild. I'd be worried someone might knock me out and kidnap you—"

His index finger presses to my mouth, silencing me. I gasp and he takes advantage, dragging his finger along the inside of my lower lip. My breaths turn choppy. His eyes flicker up long enough for me to see his wide pupils, then lower back to my lips.

"Such a pretty, pretty mouth," he whispers, sinking his finger past my teeth. "Suck."

All rational thought suspended, I close my mouth and suck, shifting forward at the same time so his finger sinks deeper. He grunts, hips twitching. The hardness behind his zipper grazes my belly. My mouth waters. I grab his belt buckle, ready to drop to my knees and finally, *finally* taste him, but his other hand seizes mine.

A whine of protest warbles in my throat. Wilder sucks in a breath, his finger curling against my tongue. "Fuck, baby. You want me in your mouth? Stretching your jaw and throat like I stretch that pussy?"

My clit throbs at the gruff words. I press my thighs together against a sudden sharp pang and nod. His eyes close briefly and he rocks into me.

"Dammit," he hisses, shaking his head. Lust and conflict sit clearly on his face. "I can't believe I'm saying this, but you're not giving me a blowjob right now. Remember where we are?"

A modicum of sense returns. I hear muted piano keys being struck in a nearby room, the bright, metallic sound of a snare, muffled voices of teachers and students. My eyes widen in horror, my libido shutting off like a faucet.

Wilder smirks as he slips his finger from my mouth, popping my lower lip against my teeth before lowering his hand and tucking it in his pocket. All the while, he watches me with that impish, cat-like precision.

"You're welcome," he murmurs silkily.

I rub my palm over my burning forehead. "Thank you. I don't know what I was thinking."

He bites his lip, a smile shining in his eyes. "I'm at least seventy percent to blame. You're incredibly hard to resist."

"So are you," I whisper.

His expression softens. "The reason I asked what you were doing tonight is the guys and I were wondering if you wanted to come over for dinner. Kind of a reunion slash catch-up situation. And a celebration, too, for signing with Indigo yesterday."

It takes me long seconds to process the words, the majority of my thoughts still on a hamster wheel of how close I came to throwing my ethics out the window.

"Um, at your house?" I finally ask.

Wilder nods, a concerned crease forming between his brows. "Despite what just happened, a big part of why I came today is because I don't want you to think sex is all I want from you."

"I don't." My quick denial causes his brows to arch. Knowing that he's a second from once again proving how well he knows me, I lift a staying hand. "I'm not saying that to avoid confrontation. I really don't feel that way. Besides, if you only wanted sex, there are a million women out there who don't have our baggage."

His lips press together, then relax. "I like our baggage. It's a little beat up, sure. Covered in peeling stickers and dents. But the insides are irreplaceable. There's only one *you*. Only one *us*. If I could take you out on normal dates, I would in a heartbeat."

My insides melt. "You would?"

He nods solemnly, but there's a telling twinkle in his eye. "As long as it wasn't crowded. And there were no fluorescent lights anywhere. And we stayed within ten feet of an exit at all times. You know... normal date stuff."

A laugh burbles out of me and he grins. Almost as soon as it forms, his smile falls. He shifts toward me, the heat of his body curling against my front. *So close. Not close enough.* When I register the intensity in his eyes, my stomach does a back-flip. My heart receives a similar memo, suddenly racing.

"Evangeline, I know it's been less than a week, but I need you to know—"

A knock on the door right beside my head makes me yelp and jerk forward. My forehead collides with Wilder's chin. We both curse.

Molly's laughing voice reaches our ears. "You guys all right? Sorry to kick you out, but April needs the room for her five o'clock lesson."

"Absolutely, sorry!" I say—too loudly based on Wilder's soft chuckle as he scoops up his guitar case. "Be right out!"

I scramble to grab my purse and water bottle, thankful for my habit of spending the last few minutes of each lesson having the student help me tidy the room. When I move to open the door, Wilder's fingers catch my wrist.

"Meet me back at your house." The low, firm tone sends a zinging shock through my body. My eyes fly to his. "We can leave your car there since it will be dark soon. I'll drive you home after dinner. I'm staying the night, by the way." He pauses for a quick breath. "Say 'Yes, Wilder.'"

The ache between my legs intensifies so fast it flirts with the border between desire and necessity. Saturday night plays behind my eyes. Behind *his* eyes, which watch me with pene-trative focus.

A much older memory rises out of nowhere, playing from

start to finish in seconds. I was six or seven. Wilder and I were caught outside in a spring downpour. My fault—I'd pestered him relentlessly to push me on the swings until his dad stepped in and told him to. Wilder was so annoyed with me that he pushed me too hard and high on purpose. Eventually I threw a fit and told him to go away.

He was halfway back to the house when the clouds opened and freezing rain poured down so fast and hard it soaked me in seconds. The sound was shocking. A vast, rushing roar that sent me stumbling away from the swings in terror—a terror that grew wings when I realized I couldn't see Wilder anymore. The house and pool had likewise disappeared. The swing set ten feet behind me was barely distinguishable behind undulating, liquid curtains.

Then the rain shifted to hail. Stinging bullets of ice struck me all over, my sweater useless as a shield. In a mindless panic, I started screaming, running blindly toward where I thought the house was.

Wilder caught me, jerking me off my feet and hugging me so tightly I could feel his ribs beneath my cheek. He yelled about the pool and how I could have drowned, but I barely heard him because I was so *relieved*. Then he covered my head with his arms. For what felt like hours but was probably a handful of seconds, I trembled in a cocoon of his wet sweatshirt and steady heartbeat as the hail battered him.

I remember thinking the world was ending, but it was okay because we were together.

Looking up at him now, I feel it again—that the world around us is a roar. A never-ending storm. But I'm safe because we're together.

"Yes, Wilder," I whisper.

THE SOUND that comes out of Evangeline on her first bite of the pasta dish Jax and Eddie prepared makes me want to throw her over my shoulder and run from the dining room, then come back and beat the shit out of my bandmates.

"This is delicious, you guys," she gushes, not noticing the sudden undercurrent at the table. Even Zander picks up on it, his eyes darting around in curiosity and speculation, lingering a bit too long on Evangeline. While it's ludicrous to be triggered by him—she doesn't have the hardware he prefers—it still pisses me off.

I glare across the table at Eddie, daring him to make the joke brewing in his laughing eyes. Lucky for him, he glances at me first. He wipes the smile off his face and lowers his head, shoving food in his mouth. *Smart man.*

Jax clears his throat, drawing my attention away from his brother. His eyes hold a mild rebuke—one I absolutely deserve. In spite of his long crush, Eddie took the news of Evangeline and me getting together with admirable maturity, even telling me he was glad we'd finally pulled our heads out of our asses. He's been nothing but supportive since, and he hasn't flirted with her once tonight. It's not his fault I feel like a powder keg rolling toward a bonfire.

I force myself to relax back into my chair, ignoring the way my skin crawls and itches. This dinner seemed like such a good idea when the guys proposed it. It didn't occur to me how difficult it would be to watch Eva, Jax, and Eddie pick up right where they left off three years ago. Their effortless, lighthearted friendship doesn't include me. It never did. I'm still the dark, cold planet orbiting light years away from their suns.

I don't know what I was thinking. That it would be different now? That I would be different? If anything, I'm *worse* now that Evangeline's mine. Every time I hear them laugh together, my fingers curl into a fist on my thigh and my teeth clench. My emotions are playing a manic game of tag and my body is no better: cold—hot—cold—hot.

My eyes keep finding the beers Eddie and Zander are nursing, both bottles still half-full. I don't understand how they can just sip them every once in a while. Why drink unless you want to get buzzed? No one loves the taste of beer that much.

Being sober fucking sucks.

I eventually take a bite of the pasta—it *is* fucking good—and decide then and there that I'm learning to cook. Someday, Evangeline will make those sounds for *my* food.

The faint fragrance of her shampoo envelops me as she leans over to murmur in my ear, "What's wrong?"

I'm a possessive, jealous fuck.

"Nothing," I whisper back, turning fast to catch her soft lips with mine. She jerks back, her already rosy cheeks darkening further as she faces her plate and scoops up more pasta.

Her embarrassment, her rejection, spreads ice through my chest. The crawling sensation under my skin worsens.

I grab my water glass and drain it, wishing it were alcohol.

"So, Eva," Jax says, his gaze flickering between us. "When are you and Lily heading into the studio?"

Evangeline answers haltingly at first but warms up as Jax guides the conversation into other topics. Eddie and Zander eventually join in, and the four of them chat easily as they eat. Evangeline is animated as she only is when she feels comfortable; there isn't even any awkwardness with Zander, the two of them spending a solid five minutes geeking out over some new keyboard that just hit the market.

No one tries to involve me. The part of me that's still rational knows they're not being rude. They simply know me. I'm not chatty, don't like being forced into conversations, and will only contribute if I feel like it. It should be a relief, but instead it stings in a way it never has before.

They know I'm not like them.

Not *normal*.

No wonder Evangeline was embarrassed when I kissed her in front of them.

The toxicity of my thoughts reaches dangerous levels, numbing the tips of my fingers and sending a snaking, burning sensation down my spine. Their voices become jarring. Dissonant.

I have to get out of here.

Grabbing my barely touched dinner, I stand fast and ignore the sudden silence as I collect their empty plates.

Evangeline scoots back her chair, but I shake my head, not looking at her. Afraid she'll see the monster in my eyes.

"I've got it."

As I walk into the kitchen, Eddie says something that makes Evangeline laugh softly, and I almost, *almost*, chuck the plates into the sink. Instead, I set them down gently, then grip the edge of the sink as hard as I can.

I can't fucking breathe.

Footsteps snap my head to the side. Jax turns the corner, the big salad bowl in his hands. He stops when he sees me, his expression twisting with concern.

"Take a minute," he says in a low voice. "I'll tell her you got a phone call or something."

My throat too tight to speak, I jerk my head in a nod. It takes a few seconds to convince my fingers to release the sink, then I flee into the back hallway. I ascend the stairs two at a time, but it still takes forever to reach the top.

A high-pitched whine fills my ears. I run the rest of the way to my bedroom. Inside, I shove the door closed right as my knees buckle.

I hit the floor hard and swing forward, my forehead smacking wood, my hands clenched in my hair.

Make it stop. Make it stop.

The Shadow's spikes close around me, sinking fast and deep. Before I'm fully aware of moving, I'm off the floor and stumbling into the bathroom. I rip open the cabinet beneath the sink and crouch to grab a plastic container full of first aid that my mom stuck in all the bathrooms when we moved in.

A strangled gasp escapes as I tear off the lid and dump the contents on the tile. My vision sparkling at the edges, I sift through the mess until I see it: a box of gauze. As I pick it up, something small and hard rattles in the bottom.

The instant relief I feel has me biting my cheek against a sob.

No, no, no.

Just one.

Don't do it.

No one will know.

200

You'll know.

You need this.

Feeling like a passenger in my body, I watch myself rip open the box and pull out the gauze to reveal the treasure at the bottom.

Two small, circular pills.

White noise fills my head.

I'm not shaking anymore.

The pills hit my palm.

I stare at them until my vision blurs.

Something wet hits my mouth.

I lick tears from my lips.

"No," I whisper. "Please."

Who I'm asking for help?

There's no help here.

Only the memory of Evangeline pulling away from me. Laughter around me, never touching me. Never mine. The cold dark. Her face wearing a thousand expressions across a lifetime. Lust and longing and hope and disgust and fear. Anger. *Hurt.*

River's resentment.

My parents' sad, worried eyes.

Shame. Guilt. Self-loathing.

It's too much.

It's all too fucking much.

Pointless.

Hopeless.

I lurch to my feet and turn on the tap, then toss the pills into my mouth and scoop a palmful of water to swallow them. Knowing what's coming relaxes muscles all over my body. I slump against the vanity and make the mistake of looking at my reflection.

"You made it fourteen days." I laugh, low and bitter, at the flushed, sweaty, tear-eyed man in the mirror. "You're pathetic. A coward and a failure. And you're a fucking drug addict."

Tears distort my sight.

The man in the mirror melts away to nothing.

CHAPTER TWENTY-FIVE

evangeline

what if I told you
I tossed the match?
Would you keep me
Or throw me back?

IT'S BEEN thirty minutes since Wilder disappeared, since Jax came back to the table with a smile that didn't reach his eyes and told me he had to take a call from their manager and would be back soon.

I'm not stupid.

There's no phone call.

I waited as long as I could, in case I was wrong, but finally asked for directions to Wilder's room. Now, as I walk down a hallway toward the closed door at the end, boulders of guilt knock together inside me.

I fucked up.

When he kissed me, I reacted badly. I should have fixed it

immediately. I *knew* he was upset, that he felt rejected. But I couldn't bring myself to do anything about it. Instead, I let him quietly implode beside me and pretended I didn't see it.

As great as it was to see the guys and reconnect, the familiar dynamic triggered old, defensive behaviors for me. Namely, my habit of relying on Eddie and Jax to buffer me against Wilder during the final months of our tour, when I was falling apart while he lived his best rock star life. Never choosing me, *seeing me*, except when we were onstage.

But that's not true anymore. And if I believe what he's told me, it wasn't true then, either. He's always seen me. Wanted me like I wanted him. He was just afraid.

I hate that I hurt him, especially after all we've shared. I hate even more that a twisted part of me enjoyed the reversal of our former roles. The power I had over *him* this time.

The admittance makes me queasy.

Dinner was a bad idea. It was too soon, our relationship too new, the potholes of our past still littering our present road.

I stop outside his bedroom door but don't reach for the handle. Closing my eyes, I breathe slowly through my nose. It takes a solid thirty seconds for me to find the courage to open his door, and I almost lose it when I see how dark it is inside. The only light comes from the hallway and from behind the half-closed bathroom door.

A shiver races down my arms as my eyes dart around the large room. Slowly, my vision adjusts, bringing into focus a king-sized bed to my left. I can barely make out Wilder, his black-clad body and dark hair blending with the bedding.

Each step into the dark ratchets up my heart rate.

"Wilder? Are you awake?" My voice is small, compressed by guilt and nervousness.

He'll forgive me, won't he?

What if he doesn't?

Wilder shifts slightly, a heavy sigh reaching my ears. I push forward until I'm fully surrounded by shadow, until my knees hit the bed. Clutching the comforter, I shuffle around the side closest to him, stopping when I see his face. The barest light from the bathroom reveals his closed eyes, but I can't tell whether he's asleep or pretending because he doesn't want to see me.

"I'm sorry about earlier," I say, my voice wavering. "Actually, I'm sorry about the entire night. I was acting like an asshole. I... I think it was just weird, being around the guys after so long."

"It's fine, Fairy."

His voice is calm, his eyes remaining closed. A trickle of relief is sucked beneath the oil-slick of foreboding. Something isn't right.

"Can I turn on a light? So we can talk?"

There's a long pause during which I try and fail to tamp down my illogical fear response to the darkness around me, to his unnerving reaction. I glance at the bathroom, at the hallway, reassuring myself there are two points of light. Two paths to escape. But I don't want to escape this—him. So I ignore the tingling in my feet that urges me to run toward safety.

"Can we talk tomorrow?" he asks finally.

"Tomorrow?" I echo, pushing the word past a stab of pain in my chest.

His lashes flicker and part, eyes absorbing the shadows and appearing black as pitch. "Yeah. I guess barely sleeping the last couple of nights caught up with me. Can you ask Jax to take you home?"

The apathy in his voice raises the hair on the back of my neck. "I don't want to leave if you're mad at me, Wilder."

He reaches out, warm fingers covering mine where they still clench the comforter. Coaxing me to release the fabric, he pulls my hand to his mouth. Soft, warm lips press to my palm.

"I'm not mad," he murmurs, breath puffing against my skin. "I understand why you pulled away. It's okay. I'm just exhausted."

He kisses my hand one more time before releasing it and rolling onto his other side, dragging the comforter over his shoulder. I open my mouth, an offer to sleep here beading on my tongue, but it doesn't come.

If he wanted me to stay, he wouldn't have told me to have Jax drive me home. If he weren't mad, he would have tugged me onto the bed and into his arms. He would have turned on the lights for me.

He wants me to go.

And if I'm honest, I don't want to stay. Not in the dark—not even for him.

CHAPTER TWENTY-SIX

evangeline

"EARTH TO EVA."

I startle, my gaze snapping away from the kitchen window where I was watching two squirrels chase each other across my back fence. Seated across from me, Lily watches me with a furrowed brow. I don't know how long I was zoning out, but her laptop is closed, her headphones lowered around her neck.

"What's going on with you? You look like a zombie and your focus is shit."

I drag a hand through my hair, wincing when my fingers hit knots. "Sorry. I didn't sleep last night."

One of her dark eyebrows lifts. "Given that you don't have the glow of a marathon sex sesh, I'm going to assume insomnia?"

I nod, unable to articulate the complex truth. How do I explain that I'm a grown woman terrified of the dark behind my own eyelids? That when I'm stressed, it gets worse. So bad I have to sleep with the overhead light on, which ends up being a snake eating its tail scenario—I need the light on to sleep but can't sleep because of the light.

The soft *clack* of headphones hitting the table pulls me out of my head again. I belatedly register the mix of sympathy and frustration on her face, but before I can think of a lie to defuse her worry, she asks, "Did something happen at dinner last night?"

Hot shame geysers through me. Avoiding her eyes, I study my hands. The sight of my ravaged cuticles makes me wince.

"If it's about Wilder, I promise I won't say 'I told you so' or anything like that. Believe it or not, I'm rooting for you two."

"Since when?" I ask, then shake my head quickly. "Sorry. You didn't deserve that."

"Eh, I probably did. I wasn't exactly Team Wilder at first but..." she trails off, color blooming on her cheeks. "Rye has told me a lot more about the bond between you guys, how you were as kids and stuff."

For the first time since getting home last night, the dense fog inside me clears a bit. I smirk. "Oh, really? Exactly how much are you guys talking?"

She palms her cheeks but not before I see them darken even further. "Pretty much constantly. Is that weird for you to hear? I've been afraid to talk about it, but I'm crushing hard. And he seems really into me, too. It's tripping me out. How is he a year younger than us and ten times more emotionally mature than every dude I've dated?"

I manage a laugh. "It's not weird for me. I saw this coming from a mile away."

She studies my face, her eyes hopeful and wary. "You're sure he's not bread-crumbing me?" she asks in a small voice. "Acting all perfect just to get in my pants and dump me after? I know he's been with a lot of girls."

"Definitely not. First of all, I'd kill him. Second, I've known him since we were both in diapers, so believe me when I say I've never seen him this into someone. He talks

208

about you nonstop. You deserve someone like him, Lil. A genuinely good guy who's loyal, stable, and kind. It's true he's been a serial dater for a few years, but only because he's a hopeless romantic searching for The One. So if you aren't looking for anything serious, you need to tell him."

She nods quickly. "We've actually talked about that a little —what we're looking for—and we're on the same page. Now he just needs to ask me out and put us both out of our misery."

I sit back with a smile. "He'll crack before the end of the week. Probably on Friday once he sees your outfit for the showcase."

Happiness flashes across her face, then a speculative focus. "And you're sure the two of you don't have unresolved romantic feelings for each other that could potentially destroy all three of our lives in the distant future?"

I mimic gagging. "Absolutely sure. Someday I'll share with you the eight million reasons why, but we'll save that convo for your tenth wedding anniversary when it's too late for you to run away screaming."

She finally laughs, looking like a hundred-pound weight has come off her shoulders. "Okay. Thanks, Ev."

I nod at her laptop. "Where were we?"

She wags a finger at me. "Nice try. I spilled my guts, so now you have to. Quid pro quo or whatever."

I groan. "Can we not?"

Not to be deterred, Lily shifts her laptop aside and leans forward on her elbows. "You have to talk to someone. Unless you've decided to tell your mom what's going on?"

I shake my head.

With a self-satisfied smile, she sits back and crosses her arms over her chest. "Tell Dr. Aoki your troubles."

I make a face. "Ew."

She stares at me, and stares some more, until I heave a resigned sigh. As uncomfortable as it is for me to talk about my feelings to anyone—even my mom—I know I need to vent before I explode. Or, in my case, implode. Unfortunately the necessity doesn't mean the words come easily.

When the silence tiptoes into the Land of Uncomfortable, I finally blurt, "It's not you. This is really hard for me. Talking about feelings. Like I'm sweating right now."

She nods, her lips twitching.

I keep rambling, my gaze bouncing around the room. "I've always been this way. Reserved, I guess? It's not like my parents ever punished me for having feelings or talking about them."

My mind latches onto an old, old memory, and it ejects from my mouth. "Wilder has a great-aunt on his mom's side. Katherine. Growing up, I was super scared of her because she'd say weird stuff all the time. Predictions that always came true."

Lily's eyes widen. "Like what?"

"All sorts of shit. One year, she said it was going to be a white Christmas even though there was no snow in the forecast. It snowed Christmas Day." I smile at that memory, then shiver at the next one. "Another time, she told my parents that Hunter shouldn't climb on the play set in the Ashburn's backyard. They laughed it off because my brother has always been super athletic and had been crawling all over that thing since he could walk. Later that day, he slipped on wet leaves inside the playhouse at the top and fell out of it. He broke his arm and had a mild concussion."

"Whoa." Lily rubs the goosebumps on her arms. "That's trippy."

I nod. "Anyway, when I was around five, I was running in the Ashburns' backyard and tripped over a root. I hurt myself pretty bad. Scraped up my knees and face and was bleeding a lot. But I just sat there in a daze. Didn't scream or cry or anything.

"Katherine was the only one who saw me fall. She didn't ask if I was okay, just sat next to me and started talking. She told me about how when you build a dam on a river, you have to make sure there are outlets and spillways. If you don't, when there's a really bad storm, the dam will overflow and eventually crack. I had no clue why she was telling me this, obviously, but I finally started crying. She patted me on the head, helped me stand, and took me inside to my parents."

Lily whistles softly. "I need to meet this woman." She folds her hands beneath her chin and grins at me. "Is that your way of telling me I get to be your spillway?"

My lips tug upward. "I guess so. But I don't know where to start."

She hums in sympathy. "The last week has probably been super intense for you."

"It really has." I take a steadying breath, my eyes stinging. "I don't know what I'm doing, Lil. What a normal relationship looks like. The three guys I've dated since high school have either dumped or ghosted me after a few months. Now there's Wilder and this... this *thing* between us. It's so big and overwhelming. I feel like I'm going crazy."

My throat clogs. I blink fast as the burning in my eyes intensifies, spreading through my sinuses.

"Keep going."

The compassion in her voice opens another pressure valve, and my voice spills through it.

"He's said so many things I've always dreamed of hearing from him. It's been amazing. Healing. And it probably sounds naive, but he means every word. I've never felt so seen and heard, so accepted. Like even my weirdest quirks are somehow amazing to him."

Lily makes a small sound. "It doesn't sound naive, Ev. It sounds like he's in love with you."

Distantly, I recognize the words should make me feel something. Hope, maybe. But they don't penetrate.

"Maybe he is. Maybe I'm in love with him, too—maybe I always have been. But can you love someone you don't really know?"

She frowns. "What do you mean?"

A few tears leak from my eyes, but my hands feel too heavy and numb to wipe them away.

"Wilder is like the deepest part of the ocean. Hidden depths upon hidden depths. There are parts of him I'm not sure he'll ever let me see, parts I don't even know if he *can* show me. But like I said, he's also opened up to me. I know he cares about me, wants to be with me. And the sex is unreal— literally unreal. I seriously thought penetrative orgasms and squirting were myths."

Her eyes widen comically. "Say *what*? Holy shit. How does it feel to be a chosen one?"

I laugh weakly. "Pretty awesome."

She sobers. "This feeling that you don't know him... it could be because of the time you spent apart. Maybe give yourself, and him, a break? It's going to take more than a few days to catch up on years." She pauses, her head tilting and a spark igniting in her dark eyes. "Or do you think he's lying to you about something?"

"No. I don't think so? Honestly, I don't know if any of what I'm feeling is real or if it's old fears sabotaging me. What if this distance I feel is all in my head? Am I'm expecting too much from him? Freaking out over nothing? Maybe I'm just an insecure idiot. Or maybe this proves that we're all wrong for each other. What if this is a giant mistake?"

I don't realize I'm crying in earnest until Lily yanks a napkin from the holder between us and hands it to me. I blow my nose loudly.

"It's been five days," I say through another sob. "This is crazy, right? What the fuck is happening to me? One second I'm fine, the next I'm freaking out."

Lily can't quite conceal her shock—she's never seen me lose it like this. "Shit, Ev. What the hell happened last night?"

I sniffle my way through a recounting of yesterday, from Wilder showing up at my work to my fuckup at dinner and what happened after. But I don't stop there, backtracking to tell her about not seeing him Sunday or Monday, the spotty texts, and how scared I was that he was getting ready to ghost me. How yo-yoing between emotional extremes has fucked up my sleep, my focus, and worst of all, my understanding of myself as a calm, rational person.

When I'm done, Lily doesn't immediately reply, her gaze on the table and her expression troubled. Knowing she won't sugarcoat her opinion, I try to prepare myself. A wasted effort, as I've barely stopped crying when she lifts her head.

"The way I see it, you have two options. Option one, you believe his explanation for pulling away the last two days—however stupid it was—and you believe that last night he wasn't upset with you, just crazy tired. Option two, you drive yourself up the wall with various worst-case scenarios. I realize option two is kind of unavoidable given your history with him, but have you considered option one? Taking him at his word?"

"I—" I close my mouth and actually think about it. "I've been fixated on the fear that he's not being totally honest with me."

213

She nods in understanding. "He yanked you around for years, Eva. Of course it's going to take time to trust him. But trust is also a choice, you know? Either you push through your fear or you decide it's not worth it."

"It's worth it," I say quickly. "I *want* to trust him."

"Then give yourself some grace as you navigate this. He says he's all in and you believe that much, right?" I nod. "Maybe setting some boundaries would help, like telling him straight-up what you need to feel safe in the relationship—communication expectations, emotional transparency, et cetera."

I rub my face, groaning. "That's not too, I don't know, needy?"

Her lips purse. "Fuck that. There's a difference between neediness and communication of your needs, and any man who can't recognize the difference is a turd. Besides, this isn't a typical new relationship with a dude you met a week ago. Your baggage with Wilder comes with extra weight fees and carry-ons."

I snort, then grimace and blow my nose again. Calmness seeps through me, as well as heady gratitude for the woman across from me.

I give her a watery smile. "Thanks for being my spillway. You're an amazing woman and an incredible friend."

To my shock, tears fill her eyes. My jaw slack, I rise halfway from my chair. She waves me back down and grabs a napkin, then dabs it delicately beneath her eyes.

"Shut up. You're welcome. Ugh. I even forgive you for threatening my mascara with that warm and fuzzy shit."

The laugh bubbling in my throat chokes off when a key rattles in my front door. Lily swivels in her chair, frowning. "Please tell me that's not Rye. He can't see me almost crying until we've dated at least six months."

I snatch my phone and check the time; when I see it, the blood drains from my head. "Oh, fuck. When Wilder texted me this morning, I told him to come over at four. I completely lost track of time."

Lily's expression morphs from worried to horrified. "Go dunk your face in cold water," she hisses.

It's too late.

The door swings open on Wilder, his head bowed as he tugs the key out of the lock. The sight of him makes my heart soar and my stomach plummet. He looks up and sees us in the kitchen.

"Hi. Sorry. I'm a few minutes early." He finally registers my tear-wrecked face and his eyes widen in alarm. "Evangeline?"

Lily stands and swiftly packs up her laptop, headphones, and phone. "Call me later," she whispers, then hurries toward the door. "Hey, Wilder. Good to see you. Coming to the Indigo showcase Friday night?"

Wilder, looking panicked and confused, moves out of her way. "Yes, I'll be there."

"Great," chirps Lily. "See you then!"

She slips past him and pulls the door closed.

CHAPTER TWENTY-SEVEN

wilder

THE THUMP of the door closing behind Lily jolts me like an electric shock. I want to follow her almost as much as I want to scoop Evangeline into my arms and kiss every inch of her blotchy, tear-stained face. My feet are likewise conflicted, remaining glued to the floor.

What happened?

Is she going to dump me?

Is it over?

I know she wanted more from me last night—starting with a different reaction to her apology—but I couldn't give it to her. With my tolerance being almost nil from two weeks of abstinence, the Oxys took me the fuck out. Making my voice sound somewhat normal during our brief conversation was next-level difficult, and there was no way I could let her turn on a light. She would have taken one look at me and known I was loaded.

My anxiety climbs so high my voice shakes when I ask, "Is this about last night? I'm sorry, Fairy. I—"

"No," she says softly.

Instead of relaxing, my heart races even faster. I take a

halting step toward her. "Then what's wrong? Did someone— is your family okay?"

She stands up fast. "No! I mean *yes*, everyone's fine." A brief, breathless laugh leaves her, and she rubs her already flushed face. She mumbles, "God, I wish you weren't seeing me like this. I'm a total mess."

I speak without thinking. "I love you messy."

Evangeline's head whips up, her eyes huge and unblinking. A second later, I realize what I said. But there's no panic.

Fuck it.

"I love you messy," I repeat as I cross the living room. My eyes absorb every inch of her: crazy hair in a listing bun, swollen eyes, baggy sweatpants, two different-colored socks, and an oversized green sweatshirt with a bleach stain on the hem and tear marks on the shoulders.

Her beauty is both suffocating and replenishing. I can't breathe—the only air I need is her.

Stopping a few feet away, I hold her gaze until I lose sight of everything else. Until there's nothing in the infinite span of the universe but us.

Her rapid breaths.

The fear and hope in her eyes.

My heart—her heart.

"I love every version of you, Evangeline. Happy, angry, stubborn, bossy, sad, tired, embarrassed, nervous... it doesn't matter. Whatever you are, I love it, because I'm hopelessly in love with you. I know my timing, as usual, is completely fucked, but it's the truth and I'm not going to cheapen it by pretending that was a slip of the tongue."

She trembles before me, eyes glassy with tears. I have no clue if she's about to say the words back to me or throw me out. In this moment, I don't care. Whatever she decides to do

217

with my deformed heart, she deserves to know the truth inside it.

Her lips part on a swift inhale. Then she blinks several times and says the absolute last thing I expect to hear.

"I'm afraid of the dark."

I dig my nails into my palms so I don't reach for her. It's not the declaration of love I was hoping for, but I know how hard those words were to say. How vulnerable she feels right now.

"I know, baby."

"I'm not talking about a few nightlights." At my lifted brows, her lips twitch. "Okay, more than a few nightlights. But it's deeper than that. It's also about the people who are closest to me. That's why I asked you to turn on the light last night. I needed to see you, to talk to you, and when I couldn't... you became the dark I couldn't find my way out of."

There's no controlling my full-body recoil.

Evangeline gasps. "I'm sorry."

"It's okay," I croak.

She shakes her head and lurches forward, wrapping her arms tightly around my waist. I hold her close, hoping this isn't the last time she lets me.

"That came out totally wrong," she says against my chest. "I haven't slept and my thoughts are all jumbled. Last night was my fault, not yours. I'm sorry for hurting you at dinner." Tears thicken her voice. "You're not the dark I'm afraid of, okay? Not even close. If I'm afraid of anything, it's my own damn head."

I *am* the dark, though, even if she doesn't know it. But I'm also a selfish bastard who doesn't want to live without her light, so I cradle her to me. Soak in my relief and her radiance. Unable to let her go even if it ends up destroying us both.

"I'm sorry," I whisper into her hair. "I'm sorry, Fairy."

She squeezes me, then lifts her head. The redness has mostly faded from her cheeks, but the skin around her blood-shot eyes is still swollen, her eyelashes wet spikes.

I'm hurting her.

I need to save her.

I can't lose her.

"What are you thinking right now?" she asks softly.

I kiss her forehead before resting my chin on her soft hair and hugging her a little tighter.

Hating myself. Loving her.

"I was thinking about you getting lost in the woods when we were kids and wondering if that's when it started."

"I think so, yes. That's definitely my first memory of being afraid of the dark." She hums. "I've never forgotten that it was you who found me. You led me out."

I led you from one dark to another.

I can't keep you safe.

You shouldn't trust me.

All the words I can't say sit like shards of glass in my throat, but Evangeline doesn't notice. She ducks her head back into my chest, rubbing her cheek against me.

"I love you, too, Wilder. So much."

A glowing wave of warmth spreads through my body. When it reaches the end of me and recedes, it leaves behind a melody. Exquisite and lovely and painful and haunting. Bright like her. Dark like me.

My heart's song as it becomes whole for the first time.

And then shatters.

CHAPTER TWENTY-EIGHT

evangeline

Pressure points thump-thumping
Beneath our fingertips
Liquid breath flowing between our lips
And yet we're still dying of thirst

RYE STRIDES toward Lily and me with his signature grin. "Twenty minutes to go, ladies. How are we holding up?"

"Super great," Lily answers, the sarcasm in her voice as obvious as the appreciation in her eyes. Even though I'll never look at Rye like *that*, I have to admit he's extra-handsome tonight in a black button-down and slacks that actually fit his giant shoulders and mile-long legs.

When he finally drags his gaze away from Lily, who looks absolutely stunning in a silvery minidress, I ask, "Did you see him?"

My friends exchange a loaded glance that makes me want to knock their heads together. Then Rye shakes his head. "I might have missed him, though. It's crowded out there."

There is a massive tent in the backyard of the opulent mansion we've been sequestered in since our sound check an hour ago.

When our new manager reached out with the invitation for a private showcase, she definitely downplayed the event's magnitude. Instead of the intimate setting we imagined, there are at least a hundred people milling outside beneath string lights and space heaters. And not one of them looks like anyone we'd see at our usual shows. Instead of jeans and T-shirts, it's cocktail dresses, suits, and champagne flutes.

I've already talked Lily out of hyperventilating twice. My own pre-show jitters are muted, smothered by a different worry. All I can think about is Wilder, who said he'd come early to see me before the show.

I check my phone for the hundredth time, but there are no new messages after the one I sent him before we came inside.

> Text me when you get here and I'll send Rye to find you. Xo

While the downstairs suite offered for our use looks like it belongs in a five-star hotel, the cell service is shit. I have no idea if he's tried to call or text me back, and when I tried to sneak back outside, a harried woman wearing a headset all but shoved me back into our room.

"Did you try calling him?" asks Rye.

I bite my cheek so I don't snap at him.

"No service," Lily answers for me, "and no one we've asked knows the Wi-Fi password."

Rye shifts his weight. "If you want, I can look again. Not sure if I can make it back before you go on, though."

I shake my head and force a smile. "Don't worry about it. I'd rather you hang here. I'm sure Wilder is out there somewhere."

He promised.

I move to the nearest window and twitch aside the curtains, squinting through fading daylight at the tent. We're too far away for me to make out faces, but I don't see anyone with Wilder's distinctive height. Not even a flash of Eddie's neon-green hair, which would at least reassure me since the whole band is supposed to be here.

Trust him.

Closing my eyes tightly, I summon memories of the last two days, wrapping them around my heart like a shield. Wilder and I spent every spare minute together. Scattered between beautifully mundane activities like playing guitar, soaking in my hot tub, and his first charmingly disastrous attempt at making me dinner, we had frank conversations about what each of us needs to feel secure in our relationship.

While there were moments I could tell he was uncomfortable—namely when I told him I want to tell my parents about us—he didn't have a single panic attack.

And the last two *nights*... even thinking about them sends currents of heat through my body. I thought sex with him had been incredible before, but having him stare into my eyes and whisper he loves me while he moves inside me? I'm forever altered by it. He's always been a part of me, but now he's in every breath I take and every beat of my heart.

The final memory I summon, possibly the most profound one, is falling asleep in his arms late last night, only to realize this morning that I'd forgotten to turn on the main nightlight in my bedroom.

He'll be here.

After heaving a sigh that fogs the glass, I turn and drop onto the couch beside my purse, tossing my useless phone into its depths.

"I need to, uh, use the restroom," Rye says, pivoting on his heel and heading into one of the adjacent bedrooms.

Lily sits next to me and hands me my giant bottle of water. I take it and fiddle with the cap as I stare sightlessly across the room.

"You good, Ev?"

Her nervous voice is a welcome gust of wind clearing my polluted thoughts. *God, I'm such an asshole.* I grab her bouncing knee, pressing down until it stills, and hold her gaze until the worry in her eyes shifts to relief.

"I'm good. All warmed up. You good?"

She nods. "I am now that your bossy-diva face is on."

I smirk. "Ready to explode some brains?"

A smile teases her burgundy-painted lips. "Hope they have a good cleaning service."

As my laughter fades, we hear voices in the hallway outside coming closer. Along with the confident tones of our new manager, Mallory Simmons, we recognize the rapid-fire speech of our equally new publicist, Anita Allman.

We make it to our feet right as the main door opens. Anita flies into the room first and beelines for us, her corkscrew blond curls bouncing around her head. Even though she's barely five feet tall, objectively cherubic in appearance, and has been nothing but sweet so far, Lily and I agree she's absolutely terrifying.

"Ladies!" she gushes, her hands fluttering around us. "Look at you two! Gorgeous, absolutely gorgeous. Aren't they gorgeous, Mallory? I can't wait to get you to my favorite stylist. He's going to have the best time elevating your look."

Feeling Lily tense beside me, I grab her hand and give it a

reassuring squeeze. Anita doesn't notice or doesn't care about our discomfort, muttering to herself as she catalogues us from feet to hair like she's taking notes on everything we need to change about ourselves. Which she probably is.

I have a new appreciation for why Wilder always hated meetings with our publicist, whose focus was invariably on him while Eddie, Jax, and I were left mostly unscathed.

"They're gorgeous," agrees Mallory in a genuine but much more subdued tone as she approaches us. "Now give them some space, will you? Your crazy energy is the last thing they need right now, and I'd like a minute with our clients."

Anita giggles, unoffended, and spins around. She squeaks when she spots Rye reentering the room. "Hello, there! And you are?" She barrels toward him and grabs his arm. "Is that a full bar? Oh my. I could use a drink, handsome. How about you?"

Rye throws us a *PleaseHelpMe* look as she tugs him toward the bar, but before either of us can react, Mallory captures our attention. "He'll survive," she says with a knowing smile. "I know Anita is intense, but I wouldn't have recommended her unless she was the best—and the best fit for your style. You'll get used to her. How are you feeling? Nervous?"

"A little," Lily says. "This isn't our usual crowd, that's for sure."

Mallory's dark eyes sparkle. "I know, but remember they're here for you, not the other way around."

"Who is *they*, exactly?" I ask. "We thought there'd be maybe a dozen people here."

Mallory chuckles and shakes her head but not in a patronizing way. Whereas Anita is a shark wearing the skin of an angel, Mallory *looks* like a shark but has the personality of a mellow, level-headed big sister. She also has a two-decade-long track record of managing successful pop artists and was recommended personally by Breaking Giants' manager, Phil, who's like a crotchety uncle to me.

"This is all Anita's doing," Mallory says, glancing toward the bar where the publicist is laughing hysterically at something Rye said. From the expression on his face, he didn't intend whatever it was to land as a joke.

"Not gonna lie, ladies," continues Mallory, "there are a lot of recognizable faces out there. Pretty much everyone who's anyone in the Seattle music industry is here, plus a handful of players from Los Angeles and New York. Producers, artists, journalists..." She trails off as she takes in our expressions.

"I'm gonna throw up," whispers Lily.

Despite my own queasiness, I pull her into a hug. "We've got this. It doesn't matter who they are. We're going to give them the exact same Glow we'd give a bunch of college kids at a house party. Okay?"

She nods against my shoulder. Behind her, Mallory mouths, "Sorry," right as Anita's high-pitched voice fills the suite.

"Just got the text, my gorgeous girls! It's showtime!"

I sigh into Lily's ear and mutter, "Guess we should've asked *her* for the Wi-Fi."

Like I hoped she would, she laughs.

CHAPTER TWENTY-NINE

evangeline

LILY AND I stand hidden from view by a wall of curtains that leads directly to the temporary stage. A few seconds ago, the lights inside the tent dimmed and those rigged to scaffolding at each corner of the stage flared brightly.

The crowd is screaming.

Screaming.

Lily stares at the sky, fading white wisps on a canvas of deep blue. "What the fuck is happening right now?" she asks dazedly.

A hysterical giggle escapes me.

The stage lights lower and the noise from the crowd spikes even higher. From the cacophony comes a familiar whistle, piercing despite my earplugs. As soon as it tapers off, I hear another welcome sound: an obnoxious, warbling scream. Laughter mixes with the ongoing cheers.

"Jax and Eddie," I tell Lily, who returns my giddy grin.

A woman positioned a few feet away waves for our attention and holds up one finger. *One minute.* We nod and look back at the stage as a shadowed figure enters from the other side and walks to the central mic. There's a gentle hum of feedback before light rises on a man—not Cory Donovan, who we were told was introducing us.

This man is well over six feet tall and wears faded black jeans, scuffed combat boots, and a leather jacket. The chaotic waves of his hair gleam darkly beneath the spotlight. His hands in his pockets and his stance relaxed, he oozes confidence and charisma. Like he was born for the stage.

My shoulder knocks into Lily's as my knees turn rubbery.

Wilder's smooth, rich voice floats across the backyard, quieting the crowd as effectively as a lullaby. "Hey, everyone. Believe it or not, for once I'm actually excited to be here with you fancy fucks."

As boisterous laughter fills the air, Lily grabs my arm and whispers, "Oh my God, I think I love him, too."

As the crowd's laughter fades, Wilder continues, "As some of you are aware, I've known Eva my entire life. Our dads are in this little rock band called Breaking Giants." He pauses for another burst of cheers and applause. "And while I've only known Lily Aoki a short time, I know she's one in a million. How? Because Eva would settle for nothing less in a creative partnership and *she*, ladies and gentlemen, is absolutely one of a kind. These incredible women have more talent in their pinkie fingers than any of us can hope to claim in our lifetimes, and mark my words, tonight we'll be listening to the birth of a legend.

"Without further ado, allow me to welcome to the stage Eva Marie and Lily Aoki of Glow!"

I barely hear Lily's squeal of excitement over the roar from the tent. Feeling like I'm floating, I follow her onto the stage and move toward the man with a grin on his face, love in his eyes, and my guitar in his hands. He lowers the strap over my head, gives me a quick kiss on the cheek, and jogs offstage.

As I face the mic and the ecstatic crowd, I still feel him. Watching me, loving me, believing in me. It hits me suddenly that even when we were apart, he was never far away. And he never will be.

No matter where I go in life, he'll be there.

As constant as my shadow.

♪

AFTER THE SHOW, Mallory leads us back down the hallway toward our suite. Lily looks as blissed out as I feel, her eyes unfocused and a small, dreamy smile on her face. My entire body, toes to fingertips, buzzes like a live wire.

Mallory is talking, wisely directing her words to Rye. "Food will be waiting in the room. They'll have forty-five minutes or so to freshen up and relax before Anita drags them back outside to mingle. Make sure they hydrate, eat some protein, and go easy on alcohol. And make sure Eva takes a vocal nap." She hands him a sheet of paper as we near the suite. "Anita already went over this with them, but here's a list of ways they can respond to questions they don't want or know how to answer. Got it?"

"Yes, ma'am."

"Cute, but if you call me ma'am again I'll make you regret it."

Rye blanches. "Sorry. Never again."

"Good man."

Mallory gives Lily and me quick, tight hugs. "Phenomenal show, ladies. I'll see you soon." She strides back down the hallway, her shimmery halter dress swishing around her legs.

Rye ushers us inside the suite. "You two back on planet Earth yet?"

Lily giggles. "Nope—oh, chocolate!" She hurries to the table laden with food and grabs a plate.

Rye follows. "Protein first!"

"Pfft," she says, a brownie already passing her lips.

I laugh, which earns me a glare from Rye. "Vocal nap!"

I roll my eyes at his bossiness but mime zipping my lips, then kick off my Converse and head to the bar to switch on the electric teakettle. My throat feels okay but I know better than to push it, especially since the night is only half over and I have a lot of talking ahead of me. As the water heats, I grab a plate off the table and start loading it up.

"I feel drunk," mumbles Lily, this time around a hunk of cantaloupe. "Drunk off how surreal that was. Did you see that one guy tearing it up our entire set? He had to be my grandfather's age. And the woman who started crying during Eva's violin solo? I saw her in a movie trailer a few days ago."

Rye nods, chuckling. "My favorite part was when Eddie tried to start a mosh pit and security almost hauled him out."

Lily chokes on her cantaloupe and spits it out so she can laugh freely. "How did I miss that?"

I shrug, my eyes watering with the effort of not laughing.

"And then there was—" Rye stops suddenly when the suite door flies open. He grins. "Hey, man! How great was their set?"

Wilder's eyes find mine as the door swings closed. He stalks toward me. "It was great. I need to talk to Evangeline."

The heat in his eyes and the gravel in his voice make me gulp. My hand shakes on my plate. I squeeze my thighs together, the throb between them a sudden, steady drumbeat.

Lily cackles, grabbing Rye's arm in one hand and her plate of food in the other. "We're going to give you guys some alone time. Explore this castle a bit, maybe get into some trouble. Grab that bottle of sparkling water, Rye."

Rye frowns in bewilderment. "Huh? But—*oof*." He rubs his stomach where Lily landed a punch, then comprehension spreads on his face along with a ruddy hue. He grabs the bottle and a giant, wrapped sandwich. "Oh, um, for sure. We'll be back in ten minutes."

Wilder doesn't look at them as he says, "Make it twenty."

CHAPTER THIRTY

wilder

EVANGELINE SQUEAKS as I lift her from the floor and guide her legs around my waist. The feel of her in my arms, warm and pliant, and the delicious, musky scent of her sweat make my mouth water. I want to lick every salty inch of her, but there's one spot in particular I'm dying to devour.

"Which one of these doors is a bedroom?" I ask roughly.

Arousal and alarm war in her eyes as she points a trembling finger. *Good.* It means she remembers the promise I made last week—the one I'm about to make good on.

I waste no time crossing the large living room and shouldering my way past a partially open door. A swift kick closes it behind us. Luckily, the lights are on, so I don't have to waste time searching for a switch. Striding to the giant bed, I tear back the gold-embroidered comforter and dump her on the sheets. Then I crawl over her on all fours, my eyes soaking in the feast beneath me. Beautiful, flushed face and eyes that haunt my dreams. Corseted breasts heaving against the long-sleeved mesh bodysuit beneath it. Miniskirt riding up with every restless swish of her legs in their artfully ripped black tights.

Fucking exquisite.

When I bend down and nuzzle my face into her neck to taste her drying sweat, her hips punch upward on a breathy moan.

"Wilder, wait. At least let me—" My palm over her mouth muffles the rest of her words.

The spark of indignation in her eyes brings a wicked grin to my lips. "No talking. If you want me to stop, you can smack my head. Better hit me hard, though, because I'll be drowning in your pussy."

Her pupils dilate, dainty nostrils flaring. I watch the war play out in her eyes—her need to have my face between her thighs battling with the bullshit societal conditioning telling her she should wash first. Like her sweat doesn't simply enhance her natural scent and make me fucking feral.

I drag my nose along hers and over one flushed cheek. "What's it gonna be, Fairy?" I croon. "Yes or no?"

She nods, a sharp jerk of her chin.

"Good answer."

Releasing her mouth, I drag my hand over her neck to her chest, where my fingers make quick work of the eye hooks of her corset. The stiff fabric sags open, revealing her bare breasts under soft, black mesh. Her nipples pebble beneath my gaze, the pale mounds jerking with her panting breaths. I flick one nipple, then the other, smirking when she slaps her hands over her mouth to trap the sound that wants to escape.

"Ever thought about piercing these?"

Her eyes throw sparks that make me chuckle and kiss her deep and sloppy and hard. When I come up for air, she looks dazed but still has the wherewithal to jab a finger at the watch on my wrist.

I cock an eyebrow. "You think I'll need more than a minute or two to have your cum all over my face?"

Embarrassment and lust turn her face bright red. Grinning, I resume my downward path, pausing on her chest until the transparent fabric shines wetly around her nipples and her fingers twist and clench in the sheets above her head. I move lower, and lower still, every stroke of my hands and graze of my tongue slowly overwhelming her brain until all she can do is *feel*.

When I find the edge of the bed, I pull her with me by the hips until my knees hit the floor. Without me asking, she spreads her legs, shimmying until her miniskirt is pooled around her waist.

"Such a good slut for me," I whisper.

She makes a small, desperate sound as I lean forward, pressing my nose to the juncture of her thighs and inhaling. *Goddamn.* My balls tighten and my patience evaporates. I grab the waistband of her tights and strip them off, then pull her thighs onto my shoulders.

"Fuck," I grunt as I lift her toward my face. "You have the prettiest, neediest pussy I've ever seen."

She's quivering ambrosia on my tongue. I savor every flavor and texture I can find with long, slow licks before finally giving her swollen clit the attention it deserves. Within seconds, her thighs begin to tremble around my head, her head thrashing from side to side. At the barest brush of my teeth, she explodes with a ragged cry, bucking against my face. Growling in satisfaction, I drive my tongue inside her to feel the fading contractions of her orgasm.

"Oh my God," she whispers, her muscles going limp.

I bite her labia—not hard, but hard enough to make her spasm. "Not my name, brat."

She yanks my face up by my hair, the burn on my scalp transferring directly to my dick. When she sees my expres-

233

sion, the irritation on her face melts to surprise. Then intrigue.

I chuckle and wipe my hand over my mouth. "You can hurt me another time, Fairy. Right now you need to eat and drink some tea. Do you want to rinse off?"

Her expression softens and she nods. She releases my hair, her fingertips trailing over my cheek and passing, featherlight, across my lips. Her eyes flicker down to the bulge in my pants.

"Can I return the favor first?"

I shake my head, bending forward to give her pussy a final kiss that makes her twitch. "Later," I murmur, avoiding her probing eyes as I get to my feet. "I'll turn on the shower. Is that your bag in the corner?"

"Yeah. Thanks."

Pain pinches my chest at her small, disappointed voice, but I keep walking, grabbing her small duffel and heading into the bathroom. The room matches the suite's aesthetics, all white marble and gleaming gold accents. I crank the dial in the glass-walled shower, leaving my fingers under the flow as it heats up. My other hand lowers to my dick, adjusting it to a more comfortable position.

Do I want a blowjob from Evangeline? Abso-fucking-lutely. But I haven't let her go down on me. And I can't explain to her why because it will make me sound like a lunatic. While the thought of her mouth on me is one of my favorite fantasies, the idea of it happening in reality gives me an uneasy feeling. Like the act is beneath her or will diminish her somehow.

There's another reason, too—at least at the moment. Despite how hard I am, it will take more time than we have for me to climax. Which has absolutely nothing to do with her and everything to do with opiates.

Self-disgust curls through me.

"Did you get my text?"

At Evangeline's soft voice behind me, I wipe the scowl from my face and turn. My IQ drops a hundred points at the sight of her standing naked before me, her toes curling into a cream-colored bathmat as she spirals her hair into a bun and secures it.

Amusement brightens her eyes. "Hello?"

I don't lift my gaze from her body. Even her belly button is perfect. There are three small moles under her right breast that remind me of Orion's belt. I want to lick them. Map them. Make my own constellations on her body with bite marks.

She snaps her fingers in my face, her voice full of laughter as she says, "Focus, Wilder."

I finally lift my gaze and hear the question she asked. "I didn't get a text from you. Actually, I was going to ask you the same thing. I called a bunch when I got here, but you didn't answer, and some jerk security bro wouldn't let me in the house to look for you."

"There's no cell service in here." She smiles faintly, and the tension I didn't realize she was carrying vanishes. Unfortunately, that tension transfers right to me.

"You thought I wasn't coming?" I keep my voice light. *Even though I promised?*

"No, I knew you'd be here," she says quickly. Too quickly. "Your intro was a nice surprise, by the way. Thank you. I love you." Lifting to her toes, she gives me a kiss, then slips past me into the shower. "God, that feels good. Hey, when you make tea, can you use the sachets I brought in my purse? It's on the couch. Oh, and don't tell Rye I've been talking, okay? He'll be annoying about it."

I smile and nod like my gut isn't churning. Like she didn't just lie to me. Like I'm not the biggest hypocrite in the world.

The biggest liar of them all.

CHAPTER THIRTY-ONE

evangeline

AFTER CLOSE TO an hour of networking at Anita's side, meeting dozens of people whose names and faces all blur together, she finally releases us to mingle on our own. Lily immediately vanishes toward where we last saw Rye, leaving me standing alone at the end of a buffet table of picked-over hors d'oeuvres.

Exhaustion creeps over me as I scan the dwindling crowd for Wilder. I don't see him, which isn't much of a surprise. After Jax and Eddie left a little past ten, he probably found somewhere dark and quiet to chill until I'm ready to leave. I couldn't be more ready, but before setting us free, Anita politely ordered us to *make ourselves available* for another twenty minutes.

"You look like you could use this," says a voice to my right.

Forcing a pleasant expression onto my tired face, I turn to find a man holding two glasses of white wine, one of them extended my way. He's handsome in a men's-cologne-ad way, with light brown hair, an easy smile, and hazel eyes. The starched white collar of his dress shirt gapes open, framing a swath of tanned skin. Despite an air of casualness, he reeks of wealth, from his shoes and watch to the suit he's wearing, which fits too well for it not to be hand tailored. While he looks vaguely familiar, I'm positive Anita didn't introduce me to him tonight.

As good as a glass of wine sounds, and as much as he doesn't *look* like a creep, there's no way I'm taking an unsealed drink from a stranger.

"Thank you, but I'll pass." Mindful of the fact I have to play nice, I soften the rejection with a smile I hope looks real. "Wine will only put me to sleep at this point."

He nods sagely and sets the glasses on the buffet table. "Coffee then," he says, offering me his arm. "Shall we?"

Irritation flashes in me. My gaze flickers around us in a futile search for a reason to refuse and snags on Anita. She's standing about ten feet away and looking right at me. For a second, I think she's going to rescue me. Then she stabs a finger toward my companion and mouths, "Talk to him."

Damn. He's someone important, then.

Swallowing a sigh, I clasp the man's forearm. "Sounds great."

The expensive material of his suit tickles my fingertips as we walk toward the bar. This close, I can smell a light, expensive cologne. When his head dips toward mine, I fight the urge to pull away.

"It's torture, isn't it?" he asks in a soft, teasing voice. "Having to be polite to strange men?"

I'm so startled I almost trip. The arm under my hand flexes, warm fingers landing on mine to steady me. "Whoa there." He chuckles, the sound warm and infectious. Drawing to a stop, he looks down at me with an indecipherable expression. Something in the realm of sympathy.

"I promise not to ask you twenty invasive questions, give you my business card, or invite you to dinner. In fact, we don't even have to talk. I just know Anita. You had about thirty seconds before she sent someone far more annoying than me your way." He shrugs. "You've been going nonstop all night, and I figured you deserved a break."

I blame my tired brain for the fact I simply stare at him until he winks and draws me back into motion. At the bar, he releases my arm and orders two oat milk lattes, then chats with the bartender as she makes them. Feeling both grateful and baffled to be ignored, I watch as he leans across the counter and whispers something that makes her blush. The sight of his cheeky grin—totally different from the polite smile he gave me—does what his words couldn't, allowing me to finally relax.

When he eventually turns and hands me a latte, I don't have to force my smile. "Thanks... I'm sorry. I don't know your name."

"Clay Eaton. Nice to meet you, Eva." He looks around us, then nods. "Follow me."

He leads me outside the tent to a cluster of empty teak chairs set around a low table, the area thankfully well lit. A patio heater radiates nearby, chasing away the chill. I settle in the chair closest to the heater, closing my eyes briefly in relief. When I open them, Clay gives me a knowing grin.

"Thanks again," I say haltingly. "My feet are killing me."

He nods and sips his drink, gaze moving from my face to roam the crowd remaining in the tent. I scan the crowd, too. But the person I'm looking for is nowhere to be seen.

"Anita's spying on us," murmurs Clay. "She's going to think I put that frown on your face. No, don't look for her. Pretend I said something funny. Or better yet, think about that grandpa's sick moves on the dance floor earlier." My soft laugh brings a satisfied smile to his face. "Knew that would work." He glances at the tent again. "Okay, we're in the clear."

I take a deeper drink of my latte, appreciating the creamy warmth and the faint bitterness of espresso, and try to relax. Easier said than done. Unlike me, Clay seems perfectly content sitting in silence with a complete stranger, his head tilted back and eyes closed.

When I catch a glimpse of Anita and Mallory staring in our direction, I'm almost relieved to have an excuse to socialize. "So did you order oat milk because you like it or because you know dairy messes with airways?"

His eyes open, humor creasing the corners. "The latter. Though I don't dislike it."

"Know a lot of singers?"

Another slight smile. "You could say that."

I tilt my head, my eyes narrowing at his evasiveness. "How do you know Anita, anyway?"

Expensive fabric whispers as he straightens. "Haven't you heard? If you throw stones at a publicist, nine out of ten times you'll hit an entertainment lawyer, too."

I blink in surprise, reassessing him. "An entertainment lawyer, huh?"

He grins. "You sound surprised."

"I am, a little. No offense, but I figured you were the son of an Indigo exec or some other industry bigwig."

His brows lift. "How so?"

Emboldened by the humor in his eyes, I wave vaguely at him. "All... that. The tailored suit. The shoes. Even the haircut is a tell. Plus, you can't be more than thirty."

He chuckles. "Well, I appreciate the compliment. Backhanded as it may be."

I grin back at him. "You're welcome."

His eyes lock on mine and his smile changes. With a spark of panic, I realize it's the same one he gave the bartender.

I blurt, "I'm not flirting with you!"

Clay laughs heartily. "Duly noted. For the record, I'm not flirting with you, either. I prefer women with fully developed frontal lobes."

I choke on laughter. "Rude."

His smile softens to a teasing curl. "That being said, if you're single at twenty-five, give me a call." My mouth drops, but he continues idly, "To answer your roundabout question, I turn thirty in June and have been practicing for almost five years. I like to think I've carved my own success, but you got me on one count—Eaton and Associates is a family business. Full disclosure: I'm only here because I stole the invite from my much more successful father's desk."

"Ah," I say with an exaggerated nod. "Then you're a *fan*."

He laughs again. "I'll admit to being a Glow convert after tonight, but the theft was at my sister's behest. She's around here somewhere. Dark hair? Crazy vibes? Also lacking full brain development?"

I roll my eyes but can't help laughing. "Doesn't sound familiar. What's her name? I don't want to leave without meeting her."

Clay opens his mouth, but then his gaze lifts over my head and he closes it. A second later, a shadow falls over me and Wilder asks, "Evangeline? You ready to go?"

"Hi! Yes, absolutely." I jump to my feet and offer Clay an apologetic smile. "Sorry. You've been great company, but I'm wiped out."

He nods, smiling affably. "Completely understand."

Wilder's chest brushes my back, a hand curling around my waist and flattening over my stomach. While my body instantly lights up, my head tumbles with surprise. Neither of our families is here tonight, but there are still people around who *know* our families. Though we didn't discuss boundaries outright, I know it's why his kiss onstage was platonic and at least part of why we separated right when we came outside.

Maybe he's jealous, whispers a small, pleased voice inside me. I slap that voice into a mental closet.

"Clay," Wilder says stiffly.

Looking between them, my confusion spikes—they clearly know each other. Clay's expression is aloof, almost cold, his eyes flat and dark. He's like an entirely different man than the one I was laughing with a minute ago. A shiver rolls down my body.

"Wilder," he says as he stands. His eyes move to me and soften slightly. "Great meeting you, Eva. Have a good night."

My tongue tangles; by the time it unwinds, Clay has disappeared back into the tent. Wilder stares after him until I palm his face, directing his gaze to me.

"What was that about?"

He shakes his head. "Nothing."

I frown. "I don't know what kind of beef you guys have, but he was perfectly nice and didn't hit on me"—*overtly, at least*—"which puts him in a very small percentage of the men I spoke to tonight."

I don't mean the words as an accusation, but I feel him stiffen. Before I can clarify that I'm not upset he couldn't stay by my side, he envelops me in his arms and kisses my forehead. I inhale a midnight rainstorm wrapped in warm leather. My body instantly relaxes, and I muse that his touch is a drug. One I'm happily addicted to.

"Don't be fooled by his nice-guy act," he says after a moment. "Clay is a manipulative bastard just like his stepsister, who ambushed me ten minutes ago."

I lift my head. "Huh? Who's his stepsister?"

His jaw clenches and releases. "Kendra."

wilder

FUCKING KENDRA.

Evangeline probably thinks I was hiding out in the dark somewhere for the last hour of the party. I kind of was. But I was also watching her. The second I saw Clay heading toward her, I was moving in her direction. Which was when Kendra intercepted me.

I knew she was at the event, of course, having spotted her lurking toward the back of the crowd during Glow's set. As the only person scowling instead of enjoying the music, she was hard to miss. Clay stood beside her. While he, at least, was bobbing his head to the music, seeing all his creepy focus centered on Evangeline set off alarm bells. No doubt he was there because Kendra wanted him to use him to drive a wedge between Evangeline and me.

That part of her plan, at least, backfired before it even unfolded. I may have a reputation as the least social party guest in history, but a life on the sidelines has made me observant as hell. Clay has a well-established type: tall brunettes who resemble his stepsister—fucking *gag*—so I wasn't worried about him hitting on Evangeline with any real intent. I was worried even less about Evangeline falling for his charming facade, not with the taste of her still in my throat and her *I love yous* filling the cracks of my heart.

I was ready for Kendra when she slithered into my path. Now she regrets every moment of pseudo-intimacy between us, when chemically induced trust led her to show me her closet full of skeletons... among them the twisted bones of her relationship with her stepbrother and stepfather, as well as a graveyard full of their corrupt dealings. I let her say her piece, listened to all the usual threats wrapped in false affection, then made it clear if she ever goes through with anything, I'll use it all—every last dirty secret she shared—to ruin the reputation of her family.

Throwing her past vulnerabilities in her face didn't feel good, but it was necessary to quell her mistaken belief that she's the only one with leverage in our fucked-up association.

Kendra may have the ability to ruin my life—she could tell the world I'm addicted to pain pills, break my family's heart, throw a wrench in Night Theory's success, *and* destroy my chance of happiness with Evangeline—but I hold an equal power.

At the end of the day, a rock musician addicted to drugs isn't nearly as sensational as the dirt I have on the Eatons.

And she knows it.

♪

IT ISN'T until we're back at Evangeline's house, showered and curled up on her couch with a movie on, that she asks the question I've been expecting and dreading.

She would have asked the second I dropped the bomb of who Clay's sister was on her, but before she could, Rye and Lily found us. The women couldn't leave before saying a round of goodbyes and thank yous. Then we had to collect their instruments and belongings from the suite and wait for a valet to bring our cars. By the time Evangeline was buckled into my passenger seat, she was half asleep, and within five minutes she was out.

Between the half-hour cat nap and a shower when we got home—during which me washing her hair turned into desperate, slippery sex—she's now sleepy but lucid. I've been pretending to watch the movie while counting down the final minutes of my reprieve.

"What did Kendra want?"

"To start a fight," I say with a sigh. "She thrives on stirring shit up and causing a scene. When I didn't take the bait, she gave up."

Even shittier than lying to Evangeline is the knowledge I brought tonight on myself. The only reason Kendra was at the showcase at all was because of me. Four days ago, I reached out to her under the pretense of clearing the air and apologizing for how abruptly I dumped her. The real reason, however, is currently buried in my sock drawer at home.

Because I'm a worthless addict.

I fucking *knew* it was a mistake to call Kendra, just like I knew she wouldn't believe me when I told her I didn't want anything from her but pills. In her messed-up head, we're perfect for each other. She doesn't see our relationship as having been toxic because she's never known anything else. But even knowing that talking to her would bite me in the ass, I hadn't been able to stop myself.

My dad's sobriety books say the first step to recovery is admitting you have a problem.

Bullshit.

The second I admitted it to myself, the line I've balanced on for years disappeared. I've fallen to the bottom of a well I dug myself, and every pill I take drops another bucket of sludge over me. I'm going to drown in the poison of my own making; it's only a matter of time.

So far, I've been able to avoid appearing visibly high around Evangeline, but my willpower wanes every time I lose the daily battle with myself. Every time I tell her I have to go home for a bit, or run an errand that doesn't exist. Every time I lie to her and to Jax, who still thinks I'm doing a dry-ninety with him.

In the mere seconds of silence as I wait for Evangeline to speak, I see a future wherein every scrap of goodness in my life burns away. Because I'm too weak to stop lighting matches.

"Is that how you met her? At an industry event because her stepbrother and father are entertainment lawyers?"

Despite how little I want to talk about the Eatons, I'm relieved at the distraction from my thoughts.

"Stepfather," I say, struggling to keep the disgust out of my voice. "And yes. Conrad Eaton gets invitations to everything. He's the guy everyone hates to need."

"Huh. I'd never even heard of the Eatons until tonight."

I twirl a strand of her clean, damp hair around my finger. Focusing on physical sensations—the slight friction of individual hairs, the scent of her shampoo—I can almost, *almost*, ignore the burn beneath my skin.

"Consider yourself lucky."

She rubs her nose against my chest and sniffs me, an adorable habit that makes me feel like the luckiest asshole in the world. I doubt she even knows she does it, and I'll never draw attention to it for fear of her stopping.

"What's so bad about them?" she asks on a yawn.

I shift in discomfort. I don't want to lie, but I also don't want to give her nightmares.

"Wilder?"

Her voice is more alert, and I wince internally. "They do all the usual shit for artists—negotiating contracts, licensing, copyright issues—but they're also criminal defense attorneys."

Evangeline sits up and frowns at me. "You're being vague on purpose."

"Because I don't want to upset you." Her frown deepens, and I sigh in defeat. "Remember when we were looking for a lawyer to negotiate our contract with Indigo four years ago? Eaton and Associates came up as an option, and I asked my dad about them. He warned me off them pretty forcefully. He didn't tell me anything specific, but I've heard enough since then to figure out why. Conrad and Clay aren't known for their integrity."

Knowing she won't stop digging until I give her something concrete, I make myself continue.

"There's a reason I didn't want you anywhere near Michael Dresden. Why whenever we're in the same place, the guys and I keep a close eye on him. Last year, two women came forward with evidence he drugged and assaulted them. Within a month, the charges were dropped and both women *just so happened* to move out of state. Clay was his lawyer."

Her lovely face twists with dismay. "My God." She pauses, and I can almost feel her mind working. "Kendra told you that?"

I nod. Kendra told me more, too. Like how Clay sent private investigators to harass and bully the women until they folded and fled.

Evangeline tucks her head under my chin. "That's so horrible. I don't even know what to say."

"Say you'll stay away from that family."

She nods. "I can't believe Clay seemed so normal. What a creep."

She yawns again, so hugely her jaw cracks.

"Come on, Fairy. Let's get you to bed."

She hums in agreement but doesn't move.

Grabbing the remote, I turn off the movie we weren't watching, then help her to her feet. Eyes half-lidded, she sways until I wrap an arm around her waist. She melts against me with a sigh, nose buried in my shirt.

"I love you, Wilder," she mumbles. "I'm going to love you forever. Just like we promised."

The words hit like a gut punch, stealing my air. Tears burn my eyes. Another bucket of sludge hits my head, burying me in more darkness.

Addict.

Liar.

Loser.

"I love you, too," I choke out. "Forever."

evangeline

DESPITE HAVING NEVER PAINTED toenails in his life, Wilder handles the tiny nail polish brush like he does chords on a guitar—with focus, confidence, and an annoying level of innate talent. He's almost done with a second coat of the dark, opalescent blue polish. A warm hand cradles my ankle, occasionally sliding up to massage my bare calf or squeeze in chastisement when I move.

Sunlight diffuses through the glass slider behind him, bringing out hints of umber in his dark hair. Outside, newborn leaves glisten on the trees and bushes in my backyard, the memory of winter fading more with each passing day. The daffodils are in full bloom, a river of white and yellow confetti along the fence.

Soft music plays around us. My Kindle sits forgotten on my lap as I cradle a mug of coffee and watch the most incredible man I've ever known carefully paint my toenails. A man who spent yesterday afternoon helping me iron out lyrics and melodies for three new Glow songs, then insisted on cooking me dinner—which wasn't even burned—and having me for dessert. The same man who woke me up this morning with back-to-back orgasms. Who followed me into the shower because he has a thing for washing me. Who made me coffee before rummaging under my bathroom sink for acetone, cotton balls, and nail polish because he noticed my pedicure was chipping.

It's not even 10:00 a.m. and I want this every Sunday for the rest of my life. I want *him* for the rest of my life.

"Come to brunch today."

I don't know who's more surprised by my sudden words. We both freeze; his fingers briefly tighten on my foot, then relax. With a final swipe of blue on my pinkie toe, he caps the polish and sets it on the coffee table. As his eyes lift to mine, I brace for disappointment.

"Okay."

"I completely understand—wait, what?"

He smiles slightly, giving my ankle another squeeze before gently relocating my foot to the floor. "Okay, Evangeline. I'll go to brunch at your parents' house." He glances at his watch. "You normally leave around ten-thirty, right?"

I close my gaping mouth. "Really? You're really okay with coming?"

He gives me a dry look. "Am I excited to face your dad? Not even a little bit. But I don't want to keep our relationship a secret anymore. Not from your parents or the public. And if we don't do it now, I'm not sure when we'll be able to. The album drops in two weeks and we announce the tour two weeks after that. Our team thinks we'll sell out fast and they're already prepared to add dates on both ends. We could be on the road as early as the third week of May."

My ears ring. He might be gone before my birthday. "That's like... five weeks from now."

"I know. And we might be gone eight months." He cracks

a smile that doesn't reach his eyes. "This probably wasn't the best time to start a relationship, was it?"

Eight months.

I have only myself to blame for the shock I'm feeling. I've purposely avoided thinking about how limited our time is before our careers pull us apart.

No more Sunday mornings. No more dreamless, deep sleep in his arms. No more forehead kisses or midnight whispers or watching him brush his teeth. Instead, he'll be on the road and performing almost every night. Surrounded by fans. By drugs and alcohol. *Women.* At the thought, a particularly vivid memory from our first tour makes me flinch.

Wilder snatches my mug and puts it on the table, then claims my hands between his. His worried eyes study my face.

"Once our schedules for the next year are in place, we'll find the time to see each other. There will be breaks on tour. I'll fly home or fly you to me." He swallows, fear brightening his eyes. "Tell me what's going on in your head. Are you... is it too much? Are you regretting—"

"No," I gasp out, shaking my head quickly. "I'm sorry. I'm being stupid. You're right. We'll figure it out. The band and tour need to be your priority, anyway."

I make to stand, to escape, but pressure on my hands holds me down. He scoots closer, lifting a palm to cup the side of my face. This close to him, my muscles can't help but relax. My mind, however, continues storming, screaming as it spirals toward the ground.

"Eyes on me, Fairy."

Unable to resist that deep, textured tone of command, my eyes immediately find his. The connection between us flares, obscuring the world.

"I love you," he says with quiet intensity. "Yes, the band is

251

a priority, but you're equally important to me. I'm not who I was three years ago. I'm not interested in partying anymore, and the only woman I want is you. I'm yours, okay? Only yours. I know it's going to be hard to trust me because of my past mistakes, but can you try? Can you let me prove I'm different now? That *we're* different?"

My mental descent slows. Stops. The storm inside me disperses so suddenly I feel dizzy.

"Yes," I whisper. "I trust you."

One cloud reforms, a dark smudge at the corner of my mind, but I keep its contents to myself.

Please don't break my heart.

CHAPTER THIRTY-FOUR

evangeline

This pressure on my bones
Reminds me of home
Where it was you and me
Together deep in the sea
Sealed by tides and seaweed dreams

But sometimes, oh sometimes
I missed the stars

HOURS LATER, Wilder and I return to my house. Neither of us spoke on the drive home, and we remain mute as we walk inside and sit on opposite ends of my couch. Quiet vibrates around us as he stares at the dark television screen and I gaze through the sliding door at a sky now clogged with gray.

"It could have been worse, right?"

His effort to lighten the mood falls short, his voice more solemn than sarcastic.

My stomach clenches, my voice emerging hoarse with agitation and lingering disbelief. "My dad wanted to drug test you."

He sighs. "He loves you and wants to protect you."

My teeth clench, catching the edge of my tongue. Copper skates over my tastebuds. Wilder reaches for my hand and threads our fingers together. Mine are freezing. So are his.

"Your grandparents like me—or at least don't hate me—and your mom hugged me when we left. Hunter and Josh were cool. It wasn't all bad." He pauses. "Your dad didn't make a scene or anything."

No, he waited until Wilder had graciously offered to clear the table and was alone in the kitchen before cornering him. Oblivious to the fact I'd followed him and heard everything.

I unclench my jaw. "What he said to you, accusing you of being high because you yawned a few times..." I drag my gaze from the stormy sky to his profile. His dark lashes are lowered halfway, his expression inscrutable. "I honestly don't know how you stayed as calm as you did. I'm so sorry."

He shrugs a shoulder. "What you told me on the drive over helped. I kept reminding myself that his reaction wasn't about me but about shit from his past. His dad... my dad. I tried to put myself in his shoes."

The nape of my neck prickles, the ennui in his voice clashing with his words. Despite the contact of our hands, he feels a million miles away. *Is this a type of panic attack? A self-defense mechanism?*

I clear my throat. "I hope you know I don't expect you to follow through on what you told him. You absolutely do not have to take a drug test to appease my father."

He lifts my hand and places a soft kiss to my knuckles. His normally warm lips are cool. "I don't want to be the reason for a rift in your family. I'll take the test." He releases my fingers and shudders; goosebumps pepper the side of his neck. "I'm going to lie down for a bit, okay?"

"Sure," I whisper, but he's already walking toward my

bedroom, his gait lacking its usual grace. The door swings half-closed behind him. I listen to the sounds of him undressing, then the familiar creak of my bed frame as his weight settles.

I'm suddenly exhausted, too. *Sad. Angry.* Tugging a blanket off the back of the couch, I curl up on my side. My dry, burning eyes fall closed, only to open a second later when, in that single moment of darkness, I realized Wilder didn't look me in the eye once since we left my parents.

Not once.

I sit up, shivering as the blanket falls to my lap. The living room is shadowed, the sky darker than it was minutes ago. Raindrops spatter against the deck. Several nightlights give off haloes against the walls, and I focus on their glow until the vise on my chest releases.

I drag in a loud, rasping breath.

"Evangeline?"

Wilder's voice kickstarts my already racing heart. I twist on the couch to see him standing in the bedroom doorway. One hand braced on the doorframe, naked except for boxer briefs. His face is shadowed, his tall, muscled frame outlined by a light in the bedroom.

My father's voice ricochets between us, eerie in its utter calm.

"Do you think I was born yesterday? You can't even look me in the eye, can you?"

I'm brittle, bubbling taffy stretched between loyalties. I have no idea what lies at my breaking point.

"Can I hold you?"

His voice is soft. Wavering with emotion.

Snap.

255

I leap up and rush into his open arms. His skin is feverish as he trembles and holds me so tightly it hurts. I hold him even tighter. My nails drive into the muscles of his back like I can open him up. Crawl inside him and expose his depths.

Even if I'm terrified of what I'll find.

CHAPTER THIRTY-FIVE

wilder

AFTER THE CLOSE call at Evangeline's parents' house, I wrestle back some control over my using. Once again, music saves my ass; in this case, the two-week runway to the release of Night Theory's sophomore album, *Fatalism*.

The stakes have never been higher for me—for any of us —and miraculously, that sense of purpose quiets my demons. I find a sweet spot where my general anxiety is manageable and my mind stays more or less sharp. No more nodding off or spiraling into withdrawals.

My free time shrinks even more, but whatever I have is spent with Evangeline. Even if it means I'm crawling into her bed at three in the morning and waking her up four hours later with my tongue. No matter what, I see her every night and prioritize texting her consistently during the day. As the world around me whips into a surreal frenzy, she keeps me rooted.

She doesn't bring up the drug test, and I sure as hell don't. I barely have time to think, much less dwell on how deeply I hate who I've become.

Every day is rigidly scheduled and sometimes lasts twelve

hours or more. Our manager, Mack Martinez, and publicist, Shelly Reeves, rule our lives via a shared calendar that links to alerts on our phones. The only consistency day to day are time blocks for rehearsing, chef-prepared meals, and forty-five minutes labeled *private time*. Eddie is convinced the latter is their way of managing us down to when we shit and shower.

As restrictive as our schedules are, aside from the occasional joke, none of us complain. It won't last forever, and we've been preparing for this for months. Years, really. We're also mature enough to understand our skills as musicians can only get us so far. Having grown up in the shadow of Breaking Giants, I'm especially aware that none of this would be happening without the dedication and tireless efforts of the people around us.

As Mack is fond of saying: "You make the cake, we serve it."

There are countless live streams. Radio and podcast interviews. A performance on a local morning television show. Surprise pop-up concerts in parks that inadvertently close neighboring streets and earn us citations. Within days of sending advanced copies of *Fatalism* to industry professionals, Mack and Shelly are flooded with interview requests from all over the country and as far away as France and Japan.

One week from release, our final and most commercially viable single, "End Times," drops. The accompanying music video—a trippy, apocalyptic mini-film—explodes the internet. When our soft-merch store launches the same day, it sells out within an hour. Preorders for a special edition vinyl sell out as well, and preorders for the standard vinyl go through the roof.

Three days before release, the most storied music magazine of all time does a feature on us predicting at least one Grammy nomination this fall.

The final Friday of April, *Fatalism* releases to the world.

In lieu of a standard launch party—which I vetoed months ago as it's the stuff of my nightmares—Saturday night we perform a release concert at the only venue in Seattle that isn't a stadium.

Eight thousand screaming fans greet us and carry us through the best set of our lives. And when I follow my bandmates into the greenroom after the show and see Evangeline waiting for me?

I've never experienced a comparable joy.

In this moment, there's no darkness at all. Only the welcome weight of her body when she jumps into my arms with a happy squeal. The impact of my shoulder with the doorframe as I clip it rushing back out of the room. The knowing laughter and whistles from the guys and our crew. The heat of Evangeline's cheek as she presses it to mine, as she squeezes me tighter.

"You were amazing," she whispers against my ear.

"That was nothing compared to what I'm about to do to you," I murmur back.

In the smallest of the three dressing rooms, the door locked behind us, we're a storm of moving hands and sucking kisses and gasping groans. She undoes my belt, yanks my zipper down, and tugs my pants and underwear off my hips. I pull up her skirt and rip down her tights, then cup the wet heat between her legs. She wraps her hands around my dick and pumps me as I kiss my way from one side of her neck to the other.

"Wilder," she moans. "I need you."

"Such a slut for me," I rumble into her soft throat.

She squeezes my dick. I bite her neck in retaliation and

259

grin when arousal soaks my hand. Sinking two fingers inside her, I pump them slowly. My thumb makes equally slow circles around her clit.

"I love your angry little growls," I say as I nip her earlobe. "Frustrated kitten, aren't you? You want something thicker? Harder? Faster?"

She growls louder. "I'm going to kill you if you don't fuck me right now."

Chuckling darkly, I pull my fingers from her body. Before she can protest, I spin her around and bend her over an empty catering table. The tights bunched above her boots have the happy consequence of keeping her legs together. Her perfect ass lifts, providing a mouthwatering view of her dripping pink center.

She wiggles teasingly—the resulting crack of my hand on one pale cheek is shockingly loud.

For a long second, she freezes. Then she moans and thrusts her ass back in the air. "Again."

"Fuck," I hiss, watching the shape of my hand form in red on her pale skin. "No more foreplay for you. Arms up. Grab the table."

She immediately seizes the edge above her head. I spank her other cheek. She yelps, then writhes. "Wilder. *Please*."

I line myself up and press the head of my cock inside her. The angle and her bound legs make it an almost impossibly tight fit. By the time I'm a few inches inside, we're both panting.

Bending over her, I growl, "Give me your mouth."

She twists her head to meet my kiss, our tongues tangling, our breaths interspersed with moans and whispers of, "I love you."

I start rolling my hips, my rhythm controlled and agonizingly slow. Every inch of me her body accepts feels like both victory and surrender. As with every time I'm inside her, I imagine more of my soul sliding into her possession. When our bodies are finally flush, powerful shivers rack my spine. I fight to stay still, ignoring the hammering voice of my need. *Take. Possess. Defile. Mark.*

I focus instead on Evangeline. She's perfectly still, her breaths shallow, her eyes tightly closed. Her teeth press deeply into her bottom lip, her fingers bleached with tension where they grip the table.

I press a shaky kiss to her temple. "Do you want me to pull out? Make you come first?"

She shakes her head. I almost smile at her stubbornness.

"Just... talk to me," she whispers.

Warmth spirals in my chest. Angling my mouth to her ear, I whisper, "You're doing so good, taking me so deep. I'm unbelievably proud of you. I love you so, so much. Being inside you is the closest to peace I've ever known. Just breathe. That's it. Take all the time you need. Tell me when you're ready."

She gasps. "I'm ready."

My body shakes with soundless laughter. She trembles, her pussy contracting so hard I choke on a groan. "I'm not moving until you relax more, baby. Otherwise it's going to hurt."

"Wilder."

I lift my head. Her silver eye blinks. Sees through me. Unmakes me. Her perfect pink lips move, the words registering a second later.

"I want it to hurt."

Fire whips up my spine. Darkness eclipses my mind—not my Shadow, though. This darkness is sparkling. Full of light. Of *her*.

I run my tongue over my teeth. "Tap my thigh if—" I lose

261

the ability to speak as she pulls herself forward and pushes back hard. Intense pleasure obliterates my hold on reason.

Her arms tense to repeat the movement, but before she can, I seize her hips and take over. I don't hold back. *Can't.* I thrust into her mercilessly. The table rocks. Grunts and gasps float atop the vicious slaps of our bodies. My gaze stays fixed on my glistening shaft as I pull out, on the singular pleasure of watching myself disappear back inside her.

All that truly matters are these moments of oneness with her.

Evangeline shatters with a breathy moan, pussy fluttering around my cock. *Not enough.* With a growl of determination, I change the angle of my hips so I'm driving downward. I know I've found the most sensitive spot inside her when she mewls in protest, fingernails scrambling on the table.

Through gritted teeth, I tell her, "If it's too much, you know how to make me stop. But if you don't tap out, you're coming again."

She curses me.

I grin as I spank her. "Now tell me the truth."

She sobs. "I l-love y-you."

"That's my girl."

Hyper focused on her body's cues, I carry her up the next peak. This time, her body seizes around my cock like she wants to break it off and keep it. This time, she screams my name as warmth gushes over my groin and drips down my thighs.

This time, I jump with her.

Seconds or minutes later, I regain consciousness after the most insane orgasm of my life. I have no idea how I managed to stay standing. My hands are planted to either side of her body, my arms trembling with strain. I heave air into my lungs. Sweat drips from my brow onto her black T-shirt.

Evangeline makes a soft sound of contentment.

In that moment, when I'm peaceful and sated and drunk off love, I make a mistake.

The biggest mistake of my life.

I whisper, "Come with me."

She yawns, then stiffens. "Oh God, we were so loud. Do you think people heard us?" She twists to look at me with wide eyes. "Can we sneak out a back door?"

She didn't hear what I said.

"Fairy."

She blinks. "Sorry, did you ask me something?"

I brush a strand of pale hair from her forehead. "Come with me. On tour."

Her brows furrow. "Huh?"

I trace the Cupid's bow of her upper lip. "Eight months, dozens of cities. It'll be amazing. We can even add encores of our old songs and perform together again. Say you'll come with me. Be with me."

She stares at me blankly for a beat, then pushes up from the table. "Let me up. Pull out of me right now, Wilder. *Now, now, now.*"

Her voice rises and sharpens with every word until she's yelling and shoving me back roughly.

Still half-delirious from performing for two hours and falling apart in bliss, I stumble backward, wincing as my body slips from her heat.

Evangeline jumps off the table and yanks her tights up her legs. She only glances at me once, hissing, "Put your dick away."

I fumble, pulling up my pants with numb fingers. Cold radiates down my body, wiping away my delusion. Revealing the wide-open darkness around me as I free-fall.

I try to say her name but nothing comes out.

She adjusts her miniskirt with jerky movements, muttering to herself. "History repeating itself. Unbelievable." Straightening, she smooths back hairs that escaped her ponytail. Her hands shake. A crystalline tear drips off her chin.

I gasp. "Wait—"

She whirls on me. I don't know what's worse, the fury on her face or the shattered look in her eyes.

"You're asking me to go on tour with Night Theory," she says in a freakishly calm voice. "To break Glow's *legally binding contract* with Indigo and drop my dream—Lily's dream—like it's trash?"

I fist my hair and shake my head. "No. Absolutely not. *Fuck.* I wasn't thinking, okay? It just came out. I swear!"

She scoffs. "That's almost worse. It means you *subconsciously* believe my dreams aren't as important as yours. That your needs and wants are superior. My feelings—my dreams—don't even matter to you. They never have."

"That's not what I said," I rasp, horrified. "I love you more than I've ever loved anything in my life. How—how could you even think that?"

Her lip quivers. For a second, I think she understands. Then her expression hardens. "I need to think. Don't follow me and don't come to my house."

No, no, no.

Black cracks spread from my edges, racing toward the center of my being. My lungs squeeze. Words jumble in my head and tangle in my throat as she walks past me to the door. In my stomach, a demon screams.

The Shadow smiles.

"I'll call you," she says softly. "Just... give me a little bit of time."

The door creaks twice. Open. Closed.

My legs give out and I slam to the floor.

White noise fills my head.

Static nothing.

I blink and Jax is grabbing my shoulders, his mouth moving.

I can't hear him.

I blink and streetlights pass outside car windows. Colorful streaks across a void.

I blink again and I'm sitting listlessly on my bed with a bottle of pills lying near my hip. My body tingles. Terror ices my mind. *How many did I take?* Shivering violently, it takes me three tries to open the bottle. I dump the remaining pills onto the comforter and count them.

My gasp of relief slices the silence.

Only three. You only took three.

Like the drug in my bloodstream was waiting for acknowledgment, intense heat spikes inside me. My muscles melt. My mind quiets. I barely manage to lift my legs onto the bed and pull the comforter over me before losing the ability to move.

I float on a warm sea. Lapping waves flush away my darkness. Drown my Shadow. Drown me.

I'm nothing.

No one.

Emptiness. Silence. *Peace.*

CHAPTER THIRTY-SIX

evangeline

Here is sucking empty
A slipping memory of your skin
Here are fingers curling inward
Seeking the source of sin

FOR THE FIRST time in my adult life, I lie my way out of Sunday brunch, texting my mom that I have food poisoning. When she immediately calls me, I don't answer.

> Can't talk. Puking

> Honey! 😟 do u need anything? Electrolytes? Saltine crackers?

> I'm good.

> Okay. I'm so sorry. Just say the word and I'll be there

I put my phone on the nightstand and flop back on my bed, wishing I actually *were* sick and my mom could come over, rub my back, and tell me everything will be okay—and I was still young enough to believe her.

I wish, too, that I had the guts to tell her the truth. That I'm not the levelheaded, confident, responsible daughter she thinks I am. I'm an insecure mess who's afraid of the dark. Afraid of everything, including love.

Turning my head on the pillow, I suck in Wilder's fading scent.

Sometime during the night, while chugging tea and journaling with every light in the house on, the inferno of anger and betrayal in my chest cooled to embers of regret.

I can't stop thinking about what my reaction blinded me to in the moment. The soft, adoring expression on Wilder's face when he asked me to come with him. His boyish excitement at the idea of us performing together again. His confusion, horror, and impassioned apology after I flipped out.

He really did speak without thinking, the words coming straight from his heart. My reaction, on the other hand, came straight from the fear center of my brain. The part of me that refuses to let go of who he was and accept him for who he is now—*again*.

Wilder isn't the same man he was three years ago or even six years ago. Every day of the last month and especially the last two weeks, he's proven that fact. Despite his insane prelaunch schedule, I never once felt like an afterthought. He texted me constantly throughout the day: quick hellos, selfies and videos of him and the guys, annoyingly funny memes about Taurus women, unfinished song lyrics, X-rated promises... And every night, no matter how exhausted he was, he found his way into my arms.

He's changed.

I'm the one who's stayed the same.

How long will I make him suffer for my inability to let go of the past? How long before he decides he doesn't want to walk on eggshells anymore or deal with my overthinking, insecure, moody self?

I owe him an explanation. An apology.

We were already planning to spend the afternoon together, his first in weeks with nothing on the schedule.

I'll surprise him with coffee.

Or better yet, a burned bagel.

I'll tell him the truth—open up to him about my insecurities like he's opened up to me about his anxiety. We'll get over this speed bump like we have others. And someday, we'll have a smooth road to walk.

Smiling to myself, I push to my feet and head to my bathroom to do something about my frizzy hair and eye bags.

♪

A PAJAMA-CLAD Eddie answers the front door. Shoving the drink carrier and bag of bagels into his arms, I rush past him into the house. He blinks at me in wide-eyed surprise, green mohawk soft and flopping over his right ear.

"There's a coffee for each of you," I say as I face the mirror in the entryway and try to fix my hair after the wind massacred it on the walk up from the curb. "I already drank mine. Bagels are in the bag. I got a variety, so have whatever you want, but leave an Everything for Wilder, okay?"

Eddie makes a strangled sound.

"Eva?" Jax stops beside his brother, looking from his full

arms to me. His mouth hangs open. "Did Wilder know you were coming over?"

"Nope. It's a surprise." I jerk my head toward Eddie. "Coffee and bagels. Is Wilder still sleeping or something?"

Please tell me he's still in bed.

Jax clears his throat. "Actually, he, uh... He's not feeling great. Should I tell him to call you later?"

My hands still, then sink to my sides. A fluttering sensation takes up residence in my throat. I face the men, finally absorbing their expressions. Eddie is unusually pale. He swallows convulsively, his eyes flickering to his brother every few seconds. And Jax looks like I caught them burying a body.

I try to swallow and choke. Cough to clear my throat. Drag in air that *burns*.

Footsteps pound down the stairs at the back of the house. "Did I hear the doorbell?" calls Zander. "Please tell me it's my food and not another psycho ex-girlfriend."

My ears ring.

Eddie closes his eyes.

Jax flushes.

Zander appears in the hallway past the kitchen. When he sees me, his eyes bug out. "Oh, shit."

My vision distorts like I'm underwater.

"It's not what you think," Eddie says quickly.

My hearing wanes like someone cranked the world's volume down. All three men are talking, but their voices are muffled. *Wah-wahah-wahh.* I touch my ears, half-expecting to find them plugged. They're not.

Suddenly, my senses turn back on.

"Tell her, Jax," snaps Eddie.

"It's the right thing to do," murmurs Zander.

Jax drags a hand over buzzed blond hair, his heavy sigh

269

the hissing descent of a guillotine. I lock my knees. My armpits prickle. Each of my short, fast breaths is sandpaper against the silence.

Jax takes a step toward me, eyes radiating sympathy.

"Just say it," I croak.

"He's not cheating on you. He's..."

The guillotine pauses.

"He's what?"

What the fuck could be worse than cheating on me?

His expression hardens with resolve. "You know what? Screw this. I'm done covering for him. Follow me, Eva. You deserve to know."

He turns and walks down the hallway toward the stairs. Muscle memory takes over, operating my body for me. Eddie gives me a wobbly smile as I pass him. Zander keeps his head down.

One step. Five steps. Ten. Down the hallway to the end.

Wilder's bedroom door is cracked. Voices come from inside. Kendra's. His.

Jax grabs my sweaty hand and pulls me to the wall beside the door.

"—really believed you'd snap out of it, Wild, but I'm done waiting. You have to choose. Me or her."

"Her."

Kendra laughs shortly. "What happens when she finds out, huh? You think Miss Perfect will accept this?" A weird, rattling sound follows.

Wilder sighs. "No, I don't."

A foot stomps. "Then why are you torturing yourself? Torturing me?"

"For the last time, this isn't about you. If you want out, fine. I'll find someone else."

She sniffles, her voice softening. "Do you really feel nothing for me?"

"I'm not doing this with you again. You don't love me, Kendra. You only think you do."

"Don't tell me how I feel!"

Wilder groans. "Just go."

"I was your girlfriend for over six months. I kept your secret and protected you from everyone trying to pull you down." She laughs again, low and caustic. "You think she'll protect you? Lie for you? No fucking way."

"This conversation is over."

There's a loud slap, then Kendra bursts into tears. "I'm sorry. God, I'm sorry. I don't understand. Make it make sense, Wilder. Please."

"You'll never understand," he says tiredly.

There's a long pause.

"You're right," she finally says, her cutting tone disturbingly at odds with her tearful outcry of seconds ago. "I'll never understand you throwing me away for a snotty, virginal bitch who's *so fucking stupid* she can't tell you're a full-blown junkie. Find another supplier for your Oxy, Wilder. I'm done with you."

If he replies, I don't hear it over the high frequency sound of my heart being cleaved down the middle. My knees give out. Jax's arm bands around my waist, his quick reflexes all that save me from hitting the floor.

The bedroom door swings open and Kendra strides out. She jerks to a stop at the sight of us, her mascara-ringed eyes widening with shock. Just as fast, they narrow, gleaming. A slow, vindictive smile curves her lips.

"Whoopsie," she whispers.

Flipping long, dark hair over a shoulder, she sashays down the hallway and out of sight.

Full-blown junkie.

My dad was right. And Kendra was right, too—I'm so fucking stupid. My hands curl into fists. Dimly, I register pain signals as my nails cut into my palms.

I defended him to my parents, to Lily. Spent weeks suffocating my own instincts in order to trust him. Tormented myself with self-doubts. Convinced myself I was the problem.

Nothing was real.

"Do you want me to stay?" Jax murmurs.

I shake my head and straighten. His arm falls away as I face the open doorway. The curtains in Wilder's bedroom are pulled aside. Sunlight fills the room, but I don't see or feel it. I'm a vortex of dark, bitter cold. But I'm not afraid.

I *embrace* the dark.

I walk a few steps into the room and stop. Wilder sits at the foot of the bed, his elbows on his knees and his head in his hands. He rocks slowly back and forth, fingers clenching and unclenching in his hair. He looks like he's in pain.

I feel nothing.

"Kendra, I told you—" He looks up and gasps. The blood drains from his face, turning his golden skin sallow. One cheek stays slightly red from Kendra's slap.

I wish she'd punched him. Broken his perfect nose or split his perfect lips.

Now that my denial has been stripped away, I see the signs clearly. Both in the present and in retrospect. Eyes that are more brown than green and slightly glazed. Eyelids a touch too heavy. Pupils that are either extremely constricted or huge. Right now, they're far too dilated for the brightness in the room. Sweat beads on his forehead. Goosebumps coat his neck and bare, trembling arms.

A word comes to me: *dopesick.*

He's withdrawing and needs a fix.

Bile coats my throat, my body clenching against an overwhelming feeling of violation. All the times he was inside me, told me he loved me, while I had no idea he was high. Sudden bouts of sleepiness blamed on his schedule. Random errands and not answering his phone. Not looking me in the eye. Manipulating me into thinking he'd changed, that he had no secrets from me. Encouraging my vulnerability while he lied.

Lied.

Lied.

Wilder stands. A small prescription bottle rolls across where he was sitting, and he shifts to block my sight of it. "This isn't what it looks like," he says weakly.

"Don't bother." My voice is empty. As cold as the endless dark inside me. "I heard everything."

"Fairy, please. Let me explain."

"I'm not your Fairy. I'm not your *anything*. We. Are. Done."

His chest convulses. "Please," he whispers. "I'll go to rehab. Right now—today. I can fix this. I can change."

Cracks spread through my frozen core, but it's not sympathy that fractures me.

It's rage.

"I don't care what you do," I snarl. "I'll never forgive you or trust you again. Do you hear me? We're through. You've lied to me for weeks, but the worst thing you did was make me believe you loved—" Stabbing pain in my chest takes my voice. My vision blurs with tears.

He moves toward me. I scramble backward and collide with the doorframe. "Stay the fuck away from me."

Features contorting, he falls to his knees. "I d-do love you, Evangeline," he says through wracking sobs. "More than anything. P-please, please don't leave me."

"This isn't love, Wilder. This is manipulation. You only love yourself and whatever's in that bottle on the bed. You *disgust* me. I hate you. I fucking hate you!"

I don't realize I'm shouting until gentle hands capture my shoulders from behind and Jax says, "Hey, it's okay. Let's go."

He pulls me out of the room and down the hallway.

Behind us is a guttural scream.

I feel nothing.

CHAPTER THIRTY-SEVEN

evangeline

NEITHER LILY nor Rye are answering their phones. Since Rye's house is closest, I drive there first. Slowly. Carefully. Every few seconds, my hands convulse on the steering wheel. I take deep, even breaths and blink rapidly to keep tears from obscuring my vision.

I slow outside Rye's house and see Lily's car in the driveway.

I drive past without stopping.

Familiar roads lead to the highway. I merge into traffic. Stay in the slow lane. Exit. Three turns. Six stoplights. A winding road.

I finally park. Turn off the car. Leave my keys, my purse. Stumble up a path to the front door and ring the doorbell.

Footsteps approach.

Wood swings inward.

Blue eyes widen.

"Eva? What's wrong?"

"D-daddy."

He catches me as I fall.

As I break.

CHAPTER THIRTY-EIGHT

wilder

MY DAD FINDS me curled in a fetal position on the floor of my bedroom, the bottle of pills clutched in my hand and my phone discarded next to me.

He drops to his knees and lifts me into a tight embrace. Like he can keep me from falling apart.

But he can't. I've lost too many pieces.

"I've got you, Wilder. I'm here. How many pills did you take?"

Words come in stutters between gasping sobs. "N-none, but I was going to t-take them all. I-I lost her. Oh, fuck, I lost Evangeline. F-forever. I can't—don't want to live without her. H-help me, Dad. Please help me. I'm so sorry."

He pulls back to grip my face in his hands. Tears track down his cheeks. Golden eyes, bright and determined, stare into mine.

"Listen to me, son. I know it seems impossible right now, but I promise it's going to be okay. You never have to feel this way again. Drop the bottle. Let it go."

My fingers spasm and open.

THE FOLLOWING days are a blur of pain over a soundtrack of misery.

My mother singing, her voice cracking every other word. My sisters crying outside my childhood bedroom. Strong, calloused hands moving my sweat-soaked body. Cold porcelain under my cheek. Cramping muscles and my teeth chattering so hard I bite through my tongue. Hot compresses and showers. Fresh sheets soaked again in minutes.

Fire inside me. Burning hotter and hotter. Melting away my sanity.

Make it stop.

Just make it stop.

Agonizing need. Yelling and begging and screaming. Pounding on a locked door.

Let me out. Out. Out.

Falling. Convulsing. Blood in my mouth.

Blacking out.

A clinical touch and unfamiliar voice.

"Whatever he told you... these are severe withdrawals. Blood pressure... dangerous..."

Hands holding me down as I writhe.

The pinch of a needle.

Darkness again.

Everywhere.

KATHERINE'S VOICE in my ear—maybe in my head.

"Find the light, Wilder."

CHAPTER THIRTY-NINE

wilder

I'M SURROUNDED by light so bright my eyes water uncontrollably. But I don't think this is what Katherine meant.

This light is from a merciless sun beating down on the California desert. Directly in front of me sprawls a single-story building of darkly reflective glass and beige stucco. My apparent home for the next ninety days.

My body is feeble, my head spiky static, my heart a chasm. The last two weeks are a grainy smear of ash and fire, the flight and car ride here a blur, the goodbye to my parents a few minutes ago almost forgotten.

I don't know if I'm lucid or in the grip of an endless nightmare.

A man stands just outside the entrance. He's wearing a suit but doesn't look stiff, and he has pale, intelligent blue eyes. There's no pity in them. No judgment, either. Just calm assurance and a hint of anticipation, like he knows something I don't and looks forward to sharing it with me.

"Welcome to Oasis, Wilder. My name is Dr. Chastain." With a soft smile, he gestures toward the door. "Ready?"

My sweaty fingers clench around the strap of my duffel bag.

Am I ready?

Yes.

No.

Maybe?

Fuck it.

I force my weak legs to carry me forward. "Yeah, Doc. I'm ready for air conditioning." I eye his dark suit. "How are you not boiling right now?"

He chuckles. "I'm used to it."

As he opens the door, cool air rushes out. Goose bumps roll over my damp, pallid skin. I manage two more steps, but my body jerks to a stop on the threshold.

I'm suspended between light and shadow, between the toxic, clinging webs of the past and the vast, terrifying unknown.

"Do you need help?" asks a low, kind voice.

My chin jerks. A hand settles on my shoulder. "One step at a time, Wilder. Together."

Deep in my darkness, a small, fragile light flickers to life.

And we walk inside.

transition

transition : *a rhythmic or melodic*
interlude between sections of a song

Life is a series of crossroads. Most of them we don't even notice and have no quantifiable effect on our lives. What we eat for a meal. What clothes we wear on any given day. If we answer a call from an unknown number or not.

Other crossroads are more obvious—they're the big life decisions. We fret over all the possible repercussions or rewards that await us depending on which direction we take.

But whether a crossroads is obvious or not, it still matters. Little ones can become life-altering. Decisions that seem momentous in the moment can shrink in importance as time passes and our perspective shifts.

Our choices, big and small, define us. Shape us and heal us.

They break us, too.

In the brief month Wilder and I were together, I faced hundreds of crossroads. Most of them only obvious in hindsight.

When I said yes to us that first night. When I swore to never regret him. When I promised to love him forever. Each kiss. Touch. Smile. The choice to trust and hope.

Every time I believed his lies... and the lies I spoke believing they were truth.

I once thought falling in love with Wilder would destroy me. I was right and also wrong. In a strange way, I'm grateful for what happened.

By embracing darkness, I lost my fear of it. I'm finally safe.

Nothing can touch me now.

LYRCIS OF "END TIMES" BY THEORY
ALBUM; FATALISM

BELLS WERE RINGING AT THE END OF TIME
THE SKY WAS ON FIRE BUT YOU WERE MINE
ASHES ON OUR TONGUES, IN OUR LUNGS
BUT YOU WERE MINE

THIS STORY'S ENDING ALREADY TOLD
STAMPED, SEALED, SOLD
BEAUTIFUL BY DESIGN
YOU WERE MINE
MINE AT THE END OF TIME

CLOSE YOUR EYES NOW, BABY
AND REMEMBER THE COLOR OF MINE
THE FIRST AND LAST TIME
YOU TOLD ME YOU LOVED ME

BEAUTIFUL BY DESIGN
(BEAUTIFUL BY DESIGN)
YOU WERE MINE AT THE END OF TIME

W.A.

LAST
CHORUS

"We all make mistakes, don't we? But if you can't forgive yourself, you'll always be an exile in your own life."

CURTIS SITTENFELD

transition

__transition__ : a rhythmic or melodic interlude between sections of a song

CHAPTER ONE

wilder

SIX AND A HALF YEARS LATER

♫

WILDER 31 | EVA 29

THE DOORBELL'S SOFT, bell-like tone echoes through the house. Even expecting it, my chest tightens and my pulse accelerates. I lower my mug of tea to the counter and close my eyes.

A normal stress response.

Breathe.

Focus on physical anchors.

My lungs push against the pressure around them as I inhale, hold the breath, then blow it out in a rush through my mouth. As I continue the exercise, I tap firmly beneath my collarbone until my nervous system calms and my heart rate slows.

Even with over six years of practice under my belt, I'm still amazed when the simple technique works. Gratitude fills me for the freedom I have now that I'm able to manage my anxiety.

The doorbell rings again.

"Coming," I mutter.

I leave the kitchen and walk down the hallway toward my visitors. The click and hum of the central heating and the creak of floorboards under my bare feet are familiar, grounding sounds. Late December, mid-morning sunlight cuts through trees on the property, diffusing through double-paned glass on my right and making the wood and white walls glow. After weeks of gray, it's a welcome sight.

As I pass the two platinum albums hanging in frames on the hallway wall, I breathe deeply again and remind myself that everything is okay, that I can handle this. That I've handled *a lot* without a drink or a drug, like writing and recording five albums back-to-back. Months upon months on the road. Sold out stadium crowds and festival fields around the world. Screaming, crying fans who have no concept of personal boundaries. Live interviews under glaring lights. And the most personally challenging career requirement: industry events and award shows where seeing *her* is unavoidable.

But the real proof I can handle anything sits in my chest: a broken heart that still, somehow, keeps on beating. That I've learned to accept, even embrace, as the ultimate proof that nothing, *nothing*, has the power to send me back into the darkness.

My fingers trail lightly across the leaves of a potted fern beside the front door, and I use the physical sensation to focus my mind on the present. One more breath, then I flip the deadbolt and pull open the door. Frigid air swirls around me and I relish the shock of it.

The couple standing on my porch regard me with starkly different expressions. Matt Sullivan is frowning deeply, hands stuffed in his pockets, shoulders high and tense beneath his coat. His wife, on the other hand, beams at me with a smile so familiar I have to make myself return it.

"Hi, Wilder," Sophie says warmly. "Thanks so much for letting us come by."

"Of course. How was the ferry?"

"Just fine," she answers as Matt grumbles, "Fucking crowded."

I glance at him—he doesn't meet my eye—before standing back. "Come on in."

Once they're inside, I close the door and lock it, then wait as they remove their coats and hang them on hooks in the foyer. As I study their body language, it occurs to me with faint amusement that of the three of us, I'm the calmest.

Sophie turns first, clearing her throat as she smooths flyaway, dark blonde hairs from her face. "How was your Christmas?"

Since she's best friends with my mom and they talk daily, it's obvious she's attempting to fill the awkward silence. I don't know exactly why they're here, but whatever the reason, it's becoming apparent that it's not a good one. My jaw clenches against the urge to ask the question that's haunted me since my mom called two days ago with their request.

"It was great," I say, my voice steady despite clanging nerves. "With River living in London and the twins down in San Diego, it'd been a while since we were all under the same roof. How was yours?"

"Just fine, thank you." Her smile falters as she glances at

Matt, who's still frowning as he stares at the floor. She nudges his arm and he finally looks at me.

What I see in his light blue eyes has me struggling not to take a step back. The familiar resentment I was expecting is nowhere to be found. He looks sad and lost.

My stomach drops.

"Thanks for seeing us," he says mutedly.

I nod, then shift back on my heels and pivot, suddenly knowing I need to be sitting down when they reveal what brought them to my door. "Come on back. Can I get you guys anything? Coffee? Water? Tea?"

"We're fine, thanks," Sophie replies.

They follow me silently down the hallway, but as we enter the heart of the house, Sophie gasps. "This is absolutely stunning, Wilder."

The open-concept living space is dominated by huge windows along the back wall that showcase a private beach and water beyond. The view is framed by the assorted pines and deciduous trees that crowd the six-acre property. One particular tree snags my gaze like it always does. It stands alone, thick trunk supporting a multitude of long, crooked branches, pale and bare for the winter.

A sycamore.

Sophie turns to me with a bright smile. "Rose showed me before and after pictures, but they didn't do this place justice. You guys did an amazing job."

A smile comes more easily this time. "Thank you. I'm pretty proud of it."

With my touring schedule, it took close to three years to finish the remodeling since my dad and I were committed to doing most of the cosmetic work ourselves. I'm more proud of this house than I am of my career success. It's my sanctuary, the first place where I've felt completely at home since I was a child. More than that, though, it's a physical embodiment and affirmation of the effort I put into rebuilding my life on a solid foundation.

Matt walks past us, his gaze trailing over the arched ceilings, sunroom-inspired dining space, modern kitchen, and adjacent living room. He doesn't say anything as he veers toward a couch and sits. Posture rigid, he stares blankly at the waterline. Sophie trails after him, perching at his side and taking one of his hands in hers.

My skin buzzes as I follow and settle on the opposite couch. It takes conscious effort not to mirror Matt's tension. I keep my arms relaxed, my hands folded loosely over my stomach.

No amount of breathing is going to help my heart rate at this point, so I do what's sometimes necessary and simply sit with the discomfort.

To my surprise, it isn't Sophie who breaks the silence.

"You're probably wondering what we're doing here." Matt laughs shortly, dragging a hand through his pale hair. *Her* hair.

Since he's cutting to the point, so do I. "I am, yes."

His throat moves. "I owe you an apology."

I wasn't aware I was fidgeting until his words sink in and every muscle in my body stills.

Sophie gives him an encouraging nod, and he continues, "I've said some really fucked-up things to you over the years. Things you didn't deserve."

Is this why they're here? The notion relaxes a knot inside me. Maybe this isn't what I was afraid of, after all.

Smiling slightly, I tell him, "Nah. I definitely deserved them."

Matt studies my face, then smirks. "You definitely did."

Expression aghast, Sophie smacks his shoulder. Matt chuckles. Surprising everyone, including myself, I join him.

Sophie glances between us, mystified. "I think what my husband is trying—and failing—to say is that we're extremely proud of you and the man you've become."

A surge of embarrassment makes my voice gruff. "Thanks, Sophie."

"That's what I said, isn't it?" Matt jokes before sobering. He pins me with a stare. "In all seriousness, I *am* sorry for the things I said. You needed support back then, but I was too caught up in my head to give it. I'll always regret that. I'm grateful you made it through, Wilder."

The gravity of the moment settles on my shoulders—not the heavy, clawed feeling of the past, but a light, comforting shroud. Goosebumps roll gently down my arms, and an old, internal scar fades.

"I appreciate that," I murmur.

Sophie squeezes Matt's hand, her eyes glassy as they shift to me. Her chin trembles, then firms. "For what it's worth, we know you didn't mean to hurt our daughter."

I've barely processed her statement when Matt says, "We know you loved her very much."

Surprise forces air from my lungs too fast, leaving me dizzy. I lift my gaze to the ceiling, seeking an anchor, and see a knot on one of the beams. In the lumpy, imperfect circle, I find a modicum of calm. And in that calm is an instinct I can no longer ignore.

Lowering my gaze to Evangeline's parents, I ask the question that's become a nonstop irritant the last two days.

"She's not okay, is she?"

Sophie's expression crumples. Matt's hardens defensively, his pale eyes impossibly bright. "No, she's not," he answers.

A thousand questions crowd my mind—*what, why, how*

—but what comes out is, "I'm assuming you've talked to Rye and Lily?"

They nod, and Sophie says softly, "They've tried. *We've* tried. But she's..." She trails off, a vacancy in her eyes I'm all too familiar with. Matt puts his arm around her and she leans into his side.

"No one can get through to her," Matt informs me. "Even knowing what fame can do to people, it's surreal. She's like a different person."

I think of the last time I saw Evangeline, in a media clip last week. She was walking into a restaurant in Los Angeles with her boyfriend. In the five seconds I managed to watch the video, I'd been focused on how much I wanted to rip his fake-tanned hand off her back.

Now I force myself to confront the image of *her*. Too thin. Too much makeup. High heels. Fake nails on the hand lifted toward the flashing cameras. Winning, superstar smile. Long hair tamed into perfect waves. A designer mini-dress in some bland color.

"I want my daughter back," whispers Sophie.

The crack in my heart widens, more debris falling silently into the abyss of Evangeline's absence.

Matt's agonized eyes hold mine. "We need your help. *She* needs your help."

Potent emotion floods me—twisted, irrepressible hope at the prospect of being close to Evangeline again. Despite knowing the hope is false, it feels too fucking real. I need to recenter myself in reality. Remind myself and them of the truth I have to live with every day.

"I want to help," I say as gently as I can. "Of course I do. But let's be realistic here. I'm the last person on the planet she'd listen to. There's an album that won five Grammys detailing exactly how she feels about me."

Matt's eyes narrow, flashing with determination and stubbornness. I see so much of Evangeline in his expression that for two seconds, I can't fucking breathe.

"So that's it? You're giving up on her?"

Sophie's head lifts, anxious eyes flying from Matt to me.

I tense. "I'm respecting her wishes—the ones she screamed at me outside your house when I came home from treatment? I'm sure you remember." I pause, reining in the emotion that bled into my voice. "It's been years. We've both moved on with our lives."

Matt scoffs. "Don't give me that bullshit. You still love her." I flinch, and he goes in for the kill. "If you don't, explain why you don't publicly date anyone, ever. Why you still write songs about her. Why *that*"—his arm swings toward the painting over the fireplace—"is on the wall."

I don't follow the line of his finger. I haven't looked directly at the painting since it was hung up on the day the house was finished.

I shift in my seat, my skin crawling. "I honestly don't know what you're asking me to do."

"I think you do," he challenges.

Standing, he draws Sophie to her feet. I rise, too, frustration punching through my veneer of calm.

"She won't talk to me. I fucking tried, Matt."

The aggression leaves his face as he sighs. "I know you did. But that was then and this is now." He pauses. "When she does answer our calls, it's like talking to a stranger who body-snatched our kid. But there's one word—just one—that gets an authentic reaction from her. Even if it guarantees she hangs up on us."

I frown, but he doesn't make me wait.

"Your name."

They turn toward the hallway.

"What the hell? How is that a good thing?"

Matt stops and looks back. I recoil when I see tears in his eyes. "It means she's still in there somewhere. *You're* still in there somewhere. You might be the only one who can bring her back."

He strides down the hallway while Sophie lingers. "I'm sorry, Wilder. We're both a little"—she sighs, glancing at Matt's dwindling form—"out of our minds. Just tell me you'll think about it? Maybe try reaching out to her again?"

She looks so heartbroken, I can't help but nod. "I'll try."

"Thank you." She smiles softly before following Matt.

By the time my leaden feet reach the foyer, their car is headed down the driveway.

I drop my forehead to the door and breathe.

Just breathe.

CHAPTER TWO

wilder

LATE AFTERNOON, my doorbell rings again. This time I rush toward it and throw it open. "About fucking time."

"Language," chirps Lily.

Rolling my eyes, I step back. "Give me a break, she's not even two."

Lily strolls past me, Rye following with my goddaughter. Closing the door behind them, I hold out my arms. Rye acquiesces to my silent demand and hands me Emma, who's already reaching for me.

Her tiny fingers immediately start tugging my hair as she chants, "Why-Why, Why-Why."

The first time Emma called me the nickname Evangeline used when she was a toddler, it felt like a knife in my gut. But exposure therapy is a thing for a reason. After hearing it innumerable times, it's now one of my favorite sounds.

"Fair warning, she's cutting molars," Rye says as he pulls off his coat. "Prepare for drool."

"Oh yeah? Show me the goods, Ems." I tickle her belly and she giggles, mouth dropping open and showcasing her collection of tiny teeth and red gums. "Ouch. That looks like hard work."

Saliva dribbles from the corners of her mouth, a thick stream dripping off her chin to my bicep. "You're so gross," I coo at her, "but I still love you."

A silicone toy shaped like a giraffe appears between us. Emma grabs it and starts gnawing on the head like a rabid animal.

"You know, if you wanted to see the baby, you could have just said so. No vague, alarmist demands necessary." Lily's light tone is at odds with the frown on her delicate features.

I look from her to Rye, whose concerned expression finally registers. "Shit. Sorry. I didn't mean to worry you guys." I adjust my grip on Emma. "Matt and Sophie came to see me today."

Comprehension sweeps across their faces. They exchange a look before Rye sighs. "We were kind of afraid they would but didn't want to say anything in case nothing came of it."

"They were talking about Evangeline like she needs either an intervention or an exorcism. What the hell is going on?"

Another loaded glance passes between them.

"Can we at least sit down before hashing this out?" asks Lily. Without waiting for an answer, she sweeps past me toward the kitchen. "You're making us dinner, by the way. One of your fancy recipes, please and thank you."

Before Rye can walk away, I grab his arm. "Just give me a scale or something. How worried should I be?"

He grimaces. "Man, I wish it were that easy. A big part of the problem is we can't get close enough to her to find out. I have better odds surviving Lily's cooking than I do getting a call back from Eva."

"I heard that!" Lily hollers from the kitchen.

Rye and I share a smirk. As we walk down the hallway, he continues in a low voice, "Do I think she's in an intervention-level crisis? No. Unless bad taste in men qualifies."

I open my mouth, then close it. Is that what Matt and Sophie were indirectly asking me to do? Break up Evangeline and her boyfriend? The idea is as wild as their assumption that I still have any effect on their daughter whatsoever.

On the other hand, the Sullivans aren't stupid. Matt especially has been in the music industry for a long time, and he's definitely heard the rumors about his daughter's boyfriend.

Clay *fucking* Eaton.

Entertainment lawyer, media golden boy, and unequivocal dirtbag who groomed and seduced his sixteen-year-old stepsister when he was twenty-three. The latter isn't conjecture, either. His stepsister, Kendra, is my ex-girlfriend, and she told me everything.

I can't even think Clay's name without wanting to break his face. Even harder to accept? That I told Evangeline he was morally bankrupt and not only did she fall for his fake charm, she's been with him for *two years*. The reason I didn't tell her about his fucked-up relationship with Kendra was because at the time, I hadn't wanted to give her nightmares. Now I wish I had.

The only reasonable—and gut-wrenching—conclusion I've come to is Evangeline must have decided that because I lied about my drug use, I lied about everything else, too.

All this time, I've clung to the silver lining that at least she had Lily and Rye. Only now I'm not sure she does.

The remainder of the walk to the kitchen is spent naming three things I can see, three things I can hear, and three things I can feel.

It barely takes the edge off.

Rounding the island, I hand a squirming Emma to her

mom. Lily gives her a smooch on the head before swapping the teething toy for a sippy cup of milk. As Rye opens the fridge to hunt for his favorite Kombucha, I head to a couch and flop down to wait for them.

They eventually settle in the same spot Sophie and Matt occupied earlier. Emma curls into her mom, drinking lazily from her cup and blinking slowly. In spite of my tension, I smile.

"She's gonna pass out."

Lily nods, smiling softly as she smooths dark hair off Emma's forehead. Her mom's touch pushes her over the edge into dreamland. Rye extracts the sippy cup from small, twitching fingers and puts it on the coffee table, then turns his attention to me.

"All right, tell us what they said."

It doesn't take long to recount the conversation. When I'm finished, Lily blows out a heavy breath.

"That's kind of messed up." She looks down at Emma. "On the other hand, I can understand their desperation."

Rye studies my face, correctly interpreting my expression —namely, how close I am to losing my shit. "It's not fair that they put this on you. Eva is different, sure, but she hasn't been body-snatched or whatever. She's still the same person, just..." He shrugs.

"Meaner," mutters Lily.

Rye counters, "She's under constant scrutiny and pressure."

From the looks on their faces, it's obvious they've had this argument before. I've never been privy to it because of the unspoken rule that they don't talk about Evangeline in front of me. I've also never pried, respecting their choice and, frankly, my own mental health. Plus, I've always assumed the rule came from Eva herself.

Lily's dark eyes throw sparks. "And I'm not under scrutiny or pressure? Really?"

"Babe, that's not—"

She cuts him off. "Last time I checked, there are two members in Glow, but only one of us is making huge decisions about the future without speaking to the other."

I frown. "What does that mean?"

Rye winces. "The Indigo contract expired a few months ago and Eva turned down a new one. Lily found out after the fact. It's been kept on the down-low so far."

My eyes widen. "What the hell?"

Lily's laugh is humorless. "My thoughts exactly. After everything Indigo has done for us? I got my hands on the new contract they offered, too. She turned down an obscene amount of money, not to mention ownership of all masters and publishing rights. It makes zero sense. And you know what she said when I confronted her? That I was being small-minded. She basically called me an idiot."

"I don't think—" Rye starts.

"Stop defending her! You weren't there."

Emma stirs with a mewl of protest. Lily visibly struggles, then relaxes with a dejected shake of her head, whispering, "It was horrible."

Rye's expression falls. I look away as he wraps an arm around her. "I'm sorry. You're absolutely right. It's not okay that she went to the meeting without you or said that to you. None of this is okay."

Lily sniffs and whispers, "Thank you," then returns her focus to me. "Obviously I'm not done being angry with her. I've also started to consider this might be the end of Glow."

More shock reverberates through me. "Seriously?"

She shrugs. "Our tour at the beginning of the year was challenging, to say the least. If Rye hadn't been able to come with Emma, I don't know how I would've managed. Our parents are getting older, too, and we want more kids. It would be nice to focus on family for more than a few months at a time, you know? Maybe even finally plan a wedding."

She and Rye share a wistful smile before she continues, "If Eva does want to call it quits, I'd be fine with it. I just wish she'd come out and say it instead of giving me some avoidant bullshit about 'waiting and seeing' and 'weighing our options.'"

Rye's tight expression tells me he heard the same undercurrent in her voice I did: denial. Lily wouldn't be fine with saying goodbye to Glow forever any more than I'd be fine with never playing guitar again.

What she wants is what many artists our age—or really, people in general—want. The best of both worlds. Family and career. And she could have it, no question. While smaller artists might suffer financially from touring less or putting out fewer albums, Glow has reached a level of success very few do. Night Theory included.

Eva and Lily have done exactly what journalist Alex Illoka first predicted. What *I* predicted. Worldwide superstardom and a fanbase of millions that grows daily—check. Over two hundred industry awards, including twelve Grammys—check. Thousands of young artists emulating them—check.

All before either of them turned thirty.

My head swimming, I ask, "Do you think she wants to go solo?"

Lily smiles weakly. "If you'd asked me that two years ago, I would have said not a chance in hell."

"What's so significant about two years ago?" As the last word leaves my mouth, realization strikes. "You think *Clay* is behind this?"

"It wouldn't surprise me. He's obsessed with her fame and what it can do for him. I've never liked him, and he's never liked me. It's not a huge stretch to imagine him pushing her to break ties."

The notion of anyone, but especially *him*, having that much influence on Evangeline nauseates me.

"Does... does she love him?" I ask hoarsely.

Rye looks ten types of uncomfortable as he shrugs. "She says she does."

Lily scoffs. "Yeah, in the same tone you use when you tell my parents I'm a great cook." Her fierce gaze moves to me. "I realize we've had a *don't ask don't tell* policy about this for years, but I'm officially over it. What happened between you guys messed her up big time."

"I know," I whisper.

Her head tilts. "Do you? Do you know that while you went to rehab, did all that therapy and figured your shit out, she was sitting awake in a dark closet all night, every night?"

Dizziness hits me as blood drains from my head. A familiar prickle rolls down my spine. Imaginary fists squeeze my lungs.

Rye shifts. "Lily, maybe—"

"It's okay," I say, sucking in a deep breath. "I'm ready to hear it."

Lily's eyes soften. "You know I love you, Wilder. I'm so glad you're sober, and you're the best godfather Emma could have. But you also broke my best friend, and a part of me will never forgive you for that."

Sharp pain slices through my chest. Rye shifts in his seat, giving me a pained look.

"You think this is my fault," I murmur.

"God, no!" She sighs noisily. "I'm sorry. I don't mean it that way. What I'm trying to say is I don't think Eva dealt with what happened between you guys. At least not in a healthy way. She pulled it together, sure. Glow was obviously a great distraction. From the outside, it looked like she'd transferred all her pain into an album and was fine. Great, even. Right?"

My tongue too thick for words, I nod.

"I thought the same." She gives me a sad smile. "Like the rest of the world, I bought the act she put on. I was convinced she'd tell me if she wasn't okay. If I'd paid more attention or asked more questions, maybe—"

"Don't do that to yourself," I interject. "Even if you'd known the right questions to ask, there was no guarantee she'd answer."

Rye cups her shoulder. "He's right. She's always been that way, always hated showing weakness. Or whatever she perceives as weakness, I should say."

My heart squeezes. "Remember the eyepatch?" I ask, and Rye laughs shortly. I tell Lily, "When Evangeline was five, she made an eyepatch out of cardboard and yarn for her gray eye."

Rye grins at the memory. "She used black and green crayons to draw an eye on the cardboard, but it was all misshapen and freaky-looking. I ran away screaming when I saw it."

I crack a smile. "You were a wuss."

"I was four, asshole."

We chuckle.

Lily sighs. "Is the point of this story coming anytime soon?"

The moment's reprieve passes, heaviness sliding back into my chest. "Sophie called my mom freaking out because Evangeline wouldn't tell her why she wanted an eyepatch. She asked for the number of the child therapist I was seeing."

Lily's jaw drops, and I wave dismissively. "Yeah, I was

already a mess at seven. Anyway, that weekend I cornered Evangeline and got the truth out of her. Some kid at school had called her a freak and hurt her feelings. I made up a story about how her gray iris meant she was related to fairies. It worked and she took off the eyepatch. But the point is, she's always locked down her emotions. Compartmentalized them."

"That's when you started calling her Fairy," she surmises.

I swallow the sudden knot in my throat. "Yeah."

A loaded silence falls, broken only by the soft, rhythmic whistles of Emma's deep breathing.

Rye's stare narrows thoughtfully on me. "Except with you."

Lily looks between us, frowning. "What?"

He turns to her. "Eva has always locked down her feelings around everyone *except Wilder*. Think about it. In all the years you've known her, has she ever really lost it in front of you? Like full-blown emotional meltdown?"

Lily sucks in a breath, glancing at me. She doesn't have to say anything. I know exactly what day she's thinking about.

I'd relapsed the night before and hid it as best I could from Evangeline. But she still knew instinctively that something was wrong. The next afternoon, I walked into her house full of shame and crippling fear. Lily was there. Evangeline had been crying, her eyes swollen and bloodshot.

After Lily left, she told me she was afraid of the dark, both tangibly and metaphorically. That when I'd shut her out the night before, I'd felt like a darkness she couldn't find her way out of.

I was too desperate to keep her to tell her she was right. I *was* the dark, and I was swallowing us both.

Memories and regrets clatter inside me. Fighting for calm, I look up at the knot on the ceiling beam. The afternoon shadows make it look like an eye. I squint, and it seems to wink at me.

Inhale—two, three, four.

Exhale—two, three, four.

I repeat the exercise until my body lets go of the fight-or-flight response. Until my heart stops racing. Until my disjointed thoughts blend and finally ring with a single, harmonious note.

Everyone close to me knows I don't carry a mere torch for Evangeline.

My entire soul burns for her.

Like I told her when we were kids: everything else, *everyone else*, will always be background noise. At least for me.

I've kept my distance for over six years out of respect for the very clear boundary she set when I came home from treatment. It was the only form of amends she'd accept. But something else is equally true: my distance was dependent on the conviction she was okay. Healthy and happy. That not only did she not want me, she didn't *need* me.

After today, that conviction is smoke.

I lower my gaze from the ceiling. "If you tell me where Evangeline will be on New Year's, I'll teach you how to make the best Nikujaga your parents will ever taste."

Lily blinks in surprise, then smiles. "Deal."

CHAPTER THREE

evangeline

your love was overrated
way too complicated
A trap to force compliance
Numb all of my defiance

Now that I've seen through you
you can take your pretty words
stuff them in your throat
And choke

LYING on my side in bed, I watch the digital clock on the nightstand creep slowly toward 4:00 a.m. Outside of its muted blue glow, the bedroom is swathed in velvety black. The dense, textured heaviness would have terrified me years ago, but now it's as familiar as the keys of a piano.

As I gaze into the dark, I think about that famous Nietzsche quote. How if you stare long enough into the abyss, the abyss stares back at you. Reaches out and touches you.

Perhaps he's right, and in some obscure way, I've become what I fear.

I can't find the energy to care.

3:36 a.m.

With twenty-four minutes before I can get out of bed without garnering suspicion, I roll over. Clay lies in his usual position facing away from me. I stare at the slope of his shoulder under the coverlet, tracking its rhythmic rise and fall.

The three feet between us might as well be a thousand. We only traverse the space during sex, something that's become an increasingly rare activity over the last six months.

I may be perpetually sleep-deprived, but I'm not blind. More than our sex life has changed since we moved in together. Outside of weekly date nights—always in public with the pressure of paparazzi watching us—we don't spend time together like we used to. No more casual nights just the two of us, chatting and laughing and enjoying each other's company.

I thought living in the same city, the same house, would bring us closer. But the opposite has happened. He works late most evenings. When he does come home at a decent hour, after dinner, he disappears into his office or our home gym. In the last month especially, the time we do spend together is set to a soundtrack of his passive-aggressive disappointment and my apathetic avoidance.

I know I should care more. Feel something... *bigger*. About him. About my life and its current trajectory. But I'm insulated underwater, dark and cold. Everything around me is slightly distorted, colors and sounds muted.

I roll over to face the clock.

3:45 a.m.

Fifteen more minutes until I can make coffee and sneak out to the pool house where I've hidden caramel creamer in the mini-fridge. Two hours until I have to choke down egg whites and toast with a smear of avocado. Four hours until—

Sheets rustle, the sound jarring in my silence-attuned ears. I wait for Clay to settle again, but instead, the mattress behind me dips with his weight. I suck in a startled breath as his arm slides over my waist. He draws my back against his front and kisses my shoulder.

"I know you're awake," he whispers. "I could hear you thinking in my dreams."

There's a smile in his voice.

I relax against him, my worry dispersing. He's not going to leave me, and I have no reason to leave him. Besides, no relationship is perfect. Intimacy ebbs and flows over the years. What we have is reliable, and that's what matters.

Deft fingers slide down my stomach and lift the hem of my nightgown. "How about an early New Year's gift?" he murmurs.

In reply, I cover his hand with mine and guide it between my legs. His touch doesn't incite overwhelming need, but that's okay. Passion isn't all that important in the scheme of things.

I enjoy making him feel good.

I can pretend.

The little lies don't matter, anyway.

♫

WHEN I STEP out of the shower an hour later, Clay is shaving at the bathroom sink. His lean torso is on display, tanned and toned. Hazel eyes track me as I towel dry.

"The stylist should be here around two so we can pick out your dress for tonight." His gaze lowers to the sink as he rinses his razor. "Hair and makeup start at four, and the car will be here at seven. Drink lots of water today, and make sure you take a nap this morning. Ten to twelve would be a good time for it. I have to do a little work, but we'll have lunch together at twelve-fifteen."

I make a sound of agreement, then trade my towel for a robe and move to the second sink to brush my teeth. As I squeeze toothpaste onto the brush, I wait for a reminder to floss. When it doesn't come—he's distracted rinsing his face with cold water—I'm almost disappointed. Not because I actually enjoy his micro-managing, though most days it doesn't bother me. Sometimes it's even a game. *If I do this, or don't do that, what will he say?*

Lily hates that Clay is so controlling. I understand her concern, I really do. It makes perfect sense why she and Rye don't like him. What they can't see, can't possibly understand, is the lure for me. The relief I feel being taken care of—and the necessity of it.

When I ran into Clay at an awards show afterparty two years ago, I was floundering. Flickering like a dying light. Eminently close to giving up on... everything.

He saved me from myself.

I spit out toothpaste, making sure to rinse all the froth from the porcelain, then use a hand towel to wipe droplets of water from the surrounding countertop. Clay snorts and shakes his head. He thinks it's a waste of time to clean up after myself when we have a housekeeper who comes daily. But he's used to it now and doesn't bother saying anything.

As I start my skincare routine, he dries his face and tosses the towel on the floor. Pausing behind me, he lifts a tendril of my wet hair and rubs the strands between his fingers.

"Did you use that new hair mask I got you?" he asks, smiling when I nod. "Thought so. Feels silky."

With a pat on my ass, he leaves the bathroom.

I wait until I hear him exit the bedroom, then grab his towel off the floor and clean the mess he left in and around his sink.

CHAPTER FOUR

evangeline

I'VE SPENT a lot of time in Los Angeles over the years—it's an inescapable leviathan of the music industry—but living here has made me lose appreciation for the climate everyone else loves.

Case in point, it's New Year's Eve and a balmy sixty-four degrees. I don't even need a coat. Which, given the minuscule dress I'm wearing, is unfortunate. It's also deeply unsettling, like my body knows something is wrong. I felt the same way waking up on Christmas morning and eating breakfast outside in the warm sunshine.

Clay says it will take time for me to adjust. Maybe he's right. But while the barely changing weather disturbs me, I doubt I'll ever get used to the migraine-inducing smog and constant traffic, or the fact there's more dirty cement here than trees or actual dirt. Or the dreaded Celebrity Tax, a joking term that really isn't funny.

While the price of celebrity certainly isn't unique to L.A., in my experience, it's more acute and constant here than in Seattle, Austin, or even New York. Anonymity is next to impossible thanks to the weather and further exacerbated by the city's culture of exploitation. Not only does the public have the right to stalk, dissect, criticize, and confront me every time I leave the house, but I'm supposed to be immune to it or at the least, never complain.

Even among those who experience the same daily pressures I do, there's no respite. Every conversation is inherently dangerous. Laden with hidden agendas and context.

Like the one I'm having right now.

Poppy Cole is a twenty-year-old pop star. Blonde hair. Piercing blue eyes. Unquestionably beautiful. Our fanbases have minimal overlap, so her barely veiled animosity makes no sense. I've literally never exchanged words with her before tonight.

"My stylist showed me that dress as an option for tonight," she says, her heavily made-up eyes flickering down my body. Her smile is fixed and completely fake.

Maybe it's the dry winds blowing across the crowded outdoor patio and irritating my eyes, or the uncomfortable heels Clay insisted I wear, but I can't summon the polite pretense required for this game. The one where I pretend we're hitting it off for the sake of appearances.

Another thing I've learned about L.A., or at least Hollywood: it's high school all over again. Cliques and social climbing and nonstop cattiness.

Poppy's eyes glitter with annoyance, probably because I'm not rising to her bait but merely staring back at her.

She makes a second attempt. "I'm glad I didn't wear it."

I take a small sip of champagne and say mildly, "It's definitely not a style that suits everyone."

When her smile freezes, I suffer immediate guilt. Fame in this city is a designer toxin for young, ambitious women. I was spared the worst of it living like a recluse in the Pacific

Northwest, but apparently the smog is slowly sucking out my kindness.

I open my mouth to apologize in the usual way, by complimenting her dress, but she speaks first.

"We should do lunch sometime. I'll introduce you to my esthetician. She's amazing at..." She twirls a fingertip around her face, eyes radiating false sympathy.

Ah, age-shaming. Nice.

"Oh, look! It's Olivia. I have to say hello. So great chatting with you, Eva. Call me!" She gives me a little wave and sashays away.

I don't bother saying goodbye.

Around me, forty or so people mingle or lounge on stark-white furniture in the cement backyard of an ultra-modern Hollywood Hills mansion. I hear Clay's laughter and track the sound to a nearby group of men. The tableau could be the intro to a joke: a lawyer, a judge, and an actor walk into a bar...

Clay glances at me, the skin around his eyes pinching when he sees I'm alone. I instantly hear his voice in my head reminding me of the importance of networking.

I paste a pleasant smile on my face, then wish I hadn't when the stretch of my facial muscles activates an urge to yawn. My scheduled nap today was a bust, and even the IV drip of vitamins, antioxidants, and electrolytes I had after lunch failed to dent my fatigue. Gritting my teeth, I overcome the reflex and look around for a friendly face. Or at least a familiar one.

What I really want is to ask Clay if we can go home. Ring in the new year on the couch in our pajamas. But I know better. He isn't a homebody like me—this is his happy place. Asking him to leave would not only ruin his night, it would worsen his growing concerns about my sleep. Or rather, my lack of it.

If I don't get a handle on my insomnia soon, I'm afraid history will repeat itself. I'll be given a choice between a stint at a private clinic or sleeping pills at home that give me nightmares and make me feel like a zombie all day.

Tension tightens my shoulders as I glance at Clay again. He's still watching me, body language projecting an intent to excuse himself and come over. If he does, I'll be stuck to his side the rest of the night, guided from group to group until my head spins.

I look around again, a bit more desperately, and sigh with relief when I spot a familiar man sitting on a couch on the other side of the patio. Maybe I *do* have one friend in this city. Seizing the opportunity, I walk toward him. If it weren't for the icepicks on my feet, I might even run.

Even surrounded by fashion-obsessed partygoers, Martin Page stands out. He wears a shimmery silver vest with no undershirt, the pale color highlighting his warm brown skin and trim physique. Snug, matching pants with fringe down the sides and white cowboy boots complete his ensemble. On anyone else, the look could easily be kitschy, but on Martin it's effortless high fashion. I'm probably the only one here who knows he likely found the outfit at one of his favorite resale shops.

When he spies me approaching, a smile overtakes his face. "Eva!" He shoves at the man next to him, who gives him an annoyed look but scoots down to make room for me.

After depositing my half-full glass of champagne on the table, I sit carefully, keeping my legs sealed so I don't flash the party. Bending as much as the restrictive dress will allow, I rub at my ankle where a tiny strap has cut into my skin.

When the sting only gets worse, I give up and lean against Martin's warm shoulder.

I whisper, "You hate my dress, don't you?"

"It's hideous," he whispers back.

I laugh over an abrupt urge to cry. "I miss you."

He drops his head against mine. "Same."

Martin was the up-and-coming stylist who took Lily and me under his wing six years ago. The instincts of our publicist, Anita, were right when she surmised we'd be perfect for each other. Over the following years, Martin became more than a friend. He was family.

My heart still aches at the memory of the day last year when he tearfully informed us he needed to part ways. Lily and I were blindsided, heartbroken, and confused. Friendship aside, our professional relationship had always been mutually beneficial. After dressing us for our first Grammys, Martin became one of the most sought-after stylists on the West Coast, and since then his name has been synonymous with edgy elegance. Until last year, his name was also synonymous with Glow.

But despite the lingering pain of his sudden departure and vague reasonings, there's no world in which I wouldn't be happy to see him.

"How are you?" he asks softly.

A lie sits on my tongue, but the truth leaps over it. "Tired."

Martin drops a warm hand to my knee and squeezes gently. "Come down to my place in Baja for a week. We'll drink margaritas and float in the pool all day. How about next month?"

I suck in a breath, my first instinct a resounding *yes*. But then I picture Clay's reaction and my chest deflates. There's no way he'd be okay with it, not with so much up in the air.

Before I can think of a way to say no, the man seated on the other side of Martin asks, "Is that who I think it is?"

Martin straightens and looks around. "Who? Is it Miley? Because if it's not Miley, I don't care."

"I can't believe it," someone else murmurs, while a woman on a nearby love seat slaps her friend's arm and says, "I knew tonight was going to be epic. Where's my phone?"

The energy of the party shifts fast, conversations dying off or lowering to murmurs as more and more people turn to observe the newcomer. I still can't see them, my line of sight blocked.

Whoever they are, I'm both grateful for the distraction and feel sorry for them. I've been in their shoes more times than I can count. While fame can be thrilling, especially at first, eventually it gets old being treated like a product instead of a person.

Lost in my thoughts, I jerk in surprise when Martin swivels toward me. His eyes are wide, lips pursed in distress.

"Honey, you're not going to like this."

"Huh?"

Frowning, I glance over his shoulder right as a group of partygoers disperses and reveals the man standing near the back door of the house.

A fiery, pins-and-needles sensation crawls over every inch of my skin.

"What's he doing here?" I whisper.

Martin squeezes my burning fingers. "Not a clue."

It's been years since I've seen Wilder in such close proximity, my exposure intentionally limited to glimpses at fifty feet during award shows or the occasional, accidental sight of him on social media or in a magazine.

I want to look away, *need to*, but I can't. I can't even blink. The sight of him has frozen every inch of me, skin to marrow.

Clearly his stance on conformity, and fashion in general, hasn't changed. He still dresses like he's twenty-five. I wish I could say the forever-casual look isn't attractive anymore, that it makes him look immature or slovenly. But it doesn't. In a sea of sparkling silverfish, he stands out like a tiger shark. Unapologetically unpolished. Magnetic, sensual, and irreverent.

Worn jeans hug his lean hips and long legs above combat boots. A faded black T-shirt showcases the sculpted contours of his chest and arms, the latter's surface almost fully obscured by tattoos. Unruly dark waves frame his face, enhancing his striking features. I'm grateful I can't see his eyes—until I see the woman he's looking down at, who's suctioned to his arm like a frilly pink octopus.

Poppy.

My jaw grinds and a spark of pain erupts behind my right eye. Through a veil of static, I register snippets of conversations taking place around me.

"...even hotter in person."

"...definitely my hall pass."

"She doesn't look so good..."

"...clearly not over him."

"...you blame her? He's a god in flesh."

I finally drag my eyes from Wilder to see people staring at me. A *lot* of people, with expressions ranging from pity to pleasure.

"Let's go inside," Martin says urgently.

When I nod, he stands and pulls me to my feet, then guides me away from the couch. I barely feel the throbs of protest in my ankles. I'm a marionette, relying on his arm around my waist to keep me upright and moving. People scatter from our path as we make our way toward the house.

Thankfully, there's another entrance closer to us, so we don't have to walk past *him*.

Then, like a different puppeteer takes control of my body, my head snaps to the left. From twenty feet away, dappled-forest eyes bore into mine.

I hate you.

And like he heard my silent scream, Wilder nods.

I know.

pre-chorus

pre-chorus : *the section of a song that builds anticipation for the chorus.*

CHAPTER FIVE

wilder

TEN REASONS TO FORGET YOU
TWENTY LIES THAT WERE TRUE
A HUNDRED WAYS OUT
A THOUSAND THROUGH
EVEN IF I COULD (REALLY SHOULD)
WON'T EVER WALK AWAY FROM YOU

I SCAN the faces around me, ignoring the rising chatter and focus of L.A.'s rich and bored. Let them stare and gossip. I don't care about them.

Nor do I care about the woman who attached herself to me like we're old friends—the intimate kind—the moment I stepped outside. She's been chattering in my face for less than a minute and I've already stopped listening.

Talon-like nails pinch my bicep. "Did you hear me, Wilder?" she asks with a little laugh. A laugh that says, *Of course you did because you can't possibly be ignoring me.*

I pause my search for Evangeline and frown down at her. Her face is familiar, but I don't know her name because she didn't bother telling me. Like she can't imagine a world where every man she meets hasn't jerked off to her photograph.

"You have such pretty eyes," she says breathily.

I extract my arm. "Thanks. What did you ask me?"

She arches her back, trying to draw my attention to her breasts. I keep my eyes on her face.

"I asked if you wanted to get out of here," she says with a sultry smile. "Celebrate New Year's our own way."

I'm almost, *almost* impressed by her nerve.

"No, thanks."

Her shocked expression makes me want to laugh. It also makes me want to buy her six months of therapy. In lieu of suggesting she consider how propositioning a stranger might not be healthy, I go back to ignoring her.

She doesn't like that, her breasts pushing against my arm. "Fine by me. We can just find a bedroom here."

Now I'm annoyed. I open my mouth to tell her to get lost, but no words come. Because in that moment, my roaming gaze finds Evangeline's profile, downturned as she walks toward the house on the other side of the patio. Martin Page is with her, his arm around her waist. He's staring at me, dark eyes glimmering like he's trying to telepathically communicate. My brows lift in question, and he shakes his head.

Utterly confused, my gaze falls to Evangeline. The second it lands on her, her head jerks up and turns. Mismatched eyes lock unerringly on mine.

My breath stills.

My heart seizes.

It's the first time in over six years she's looked directly at me and nothing has changed.

She hates me.

I swallow. Nod in acknowledgment. She and Martin disappear into the house.

WHEN LILY and Rye asked me what my plan was for tonight, I told them I didn't have one beyond seeing Evangeline for myself, maybe observing her for a minute before bailing. It was true—*was* being the operative word.

Now that I've seen her, I'm incapable of walking away.

Even harder to swallow than her gaunt cheeks and the almost brittle way she moved was seeing the absence of what always made her *her*. That intangible aura that ensured she was the center of every room even when she was hiding in a corner.

She didn't look like someone at the peak of professional success, whose lifelong dreams have come to fruition.

She looked empty.

The only thing familiar about her were her two-toned eyes and the loathing in them. In every other way, she barely resembles the girl I grew up with. The woman I loved, whose heart I irreparably broke.

I wander the party in a daze, waiting for Evangeline to come back outside or for an ability to leave to manifest. People talk to me. I talk back. Smile and nod and fulfill the demands of small talk.

"What brings you to L.A.?"

"Just escaping the rain for a minute and visiting some friends."

"Did Night Theory break up?"

"Don't believe everything you read. We'll be back in the studio soon."

All the while, I fight the instinct to find Evangeline.

When I reach my absolute limit of socializing, my smile a grimace and my ears buzzing faintly, I retreat to the shadows at the edge of the patio where a waist-high fence separates

329

the home's backyard from a terraced hillside. In the distance, downtown L.A. shines like a gold-dusted circuit board.

I look up at the sky, clear but disturbingly starless, like even the air here holds dreams just outside of reach.

She doesn't belong here.

"Wilder?" asks a tentative male voice. "Can I talk to you for a minute?"

I turn, a polite refusal ready, but choke the words back when I see who it is. "Sure."

Martin Page approaches the fence a few feet away from me. He doesn't say anything right away, just stares outward much as I'd been doing. Tucking my hands in my pockets, I wait, braced for him to tell me off on Eva's behalf.

"I don't know if you remember me, but we've met in passing a few times."

The thread of nervousness in his tone makes me blink and swiftly reassess. "I remember you, Martin. Good to see you."

His head turns, eyes scanning mine, and he gives a little laugh. "It's so weird. I feel like I know you, but this is the first time we've had a conversation."

For a second, I think he means Evangeline talked about me over the years, but then he continues, "When my little sister was first getting clean, about three years ago, I went with her as support to a sobriety convention in Seattle. You were one of the main speakers."

All I can manage is a weak, "Ah."

I remember that convention well. How I'd wanted to refuse the invitation, but my sponsor convinced me—or rather, bullied me—into doing the forty-five-minute talk. I'd been nervous as hell leading up to it, the task of sharing my story with a ballroom full of recovering addicts seeming infinitely harder than performing for thousands.

In some ways, it had been. But there's also nothing quite like having hundreds of people from all walks of life nodding and laughing in solidarity as you talk about the most fucked-up time of your life. More than any therapy or one-on-one conversation, the experience convinced me that I'm not alone —or even remotely unique—in my struggles with addiction. And there's massive relief in knowing that.

Afterward, I was glad I'd done it, but I've also never accepted another invitation to speak at a large event. As much as I've grown to appreciate the sense of belonging I feel when I'm with other sober people, I'm still not much for group activities or crowds. Without a guitar in my hands, that is.

"I didn't mean to make you uncomfortable," Martin says. "I know it's all anonymous for a reason. I swear I've never told anyone about seeing you or shared what you talked about."

I smile wryly. "It's all good. My sobriety is an open secret, anyway. But I do appreciate the discretion. How's your sister doing?"

His face lights up. "Amazing. Still clean."

"I'm glad to hear it."

Martin glances toward the house. "So, uh, there's another reason I wanted to talk to you."

My pulse kicks inside my throat. "You want to dress me, don't you?"

His laugh is a tad shrill. "Talk about a dream come true. But no—I can't because... well, you know."

I nod slowly. "Because of Eva."

He gives a wincing smile and a nod. "She's actually who I wanted to talk about. I realize this is insanely presumptuous, so feel free to tell me to fuck off."

"Not gonna do that," I murmur.

Whatever he sees on my face seems to encourage him, but then his gaze darts anxiously toward the house again. It belatedly occurs to me that he's worried we'll be seen together, that it will get back to her.

Where we're standing is pretty dark and a good fifteen feet from the closest person. It's also past eleven and from the increasing sounds of revelry, everyone's pretty trashed. But I still shift a few steps back until Martin's shorter, slighter frame is blocked by mine.

When he realizes what I've done, he looks embarrassed but also relieved. "Thanks. If she finds out I'm talking to you, she'll never speak to me again."

I should be used to hearing confirmations of her continued enmity, but I'm not. Every one is a fresh blow to my chest.

Before I can think better of it, I ask, "She still hates me that much, huh?"

"I don't think it's you she hates," he says with a sigh.

My brow furrows. "What does that mean?"

Martin shakes his head like he either doesn't have an answer or can't tell me. He clears his throat. "I stashed her in a bedroom and told her I'd look for Clay. But I don't see him. Do you?"

Confusion deepening my frown, I turn and scan the throngs of people. I haven't seen Clay at all tonight. While wandering the party, I was half-expecting him to appear and try to get me to leave. I can't say I'm not glad I've avoided him so far, but...

My gaze snaps back to Martin. "What are you getting at?"

His jaw firms. After a few seconds of internal struggle, he says tensely, "He went inside before you got here. I didn't see him in the house, which means he's probably in a different bedroom."

"What—" I start, then stop as the words click. Rage

unfurls under my skin. "He's cheating on her at a party they're attending *together*?"

Martin gives an agitated shrug. "Even if he isn't, he's still the piece of shit who threatened to end my career if I didn't quit working for Glow. More to the point, he's a toxic asshole who doesn't deserve Eva."

Reeling, I open and close my mouth a few times, finally asking, "Does Eva know? About him threatening you?"

Martin's eyes glitter with feeling as he shakes his head. I'm somewhat relieved until he says, "I've been where she is —with a partner like him—and knew there was no point in telling her. That's not to say I didn't try early on to get her to dump his ass. The red flags were waving from the beginning, if you know what I mean."

Cold snakes down my spine. "I don't, actually."

Martin's eyes probe mine. "Do you still care about her the same way you did when you gave that talk?"

"Yes," I say without hesitation.

His sad smile makes me think he can see the fractured heart beating in my chest. "I figured when I saw the way you looked at her tonight. You've got the whole broody, pining thing down pat."

I huff a humorless laugh, and his gaze shifts to the lights of downtown.

"I'm ashamed to say it took me a while to see what was happening. Clay is really good at camouflaging control as care. Better than my ex, that's for sure. But after months of perfect behavior, he started slipping up when I was in the room. Making comments about her diet, clothing, who she was spending time with."

"What the fuck," I whisper, but Martin doesn't seem to hear me, his gaze turned inward.

"Eva started second-guessing herself over the littlest

things. Withdrawing from me, from Lily and Rye, and relying on Clay's opinion for everything." His haunted eyes find mine. "She doesn't see it because she can't. He spun his web around her so slowly she didn't notice, and now she's wrapped up tight. Dependent on him. I don't know what to do."

Mud replaces blood in my veins, making my heartbeat sluggish. I stare at the lights of downtown, wavering like a mirage—like my entire reality.

This is a lot fucking worse than I thought. Than Lily and Rye thought. And Sophie and Matt's distress suddenly makes a lot more sense.

"I just spoke to Lily and Rye a few days ago," I murmur. "They're not fans of Clay's, but they have no idea it's as bad as you say."

Martin hears my unspoken question. "When Clay came into the picture, Lily was about to pop out a baby. She was nesting and shit. I was around Eva a lot more." His mouth pinches with guilt. "When I saw them in Seattle last year, before I quit, everything seemed great. *Eva* seemed great. I convinced myself it was all in my head, that I was projecting my own trauma onto her. And I stupidly let it go, forgetting how good these motherfuckers are at playing the long game."

Dipping his chin, he makes a choked sound. "I didn't even know Eva moved down here until I read it online. She hasn't returned my calls for months. When I saw her tonight, I wanted to throw up. She looks unwell. There's no spark in her eyes. And that dress and those heels? Come on. My Eva would never. God, I don't know what to do." He covers his mouth, muffling a sob.

Bouncing thoughts coalesce into a roiling mass of fear. My scalp prickles in warning right before vertigo hits. I swing forward, bracing my hands on my knees.

Breathe in. Hold. Breathe out.

Miraculously, my panic stalls at a rolling boil instead of overflowing into a full-blown attack.

"Oh God, are you okay? Shit—I'm an idiot. I was already planning on calling Lily tomorrow, but then I saw you..." He makes a shrill, distressed sound.

"I'm okay," I grunt.

Martin pats my back. Hesitant, light taps like he's afraid I'll take a swing at him. The thought brings a burst of caustic hilarity, which in turn dials my anxiety down another notch.

Waving him off, I straighten my spine one vertebra at a time. When I'm upright, I dig my fingers into my hair, clenching them and concentrating on the slight burn until my mind clears.

"I'm really sorry, Wilder. I shouldn't have dumped all that on you. Especially since—"

"I'm fine. Just got dizzy."

He doesn't look convinced but thankfully doesn't continue his thought, which I'm sure was something along the lines of, *Especially since there's nothing you can do or say to help her because she can't even stand to look at you.*

My breath hitches in my still-tight chest. "I'm only here in the first place because you're not the only one worried about her. So I came to see for myself. What you've said is a lot to take in. What I *saw* is a lot..." I trail off, unable to put words to the tangled knot of guilt and worry inside me.

"Hey. This isn't your fault. You know that, right?"

I'm surprised for the few seconds it takes for me to remember he heard me speak at the convention. I might not have said Evangeline's name, but I shared candidly about the guilt I carry—will always carry—for hurting the girlfriend I loved deeply. And like my sobriety, Evangeline's and my shared history is an open secret.

I look away from the knowing glint in his eyes.

"Left down the main hallway. Second door on the right." Martin's voice is low, vibrating with sudden fervor. "I left her wrapped in a blanket on the bed and half-asleep. I'll run interference if I see Clay."

My head whips toward him. His brows lift expectantly, an unmistakable challenge in his eyes.

I bark a disbelieving laugh. "Are you for real? She literally fled when she saw me. Better that I bring what you've said to her parents, to Lily and Rye, and they—"

"Maybe you're right," he interjects, his expression torn between worry and conviction. "But can you really leave without trying?"

I huff and drag a hand through my hair again, no doubt making it even more chaotic than usual. "Think you know me, huh?"

His lips twitch. "Pretty much."

I look at the house, at the door leading inside.

To her.

"Fuck it."

As I stride away, Martin calls, "Thatta boy!"

I flip him off over my shoulder, his startled laugh swallowed by voices as I part the crowd with my steps.

CHAPTER SIX

evangeline

CURLING FURTHER into an unfamiliar blanket on a stranger's bed, I bring my fists against my breastbone and press toward the ache beneath.

I don't actually hate Wilder.

I wish I could.

Maybe if he were still a drug addict, leaving the wreckage of his selfishness scattered in his wake, it would be easier. But since I'd never wish a relapse on him, I'm left instead in the itching intersection between a grudge I can't let go of and a maudlin longing that time has reshaped but not erased.

At least the years have granted me *some* clarity. Enough that I know it's not him I miss so much as the person I was before I fell in love with him. Seeing him just reminds me of that loss.

But as with everything tied to Wilder, even my clarity on the matter isn't simple. It has depth and weight. A history full of tangled shadows and glimmers of inescapable light.

No matter how much I might want to at times, I can't pull up the roots he planted inside me when we were young. They're too deep. He'll always be the boy I worshipped as a child. The teenager who read my poetry, picked up a guitar, and changed the course of our lives. The unique, complex man who opened my world with equal parts conflict and communion.

He'll always be a part of me.

I can't *not* be happy he got the help he needed and turned his life around. That his career took off and his music has garnered both success and acclaim. That he's sober, stable, and by all accounts thriving.

But feeling happy for him from afar, buffered by the life I've built for myself, is one thing. Being close enough to see the freckles in his eyes is, as tonight proved, drastically different.

It took years for the high, piercing note of my heartbreak to fade. For me to let go of Wilder, of who I thought I was to him—who I thought we were to each other—and move forward with my life.

But I did. I fucking did.

Didn't I?

My erratic thoughts clash and reform, providing a new, unwelcome dimension to my acceptance that Wilder will always be a part of me. Because if that's true, then parts of *me* were displaced as he grew. I'll never be able to heal the gaping cavities his roots dug inside me.

He'll always be my weakness.

My forever wound.

A small, pained moan shocks my ears. My gaze flies around the room for a good five seconds before I realize the sound came from me. When I do, I make another one—a hoarse laugh.

I'm officially losing it.

I have no idea how long it's been since Martin left to find Clay. There are no clocks in the room and my phone was left at home. Is it close to midnight yet? Why hasn't Clay come?

Please get me out of here.

Despite my desperate desire, when I finally hear the soft creak of the doorknob, it's not relief I feel but panic at the thought of Clay seeing me like this. Heady adrenaline shoots through my veins. I wrench upright, throwing my legs off the bed and tossing the blanket to the side.

My stomach swoops as the door swings inward, then drops like a lead weight when it isn't Clay who steps inside but a stranger paradoxically more familiar than my own reflection.

Wilder gives me a slight, close-lipped smile and shuts the door behind him. "Hey."

Speechless, I watch him sidestep a few paces before sliding to the floor. He braces his arms on his bent knees, drops his head back to the wall, and closes his eyes. The thick tendons in his forearms jump beneath black-and-gray tattoos as his long, elegant fingers move restlessly, playing a song only he hears.

Less than five feet of carpeted floor separate our toes.

"I fucking hate parties," he mutters.

I blink hard, half-expecting him to disappear, but instead he becomes more real. *Excruciatingly so*. Airbrushed memories of him collide with reality and tear something deep in my chest.

At twenty-five, he was almost ethereally beautiful. Now he's... devastating. Somehow both rougher and more refined. Potently masculine, mature, and *healthy*. Smile lines crease the skin around his eyes, the shadows of his dimples now permanent fixtures, the slope of his clean-shaven jaw even sharper. His body has changed, too, still lean but more densely muscled, his light olive skin radiant.

Movement brings my gaze to his throat. As he swallows, the wings of a gorgeously detailed moth ripple in mimicry of flight. He shifts against the wall, sighing, and a hint of his midnight-rainstorm scent reaches me. Seductive and threatening. A siren's haunting call.

I want to light him on fire.

I want to suck him in like water and drown.

He's thirty-one years old.

It's unbelievable, suddenly. So wild a notion that I choke on the urge to giggle, the pressure of holding it in nearly unbearable.

"W-what are you doing?" I finally ask. My voice is ragged. Breathy and dismayed.

Dark lashes parting, his gaze lowers to my face. His expression is inscrutable, but there's a glimmer in his eyes. One that sends more adrenaline into my system.

"Taking a break from all the drunk, annoying people outside. What are you doing?"

The casual familiarity in his voice pulls the plug on my thoughts. They pour away in a torrent, leaving a buzzing silence behind.

Wilder's lips curve to one side, deepening the adjacent dimple. "Better close your mouth before you catch a fly." His eyes flicker down. "Legs, too."

I snap my knees together, simultaneously grabbing the discarded blanket and bringing it over my lap. Embarrassment sears my face and chest—another shock, nearly nauseating in its intensity.

I can't remember the last time I blushed.

"Get out," I whisper.

Head tilting, he cups a hand behind his ear. "What was that?"

My teeth clench. "Get. Out."

He stretches his legs, crossing them at the ankle, and folds his arms over his chest. "Nah, I'm good here." He smiles slightly. "How's life these days?"

I can't speak.

Can't think.

Air rasps in and out of my lungs. My arms tremble uncontrollably.

"Did you know Emma is cutting molars?" he continues, eyebrows arched inquisitively like I'm not having a fucking aneurism five feet away. "She's the coolest. I still can't believe she calls me Why-Why. Such a trip."

My breath stills. "She does?"

"Yeah." His eyes turn so soft and warm, I have to look away. "Gotta say, though, I kind of miss her calling me Poop."

A strangled sound leaves me. "Poop?"

He hums in confirmation. "No idea how that one started." I arch a brow and he chuckles. "Fine, there was an incident. I might have had an adverse reaction that Emma thought was hilarious. In my defense, it was my first experience with explosive baby diarrhea."

I grimace. "Gross."

"The grossest. But at least she decided on calling me Poop instead of picking one of the other words I used in the moment. Lily would have freaked if she started calling me Fuck."

I bite my cheek. "She's definitely militant about the no-profanity rule."

At the thought of Lily, my flash of humor dies. My relationship with her, Rye, and Emma has changed over the last year, most drastically in the last six months. I want so badly to fix what's broken, but I don't know how. Not without making a sacrifice I'm not sure I'll survive.

Wilder's stare is heavy and probing. I look down to hide my expression, but it's too late.

"You don't belong here. This city is a vampire sucking you dry. Come home."

Anger roars through me, the welcome firestorm burning away my melancholy. "You have no idea where I belong. You think you have the right to say that? Why? Because I followed you around as a kid or because we fucked for a few weeks a million years ago? Get over yourself, Wilder. You're a footnote in my life."

His jaw hardens, arms falling to his sides as he sits up and leans forward. For a moment, I think he's going to spew equal vitriol back at me. I *want* him to—want him to say something as awful as what just came out of my mouth so I don't have to acknowledge the stinging precursor of guilt. So I can hate him again, if only for a moment.

What he says instead, in a dangerously soft voice, is worse.

"Lie to yourself all you want. I'll *always* know you. You're inside me forever, just like I'm inside you. And you belong where you always have, with your feet in the dirt between water and giant trees, moonlight shining in your hair."

The absurd words shatter like glass inside me. Tiny, bleeding wounds open all over my heart.

My belated scoff sounds alarmingly close to a sob. "I don't know what your angle is, but let's get one thing straight— you're deluded if you think I'll ever fall into your bed again."

He laughs.

The motherfucker *laughs*.

Then he stands up, stretching his arms over his head and bending from side to side like we're in a goddamn yoga class. The hem of his T-shirt rides up, exposing a few inches of skin above his belt. I tear my eyes away, but not fast enough to prevent the sight from burning itself into my brain. Two sharp, shadowed valleys of muscle arrowing toward his groin. Tattoos I've never seen before. That trail of coarse, dark hair I wish I didn't remember the feel of grazing my belly.

When he stops flaunting his stupid, ripped body, I shift my glare back to his face. He wears a knowing smirk that makes me want to kick him in the nuts.

"You thought I was flirting with you?" *Tsking*, he shakes his head, eyes bright with laughter like the joke's on me. "You've never even seen me flirt. In any case, I think we can agree that ship has sailed."

My jaw drops.

His devilish grin widens. "It was good chatting with you. Happy New Year." He opens the door, then glances back at me. "See you around, Evangeline."

He's gone before I can gasp my next breath.

CHAPTER SEVEN

evangeline

NEW YEAR'S Day dawns bright and clear. Not unexpected. What *is* unexpected is the fact I missed dawn for the first time in months. I'd blame champagne for knocking me out, but I didn't even finish my first glass.

For the last half hour, I've been sitting at the glass-top table on our terrace, nursing my second cup of coffee and picking at half of a tart grapefruit. Neither has dented my grogginess.

The kidney-shaped pool we never use glitters in the sunlight, smaller reflections dancing off damp blades of grass beyond. For once, there's an actual bite in the air. Occasional currents of cold slide beneath my robe and coil around my bare legs.

I'm still too hot.

Fuzzy-headed and floaty.

A bird lifts from a nearby palm, its passage bringing a flash of memory. Inked wings moving on golden skin. A rough shake of my head sends the errant thought away.

Focusing on the pool, I fantasize about jumping in. The water can't be more than fifty degrees, and my Pilates instructor is always talking about cold plunging and how beneficial it is. Would it feel invigorating or terrible? More importantly, would it wake me up?

My musings are derailed by the crisp, measured clicks of designer men's shoes on tile. Smoothing my expression, I turn my head toward the house. Clay approaches me, his attention on the tablet in his hands. While I have yet to change out of my pajamas and robe, he's dressed in his typical winter casual wear: pressed slacks and a lightweight cashmere sweater.

A greeting dies on my tongue when he lifts his head, revealing the scowl on his face.

I should have jumped in the pool.

"I'll get dressed in a minute. Just finishing breakfast."

Without saying a word, he sets the tablet on the table beside my plate with its listing grapefruit husk. I blink down at the screen, my pulse jumping when I see the side-by-side photographs at the top of an article from a popular magazine.

Suddenly, I'm more awake than I've been in months.

The photos are red carpet shots from the Billboard Music Awards a few months ago. One photo is of me. The other is of Wilder.

In reality, we didn't cross paths that night, and I made sure to be using the restroom when Night Theory was onstage. But whoever picked and aligned these particular photos did a masterful job at manipulating perception. We look like a couple, both in all black, similar faux-serious expressions on our faces. Even our bodies are angled toward each other, giving a subtle impression of togetherness.

My already erratic heartbeat rattles as I read the headline.

Music's Favorite Star-Crossed Lovers Spotted Together New Year's Eve

I read the opening paragraphs, my stomach dropping further with every word. Multiple people apparently saw me go into a bedroom and Wilder slip inside after me. There's no mention of Martin, who was in the room with me far longer than Wilder was, or the fact Clay found me just minutes after he left and we shared a public kiss at midnight. Because facts have no place in clickbait.

I open my mouth to say as much, but Clay snaps, "Keep reading."

The back of my scalp tingling in trepidation, I continue scrolling and realize this isn't some short fluff piece with no purpose but to generate website traffic to ads. The article is long, dense, and annoyingly well written.

First is the expected regurgitation of history: our fathers being best friends and founding members of Breaking Giants, how we grew up together and formed Night Theory in our teens. The moderate success of our first album and tour. Our electric stage chemistry and how I shocked fans when I suddenly left the band. That I didn't leave because of creative differences like our label said but because of rising conflict with Wilder. How after a three-year estrangement, we had a brief, intense affair followed by an explosive breakup. Wilder went to treatment for drug abuse. I cut him out of my life.

The accuracy of it all is jarring but not really surprising. For better or worse, we're both autobiographical songwriters and public figures. Anyone with access to the internet and time to kill could piece the same story together.

But then the article takes an unexpected turn, going from annoying to a *fuckmylife* level of alarming. According to the author—someone named Angie Irving, though it's likely a pseudonym—Wilder and I are still in love with each other. How does she know? Well, apparently every album we've written and released since our breakup is part of an ongoing love letter between us. Her theory is backed up with a shockingly thorough analysis of our individual discographies over the last six years.

It's both complete bullshit and perfectly crafted to be convincing as hell.

Fuck. This is really bad.

I lower the tablet to the table, making sure it connects silently with the glass. My senses return slowly. I become aware of my cold fingers and toes. An itch on the back of my neck. Gusting breezes whispering through bushes and trees. Birdsong and the neighbor's sprinklers. Water gurgling through the pool's filtering system.

"I've already talked to Anita," Clay says in a monotone. "A retraction isn't likely, but I might slap the magazine with a suit anyway just to make their life miserable."

When he doesn't say anything else, I know it's my cue to explain myself. But right now the only coherent thought in my head is that I hope Angie Irving and her so-called credible sources from last night are stricken with incurable rashes on their assholes.

I take a few sips of cold coffee, ignoring its bitterness, and try to come up with something to distract Clay. I need to buy myself some time to get my thoughts in order.

"I really loved that dress," I finally say. "The one from the BBMAs."

I wore the long, edgy black number against his wishes. He was pissed for days and has yet to overlook an opportunity to remind me of how ugly he thinks it was.

Sadly, he doesn't take the bait.

"Don't make me ask, Eva."

As I set down my mug, I remind myself to stick to general facts and avoid sounding defensive.

"He walked in uninvited. We had a brief conversation about Emma before I questioned his motives for speaking to me. He reassured me that he has no romantic interest in me and was merely taking a break from the party. He left. You came in a few minutes later."

There's a weighted pause. "Look at me."

Forcing myself to remain relaxed, I shift my gaze to his face. Even expecting the coldness in his eyes, it still shocks me. They used to be warm all the time.

"Is that all?" he asks.

"Yes."

He frowns at me for another moment, then looks across the backyard. "Maybe that's the spin. Childhood friends catching up." Nodding to himself, he adds decisively, "If I can't figure out a faster fix, at least we have The Golden Globes next weekend. I'll ask Anita to find out who's working the carpet and prep some questions for them. We'll rehearse your responses."

I have zero interest in attending The Golden Globes, in being photographed and dissected for consumption by the masses, but there's no point trying to get out of it. Clay's social standing, cultivated meticulously over a decade, means he's invited absolutely everywhere. Last week, he was invited to a ribbon-cutting ceremony for a butcher shop. So I guess I should be grateful he's selective about our appearances.

I make a noncommittal noise and fiddle with my robe, pulling the fabric over my knees.

Another heavy sigh floats over me. "You should have told me last night." His voice is soft now, thick with hurt that makes my blood instantly boil.

Before I can stomp the impulse, I retort, "I was distracted by the taste of someone else's lip gloss during our New Year's Eve kiss."

We both go preternaturally still.

I can't believe I said that.

Fingers grip my chin, lifting and turning my face. His eyes scan mine. "It was a forgettable mistake."

His version of an apology, as well as a reminder of how discreet he is normally. Like the fact he doesn't routinely wave his infidelities in my face means I don't have a right to be offended.

To him, our dynamic is normal. He's merely repeating patterns he witnessed between his parents when he was a child and again between his father and stepmother during his teens. Even among his colleagues and friends, I don't know of a single relationship that's monogamous.

There have been times recently that I've even wondered if what I saw growing up, what I've always wanted for myself, is nothing more than a fantasy. An aberration of modern love.

Clay's grip on my chin tightens. "Maybe if you actually enjoyed sex, I wouldn't need to find relief elsewhere. Have you considered that?"

The fire inside me burns brighter. The flame is black, though. Toxic. Biting my tongue so hard I taste copper, I roughly pull my chin from his hold and scoot my chair back. I stand and gather my plate and mug.

"I'm going to take a shower," I say as I move past him.

"Do we need to discuss this further?" he asks sharply.

What I hear instead is what he really means: do I need to be reminded of how well he takes care of me?

I shake my head, my shoulder blades squeezing together as he follows me inside. I set my dishes beside the sink, knowing that if I rinse them and put them in the dishwasher, it will set him off. There's no way I can handle one of his rants right now.

As I walk toward the hallway, he asks, "Did you take a sleeping pill last night?"

Caught equally off guard by the question and the lack of animosity in his voice, I look over my shoulder. "No."

Familiar and seductive warmth sparkles in his eyes. The sight of it ruptures my psyche, half of me relaxing while the other half remains hyper alert.

A smile curves his lips. "That's great news. How do you feel?"

Like the blade of a serrated knife, thanks.

"Good," I lie.

He tilts his head. The smile stays, but the warmth in his eyes disappears. "I hope that means you're feeling up to calling Lily today."

My stomach turns to lead even as I smile back. "Maybe."

Turning on my heel, I walk from the room.

CHAPTER EIGHT

evangeline

I have no questions left
No air to feed my breath
Emptiness the price I pay
For the love you took away

AFTER MY SHOWER, I throw on old sweatpants and a T-shirt without thinking. Halfway across the bedroom, I come to my senses and change into a gray athleisure set Clay gave me for Christmas. I'm not a fan of the style, but at least the fabric is soft.

In the hallway, I hear his voice coming from his office at the opposite end of the house. Lighthearted, charming tone. Infectious laugh. It's the voice he uses to seduce clients... and women.

It certainly worked on me.

The thought causes a flare of uncomfortable, sticky heat beneath my skin. My teeth clench.

I need to calm down before I face him again, and there's only one room in the house that's truly mine. Walking lightly so he doesn't hear my steps, I quickly head downstairs.

The bulk of the lower level is a lounge with game tables, a bar, and a widescreen TV that Clay and his friends use for their bi-weekly poker nights. Down a hallway to the left is a movie room, complete with theater seating, as well as our home gym, a guest suite, laundry, and a full bath. But tucked off a smaller hallway to my right is my studio.

Formerly a storage room, Clay had the space remodeled before I moved in. I think I've been in it a grand total of four times in six months, a fact he likes to weaponize whenever he perceives me as ungrateful.

I slip inside the room and flip on the lights, dimming them immediately when the brightness makes me wince. The door thumps closed behind me. I swiftly lock it, and my lungs expand with a deep breath. Possibly my first of the day.

The space is pretty bare-bones. Soundproofing panels. Low-pile carpet. Some basic recording equipment, none of which is plugged in. A desk, laptop, standing mic, audio interface, speakers, a mixer. My keyboard, still packed away in its giant case. Three guitars, two acoustic and one electric, likewise collecting dust.

The back wall is lined with boxes I haven't unpacked and don't care to. Bubble-wrapped, framed album art, articles, and accolades. All of Glow's awards, including a dozen Grammys.

In the living room upstairs, Clay has empty glass shelves ready to display the gold gramophones. He bugs me about unpacking them once or twice a month but hasn't demanded it yet. I'm dreading the moment. I would have left them in storage in Seattle if he hadn't personally packed them.

I can never tell him why I don't display them. Why I don't even like looking at them.

Because of Wilder.

"I can't wait to remind you of this moment twenty years from now when I'm putting up yet another shelf for your awards."

The memory makes me flinch and focus elsewhere. Unfortunately, what my eyes land on next are three boxes stacked beside the desk. They're older, the cardboard wrinkled, the tape peeling. They were definitely supposed to end up in storage, but I'd forgotten to mark them with the right label before the movers came.

Without permission, my feet carry me to them. I finger the tape on the top box, then peel it off.

Haphazardly stacked journals stare up at me, all different colors and sizes, all filled front to back with my teenage ramblings. My heart pounding, I pull a few out and set them on the desk. Then a few more. Before I can stop myself, I've removed them all to reveal what's hidden at the bottom.

Memories drift around me like distant music as I stare at the black, sticker-covered memento box. My fingers tremble as I lift it.

An unsteady step backward brings me to the desk chair, the leather sighing as I drop my weight and settle the box on my knees. The lid is warped from sitting under the combined weight of the journals. I tug until it comes free, then toss it on the desk and look inside the box for the first time in close to a decade.

There are loose, lined pages folded in fours, covered in messy words. An assortment of ticket stubs. Paper napkins littered with bleeding ballpoint ink: doodles and notes and disjointed lyrics. Sycamore leaves in various stages of life preserved by thick, yellowing tape. Cheap guitar picks and curling band stickers. The very first Night Theory fliers, which Eddie and I printed on bright pink paper to annoy Wilder. A few of our demo CDs, the plastic casings cracked and the labels faded.

My eyes land on a palm-sized, dark green journal tucked against the side. The edges are worn, softened by countless hours spent in backpacks and purses and pockets.

I grab it without considering the consequences, opening the cover to read the first page.

THIS JOURNAL BELONGS TO WILDER AND EVANGELINE.
IF YOU AREN'T US, FUCK OFF.

You're so dramatic.

I close it fast, my shuddering exhale fracturing the quiet. My fingers curl, clenching until the journal curves. When the binding crackles ominously, I throw it back in the box. Shoving the lid on, I waste no time loading it and all my journals back in the original box.

If I had packing tape, I'd reseal it. If I had a blowtorch, I'd burn them all.

Jerking to my feet, I walk around the room a few times. Consider and discard the idea of setting up my keyboard. Pause to open a guitar case, then close it when the sight of my custom Gibson acoustic makes my stomach bottom out. All while the pressure inside me builds and builds.

I resume pacing, back and forth from desk to door, faster and faster until I feel the claustrophobia that was missing when I entered the room. My thoughts churn with my legs, thrashing against their containment. Against walls I knew were there but for the first time can actually *feel*.

God, it fucking hurts.

Thanks to opening that stupid box—thanks to last night and Wilder's goddamn mouth, his unbelievable arrogance in telling me where I belonged—I *remember*. The girl I was. The girl I wanted so badly to protect but ended up caging and muting instead, little by little, over the course of years.

In hindsight, it's clear how my prison was crafted, another brick added every time I felt too much—too vulnerable or uncertain, hurt or angry or lonely. More bricks after each brief, disappointing attempt at a relationship. After lackluster sales reports, poor reviews from respected sources, a particularly vicious media cycle, a flood of critical comments online...

Every time I smiled when I wanted to scream. Said I was fine when I was flailing. Pushed forward when I wanted to rest. Avoided when I wanted to confront.

I built my mental cage to protect myself. To *save* myself. But now I'm trapped inside. Cut off from the bonds that used to give my life depth and vibrancy—my friends, my family. I'm disconnected from my own voice. From *music*.

There's only darkness and silence inside me now.

I know Lily believes I rejected the Indigo contract because of Clay's influence, but I did it out of desperation. Out of deep fear and shame for what I've been hiding from her.

The only person who knows I haven't written new material in over a year is Clay, but my confession didn't faze him. He said it doesn't matter. That when I go solo, the best songwriters in the business will jump at the chance to write for me.

When I told him I'd rather give up music altogether than perform other people's songs, he laughed and said I needed to grow up. *"Stop thinking of yourself as an artist, Eva. You're a business."*

More walls shift forward in the fog around my mind. Different dimensions of the same prison demanding acknowledgment.

I suddenly see it—who I've become. Who Lily and Rye see. My parents and brother, too.

But mostly, I see myself through Wilder's eyes.

And I hate her.

CHAPTER NINE

wilder

FRANK CLARKE WIPES a napkin roughly over his mouth, causing his bushy gray mustache and surrounding beard to expand like porcupine quills. With an exaggerated groan, he leans back in his chair and belches. Disgusted looks are thrown our way from the nearest table, but Frank just grins at me and winks.

I roll my eyes at his antics. I'd wanted to meet at the house I'm renting, but he'd breezily suggested lunch. After years of him pulling this exact shtick whenever we're both in town, I didn't bother trying to dissuade him. At least the restaurant he chose this time doesn't have a dress code and didn't require renting a plane.

The quaint, Santa Monica café may be casual, but in keeping with Frank's tastes it's highly exclusive. I hadn't even bothered with calling for a reservation myself, knowing they'd think I was lying about who I was, and instead texted my PA to do the honors.

Normally I get a kick out of bringing the burly, aging biker into social spheres he wouldn't otherwise be able to access. But the last hour has been a struggle. I'm bent out of shape about last night, exhausted and impatient. So while he's decimated his food and talked nonstop, I've barely touched mine and most of my responses have been monosyllabic.

Frank slurps his Americano contentedly. I continue pushing food around my plate, ignoring curious stares from teenagers whose wealthy parents have dragged them out for New Year's brunch.

After a few more minutes of torture, Frank finally sets his cup down and folds his hands over his belly. "Okay, champ. Why don't you tell me what's on your mind?"

I glance around one more time, reassuring myself that the closest tables are actually pretty far from us and no one is pointing a phone in our direction. I still speak softly and don't use names as I tell him everything from Matt and Sophie's impromptu visit to what happened last night.

Even without names, Frank knows exactly who I'm talking about, having been on the receiving end of my verbal vomit more times than I can count. Sober himself for three decades, he's been a drug and alcohol counselor almost as long.

I met him at Oasis, the desert treatment center where I spent three months and where he works as a group therapy facilitator. In my first week there, he took a liking to me. Apparently how deeply pathetic and ornery I was reminded him of himself at my age.

Our unlikely bond grew and was solidified when, a few days before leaving Oasis, I had a severe panic attack. Despite all the work I'd done, despite feeling mentally stable and even hopeful about the future, the impending leap back into my life—and all it signified—hit me like a train.

What sent me spiraling wasn't the impending start of Night Theory's delayed world tour; I was amped to play music again. Nor did I really care about what the press was saying about me. The problem was everything else. All the consequences of what I'd done to Evangeline, to my family, to my supportive but rightfully resentful bandmates, and the fact I'd have mere days to start repairing all my relationships before touring for months with temptations everywhere.

I was still shaking from the effects of the attack when Dr. Chastain called for Frank to join us in his office. I didn't know what was happening until Frank appeared like a prison-tattooed Santa Claus and in his usual, gruff way said, "I haven't been a roadie for forty years, but if you want some company on tour just say the word."

And that was that. With Chastain's support, Frank took a leave of absence from Oasis and came on the road with me for seven months. He's been my sponsor ever since. By the end of that tour, I'm pretty sure my bandmates and our road crew liked him more than me. My family, too. Not really surprising in hindsight. I was legitimately fucking nuts for the first year of my sobriety, on a daily rollercoaster of emotional highs and lows.

Kind of like right now.

When I've finished unloading the chaos of the last week on him, Frank studies me in silence, his lips working against the scraggly ends of his mustache. The objectively nasty habit is his tell that he's about to impart some wisdom I don't want to hear.

"She's not yours, Wilder." When I stiffen, he lifts a hand. "Before you get your panties in a twist, I'm not saying you shouldn't care or even that you shouldn't try to help, but if you only want to help her because she might fall in love with you again... well, that's selfish as shit, isn't it?"

My abdominals clench against a blow that bypasses them

and lands deep in my gut. Rubbing my hands over my face, I mumble, "What am I supposed to do?"

"The only thing I'm qualified to give you advice about is how to stay sober and not be a dick."

I drop my hands to glare at him.

He heaves a sigh. "I won't sugarcoat this for you."

"I don't want you to."

He shifts in his seat, wrinkles deepening around his eyes. "Your friend seems to be in a tough spot. Between what the man last night told you and what you observed, there are a lot of markers pointing to psychological abuse." He pauses for another round of mustache chewing. "Statistically, it takes an abuse victim seven times to leave their abuser for good. Do you know if she's tried to leave him before?"

I shake my head, my stomach roiling. "I don't. I guess I can ask…" I trail off, thinking about my phone call with Lily and Rye this morning. Their stunned silence after I told them what Martin said and what I saw with my own eyes.

They judged Evangeline harshly. Had all but written her off. And now they're sitting with the knowledge that her withdrawal and hurtful behaviors might have been cries for help.

All I could do was tell them it wasn't their fault. How were they supposed to know? Evangeline has always been a fortress, and they aren't mind readers. It's no one's fault but Clay's—and maybe mine.

Logically, I know I don't have that kind of power. But I still *feel* responsible. What if what I did to her made her more susceptible to Clay's abuse somehow?

I'm haunted by the image of her when I walked into the room last night. How she sat so still, pale and rigid on the bed. Like a broken doll, her eyes lifeless.

Frank grunts, and I realize I've curled my fingers around a

knife on the table. I release it so fast it spins and clanks against my plate.

"I want to hurt him," I confess.

"I know, bud, but you won't. Because you want to help her more."

"How?" I demand. "How do I help her?"

He shakes his head sadly. "I know you want a straightforward answer, but I don't have one other than don't confront her. Given your history, I can guarantee it won't end well."

"Agreed," I grumble, thinking about what triggered her anger last night—my ill-conceived comment about how she didn't belong in Los Angeles. I can only imagine her reaction if I told her she should leave her boyfriend because he's an abusive piece of shit.

God, the irony. It fucking *stabs*.

I was her abusive boyfriend once. Lying to her. Manipulating her to keep her at my side.

Dark emotion coils and tightens around my heart. I see it in my mind as a thick, black-scaled snake. Old and tired but still powerful. Selfish. Covetous and borderline amoral.

I'm not a perfect person just because I'm sober. Far from it. Last night I did something I swore I'd never do again—I lied to Evangeline. I told her I wasn't interested in her anymore, pretended that the idea of me seducing her was laughable.

In the moment, I hadn't wanted her to see me as one more person who wanted something from her. But I do want something. I want *everything*.

A handful of times, most recently when I heard she was dating Clay and freaked out, Frank has asked me to consider the possibility that my feelings might collapse in person. That they're not actually real. That maybe I've been holding onto the idea of us all these years to avoid facing vulnerability with someone else.

He isn't the only one who's suggested it. My parents have voiced similar concerns. Jax, Eddie, and Zander have as well. And it's been implied in one way or another by every person I've been romantically involved with over the years—usually accompanied by anger—when they invariably realize I'll never fall in love with them.

But after last night, I know they're all wrong. Ten seconds in the same room with Evangeline was all it took. No matter how much she's changed, how much I've changed, my feelings haven't. I felt the same old fire in my gut, my bones, my cock. In my fingers, itching to touch her. My tongue, burning to taste her.

I still want her. All of her. Her secrets and truths. Every thought and word, sigh and gasp. Every smile and frown and tear. If anything, my obsession is *more* now. Clearer. Purer. Unsullied by my inner conflict of the past. By my addiction, my self-hatred, my demons.

And she still wants me, too. She'd no doubt deny it, but I saw the proof. The goosebumps on her arms. The fevered intensity in her eyes as they roamed my body. Her expanding pupils. The thumping pulse in her neck. The blush that billowed like a rosy cloud over her chest and face.

Our bodies and souls still sing for each other.

Like Frank is privy to my thoughts, he says softly, "Be careful, Wilder. These situations are delicate and volatile. They're not dissimilar to the progression of active addiction in the sense there needs to be a rock bottom situation of some kind. Something that activates an urge to seek help. The only thing you can do is the same thing I'd counsel loved ones of an addict to do. Don't enable but don't judge or shame. Maintain healthy boundaries while providing a safe space for them to come when they're ready for change."

My mind latches onto two words: *safe space*. I want to be that for her so fucking badly. Can I? Is there a way to become again what I once was, before all the pain and hurt? Her confidant... her friend?

Frank drops his fist against the table. Not hard enough to alert other diners but still hard enough to jolt me from my thoughts. My gaze flies to his face. Twitching mustache. Knowing eyes.

"Stop scheming," he says gruffly.

The admonishment lands like an anvil. Annoyed by how easily he pinned me, I quip, "Yeah, yeah. The only person I have control over is myself. Can't help anyone if I take my oxygen mask off. Stay on my side of the street, et cetera."

Frank only huffs in amusement, stroking his beard with thick fingers before draping his arms on the table and leaning forward. His expression turns grave.

"Your friend didn't choose this, not like we chose drugs and alcohol. You get me?"

I nod weakly. "She's a victim."

"That's right." The sudden worry on his face makes my heart beat faster, and I know what he's going to say before he says it. "It's been a long time. Your feelings may not have changed, but..."

My mind fills in the blanks.

...but her feelings might have.

...but you're setting yourself up for heartbreak.

...but you're risking a relapse if this spirals.

...but she isn't yours.

I drop my gaze, unable to hold his. "I hear you."

Frank coughs. "I hate to bail on you like this, but I've gotta get back to Oasis." He pauses, shaking his head in mingled exasperation and fondness. "For fuck's sake, next time let me know right out of the gate that you need a serious one-on-one. I wouldn't have dragged you out to lunch or yapped so much."

I crack a smile. "Fair enough."

Part of me wishes I could go to Oasis with him. Back to the place and time when all I had to worry about was putting one foot in front of the other. Eating three meals at set times. Walking a dusty, rock-lined labyrinth at dawn and dusk. Swimming laps until my muscles burned. Learning about my anxiety, the root causes and triggers, and how to manage it sober.

In many ways, those three months were the hardest of my life. Dr. Chastain tore my head and guts apart before helping me put myself back together. But despite how painful it all was, there was a beautiful simplicity to the process.

Best of all, back then I still had hope. Naive, selfish hope that my broken heart was temporary. That when I got out, I'd make amends to Evangeline and in time she'd forgive me. Because surely our love was too big and perfect for her to walk away from.

Only it wasn't.

I thought I'd learned that lesson when I returned to Seattle, when she said all that shit on her parents' front lawn. When she took the pieces of my heart and stomped them to dust.

But apparently I'm hardheaded as fuck. Or a master of denial still clinging to a single remaining sliver of hope.

Still addicted to her and unable to let go.

"It's going to be okay, Wilder."

I nod, not meeting Frank's eyes, and signal for the check.

CHAPTER TEN

wilder

I FOLLOW Frank to the front of the restaurant, where he pauses near the host station to chat with the woman there. I stop as well but don't pay attention to their conversation, distracted by all the notifications on my phone that weren't there an hour ago.

There are texts from pretty much everyone I know, but what spikes my blood pressure are the missed calls and voice-mails. Two are from Night Theory's manager—concerning because Mack is currently in Barbados with his longtime girl-friend and his last words to me were, "Have a nice break and don't fucking call me unless someone dies."

But far worse are the six missed calls and three voicemails from our publicist.

Shelley isn't known to overreact.

My heart racing, I unlock my phone and open my text messages, bypassing my sisters and mom in favor of Jax.

His most recent message reads,

Anything you want to share with the class?
Did she actually talk to u??

Attached is a link to an online article from a big gossip magazine. The preview shows side by side images of Evangeline and me from the BBMAs, along with a headline that makes my eyebrows jump. A flare of satisfaction warms my chest, smothered almost immediately by alarm when I think about Clay reacting to this.

Has he seen it? Has *she* seen it?

Given the calls from Shelley, my guess is yes and yes.

Fuck.

Before I can click on the link, a voice asks, "Mr. Ashburn?"

I look up at Frank and the woman, who wears a gold pin on her black button-down that says MANAGER. Frank's lips are folded inward, his eyes laughing. The woman, conversely, looks like she's ten seconds from a mental breakdown.

"Yes?"

Before she can answer, the heavy front door opens and a familiar man slips inside. Sam is my usual driver-slash-security when I'm in the city. He's ex-military, mid-forties, with biceps as big as my head. His normally placid expression is intact, whereas mine has no doubt shifted to horror after what I just glimpsed outside.

Hell in the form of a swarm of hungry, buzzing paps.

Double fuck.

"Good timing," Sam drawls at me. "I was just coming in to discuss the situation. Car's out front already, but there's fifteen feet of exposure between the door and the curb."

He doesn't have to tell me they're here for me. I can hear them shouting my name now. Someone must have seen me when the door opened.

The woman steps toward us, wringing her hands nervously. "On behalf of the entire Rhubarb family, I'm so sorry about this, Mr. Ashburn. Rest assured, we're already investigating to make sure no one on our staff is responsible. If you'd be willing to wait a few more minutes, more security is on the way to assist you to your vehicle."

Frank pats her shoulder. "Don't worry, Belinda, he's not going to blame you. Ain't that right, Wilder?"

"Yeah, that's right," I say, then look away, uncomfortable with the acute relief on her face. It was probably one of the teenagers inside posting to their socials, anyway. "Is there another exit?"

Sam answers for her. "They've got that covered, too."

I sigh. "All right. Let me make a quick call, then we're out of here whether or not we have backup. I can make it fifteen feet."

He nods and shifts so he's blocking the front door. Technically, as members of the public paparazzo have the right to enter a restaurant, though they rarely do because of harassment and privacy laws. I'm still glad Sam is in the way. I'll have to deal with the vultures soon enough.

Frank claps me on the shoulder. "My bike's parked around back, so Belinda's gonna show me out. Call me, okay?"

"Will do. Thanks, Frank."

"Good luck, champ."

When he's gone, I skirt around the host station into a short hallway and dial Shelley. She picks up on the first ring, not bothering with hello.

"Happy New Year, right? Good news and bad news. The bad is that I'm hungover and my phone won't stop ringing, so thanks for that. The good news is the article is flattering. Well, maybe not flattering since it implies Eva cheated on Clay Eaton with you last night. But as I see it—"

"Hold up," I bark. "Cheated? We barely spoke for five minutes. Who the fuck said this?"

There's a minuscule pause and an equally short exhale. "You haven't read the article. Okay. In summary, unnamed people saw you and Eva sneak off to a bedroom last night. There are no photos, which is good. Also good, streaming numbers for both Night Theory and Glow have skyrocketed—"

"Nothing about this is good, Shelley," I say through my teeth. "You know there's a double standard for this shit. Even a rumor of Eva cheating will follow her in the press for years."

Her tone softens. "I know. I have more news on that front. I spoke to Glow's publicist, Anita Allman. Super weird convo, to be honest, but the moral of the story is she wants our help redirecting the narrative. I have a feeling you won't like the ask, though."

"What is it?"

"She wants you to have lunch with Eva and Clay tomorrow at Café Doux in Beverly Hills. The spin is that last night was childhood friends running into each other and catching up. Vibe for lunch is smiles and laughs all around—documented, of course. Voilà, heat's off and cheating rumors are dead in the water."

As her words sink in, my skin starts crawling. The mere thought of having to sit across from Clay and pretend like I don't want to murder him has me slumping against a wall. What if he touches her? *Kisses* her in front of me?

I don't think I can do it. I'm not that good of an actor.

When I'm silent too long, Shelley says softly, "From a PR standpoint, I have no problem with you declining. We can mitigate the backlash another way. Release a statement of our own, accept a few interview requests. Whatever you feel comfortable with."

I press a thumb to the spiking tension in my forehead. "Are you sure Eva's on board with this? With lunch?"

Shelley's voice lowers again. "That's the weird part. With the history between you guys, I was surprised she agreed. No offense."

I grunt. "None taken. Why is it weird?"

"Well, since I was so surprised, I fished a bit. Anita was cagey at first but cracked. She didn't speak to Eva at all. This is coming from—"

"Clay," I finish, his name a bitter burst in my mouth. "He's definitely orchestrating this. Dude hates me. He's probably hoping I say no so he can blame me for any fallout."

"Huh. I didn't realize you had history with him, too."

I almost smile at the poorly veiled curiosity in her voice. Knowing the details won't leave our phone call, I offer, "I dated his stepsister years ago. Around the same time, she stopped sleeping with him. He blames me for her change of heart."

Shelley chokes on air and coughs for a good ten seconds, then finally gasps out, "What in the daytime drama?"

"Less soap opera, more *Dateline*." I bite my cheek before I tell her the whole truth. "Trust me, he's not a good person."

"He sounds like a nightmare," she says seriously. "My call with Anita suddenly makes a lot more sense. She definitely doesn't like him. Is this one of those toxic-boyfriend-becomes-manager situations?"

I wince, regretting opening my mouth. "Maybe. I honestly don't know. Can we move on?"

"Of course," she says gently. "What are your thoughts about tomorrow?"

Movement down the hall turns my gaze to Sam, who jerks his thumb toward the front door. "I have to go," I tell Shelley. "Leaving a restaurant surrounded by paps."

"Ah, how delightful. Not that you need the reminder, but—"

"Neutral expression and keep my mouth shut," I say dryly.

"Exactly. Call me in ten?"

I move toward Sam. "My brain doesn't work at your speed, Shelley. Give me an hour to think it over."

"You got it. Oh, and don't worry about calling Mack. That was my bad. I forgot he was on vacation when I was trying to track you down. Talk soon."

She hangs up just as I reach Sam and two nervous, rent-a-cop-looking guys, presumably from the restaurant's security company. The noise from outside has definitely increased in volume. I wince when a woman's scream confirms that the crowd now includes fans—rabid ones who will drop everything and risk speeding tickets to get wherever I've been spotted.

Belinda hovers before the archway leading to the dining room, a forced smile on her face. Standing beyond her is a family clearly waiting to leave. The kids gape at me while their parents give me double stink-eye.

"Sorry about this," I tell Belinda. "I'll be out of your hair in a sec."

She rejects my apology with another one of her own, but she's clearly frazzled and wants me gone.

The security guys introduce themselves to me as the four of us approach the door. I forget their names as soon as they're spoken, a hundred percent of my mental effort focused on preparing myself for extreme sensory overload.

Inhale. Hold. Exhale.

When Sam looks back at me, I nod. He opens the door and pandemonium erupts. Shouts and screams and bodies rushing, pressing, shoving. Every step toward the black car at the curb feels like a mile-long sprint. My breath is shallow, muscles tight, heart racing, but my face reflects none of my inner turmoil.

"Wilder! Wilder, over here!"

"Are you in L.A. to see Eva?"

"Look this way!"

"What happened in the bedroom last night, Wilder?"

"MARRY ME, PLEASE!"

"Wilder! Is Eva leaving Clay Eaton for you?"

When the car's back door opens, I manage to slip inside calmly instead of diving. Sam forces his way around the hood while a crying woman yanks on the handle of my locked door and people jostle each other to get a good camera angle through the windshield.

Sam makes it inside, cursing as someone tries to crawl in with him. When he finally gets his door closed sans interloper, his eyes meet mine in the rearview.

"We'll have to take the long way home."

Meaning, he'll have to lose however many cars are already waiting to tail us or risk leading them to my rental.

I want to tell him to take me straight to the private airport in Van Nuys. Every instinct is screaming for me to go home. But I can't. If I bail now, it means abandoning Evangeline to deal with the mess I unintentionally made in her life last night. Poisoning her mind further against me. Leaving her at the mercy of Clay and the rumor mill.

So instead of taking the easy way out, I smile faintly. "Figured. Thanks, man."

"You got it."

The security guys clear the crowd enough for us to pull away from the curb. It's slow going for a block, the main road congested by people slowing to gawk. As soon as traffic opens up, Sam's takes advantage and does what he does best, taking

371

our followers on a merry chase until, close to an hour later, we're in the clear.

By the time he pulls through the gate at my rental, I've read the article several times and cycled through an emotional spectrum ranging from joy to despair. I also texted with Jax and Rye and called my mom, who I shamelessly tasked with updating Evangeline's parents.

When I walk inside the house, I finally call Shelly back with an answer about tomorrow. She isn't thrilled but neither is she surprised.

No part of me is looking forward to sitting under the scrutiny of cameras while pretending I'm happy to share a meal with the woman I love and her abuser.

But for Evangeline, I'll do it.

I'd do much worse for her.

A few minutes after I hang up with Shelley, she emails me two documents bearing the logo of her PR firm. *Smalltalk Prompts and Socializing Tips for Introverts*, and *Body Language in the Public Eye*.

The attached email is brief and almost makes me laugh.

No, these weren't written with you in mind. Okay that's a lie. They're totally about you.

You'll do great. Just be yourself.

Being myself tomorrow will mean leaving the restaurant in handcuffs. Since I'm not down to spend a night in jail—or more likely, the rest of my life—I guess that means I'll have to be someone else.

I'll have to lie. Again.

And hope someday Evangeline will understand why.

CHAPTER ELEVEN

evangeline

WE'RE GOING to be late.

Since Clay is never late unless he intends to be, it's a power play. He wants Wilder to have to sit alone and wait for us. I have no idea what advantage he thinks it will bring, but either way it's asinine.

Not that I'm in a hurry. But I also want to get this over with.

"You didn't come to bed last night."

They're the first words he's spoken to me since we left the house and the third sentence today. No concern evident in the tone, just reproach. Like I'm a defiant child who intentionally stayed up past bedtime.

I'm not the only one who picks up on the immediate tension in the car. Our driver, Phillip, glances at us in the rearview before turning on the radio to give us an illusion of privacy. The Escalade is spacious but not *that* spacious.

With an internal sigh, I turn from the window to face Clay. He doesn't look at me, continuing to scroll through sports statistics on his phone. But he's waiting.

"I lost track of time in my studio and crashed in the bedroom downstairs."

I don't care whether or not he believes me. It's his fault I couldn't sleep in the first place, since he agreed to this insanity on my behalf. There was no way I was going to be able to turn my head off last night, so I didn't even try.

I ended up watching mindless television for hours to avoid thinking about this ridiculous PR stunt. About Wilder. About the flood of messages and voicemails on my phone since the article came out. From Lily and Rye, Martin, my parents, my brother. From my publicist, manager, and my PA, Sandra.

Most of all, though, I needed distraction from the disquiet I've felt since opening that box in my studio—the eerie feeling that maybe my insomnia isn't actually an inability to sleep, but sleep of a different kind. One I can't wake up from. One that has slowly taken me so far from myself I no longer know who I am.

Clay tilts his head at my answer but otherwise doesn't respond. If I wasn't adept at reading his micro-expressions, I'd believe he was relaxed right now. Ambivalent about going to lunch with Wilder. But there's strain around his eyes and his left pinkie twitches intermittently against his phone.

He's just as anxious as I am.

"This is pointless," I mutter, tugging on the hem of my too-short dress. "I'm honestly shocked Anita suggested this."

I'm likewise shocked Wilder agreed to it. Six years ago, he wasn't a fan of Clay's. I don't quite remember why, only that he told me he didn't like him on the night of Glow's first showcase. Maybe something to do with his ex, Kendra, and the fact Clay is her stepbrother?

That whole evening is a blur in my memory. Mostly because it was so intense for Lily and me, but partly because it exists in a padlocked mental closet along with the majority of that month of my life.

Maybe Wilder doesn't care one way or the other about Clay these days, but I know for a fact Clay despises him. I also know why.

Despite their seven-year age difference, Clay and his stepsister were extremely close growing up. They remained that way until Kendra met Wilder. She fell in love with him. He got her hooked on painkillers before dumping her... for me. Not long after, Kendra left Seattle. She hasn't spoken to anyone in the family for years. All Clay knows is that she's been in and out of rehabs since and is living back East somewhere.

If there's anyone who has a reason to hate Wilder, it's Clay. Which means he isn't doing this for himself. He's sacrificing his peace because he thinks it's best for me, for my reputation.

My irritation softens and fades. I reach across the back seat and touch his thigh. He finally lowers his phone, shifting cold eyes to my face. I ignore the instinct to retract my hand.

"We don't have to do this, Clay."

"Yes, we do," he says, his voice low and rigid.

I make myself smile. "This will blow over soon enough. Tomorrow there will be a new story, a different drama."

He scoffs. "I won't be cuckolded by the media, Eva, and definitely not by the waste of oxygen that is Wilder Ashburn. So put a smile on your face and play the part. Consider it your due for landing us in this situation to begin with."

Dumbstruck, I recoil to my side of the back seat. He returns his attention to his phone. I study his profile, searching for *something*, but he's wearing his courtroom expression. Perfectly composed and aloof.

Another one of my mental walls crumbles. More awareness floods in.

I swim through tangled, murky thoughts until Phillip pulls up to the entrance of Café Doux. Then I shove the mess in my head behind a mental door and slam it closed.

By the time I exit the car and walk inside with my arm wrapped around Clay's, I've become who I need to be. The transition is surprisingly easy, fueled by the adrenaline pouring through my veins. The incessant butterflies in my stomach are just a side effect.

It doesn't mean anything that those butterflies multiply exponentially when the hostess leads us to a private, shaded patio and I see the man sprawled in apparent ease at a corner table. A man who turns his head as we approach. Who rises gracefully to his feet, a welcoming smile on his face.

Wilder's smile never falters as he shakes Clay's hand. They exchange pleasantries, and several people stationed discreetly around the otherwise empty patio take photos. The men laugh. Camera shutters click rapidly.

This can't be real.

Wilder turns to me with an easy grin. It looks so effortless, so *unlike him*, that for a moment I'm convinced I'm asleep. The feeling intensifies when I blink and see a flash of light— an instant sunrise behind my eyes—and hear leaves rustling in an imaginary wind.

"Great to see you, Eva."

His hands cup my shoulders, twin flashpoints of heat. His kiss to my cheek is there and gone, the flutter of passing wings after a midnight rainstorm.

Still not convinced this isn't a nightmare, I smile at him with counterfeit joy. "You, too. I'm so glad we could squeeze in a lunch while you're in town."

There's a flash of wry amusement in his eyes, so fast I

wonder if I imagined it, then he's sitting back down. We're all sitting. Ordering iced teas and appetizers. Chatting about the weather and traffic, about the city's ongoing efforts to rebuild after the devastating fires a few years ago.

Clay holds my hand. Touches my back. Strokes my thigh. I ignore the way my skin hums with discomfort. When he nuzzles my ear and kisses my cheek in the same spot Wilder did, I smile like his casual affection is normal and welcome. Like it doesn't rub against the emotional bruise left by our conversation in the car.

Wilder tells a story about remodeling his house and a family of ducks that put construction back months.

We laugh.

Clickclickclick go the cameras.

Over our meals—steaks for the men, a dressing-free salad for me—Clay brings up the Grammys next month, congratulating Wilder on Night Theory's nomination for Best Rock Performance for their song, "Gray Matter." Then he asks if he thinks they'll win.

Wilder's eyes sharpen; Clay's smile widens. I stiffen, my gaze flickering to the nearest cameraman and the phone sitting on the table beside him. We all know our conversation is being recorded, that whatever Wilder says could very well end up in print.

I hold my breath until Wilder chuckles and says offhandedly, "We're up against some of my favorite songs and artists from last year, so I'll be happy no matter the outcome." Forest-toned eyes slide to me and soften. "Glow's up for three, right? Ready to add another shelf?"

My heart cartwheels in my ribcage, elevating my pulse and sending a wave of warmth up my neck. In my head, a locked door rattles ominously.

As I suck in a breath, I finally accept that I'm undeniably and unfortunately awake.

Clay's fingers tighten on my thigh to the point of pain, eliciting another gasp. Wilder's eyes narrow. He opens his mouth, but Clay interjects brightly, "You'll be thrilled for whoever wins, won't you, my love?"

"Absolutely," I intone, then place my napkin beside my plate. "If you'll both excuse me? Too much iced tea."

I push my chair back, forcing Clay to release me or risk an awkward struggle. He flashes me a sharp grin. "Hurry back."

I nod.

Smile.

My thigh throbs as I walk away.

CHAPTER TWELVE

wilder

EVANGELINE'S ACT IS FLAWLESS, but I see right through it. Maybe because I learned how to behave through observation and mimicry as a child, I'm able to recognize when someone else is presenting a false front. Pick up on subtle cues others would miss. But I think the truth is both simpler and more convoluted.

I just know *her*.

The broken, angry woman on New Year's Eve was miles closer to the real Evangeline than the version striding away from our table.

Four-inch heels clack expertly over tile, the muscles in her calves bunching starkly on each step. Shiny, white-gold hair bounces in its high ponytail.

In no world can she be comfortable. Not in those shoes. Not in that tight white dress that does nothing to conceal the jut of her ribs. And the fact she ordered a salad without dressing? Iced tea with no sugar? It's beyond disturbing. Like seeing a snow leopard declawed and defanged, brainwashed into thinking they're a gazelle.

But then I recall her gasp and the flash of pain in her eyes when I asked about Glow's Grammy nominations. The clenching of her jaw when Clay answered for her.

She's still in there... somewhere.

"We're done for today."

Clay's words are for the photographers, who obediently pack their equipment and file from the room. I watch him warily as he lifts a finger to beckon our dedicated server.

"Scotch on the rocks."

The man's eyes move to me. "And for you, sir?"

"Nothing, thanks."

With a polite nod, the server turns to leave, but Clay stops him with another arrogant lift of his finger.

"Hold the drink for five minutes and close the doors. If she tries to return, have the chef give her a tour of the kitchen or something."

"Very good, sir." Eyes lowered, he slips across the patio on silent feet. On his way out, he closes glass-paned French doors.

Here we fucking go.

Clay wastes no time dropping the pretense of friendliness, shifting instantly into what Eddie would call Yacht Guy Dickhead Mode. Draping an arm over Evangeline's empty chair, he manspreads in his designer slacks and sighs like his balls are relieved. But the key to the personality type—which Clay nails—is looking relaxed *and* like there's a baseball bat shoved up his ass.

As I wait for whatever intimidation tactics he has planned, I'm extra grateful for my hour-long meditation this morning and the phone calls with Frank and my dad. But what really allows me to stay calm in response to his smug smile and air of superiority is the primal, unspoken communication between our egos.

We both know my dick is bigger than his.

Eventually Clay realizes he won't win a staring contest with me. His chin lifts imperiously. "I hope you know what's happening here."

I smirk. "Aww, are you trying to thank me?"

His smile vanishes. "I should have known you'd be too stupid to understand."

I roll my eyes. "Why don't you enlighten me."

Lowering his arm, he leans forward. "This will be the last time you speak directly to Eva. She belongs to *me*."

Rage unfurls in my gut. I let it out in a slow exhale so it doesn't taint my next words. "Wow, Clay. Join us in the current century. These days we don't own women." I tilt my head. "I wonder how Eva would feel about what you just said?"

"You actually think she's capable of thinking for herself? That's precious."

Even aware that he's baiting me, I still tense. "If you believe that bullshit, you don't know her at all."

With an unnerving smile, Clay relaxes back in his seat. "To the contrary, it's you who doesn't know her. Let me let you in on a little secret. Eva thinks and does whatever I tell her to because unlike you, I have her best interests in mind. I know exactly what she needs."

My molars grind. "Is that right? Let me guess, she needs you dictating her career like you already dictate her personal freedoms. You want to launch her as a solo act. Turn her into another boring, overproduced pop star. I bet you already have the Big Three chomping at the bit to sign her and a dozen brand deals in the pipeline, huh?"

He doesn't bother faking offense, instead shrugging casually. "What can I say? I have a gift for the big picture, and I've had my eye on this particular one for years. Thanks, by the way, for removing yourself from view early on. A little disappointing how long it took her to get her shit together afterward, but it worked out in the end. In fact, you primed her quite well."

I hate him. I really, really fucking hate him. And he knows it, his smile turning even more smug.

"Realistically, Eva has another four, maybe five years of peak marketability. I plan to use them. Then, of course, there will be residencies and other ventures. Who knows, maybe a Glow reunion album or two. And let's not forget the two kids raised by nannies and the vacation home in Turks and Caicos."

Fury and helplessness bleed my thoughts red. My knuckles itch to punch the smarmy look off his face.

I need to end this before I end *him*.

"Does she know all you care about is objectifying and commodifying her?"

His eyes glitter with malice. "What she knows is her place, which is doing exactly what I fucking say. And it's past time you learned your place, Wilder. Let me put this in plain terms: if you come near her again, I'll gladly destroy your reputation and end your career."

And... I'm done.

I hit Stop Recording on the phone in my lap, then tuck the device into my pocket and stand.

"Threats from an Eaton, how tediously familiar. Sorry to cut this short—really, I'm enjoying myself—but your five minutes are up."

I saunter around the table, forcing Clay to either stand or be at eye level with my crotch. He shoves his chair back and rises, then plants his feet and puffs up his chest like he's a tough guy.

I invade his personal space until I'm close enough to smell his overpriced cologne and hair wax. Close enough for him to be painfully aware of our height difference, how I'm looking *down* at him. Then I let my mask drop, revealing how close I am to letting myself off the leash. That if it weren't for Eva, his physical health would be in serious fucking jeopardy right now.

When I brush imaginary lint off his shoulder, he flinches.

It makes me smile.

"Speaking of Eatons, how *is* Kendra these days?" I pause, enjoying the vein that begins to pulse in his temple. "Ah, that's right. You wouldn't know, would you, *big brother*? Well, I'm sure you'll be relieved to hear she's doing great. She's happy, and more importantly, she's safe."

At the unmistakable ring of honesty in my words, the blood drains from his face. Then rage brings it right back in an unflattering flush.

"You piece of shit," he spits. "Tell me where she is."

Grabbing the top of his shoulder, I slowly increase the pressure of my grip as I angle my mouth to his ear. "I will never fucking tell you where she is, but I'll let *you* in on a little something. She still has the Eaton box of secrets. So how about this? You never threaten me or tell me what to do again, and I won't send Eva the recording I made of our fun little conversation... today, at least."

He jerks, muscles bunching as he tries to break my hold. I just squeeze harder, slapping his hand away when he tries to grab my arm.

"Do we have a deal, Clay?"

"Fine," he hisses, "but mark my words, you're going to regret this."

I chuckle darkly. "That's just one of the many differences

between you and me. I'm not afraid of bad press. And we both know there's nothing you can throw at me that I can't return doubled. *With receipts.*"

Releasing his shoulder, I give it a final pat, hard enough to make him stumble back. I watch dispassionately as he struggles for composure, his nostrils flaring, chest heaving, hands clenching and unclenching. Sadly, this is likely one of the few times in his pampered life that he's felt powerless.

At the sound of the patio doors opening, I look up and smile at Evangeline. She pauses on the threshold, her eyes narrowing on us. Our server shifts nervously behind her, Clay's scotch in his hands.

"What's going on?" she asks, her gaze sliding to Clay's back. He doesn't turn around, likely because his balls are in his armpits and his face still resembles an eggplant.

My smile softening, I walk toward her. "Just thanking Clay for lunch. I have a flight to catch."

The closer I get to her, the more her body reacts. I relish the small hitch in her breath, her subtly dilating pupils, and the ribbons of rose that sweep across her cheekbones.

For the first time today, her control over her expression falters. Vacuous neutrality vanishes. Bemusement shifts to wariness, which turns into a scowl of defiance. Her chin juts up, eyes flashing as I stop right in front of her.

There she is.

A sense of rightness warms my chest. I'm still the only one she can't hide from. The only one who can read her music.

She knows it. I know it.

The whole fucking world knows it.

Giving in to impulse, I gently cup her head and place a soft kiss on her brow. She tenses. And when I drop my mouth to her ear, she stops breathing.

"410 Coves Lane, Madrone Island," I whisper. "Anytime, for any reason. No expectations or strings attached. I will always be here for you, as a friend, no matter what."

Releasing her, I allow myself a final glimpse of her face: searching eyes, flushed cheeks, lips parted in shock.

Then, against every instinct, I walk away.

chorus

chorus : *the section of a song that encapsulates the lyrical message.*

CHAPTER THIRTEEN

evangeline

Turned out the lights
Lost all my lessons
Sunk into shadows
And now here I am

In the darkness
In the empty
Again

IN THE WEEKS since that excruciating lunch, things have been different between Clay and me.

Clay has been different.

I was on edge for days afterward as I waited for him to share all the flaws in my performance. For him to accuse me of smiling too often, talking too much or not enough, or not hiding my disgruntlement at eating a dry salad while the men had juicy steaks.

My biggest fear, though, was that he'd demand I tell him what Wilder said to me right before he left. I crafted a dozen potential responses. A dozen ways to deflect. But he's only brought up lunch once, and that was an offhand comment about the success of our ploy.

Instead, from the moment we got in the car to drive home, he's been kind. More than kind—he's been warm and charming and engaged, just like he was when we first started dating. There have been no critiques of my body, clothes, or sleep habits. No coldness, indifference, or disdain.

When I come down with a horrible cold right before The Golden Globes, he shrugs it off and stays home, plying me with medicine, tissues, and soup. When I have a particularly painful period and spend all day in pajamas in front of the television, he doesn't insinuate that I'm lazy. He brings me my favorite chocolate and a heating pad.

There have been other changes, too. He's started coming home from work in time to have dinner with me. He hasn't dragged me to parties or events. He doesn't bring up Glow or my standing appointment with a Sony music executive.

I'm not proud of it, but I test the boundaries of our new peace a few times. But nothing ruffles him. Not when I tell him I'm tired of toast and want more breakfast options. Not when I go shopping and come home with a bunch of black clothes.

Even though part of me stays wary and waiting for the other shoe to drop, as weeks pass, I begin to relax. My sleep improves, which does wonders for my energy, stability, and clarity. Slowly, I step back into my life.

My parents are overjoyed when I begin calling them a few times a week. Receptive to my unwillingness to talk about myself, they stick to safe topics like my brother's newest girlfriend, the painting my mom is working on, and my dad's new whittling hobby that will last, at best, another month or two.

One day, I impulsively send Rye a meme. He sends one

back, and before I know it, we're exchanging them daily. Around the same time, I ask Lily for photos of Emma, which become routine video calls. At first, my goddaughter doesn't seem to know who I am—a fact that hurts more than it should since she's literally a baby. But it doesn't take long for Lily to start sending me videos of Emma asking if "Aun-jelly" can sing to her.

I start playing guitar again, too. For a few minutes a day at first, then a few hours. My calluses reform. Soreness in my arms and back peaks and fades.

The more I play, the more I *listen*, the more I come to understand that music never left me. I was the one who turned my back on music. And with that realization, a floodgate opens.

I overflow lyrics and melodies.

Mixed with my relief is guilt over keeping the news from Clay. I tell myself it's because I don't want to jinx the return of my muse, but it's really because I'm not writing solo pop songs.

I'm writing the next Glow album.

Telling him would be more than a test of our relationship—it would be a crucible. And although there are moments wherein I sense the crossroads ahead of me, I'm not ready to face it. Not yet. Not even as every song I write pulls down another wall inside me. Opens another door of memories.

I'm remembering myself, who I was before I became the very thing I was most afraid of—the endless, uncaring dark.

And if I'm remembering someone else at the same time? Seeing our past anew through a wide-angled lens? Finding comfort in his promise the last time I saw him?

There's nothing I can do about it.

He is, after all, a part of me.

♪

TUESDAY EVENING, the week of the Grammys, begins like every other recent night. Clay comes home from work, spends forty-five minutes in the gym, then showers and joins me in the formal dining room with its too-large table and uncomfortably stiff chairs.

Over salmon with mushroom risotto—I hate mushrooms, but it's Clay's preferred Tuesday meal—he tells me about winning a copyright case in court today. I respond exactly as I'm supposed to, with effusive praise, while ignoring the dread and determination sitting side by side in my chest.

When Clay finishes eating, he signals to our chef, Paul, who moves forward to clear dishes from the table. I shift in my seat, uncomfortable as always with the power differential.

In his late sixties, Paul works tirelessly for us every morning and most evenings. On Sundays, he's here almost all day, prepping lunches for the week. He does his best to make my restrictive menu flavorful, sneaks me chocolate chip muffins a few times a month, and chats with me whenever Clay isn't home.

Lifting my plate, Paul eyes my untouched pile of risotto like it personally pains him. Before he can ask to make me something else as he does every week, I smile warmly and shake my head. It's hard enough sitting here while he waits on us; no way am I making him work more than he already does. No matter how hungry I am.

"It was delicious Paul, thank you," I murmur, and he gives me a soft smile. "Have you thought any more about a vacation? I bet Laurie would love a trip to see your grandkids."

He glances furtively across the table. "I haven't, no." He beats a hasty retreat. I open my mouth, then close it and frown.

"Inciting rebellion among the staff?"

Clay's smile is teasing, but there's a coolness in his eyes I haven't witnessed for a few weeks. The sight is oddly comforting, like slipping back into a familiar, if painful, reality.

"Just making sure they're happy," I say flippantly, then continue before I lose my nerve. "I know it's game night and the guys will be here soon, but can we talk about this weekend for a minute?"

His smile brightens. "Have you changed your mind about Friday night?"

"Ah, no. I haven't."

Goodbye smile.

"I'm disappointed to hear that. You already turned down the invitation to perform, but skipping the gala, too?" He shakes his head. "Terrible decision, not to mention lazy of your manager to allow it."

I have no idea why, but I want to laugh. His tone is so autocratic it's theatrical. Resisting a childish urge to mock it, I reply, "Regardless, I haven't changed my mind."

Clay lifts his wine glass, swirling the dark liquid before taking a sip. "This casual throwing away of free publicity," he murmurs, eyes flashing up to mine, "is it going to become a habit?"

My internal levity disappears. "I've worked myself to the bone for years, Clay. I've earned some rest. Mallory knows this."

He sniffs. "Moving on. What did you want to talk about?"

Steeling myself, I forge ahead. "As I've already mentioned, Lily and Rye are renting a house at the beach this weekend. I've decided to spend Sunday with them and get ready there. You're welcome to join us, or if you'd rather not, we'll be ready for the limo at three."

For five long seconds, he doesn't say anything. While I

can't see his anger, I can feel it, clawing and crawling all over me. I sit still, my heart pounding in anticipation of an argument.

But then he smiles and shrugs. "That's fine. Send me the address, and I'll pick you guys up at three."

I don't relax.

Not when he tosses his napkin on the table and stands. Not when he drops a kiss on my head, squeezes my shoulder, and tells me he's going to get ready for game night. Not even when he leaves the room.

As Paul returns to clear the silverware, I stare at the wood-grain surface of the table and ignore his worried glances. I wait to feel what I *should* feel. But there's no sense of victory. No relief.

Instead, a memory slips into my mind. The voice of Wilder's great-aunt, Katherine, speaking to five-year-old me after I fell and hurt myself playing outside.

"Did you know that when dams are built, they have to have outlets and spillways? No? Well, I want you to imagine a very bad storm, or even just lots and lots of rainy days. If there are no outlets for all that unexpected water, the reservoir behind the dam will overflow and flood the area. Eventually, the dam itself will crack under the pressure of everything it's holding back."

I'd barely understood what she was saying, but I remember vividly how I'd felt. Pressurized and overfull. Poised on the cusp of violent expansion.

I feel the same way now.

But unlike back then, no tears come. There's no spillway. No parents waiting to fuss over my skinned knees and face, no seven-year-old Wilder to tell me I'm going to have cool scars and make me laugh.

I'm alone at my breaking point.

"Eva?" asks a gentle voice. "Can I get you anything else?"

I blink up at Paul. "I'm fine, thank you."

He hesitates, radiating fatherly concern, and I manage a smile. "You should take a vacation, Paul."

He winks. "I will if you do."

I laugh, and though it's mostly for his sake, when he leaves the room, he goes unknowing of the gift he gave me with those few kind words.

A tiny spillway—a reminder I'm not alone. Or rather, that I don't have to be.

CHAPTER FOURTEEN

wilder

TELL ME YOU FEEL THIS
HEAR ME SCREAMING
AS I CARVE OUR NAMES
IN THE SYCAMORE TREE

"I SHOULD LEAVE before she gets here, right?"

Rye throws a handful of peanuts in his mouth, chomping them as he tracks me with squinted eyes. "First, you've gotta stop pacing. You're making me dizzy and blocking my ocean view. Second, where are you going to go? You're literally staying in the house with us."

"The guys have suites near the arena. I can go hang with them." I stop at the corner of the couch he's sprawled on. "Hasn't anyone told you it's gross to talk with your mouth full?"

Lily's disembodied voice answers, "A million times, Wilder!"

Rye rolls his eyes, brushing peanut dust off his chest. "Hilarious, my love," he calls back, then says to me, "Don't trust her. Last week she put leftovers in a cabinet instead of the fridge, then freaked out when there was an unidentified smell in the house. She wanted me to call nine-one-one because she was convinced it was a gas leak."

"I heard that," Lily says as she chases a giggling Emma into the living room.

Rye's mom, Kat, follows the pair. With deft precision, she circumvents her daughter-in-law to pick up the nap-escapee. She murmurs to Lily, then gives us a cheerful wave before carrying a squirming Emma back down the hallway.

Lily flops onto a love seat. "Your mom is a godsend, full stop."

Rye, his mouth full of peanuts again, wisely nods instead of speaking.

"Sleep regression is brutal," Lily says to me, then yawns so hugely her jaw cracks.

My mind still mid-spiral, I squint at her. "Sorry, sleep-what?"

"Regression. Remember when you watched Emma last week and she refused to nap? Imagine that twenty-four seven. We're a minimal-sleep household at the moment, hence the leftovers in the pantry."

"Also why we told you to pick the farthest bedroom from us," adds Rye. "You're welcome, by the way."

"Ah. Thanks." I glance at my watch. "Not to be totally self-centered—sorry about your parent life—but can we get back to my question? I don't want to make Evangeline uncomfortable. Do you think I should leave?"

Rye grins. "No way. If you bail, it'll be super obvious to everyone that you're a big baby chicken."

"Wow," I deadpan.

Lily snorts, then tells me, "Stay. She knows you're going to be here. And you want to see her, don't you?"

I palm the back of my neck, squeezing to relieve the tension that's been there since I woke up. "Of course I want to see her."

Rye sits up, finally realizing I need him to take me seriously. "What are you worried about?"

"I just have a bad feeling," I admit. "I know you said she's been acting more like herself the last couple of weeks. Sophie and Matt told me the same thing. But you guys heard the recording—all the foul shit Clay said about her. And now suddenly she's writing Glow's next album, wants to come up to Seattle to record this summer, and is hanging here solo all day? Something isn't adding up. What's changed?"

Lily chews her lip. "I don't know. I haven't asked about Clay because I haven't wanted to scare her off. At the risk of sounding naive, maybe she's finally realizing what a monster he is and is gearing up to leave him?"

"Maybe." Though I try, I can't keep the skepticism from my voice.

Rye glances between us. "Let's hope for the best."

Not wanting to kill the mood any more than I already have, I nod a few times before turning to gaze out a giant picture window at the ocean.

When I heard Evangeline was reaching out again to her friends and family, that she was working on Glow songs, I was initially optimistic. Unfortunately, overthinking is my brain's default mode. It wasn't long before I was chewing on other, darker possibilities, the worst of them being that because of my meddling, Clay changed tactics. I know damn well he didn't trip and land on how to be a good person. What worries me is that he's pretending to be one and she's falling for it.

Beyond the glass, the Pacific glitters in the morning sunlight, blue water mottled by stretches of foam, seaweed, and darker currents. I follow a set of waves, tracking its transformation from distant swells to whitewater on the beach. Then I find another set and another.

My awareness of the room fades, the vastness and rhythm of the ocean reminding me that I'm one fleeting, fragile life on a planet four and a half billion years old. Measured against the scope of time, my worries are minuscule and absurd.

But I guess that's part of being human—the intrinsic struggle between irrelevance and ego. Even though I can accept that my emotions aren't facts, they often feel tangible. Powerful and overwhelming, like a never-ending set of waves pummeling my shore.

Lost in a mini-meditation where I imagine that instead of sand, I'm a wave indifferent to fear or heartache, I miss the soft chime of the doorbell. I don't notice Rye and Lily leaving the room. Nor do I hear a single set of footsteps approaching me.

But then, like my cells are coded to react to Evangeline's nearness, I sense her. My skin vibrates, the hairs on my neck lifting. My lungs instinctively expand to bring her closer.

My missing piece.

Her advance is tentative, with several long pauses during which I struggle not to turn around. As hard as it is, I wait.

Come here, baby, I coax silently. *I won't bite.*

When she finally appears a few feet away, I give myself permission to look at her. Baggy sweatpants, white T-shirt, and flip-flops. Hair in a messy bun, no makeup covering the sprinkle of freckles on her nose. Arms crossed tightly over her chest. Eyes on the ocean. Chin slightly uplifted. Lips lightly pursed.

You're so fucking gorgeous, Fairy.

Like she hears my thought, her gaze flickers to me. The moment our eyes meet, hers snap back to the window.

"Great view," she says.

My face spasms as I hold back a grin of triumph. "Yep. Pretty much the only thing I like about this city."

"Hating L.A. is such a cliché, Wilder. What's not to love? We have sunshine and beaches. Oh, and don't forget smoothies and avocados."

The thick sarcasm in her voice has the unfortunate side effect of sending blood rushing to my cock. I quickly tuck my hands in my pockets to minimize the evidence, grateful I traded sweats for jeans this morning.

"I don't actually hate it here," I murmur. "I probably just resent that I can't experience it. I wish I could hit up a taco truck and spend an afternoon at the beach." I pause, wincing. "That probably sounds super whiny and ungrateful."

Surprising me, she shakes her head. "No, I get it." She hesitates, and I hold my breath until she continues. "Do you think if our dads weren't our dads, we still would have felt the compulsion for all this? The career, the fame, this... life?"

Facing her, I lean a shoulder on the window frame. Casual, like this is no big deal. Just your average, deep-as-fuck conversation between lifelong friends.

Inside, I'm exploding.

"I think so," I say carefully. "I've wanted to make music from the moment I first held a guitar, and I vividly remember you singing before you could even talk. That being said, it would have been a lot harder for me to make it to this level."

She gives me a dubious look. "How so?"

"If certain doors hadn't already been open because of my dad, I think we both know my personality would have been a major roadblock."

The glimmer of humor in her eyes makes me glad I'm already leaning on something.

"You seem to do okay with the whole *peopling* thing nowadays."

I grin at her. "Are you agreeing I was an asshole?"

Her gaze returns to the window, but her lips curl in the cutest little smile. "Maybe."

My chuckle reaps an immediate reward: her answering shiver of awareness. It's a challenge not to entertain a fantasy of mapping her goosebumps with my tongue. Good thing I'm a pro at abstinence.

Pulling my gaze from her, I find a wave to focus on. "That compulsion you mentioned—I think everyone has it. We all want to be known and heard, validated and loved. As artists, we simply have a public, defined space to ask for that feedback. The key to staying happy, at least for me, is maintaining perspective. My music is a reflection of me, sure, but it's also just one part of the whole. So I try to remember that no matter how loud a million strangers are, their feedback isn't nearly as valuable as the voices of those who see all of me."

Feeling Evangeline's stare, I glance at her and immediately tense. She looks horrified.

"What is it? What did I say?"

To my shock, she laughs. "Nothing. That really profound, is all."

The stranglehold on my lungs releases, then re-clamps twice as hard when she *fades* right in front of me. Her smile falls, shoulders curling inward. Her eyes turn distant right before she looks down.

When she speaks, her voice sounds *wrong*. Timid and sad. "I'm happy you're clean and sober, Wilder. I'm sorry I've been too cowardly to tell you that." She makes a soft, derisive sound. "Let's be honest, I've been too much of a coward to even acknowledge you for the last six years."

My ability to speak is shredded, her name a puff of air she doesn't hear. She hugs herself tighter, making herself even smaller, and closes her eyes.

"In the beginning, I avoided you because I was angry and my heart was broken. But even when I didn't feel that way anymore, I kept avoiding you. Probably because deep down I knew your voice mattered more than most. And if I listened to you, I'd have to face shit I wasn't ready to face."

The cracks in my heart widen, and I can't take it anymore. Closing the distance between us, I wrap my arms around her. She stiffens at first, but then a miracle happens. Her weight drops against me, forehead thudding on my chest. And while her arms stay between us, the extra space is a good thing— my stupid cock doesn't care that this is an intense and tenuous moment.

"I'll never judge you," I whisper into her hair.

A tremor wracks her body. I hold her as close as I dare, rubbing circles on her back with one hand and cupping her head with the other.

"I'm jealous of you," she mumbles. "You've got it all figured out while I... well, I don't. Not even close. I don't know what I'm doing anymore. Nothing makes sense. Nothing feels right."

This feels right.

I keep the thought to myself and rest my chin on her soft hair. "I definitely don't have it all figured out. Believe me, I've felt the same way you do more times than I can count. In my case, it's usually expectations that trip me up, specifically the ones my younger self had. I get stuck comparing how I thought my life would look to how it really does, and I lose sight of what matters."

Her breath waterfalls against my chest, warming the skin over my heart. She says tartly, "It's really weirding me out how mature and wise you suddenly are."

I shake with a soundless laugh. "I have my moments, I guess. Catch me on a different day, and I'll be the same immature freak you've always known."

"Somehow I doubt that."

I hum a low, soothing note, gratified when she relaxes even more. "There's one thing my younger and current self agree on, though. A truth I accepted in childhood that has never been challenged."

"What?" she whispers.

"You," I say just as softly. "The truth of Evangeline Marie Sullivan. From birth, you've been a force to be reckoned with. I know you feel lost right now. That's okay. Feel what you feel. But someday soon you're going to remember how powerful you truly are."

She trembles, and I pretend I don't notice as her tears soak through my T-shirt.

"Damn you," she croaks.

My grin is involuntary. "I know," I say, my voice thick. "I'm still the worst."

Her laugh is strangled.

Movement across the room brings my gaze to the hallway connecting to the front of the house. Rye and Lily take us in, their expressions a mix of pain and relief.

When Rye's gaze moves to my face, I widen my eyes, hoping to communicate that I desperately need his help. My arms don't want to let go of Evangeline, and I'm seconds from ruining the moment with an inappropriate confession of my feelings.

He leans down to whisper in Lily's ear. She nods and backs up until she's out of sight.

I hold my breath.

"Hey, Lily!" Rye throws the jovial words over his shoulder. "You're not gonna believe this, but it looks like grandma and grandpa are friends again."

I groan.

Evangeline giggles and rubs her snotty nose on my chest.

Thank fucking God for Rye.

CHAPTER FIFTEEN

evangeline

RYE'S obnoxious comment comes at the perfect time, interrupting the equally unbearable and euphoric experience of being in Wilder's arms again.

I'm likewise grateful when not five minutes later, Anita, Sandra, and the team of stylists arrive. Despite coming straight from the airport, our publicist and PA barely stop to greet us. Anita herds everyone to the master suite while Sandra runs through our timeline for the day, including where we'll change after the event and the afterparties we're expected to attend.

My last glimpse of Wilder is of him talking quietly to Rye near the windows. I shouldn't be surprised when he turns his head, but I am. Our eyes meet, his crinkling in a subtle smile. Then Sandra's arm steers me around a corner.

As chaos cyclones around Lily and me, I don't miss the disgruntled looks she throws me. But there are too many strangers in the room for her to grill me about Wilder—a gift I'm glad to accept. I'm not sure I'd have the fortitude to deflect her questions or downplay the gravity of what happened.

Wilder holding me.

Me, voluntarily being held.

Soon enough, the mayhem settles into a well-oiled machine. Anita and Sandra come and go, phones glued to either their hands or ears. Lily takes pity on me, drawing me into a familiar rhythm of lighthearted banter as the stylists have their ways with us.

As we chat and laugh, more walls fall inside me, and I remember what having a best friend feels like. What having *Lily* feels like. And I don't know how I survived the last six months without her.

There's only one serious moment between us. We're sitting on a couch with curlers in our hair and sheet masks on our faces. During a lull in conversation, she catches my eye and whispers, "I've missed you."

Emotion floods me and I'm forced to blink rapidly at the ceiling to keep tears from spilling over. The facialist rushes over in a tizzy, worried that product has dripped in my eye. It takes me a while to convince her I'm fine, which Lily finds hysterical. She then laughs so hard she somehow gets product in *her* eye.

It isn't until the makeup artist goes to work on my face and I'm forced to stay still and silent that thoughts of Wilder intrude.

For the next forty minutes, I relive every second of this morning on a loop. From my first sight of him at the window against a backdrop of blue, to my overwhelming impulse to see his face and talk to him. His clear eyes, the compassion and tenderness in them. His shockingly insightful replies to my questions and confessions.

When he hugged me, in the moment all I felt was the comfort and rightness of his embrace. I felt sheltered. Safe. Only now, in hindsight, does dangerous awareness bloom.

Sitting motionless becomes increasingly difficult as I experience a delayed physical response to his touch linked to older, still potent memories. His bare, sweat-slick chest against mine. The flex of his hips between my thighs. Fingers clenched in my hair. A hot palm on my throat.

Low, rasping whispers in my ear.

"That's my girl. Such a good little slut, dripping all over my cock. Fuck, baby. You're the most beautiful mess I've ever seen."

Memories spiral out of control, turning my face and chest red and blotchy. My makeup artist has a silent panic attack.

"Can we turn the A/C on?" I ask weakly.

Seated a few feet away, Lily takes one look at me and her eyebrows disappear beneath her bangs. I avoid her laughing eyes and narrow my focus on the movement of brushes on my face. Then on the stylist showing me options for shoes and purses. On the cheerful woman who steps forward to style my hair. On Lily as she shares the woes of sleep regression with everyone in the room. On Anita when she reappears to prep us for questions on the red carpet.

But no matter how hard I try to stay present, Wilder is everywhere inside me. Waiting behind every blink, in every silent moment. He's smoke seeping through all my cracks. A skeleton key opening all of my locked doors.

"I know you feel lost right now. That's okay. Feel what you feel. But someday soon you're going to remember how powerful you truly are."

After all this time, he still believes in me. And I can't for the life of me understand why.

Justified or not, I abandoned him at the lowest point in his life. And when he graduated from rehab and came to my parents' house? When he tried to make amends to me? I had no compassion at all. I couldn't *see* him. I could barely hear him.

In the three months he was gone, beyond shaping my pain into songs that would become Glow's most acclaimed album, I didn't process my heartbreak. I chewed on it. Magnified it. *Drowned* in it. Outwardly, I put on a brave face. Acted like I was coping. Internally, I was digging and laying the foundational bricks of my first, highest wall, behind which I hoarded my misery.

I became fixated on my nyctophobia, convinced that overcoming my lifelong fear of the dark was somehow synonymous with healing. Every night, I'd crawl into my closet and sit in catatonic terror until dawn. Eventually, I grew desensitized to the phobia. But there was no healing. I hadn't liberated myself—I'd saturated myself with darkness.

When I saw Wilder again, it was the morning after a particularly bad night. Mentally, I was still in my dark closet. So when he took accountability for his actions and asked me what he could do to make it right, I laughed in his face. I said heinous, unforgivable things—things that make me cringe to think about now, that stunned my parents so badly they barely spoke to me for days afterward.

But Wilder just stood there and accepted my hostility. He didn't defend himself, not even from my worst, wildest accusations. When I ran out of steam, he said only, "I hear you," and walked away from me like I had from him.

Or I thought he had.

As impossible as it seems, he stayed my friend from afar. My faithful shadow, even when it was so dark I couldn't see him.

"You didn't take your allergy medicine, did you?"

Lily's overly bright voice brings me back to the present as I'm being zipped into my dress. I frown, about to ask what she's talking about, then realize my eyes are burning with tears.

I sniff them back and groan. "Damn. I forgot."

Within a minute, four people have produced antihistamines. As Lily holds in laughter, I thank them and quickly fabricate a story about the medicated eyedrops waiting for me in the limo.

The topic is quickly forgotten when someone else points out the time. There's a flurry of finishing touches to our hair and makeup. We step into our shoes. Transfer our phones and mini-cosmetics into clutches. A smiling woman who arrived twenty minutes ago unlocks a case of fine jewelry for us. Lily and I choose a few pieces to wear, giggling because playing dress-up still hasn't gotten old.

Anita gives us air kisses and leaves to meet us on the red carpet. Sandra oversees the room being packed up.

In the living room, Rye waits in a charcoal suit to match Lily's dress. She admonishes him for looking so good while she's ovulating. He gushes over her ethereal beauty. I laugh at their antics, feeling joyful by proximity. But when they start playfully groping each other and whispering, the brightness inside me dims.

Looking away, I stare toward the windows, the space before them now empty.

"Did Wilder already leave?"

As the question slips out, my face heats. The shocked silence behind me magnifies not only the disappointment in my voice, but the incongruity of me asking in the first place.

With a sigh, I turn to face my friends in time to see Lily land a solid punch to Rye's stomach. He winces and attempts a neutral expression. But his blue eyes are too bright.

"Never mind," I say quickly. "Stupid question."

Obviously Wilder left to meet his bandmates. It's not like he could have ridden with us, arrived at the event with us.

The sense of loss I feel is completely irrational. So is the fact it lingers until Clay arrives. Then shame takes center-stage inside me, followed swiftly by a dance of irritation and hurt when he says, "I thought we agreed on the cream chiffon dress, not this Morticia Addams shit."

I pull away from him, glad Lily and Rye are saying goodbye to Emma down the hall.

"For fuck's sake, Clay. This is vintage Versace."

His eyes flash and narrow, but before he can say anything, Lily and Rye return. He's immediately all gracious words and smiles. My irritation simmers as we file out to the limo. When Lily heads for the bench behind the driver, I take the seat beside her. Clay's reaction is brief—a clenched jaw and searing glance—before he starts talking sports with Rye.

What happens next is my fault.

I'm not paying enough attention to the conversation, focused mostly on quelling my internal chaos as I gaze out my window at passing scenery.

Then Rye says, "I had no idea you were into baseball, man. We should catch a few Mariners games this summer."

"This summer?" echoes Clay.

I whip my head around, but it's too late.

Rye smiles and nods. "You'll be coming up with Eva, right? God knows we'll barely see them the first few weeks they're in the studio. Plenty of time for us to catch a game or two."

My body flashes cold, every muscle locking, my mind blanking.

Clay's laugh is a harsh, truncated burst. "What are you talking about? They're not recording this summer."

Lily sucks in a shocked breath.

Rye's eyes dart to me. He blanches, then coughs. "I mean, I, uh—just some wishful thinking on my part. Wouldn't that be cool?" No one acknowledges the obvious lie.

If I were braver, if I had a voice at all right now, I'd tell Rye this isn't his fault. I'd take accountability. Come clean to Clay, to my friends, all three of whom I've wronged.

For weeks, I've offered and omitted pieces of myself as needed. All to maintain a laughable facsimile of control over my life. Now Clay knows I've been lying to him, and my friends are probably confused as hell.

"Explain yourself, Eva. Right. Fucking. *Now.*"

Scratch that—now they know something is seriously wrong with my relationship. For the first time in front of them, Clay has dropped all pretense. His voice oozes so much menace that I flinch, Lily gasps, and Rye turns toward him with a furious glare.

Before they can come to my defense and make everything a thousand times worse, I force my numb lips to move.

"Later." I gesture weakly to his window.

Clay glances outside to see that we're nearing the arena. For the rest of the short drive, he stares at me and seethes.

No one says a word.

CHAPTER SIXTEEN

wilder

I MADE A MISTAKE
TASTING YOU
BEFORE I KNEW
WHAT STARVING WAS

FIFTEEN FEET AWAY, on the other side of Chateau Fontaine's upscale bar, Evangeline sits with five other famous faces in a horseshoe booth. The lighting is dim, the music loud, and it's close to two in the morning.

Besides the waitstaff, I'm the only sober person in the place.

The luxury hotel in West Hollywood is the last stop on Glow's afterparty tour, and thank fuck for that. I'm exhausted, my senses overloaded to the extreme, and Zander is at the end of his rope from me dragging him all over the city. Or he was until a few minutes ago. Now he's flirting with a nerdy-looking dude I vaguely recognize from television.

Evangeline throws her head back in a laugh. I can't hear it, but I don't need to in order to know it's fake.

The bad feeling I had earlier is back with a vengeance.

Something happened after I left the house. I have no idea what, since Lily and Rye have avoided me like the plague all night. But they've also avoided Eva. Or maybe it's Eva who's been avoiding them.

My gaze narrows on what I can see of Clay's face. He's currently at the bar, his back to Eva's booth. He's chatting with two men—one of them a recognizable music producer —and sipping a bright green martini like a dumbass. He looks even more smug than usual. Not surprising, since Glow took home two more Grammys tonight and Clay's deluded enough to think they're his by proximity.

But I haven't missed the fact that besides arriving and leaving together, he's kept his distance from Evangeline all night, too.

"You good if I head out?" asks Zander. A quick glance behind him reveals the blushing actor.

Smirking, I nod. "I'm not going to stay much longer. Thanks for hanging." Leaning toward him, I lower my voice. "Have fun polishing your new Grammy."

Zander laugh-groans. "You're such a loser. Speaking of, have fun with your stalking."

I roll my eyes and wave him off. When they're gone, I look back across the room just as a scowling Lily walks in from the other side. I don't see Rye, but he's probably not far behind.

I straighten from my slouched position against a wall. Before I can decide whether or not to approach Lily, she beelines for Evangeline's booth. Leaning down, she whispers something to Evangeline, who rears back, shaking her head and laughing. Lily tries again. This time, she's able to tug Eva to standing.

413

It's immediately apparent that Evangeline is wasted. She stumbles in her high heels. Lily reaches out to help her, but she jerks away and almost falls again. When she finally balances, she does a little bow that makes everyone in the booth laugh.

Lily steps forward again, urgency and worry clear in her expression. She says something that causes Evangeline to frown, and I watch her lips shape the words, "I can't, Lily."

After a pause fraught with enough tension that I feel it across the room, Lily spins on a heel and stalks away. Evangeline stares blankly after her, swaying on her feet.

A quick glance toward the bar tells me that Clay hasn't noticed the drama. But others have.

I'm walking before I've processed the thought. Just as Evangeline turns to sit back down, I curl my fingers around her bicep. Startled, she looks up at me with wide eyes.

"Can I talk to you for a sec?"

She nods, her gaze lowering to my mouth. I tell myself I'm only imagining the heat in her eyes, that the increased glassiness is from booze and not lust. My body, of course, decides differently.

Ignoring my suddenly tight pants, I slide my hand down to her elbow and guide her into a nearby hallway. She's so out of it, she doesn't comment when I pull her into a family bathroom.

Given the luxury of the attached hotel, it's no shock the space is huge and spa-like, with a separate seating area, high-end finishes, and mood lighting. On the double-sink vanity, there are baskets of toiletries and a pitcher of ice water next to a stack of sparkling glasses. The toilet is off to the right, the partially open door confirming that we're alone.

I flip the deadbolt on the main door, then steer Evangeline to a leather couch. She sits—or rather, falls—then topples to the side until her cheek is smooshed on a cushion.

Her eyes flutter closed. "So cold," she mumbles. "Feels good."

Swallowing a sigh, I head for the water dispenser and fill a glass. Then I crouch next to her head.

"Can you sit up for me?"

"Nopity nope."

Despite my frustration, my lips quirk. "Evangeline, come on."

"Pfft." Eyes still closed, she squirms, bare legs scissoring until her high heels thunk to the floor. "Thas better."

She rolls onto her back and stretches with a hum of pleasure, completely oblivious to the fact her silver-beaded minidress isn't stretching with her. The hem rides so low over her chest, I can see the small mole above her right nipple and a hint of pink areola.

My cock, already stiff against my thigh, pulses in agonized want.

Out of desperation, I snap, "Fairy."

Her eyes pop open. Glazed, they roam my face before stalling on my mouth. "I thought I dreamed you."

Jesus fucking Christ, I'm not strong enough for this.

I'm still reeling from the longing in her voice when her eyes suddenly widen. She laughs, the sound soft, throaty, and designed to torture me.

"Remember asking me if I'd ever pierce my nipples?"

The water glass almost slips from my hand. Setting it down quickly on the end table, I look up at the ceiling and start counting down from a hundred. When I get to seventy-three, my balls stop throbbing. At sixty, I find the willpower to lower my gaze back to her.

"Evangeline, I—"

"Do you remember?"

She's not laughing anymore. Her eyes are more lucid, the look in them brave but resigned. Like she's expecting disappointment. Like she's used to it.

It fucking hurts. Even if I understand why. Even if it's my own damn fault she's ever doubted that our time together was as real for me as it was for her.

I've never had a chance to explain that by the end of my using—which she had a front-row seat to—I was lucky if I managed to stave off the full brunt of withdrawals every day. Actually *feeling* loaded was rare. As weird as it sounds to most people, it hadn't even been a priority. If it had been, I would have stuck to drinking.

I have no doubt alcohol would have taken me to rock bottom eventually, just like it did my dad. Opiates got me there first because they did what alcohol couldn't. They turned down the volume on my anxiety and—most importantly—helped me function like a somewhat normal person. Initially, at least. Until my addiction progressed. Until I was walking a fraying tightrope of lies, avoidance, and denial.

Until I lost her.

I was a junkie, no question. Enslaved to my physical craving and mental dependence. But the times I was impaired enough to forget a single moment from that month of my life?

Zero.

Maybe someday I'll be able to tell Evangeline everything. Maybe it will matter to her, or maybe it won't.

But at least I can fix one misconception right now.

"I remember asking more than once. You finally told me that if I shut up about it, you'd let me take you to get pierced on your twenty-fifth birthday."

She looks away, flushing and blinking fast. Probably remembering the other part of the deal, just like I am—that if she went through with it, I'd owe her twenty-five orgasms. And ice cream.

My thoughts are sluggish, bloated with memory and desire and regret. When she grabs my hand, I don't understand what's happening at first. And when I finally do, I'm incapable of resisting as she guides my fingers to the peak of her breast.

Fuck me sideways.

Even with all the beads on her dress, I can feel the metal beneath. Adjusting her grip, she guides the tip of my index finger from one side of the petite barbell to the other.

I'm concentrating so hard on not nutting in my pants that when she speaks, I barely register her soft, forlorn voice.

"Everyone's mad at me. You should be, too. I'm... I'm not a good person. I used to be one, I think. Was I, Wilder? A good person? I've been trying to remember, but all I can really remember is you. What we were. What we did to each other."

There's a delay while my bloodless brain processes the words. Then I'm suddenly, acutely clearheaded. Slipping my hand from beneath hers, I sit back on my heels and heave air into my lungs.

Evangeline turns her face toward the back of the couch. A thick section of her pale hair falls off the edge and lands on my thigh, light as a feather and heavier than lead. I clench my hands to keep from touching it.

"S' okay," she whispers. "I wouldn't want me anymore, either."

"You have no idea—" I clench my teeth to hold back the rest. Nothing I say is going to land right now. Chances are she won't even remember this conversation tomorrow.

I reach for the water glass, determined to at least have her drink some before I decide what to do. I don't want to send her home with Clay, especially without knowing whether or not it's safe for her. But Lily and Rye are ignoring me, and I can't exactly carry her out of here myself. Not without serious consequences.

A sudden vibration in my back pocket threatens my grip on the water again. I put it down for the second time and yank my phone out, sighing in relief when I see a text from Rye.

RYE

Not avoiding u on purpose. Shit went off the rails after u left. Been trying to keep Lily calm all day. Headed back to house now

WILDER

Wtf happened?

He types, and types some more. In the interim, I lean forward to peek at Evangeline's face. She's passed out and drooling.

Finally, Rye's texts come through.

I stuck my foot in my mouth in the limo. Said something about Eva being in Seattle this summer to record. Clay was like "haha what? No, she's not."

Eva got so pale I thought she was gonna pass out. Clay told her to explain herself in this super psycho voice. I almost put his face through the window. I can't explain it. My skin was legit crawling from the look he gave her

We tried all night to get her to talk about it and come home with us but she wouldn't. Lily finally lost it. I had to get her out of there before she went postal

My adrenaline skyrockets, my muscles quivering with the desire to break Clay's bones. When I look down at Evangeline, a different need rises. One just as implausible, just as reckless. But far more appealing.

I want to carry her out of here and straight to the airport. Fly her home. Lock her in my house. Never let her out of my sight again.

"Fuck," I whisper. "Fuck. Fuck."

Clenching a hand in my hair, I look wildly around the bathroom.

Three things I can see. Three I can touch. Three I can hear.

Inhale. Hold. Release.

My phone buzzes again

> U there? Pls tell me you haven't left the party

>> I haven't. With Eva in a bathroom. She's trashed and passed out on a couch

> Thank god. Don't let her leave with Clay ok? I'll drop off Lily and come back. We'll figure something out

>> K. No way in hell she's leaving with him

I toss my phone to the floor.

Eva stirs. "Wilder?"

"I'm here."

Unable to help myself, I stroke the hair off her forehead and temple. Her eyes are still closed, but tightly, as though she's in pain.

"Need you to know something..."

I lean closer to hear her faint voice. "Yeah?"

"You weren't a footnote. You were the title of my favorite book."

Her whole body tenses.

Then she lurches toward me and vomits all over my lap.

CHAPTER SEVENTEEN

evangeline

THE SECOND I WAKE UP, I remember how much I hate alcohol. My mouth tastes like a trashcan, my stomach is on a boat, and my heartbeat thuds in my eyelids.

Rolling away from sunlight that burns my face like a chemical peel, I search blindly for a pillow to put over my head. After a few seconds, I give up with a groan of defeat. Even if by some miracle I was suddenly the type of person who could fall back asleep easily, the ache in my bladder would negate the option.

Nevertheless, opening my eyes is a mistake. For several reasons.

First, my eyelashes have glued themselves together in retribution for me not taking off the eight pounds of mascara I wore yesterday. By the time I force them to part, my eyes are stinging and watering.

Second, I can no longer ignore the fact my bedroom is south-facing and doesn't get direct sunlight—the kind blasting on my back right now.

And lastly, the man sleeping in an oversized armchair

beside the bed, clearly having kept an eye on me all night, is *not* Clay.

Wilder's arms are crossed over his bare chest, his head propped awkwardly on what looks like a bunched up T-shirt. His long legs, encased in plaid pajama pants, are crossed at the ankle on an overturned luggage case. Dark hair falls artlessly over his brow. His lips are slightly parted, his breathing deep and even.

My physical misery now has a challenger—absolute panic. They go to war as I sit up too fast and almost hurl. Cold sweat breaks out on my body. Swallowing bile, I look around and recognize the style of the room. I'm back in the Santa Monica house.

What the hell happened last night?

As if waiting for the mental cue, flashbacks unfurl like a row of middle fingers eager to extend a *fuck you* to what's left of my mental stability.

What happened in the limo. Surviving the red carpet and Clay's touches through sheer willpower. The cool satisfaction in his eyes when I sat down after Glow's final win. Changing in a hotel room and dodging Lily's attempts to talk. Avoiding her and Rye the rest of the night. Laughing and pretending everything was fine. Drowning my despair with alcohol.

My memories melt somewhere between Lily's final attempt to speak with me and Wilder's hand on my arm as we walked somewhere.

My panic reaches new heights, manifesting as a high-pitched note in my ears. I scramble off the bed, almost eating floor when my feet are momentarily caught in the comforter. My tangled, product-encrusted hair whips around my face as I dart erratically around the room. In the attached bathroom, I locate my dress—damp for some reason—hanging over a towel rack. But my clutch is nowhere to be found.

I run back into the bedroom.

"Wilder, wake up! Where's my phone?"

He jerks upright with a grunt, then winces and grabs his neck. "Shit. Why are you yelling?"

His sleep-roughened voice arrows right between my legs. Before I can recover, he stands, visually punching me with the mouthwatering sight of his bare upper half.

No one should have that many abs. It's not natural.

Wilder's rapidly clearing eyes scan my face, drop down my body, then snap back up. He drags a palm over his mouth, his brow pinched. Air leaves his nose in a short burst.

That's when I realize I'm wearing a thong under one of his T-shirts, which just so happens to be soft, thin, and white, and that the sun is behind me. Not only can he see how tightly my thighs are squeezed together, he can see everything else, too.

Another flashback hits. Mortified, I slap my hands over my face and shake my head, not caring that the violent movement magnifies the pounding in my skull.

"Please, please tell me I didn't make you touch my nipple."

He coughs over a sound suspiciously close to a laugh. "You totally did."

"Why didn't you lie?" I wail.

Now he's for sure laughing. "I make an effort not to these days. Besides, you were shitfaced. It's not like I took it as an invitation." He pauses. "Do you remember anything from after that?"

I slowly lower my hands, turning my back to him at the same time so I can stay sane. "Not at the moment, no. Why? What else do I need to be humiliated about?"

"Absolutely nothing," he says, quick and firm. "I just wondered if you knew how you got here."

I shake my head. Panic creeps back in. "Do you know where my phone is? I really need it."

I listen to the familiar sound of him pulling on a shirt, then his soft footsteps approaching me. They pause a few feet away.

"Your phone is in the kitchen, but before you bolt, listen for a sec. Everything is okay. After you passed out, Rye and Lily came back to the party. Lily stayed with you while I went outside to meet my driver. Rye found Clay and told him they were bringing you here. He was fine with it."

Too relieved to acknowledge the edge in his voice, I whisper, "Thank God."

His following sigh is weighted with intent. A whole different level of anxiety ripples through me, shortening my breath.

"Evangeline..."

Turning fast, I dart around him toward the bathroom. "About to pee my pants, sorry!"

After closing the door and locking it, I brace my hands on the vanity and try to catch my breath. My body shakes intermittently, cramping with so much tension that my bladder has gone into hiding. The mirror tells me I look as bad as I feel. My bloodshot eyes are ringed by melted makeup. A section of my hair sticks up in defiance of gravity, the rest flattened and tangled in chunks. My skin is grayish-white, my lips bloodless.

There's a soft thud on the door that I instinctively know is from Wilder's forehead meeting the wood. Sure enough, his low voice slips around the frame and curls into my ears.

"I know about what happened in the limo. Why you got so drunk."

Another thud.

"This might make you hate me again, but I have to say it.

Juggling lies, partitioning off parts of yourself, avoiding the truth screaming in your gut... it's no way to live. I should know. I also know how scary it is to break free of the bullshit and let it all go. Feels kind of like jumping without a parachute. But you *can* take your life back."

There's a long pause. My stomach churns, and it's not from the hangover this time. I can feel what's coming, sense it in the same way you smell ozone between lightning strikes.

Because no matter how drastically storms have altered our topography as adults, the structure of us as children still stands. Within those unassailable walls, Wilder remains my silent protector and reluctant hero. Challenging me to be brave even as he tries to shelter me from pain. And always, always finding me when I'm lost.

"I've broken promises to you, Evangeline. I broke *us*. I'll never forgive myself for it. I don't expect you to forgive me, either. But you have to know... even if you don't want me to be, I'm in your corner. Forever. That's one promise I will never, ever break."

There's a final thud of his forehead on the door before his footsteps move away.

I don't know how long I stand there unmoving, covered in goosebumps and staring blankly at the door. It could be a minute or ten before Lily knocks and tells me she's leaving a change of clothes on the bed, and that I'll find toiletries, including ibuprofen, under the sink.

Her calm voice cracks the plaster on my limbs. I open the door, stalling her retreat from the room.

"I'm sorry, Lilly. For so much. The Indigo meeting and what I said to you after. Shutting you out. Being a shit friend and godmother. I've never wanted to leave Glow. I'm *not* leaving Glow. I just..."

My voice hits an emotional blockage in my throat.

425

Her chin quivers before firming. "I'm sorry, too. I haven't been a good friend to you, either. I was too wrapped up in my own life to see what was going on, and I wasn't there when you needed me."

"W-what are you talking about?"

But I already know. I fucking know because like Wilder said, it's the truth screaming in my gut. The one I've been terrified to face for longer than I can admit to myself.

"I'm talking about Clay. He's abusive. Some part of you must know that."

My chest tightens, burning. More pieces of the walls I've been dismantling rip free, falling and shattering. Tears fill my eyes. Suddenly dizzy, I grab the doorframe.

Then I force out probably the hardest words I've ever had to speak.

"I know."

Lily's expression softens, the sympathy in her eyes half balm, half acid on my heart.

"Leave him, Eva. You can do it. We'll help you. Anything you need."

Panic rises again. I break out in a sweat. "I-I want to. I... I've tried. I'm trying. Please believe me. I'm sorry."

She closes the space between us and wraps her arms tightly around my waist. "It's okay. I understand. I love you, and when you're ready to talk about it, I'll be here." Stepping back, she wipes tears from her cheeks. "Right now the only thing you have to do is shower. Please. Between your pits and your breath, I'm about to pass out."

I laugh, sniffing back tears. "Ugh, you're right. It's so bad." Another memory abruptly appears, and I groan in mortification. "I puked on Wilder, didn't I?"

She nods, failing to hide her amusement. "A few times. I

cleaned you up and got you out of your dress, though. In case you were worried."

I nod, wincing. "I'm remembering now. Thanks for doing that."

"Sure. I would have stayed up with you, too, but I literally couldn't keep my eyes open, and Emma..."

"No, no. I completely understand." I laugh weakly. "I can't believe Wilder babysat me all night. What alternate dimension is this?"

She smirks. "A good one, trust me. Just wait until you try his French toast."

CHAPTER EIGHTEEN

evangeline

FOUR IBUPROFEN and washing my hair three times in the world's longest, hottest shower bring me most of the way back to the land of the living. Fresh clothes and minty breath do the rest. I'm still hungover, my eyes aching and limbs weak, but at least I'm clean.

Dressed in a pair of stretchy black leggings and a baggy, faded T-shirt from Glow's first tour, I venture out of the bedroom. I make my way through the quiet house to the kitchen, where I find Rye sipping coffee. When he sees me, he stands and gestures to a stool at the island, then moves to the oven.

I sit, murmuring thanks as he sets a warm plate of thick, browned brioche slices in front of me and slides three small bowls my way. Powdered sugar, maple syrup, and fresh blueberries and raspberries. Despite lingering queasiness, my stomach growls.

I pop a berry in my mouth. "Where is everyone?"

"My mom took Emma down to the beach for a bit, and Lily's showering. Coffee?"

"God, yes. Thank you."

He pours me a cup, topping it with half and half before sliding it my way. I take an eager gulp as he hops back onto his stool.

"And where's... the chef?"

Rye's smile doesn't reach his exhausted eyes. "He went to see some friends."

I glance at the clock on the oven. "Before nine on a Monday?"

He takes a sip of his coffee, avoiding my eyes. "Wilder went to a meeting, Eva. The sober kind. He should be back soon."

Realizing I'm drowning my plate in syrup, I hastily set the bowl down. "Oh. Well, it was nice of him to cook breakfast." We both wince at my too-cheerful tone. Thankfully, he doesn't comment.

I distractedly cut into my French toast. Did Wilder go to a meeting because of me? I hadn't considered that dealing with me drunk might have been triggering for him.

Of course it was, idiot.

My appetite fades, but I make myself take a bite.

"Holy shit," I mumble.

Rye snorts. "Right?"

I chew and swallow. "Are you guys still going to Disney today?"

"As much as it pains me to say it, yes. Leaving in thirty if you want to join."

"I'd rather stab myself."

He smirks. "Wilder said the same thing."

I swallow another mouthful. "Did he seem okay? When he left?"

There's a flash of something on Rye's face. Something I've never seen there before, at least not directed at me. A mix of disappointment and resentment. My heart pangs.

"He's fine."

I manage a few more bites. Even oven-warmed, the French toast is hands down the best I've ever tasted. I have no idea whether it's because I'm hungover or it's actually that good, but I suspect the latter.

Setting down my fork, I reach for my coffee and courage. "I'm sorry, Rye. For what I put you through yesterday. And for... everything."

Eyes on his mug, he shakes his head. "We're not doing this right now," he says tightly.

My stomach drops, my eyes instantly on fire. I blink fast. "O-okay. Sorry."

I make to push back from the island, but Rye quickly turns toward me. His blue eyes are beseeching. "I'm not mad at *you*, Eva. I'm mad at... all of it. Mostly, though, I'm mad at your—" His lips seal, but the word *boyfriend* floats between us.

Lily must have told him about our conversation. How when I tried to talk about Clay, I could barely form a sentence. I lower my eyes to my plate, my neck heating as I imagine them talking about me. Their *pity*.

I try to stay calm, but it's no use. An ugly trifecta of humiliation, emotional nakedness, and defensive anger swallows me. My spine stiffens, fingers curling until my nails bite my palms.

"I bet you both think I'm some hapless victim, huh? Poor Eva, too weak and clueless to know her boyfriend is a raging asshole. How long has this been going on?" I lift my gaze to Rye, whose freckles turn stark as he pales.

"Eva—"

I cut him off with a low, bitter laugh. "I should have known something was off with how you guys were acting. Like nothing has changed between us. Like I haven't been ignoring your calls for months and didn't completely fuck over Lily at the Indigo meeting." Thinking back over the last couple of months, I land on an explosive conversation with my dad when I told him I wasn't visiting for Christmas. "My parents are behind this, aren't they?"

They've never liked Clay. My dad especially. The first time I brought him to meet them was a disaster. When I confronted my dad afterward, he justified his borderline rudeness by telling me a bunch of old rumors about Clay's father.

I was stunned and instantly defensive. Clay had swept me off my feet a few months prior, at a point in my life when I'd been battling listlessness and rapidly worsening depression. Suddenly I had a mature, confident, supportive man in my life. Someone who wasn't threatened by my career or schedule, who had his own life in Los Angeles. We talked daily and saw each other once a month, spending long weekends together. He was the brightest spot in my dim world.

I accused my dad of condemning the son for the actions of the father, callously adding I would've thought he'd be the last person to do that.

Hindsight is a real bitch.

My dad *was* wrong to judge Clay based on rumors of his father, but his concern was justified all the same. I just didn't know it for another few months. By then, however, I'd already begun distancing myself from my family. Not seeing or calling them as often to avoid talking about my relationship.

The first few times I cried myself to sleep over something Clay said to me, I wanted to call my mom badly but talked myself out of it. She has PTSD from a relationship in her early twenties, and I convinced myself I'd only be triggering her trauma. My situation wasn't nearly as bad—Clay was mean sometimes, and controlling, but he wasn't physically abusive. Plus, if I told my mom, she'd tell my dad, and I didn't want to deal with his militant, overprotective mode.

But what really kept my mouth shut was pride and its shadow, shame. I couldn't bring myself to admit that despite being raised to recognize red flags, I'd missed them all. *Again.* And that my second serious relationship was somehow even more toxic than the first.

By the time Clay and I celebrated our one-year anniversary, I was already numb to the cycle. The slow build of tension. Scattered, tiny hurts escalating into a deeper betrayal. Confrontation and misery. Apologies and a period of repair and comfort, which invariably degraded as tension built again.

My oldest friend stares at me, eyes wide and searching like he can see the emotional sewage leaking out of me.

"It's a simple question, Rye. Did my parents put you up to this?"

He swallows thickly. "They're concerned. We all are."

Something in his tone connects more dots in my mind. When I see the line that forms and understand what it means, the pain I feel is indescribable. A thousand savage cuts.

I jolt to my feet, my nerves on fire.

"They went to *him*," I choke out. "That's why he showed up at the party on New Year's Eve. It wasn't a coincidence at all. It was manipulation. Wasn't it?"

The answer comes from behind me.

"Yes."

Before I can turn, Rye stands and snaps, "Your parents wouldn't have gone to Wilder if you hadn't turned into someone none of us recognize!"

I gasp, swaying against the edge of the island.

Wilder says quellingly, "Enough."

"I'm sorry, Eva." Rye's voice is muted, his following steps swift as he leaves the room.

Then it's just us. Wilder and me. But there's none of the sparkling warmth I felt yesterday or this morning. No connection or comfort in his presence. No childhood bond or tentative new friendship.

I'm still alone.

CHAPTER NINETEEN

evangeline

"DON'T BOTHER TRYING to explain, Wilder. Just leave me alone."

I load the condiment bowls onto my plate, then grab my mug and carry everything to the sink.

Wilder, *being fucking Wilder*, ignores my demand, following and leaning a hip against the counter a few feet away. Refusing to look at him, I turn on the hot water, then grab a sponge and squirt too much soap on it.

I hate that he doesn't tell me not to wash the dishes.

I hate that the last two years have proven to me, over and over again, that he and Clay could not be more different.

Yes, Wilder hurt me when we were younger. Both with his words and actions. In the months before I left Night Theory, he was a total dick, and his behavior afterward was atrocious. Then, after ignoring me for three years, he seduced me on a false premise of honesty. Overwhelmed me with mind-blowing sex, intimacy, and promises of forever. All while he lied about his drug use, a fracture of trust that shattered my heart and tainted every second of our time together.

But in spite of being an asshole intermittently from nineteen to twenty-five, Wilder has never, *not fucking once,* made me feel as small, empty, and worthless as Clay.

"Will you look at me?" he asks softly.

I shake my head and keep scrubbing. The dishes are clean, but I can't make myself stop.

"I'm sure this won't be a surprise to you, but I've always felt different, even as a little kid."

Wilder's voice is just loud enough to be heard over the faucet. I pour more soap on the sponge and keep scrubbing.

"In some ways, it was probably natural for me to compare myself to others. To look for a place I fit. But my units of measurement were wrong. I was comparing my insides to everyone else's outsides. They never matched, so I invariably felt less than."

I still don't look at him, but my hands stop moving. Against my will, every part of me is listening.

"I have so many memories of watching you, Rye, and the other kids playing, laughing... I wanted to be a part of your joy, but my own conviction that I wasn't good enough held me back. It happened in school. With Night Theory, too. In focusing on how different, how alone I was, I suffocated myself with shadows of jealousy, self-loathing, and fear."

I didn't notice him move, but he's suddenly so close his chest brushes my shoulder. Heat spreads from the contact, radiating down my right side. I suck in a breath on reflex, inadvertently saturating my senses with him. A hint of coffee beneath mint. A whisper of soap over his natural scent, that improbable fusion of dark forest, rain, and lightning.

A muscled, tattooed arm reaches into the sink. His fingers close around mine, squeezing them and the sponge I'm still holding. Suds explode, thick and silky.

His lips graze my temple. "I think it's easy to forget we're all just human. Inherently fallible. We think admitting weakness makes us weak, but it's the opposite. Only the strong admit their failings and confront the deeply uncomfortable work of growing."

A thumb wedges itself against my palm, rubbing slow circles. Gasoline hits the fires inside me, detonating in my chest, my face. Between my legs. My head empties, overwhelmed by the sensation.

I stop breathing as he shifts to stand behind me, then gasp as his other arm slips beneath mine to cage me between his body and the sink. His second hand joins the first, both of them now spreading slick bubbles over my hands and up my wrists. Strong thumbs knead tiny pressure points. Calloused fingertips enclose and twist around mine.

My breaths are staccato, my heart galloping, my pussy throbbing.

"Wilder?"

"What?" he whispers back, the teasing tone so unexpected that it takes me a few seconds to answer.

"W-what are you doing?"

"Am I not being obvious enough? Here, let me fix that."

He erases the space between our bodies. The counter digs into my stomach, but I don't notice. All I feel is his hands, still moving over mine, and the heat of his chest down my spine. Ninety-nine percent of my awareness, though, is now on my lower half. Specifically my ass, against which presses undeniable evidence that he's still attracted to me. Thick, rock-hard, searing evidence.

Deep inside me, behind a rattling door, is relief so sudden and potent that if I dared to feel it, I'd probably sob for hours.

He murmurs, "The second part of my answer to your question, Evangeline, is that I'm turning off the noise in your head so you actually hear me. Ready for the hard part?"

My mind blank, I nod.

"First and foremost, have you even met me? No one can *make* me do anything. Yes, your parents showed up at my house a few days after Christmas. Completely blindsided me." A silent laugh huffs in my ear. "Your dad apologized for being a jerk to me years ago. I told him I'd deserved it. We had a bromance moment. It was great."

My lips twitch, then compress as he continues, "Then they dropped a bomb on me. They told me you were in trouble and asked me to try to help you."

When I immediately stiffen, he pulses his hips. Caught on the rougher fabric of his jeans, my leggings drag upward, pulling the seam tighter between my legs. A small, choked whimper leaves me.

"Listening ears back on?"

Annoyance pierces my sensory overwhelm. "Asshole," I hiss.

My back vibrates with his low chuckle, but there's more threat than humor in it. "You're right. I'm such an asshole. Only an asshole would be sick with worry for a woman who told him he might as well have overdosed because he was as good as dead to her."

A hammer hits my heart, making me gasp. "I didn't mean that."

He counters calmly, "I never held it against you. Honestly, I felt like I deserved worse for what I did." A sigh ruffles my hair. "Regardless, you're not wrong. I'm still an asshole. I've decided to disregard your request to leave you alone. It's been almost seven years. I'm done playing dead. Done pretending my heart will ever stop belonging to you."

A different hammer hits my chest, this one spiked.

Catastrophic.

"No. You can't say that. You don't mean that. Let me go."

Water and soap fly over the counter and backsplash as I

struggle against him. But he only holds me closer, tighter, as he speaks in a voice of gravel and iron.

"Right now you have two choices. One, you shut your beautiful mouth and listen because I haven't finished. Or two, I take you to the nearest bed and fuck the stubbornness out of you."

My whole body shudders, my clit pulsing so incessantly I know a purposeful touch would send me over the edge. A moan rockets up my throat. I manage to catch it before it escapes, but I'm powerless to stop my hips from searching for friction.

Wilder muffles a groan on my shoulder. "Stop that. This is hard enough without coming in my pants." He pauses, then chuckles. "Punny."

On a breathless note of hysteria, my head falls forward and I sag against the counter. Sensing the fight leaving me, Wilder nuzzles my neck. He inhales deeply, humming when I tremble.

"Option one it is," he whispers.

I stare into the sink, musing that my sanity is draining away with the last of the soap. At the thought, a vague guilt pricks me for wasting so much water.

Wilder slaps the faucet off.

My mouth drops open. "What, are you psychic now?"

"Runs in the family," he replies lightly, like he didn't just threaten to fuck me, laugh at his own pun, then read my mind. "Suffice to say, when your parents left my house, I was pretty freaked out. They were vague about why you needed help. Lily and Rye didn't have answers, either, at least not ones that were good enough.

"I needed to see you in person, to draw my own conclusions. So I found out where you'd be on New Year's Eve and yes, I ambushed you. But you ambushed me, too. Because instead of finding the indomitable Evangeline-fucking-Sullivan, I found one of those wooden dolls that hide a bunch of smaller dolls inside it."

"A Matryoshka doll," I say in spite of myself.

"Exactly. You'd covered yourself with a dozen protective layers, thinking no one would notice." His voice lowers to a rasp. "Did you think for one fucking second I wouldn't see all the way to the center of you?"

Closing my eyes, I shake my head helplessly. "Why are you doing this? What do you want from me?"

"You know what I want."

The undisguised need in his voice sends a wave of blistering heat beneath my skin. I'm seized by longing so intense it scalds, so bright it spears into the deepest shadows of my psyche.

For a single moment, I imagine it. *Us.* Then what lives in those shadows—complex knots of memory and pain—rears up in defense of itself.

"I can't." My voice is reedy, naked with fear. My heart whispers the rest: *I won't survive you twice.*

Wilder tenses, his exhale harsh on my neck, then straightens and steps back. My body immediately protests the loss. Locking my knees, I transfer my pruned hands to the lip of the sink.

I don't have the courage to face him, a weakness I'm grateful for when he says the same thing, in the same empty tone, that he did when I told him I wished he were dead.

"I hear you."

I flinch. "I-I'm sorry."

"Evangeline, no." Dry amusement and self-deprecation tangle in the soft words. "As far as I'm concerned, you're exempt from apologizing to me for anything, for all time. I shouldn't have said that. And it doesn't matter, anyway. It doesn't change anything. I'm not going anywhere." After a moment, he adds, "As your friend."

"What if I hit you with a car? Should I apologize then?"

There's a beat of silence, then his smiling reply, "Just say 'oops' or something."

I bite my cheek to keep from laughing, knowing the sound won't resemble anything sane. There's also a chance I'll sob, risking the delicate boundary just restored by inviting his physical comfort. And while my skin hums at the prospect, muscles deep within me clenching in agreement, I breathe through the sensations.

What I feel now merely confirms what I've always known. Nothing will ever diminish my desire for Wilder. Not pain, time, or distance. My ears will always long for his voice, my eyes for his face, my body for his.

He's like the eczema on the back of my knees—even when it's dormant for long periods, it's still there, just waiting for the right conditions to flare up.

I reach for a nearby hand towel and start wiping up the small puddles around the sink.

"Is the hard part over?" I ask, attempting levity.

There's a pause, then I hear the familiar, whispery *swish* of his fingers dragging through his hair. And I know what he's going to say before he says it.

"Not quite."

The water is gone, the sink clean. But I keep wiping, my movements rote but necessary, providing a tiny buffer between my body and mind.

"Just say what you want to say, Wilder. I have to get going soon."

"Your parents came to me as a last resort, probably because they knew I had nothing left to lose. What was the worst thing that could happen? You tell me you hate me, to fuck off? Been there, done that."

His amused tone lessens the sting of his words, but I still stiffen.

He clears his throat. "If it makes you more comfortable to believe I'm here because your parents guilted me, go right ahead. But it was only a matter of time before I showed up. You think I didn't notice your light dimming over the last two years? You think I didn't know why? I wish I'd come sooner. I *should* have. I should have let go of my stupid attachment to the idea that staying away from you was the only way I could make amends."

I turn before I can stop myself. "This hero-complex shit is getting old. I don't need you or anyone else to save me."

His jaw works. "I'm not trying to save you," he grinds out. "I'm trying to give you a weapon that will help you save yourself."

I toss the towel down and cross my arms. "And what's that?"

The forest of his eyes turns dark. "Clay has a history of preying on young, vulnerable women. Once they're seduced, he begins slowly undermining their self-worth. Forcing them into smaller and smaller versions of themselves. Gaslighting them until eventually they start thinking *they're* the crazy ones. Sound familiar?"

I swallow thickly.

"Ask me how I know, Evangeline."

CHAPTER TWENTY

evangeline

Been breathing underwater
waiting on a slaughter
Shaping sand like it was clay
Hoping it would stay

Forgot how to be honest
(even though I promised)
Forgot how to be strong
(somewhere I don't belong)

But I remember now

WILDER'S DRIVER, a giant and kind-faced man named Sam, takes me home an hour later. Besides asking me if I'd like air conditioning, he leaves me alone with my thoughts.

The world outside the tinted windows is a blur of faded greens, grays, and browns. I watch it streak past, feeling surprisingly serene. Or I could be numb. Overloaded and shutting down. But regardless, I feel lighter. As though despite not speaking a word of my own experience, hearing Kendra's history with Clay somehow unburdened me.

"He was twenty-three when he seduced Kendra, who'd just turned sixteen. He played the perfect prince and made her fall in love with him. Then it started. Insults wrapped in justifications about how much he cared, withholding affection like food until she starved. Manipulating her emotions until she felt crazy, then turning her reactions around on her as proof that she was the problem.

"He dumped her the day she turned eighteen, then continued toying with her off and on for the next five years whenever he was single. She was so fucked up over the whole thing, by the time I met her she was hooked on speed and painkillers. When we dated—if you can even call it that—she was just starting to face the abuse."

As Wilder spoke, each word precise and ringing with truth, it was like a crooked painting was being slowly straightened and brought into focus.

On some level, I must have always known Clay was lying about him being responsible for Kendra's drug use. About him being the reason she disappeared and shunned her family.

"It's a game to him, one his father taught him how to play. Kendra even overheard them laughing about it once. Conrad was congratulating Clay for doing to her what he'd done to her mother. Clay joked that it had been too easy. He said he was going to stick to women over twenty-five from then on because a 'fully developed brain' would be more of a challenge.

"All he cares about is power and control. In Clay's mind, you're the ultimate catch. Someone strong enough to provide a long-term challenge while also giving him access to circles of higher influence.

"These are Kendra's words, by the way. I'm merely the

messenger. She suspected he'd be drawn to you years ago based on your potential alone. It's why she brought him to your show-case—something she deeply regrets and hopes to apologize for someday.

"He hunted you, Evangeline, probably from that first night. Watched and waited for the right time to lead you into his care-fully laid trap. And if you need even more confirmation, hear it from his own mouth."

He played the recording he made of Clay at lunch last month. When it stopped, I calmly asked him to play it again. I didn't cry or shout or deny. Instead, the oddest thing happened.

My entire body relaxed.

Wilder noticed. With a small, soft smile, he said, "It's cathartic, isn't it? When you finally realize you're not crazy."

He told me he felt the same way the first time his sponsor, Frank, shared the story of his own youth, struggles with addiction, and eventual recovery. On the outside, his and Wilder's life experiences were starkly different. But their emotional experiences growing up were eerily similar.

I may never have warm and fuzzy feelings toward Kendra, but Wilder was right. I feel a kinship with her now. Her expe-rience validated mine. Because of her, I know I'm not crazy.

I'm glad she's safe now. Sober and healing far away from those responsible for her abuse.

I'm even glad she and Wilder reconnected and were able to resolve the toxicity of their shared past to become friends —a sentiment I'll never admit has far more to do with Kendra being happily married to a woman than my emotional maturity.

♪

AS WE PROGRESS up a long driveway bordered by skinny palm trees, the last of my fluttering thoughts fade away.

There's no confusion left.

Only resolution.

The car stops. I thank Sam and step out. He tips an imaginary hat to me, then does a U-turn and heads back down the drive. I watch him go, allowing myself a moment to think about how his next journey will be taking Wilder to the airport.

When the car turns onto the street, disappearing behind a hedge, I face the house.

The sun-warmed concrete soothes my bare, aching feet as I walk toward the front door. The air smells of freshly mowed grass; beneath it, the dry earthiness of the desert and a touch of alkaline from the smog layer.

I'm not surprised when the door opens before I reach it. Given the event yesterday, I knew Clay would be working from home. And given what happened in the limo and last night, I knew he'd have his eye on the exterior cameras.

He doesn't say anything as he holds the door open for me to pass. I walk across the foyer into the living room I've never liked, with its dark walls, overpriced art, and empty glass shelves framing the television.

Not bothering to sit, I turn and lean on the back of one of the boxy leather couches.

"We need to talk."

Clay stops a few feet away. Murky eyes take me in from messy hair to bare feet. There's a flicker of disapproval, but that's it.

There was a time I thought his ability to appear supernaturally calm was a defense mechanism leftover from an emotionally neglectful childhood. But that was me trying to humanize him. The skill is merely another weapon in his arsenal, one he exchanges as needed for anger, humor, disappointment, affection, et cetera.

I'm not sure he *has* real feelings.

Wilder's face flashes in my mind. His mood-ring eyes with their shifting greens, golds, and browns. The way even his micro-expressions are easy for me to decipher. How even when he looks perfectly calm or happy, I've always been able to tell when he's actually sad, or overstimulated, or annoyed—

"I don't have all day, Eva. Go ahead and talk."

I inhale slowly, then meet Clay's frosty stare. "I'm moving out."

His features rearrange into a facade of exhaustion. "I was hoping for an apology, but I can't say I'm surprised. You're clearly hungover and emotional right now. I'll set up a massage and an aromatherapy treatment."

"I'm only here to pack a few things. I'll arrange for a moving company to come this week."

His aggravated groan sets my teeth on edge. "Jesus Christ, do we have to go through this again? Let's just skip the part where you throw a fit and issue empty threats. If you want some space, fine. I'm due for a golfing trip to Palm Springs, anyway. I'll leave tomorrow and come back Friday. How's that sound?"

I almost laugh. What comes out instead is, "The night we ran into each other two years ago, did you really not remember me from the first time we met?"

His brow furrows. "What?"

"We met at Glow's first showcase."

"Why are we talking about this again? I told you I vaguely recall being there but not meeting you."

I tilt my head to the side. "I don't remember much of that

night, either. But I have the strangest memory—funny, really —of you telling me that you only dated women with fully developed frontal lobes. That if I was single at twenty-five, I should call you."

Apprehension flickers in his eyes, along with a touch of what looks like fear. If I didn't know better.

I'm no longer relieved, resolute, or even resigned. I'm a category five hurricane of disgust and rage. The impulse to scream at him is so powerful I have to bite my cheek. I want to expose him. Tell him I heard the recording, that I know what he did to Kendra. I want to make him crack, unravel, and admit it all.

But he won't.

There will be no restitution. No consolation prize for my awakening. Only a truth so bitter it burns.

I let this happen to me.

Clay takes a step forward, his face a mask of concern, hands lifted like I'm a wild animal.

I feel like one.

"Eva," he says in a placating tone. "We've been through this before. You're not leaving me. Think about it. Think about everything I do for you. Who else is going to put up with your moods? I'm the only one who understands what you need. I take care of you, remember?"

A wave of lethargy hits me.

I feel myself sinking, water closing over my head. I'm powerless to fight it, incapable of swimming a second longer.

The doorbell rings.

Clay stares at me another moment, then stalks from the room. The front door opens. I hear voices, the words muffled by the white noise in my ears.

Movement in my peripheral vision turns my head toward

447

the nearest doorway. I blink in surprise at the sight of Paul, a hand towel twisting between his hands.

Features set in worried lines, he whispers, "Leave him, Eva," then backs away as Clay's footsteps pound toward me.

Another set of footsteps follows his. Lighter and faster. And suddenly, I remember how to swim.

"Eva, what the hell is—"

"Shut the fuck up, Claybee," trills Martin, skirting around him to plaster himself to my side. Arm around my waist, he pulls me up until my knees lock. "Get it? Claybee like baby, because you're a whiny little bitch."

I snort.

Clay flushes, his features twisting with rage. His mouth opens.

"By all means," Martin says, lifting his phone to show he's recording video. "Show the world exactly who you are."

Air hisses through Clay's teeth. He gives me a long look that should probably scare me but doesn't. Then he spins on a heel and leaves.

Martin exhales noisily.

"Thank you," I whisper.

"Honey, thank *you*. I've wanted to call him that for years." He palms the side of my face, his dark eyes glistening. "I'm so fucking proud of you. Let's pack a bag and get out of here, okay? You and me and margaritas on the beach."

I blink away tears and nod.

CHAPTER TWENTY-ONE

wilder

TWO MONTHS LATER

SOFT MUSIC FLOATS amidst the voices and laughter at my dining room table, cutlery and glasses clinking in an irregular but melodious percussion line.

I never thought I'd be someone who hosts and enjoys dinner parties, but here we are.

"That was phenomenal, Wilder."

Smiling, I raise my water glass toward Jax's wife. "Thank you, Shannon." Then I give my bandmate a pointed look.

He rolls his eyes. "Yeah, yeah. The student has surpassed the teacher. Great lasagna."

"Pastitsio," I say with a smirk.

"Just accept it, bro," Eddie chides. "He's been in another league for years. Do you even know what a béchamel sauce is?"

After a beat of silence, Eddie's girlfriend, Holly, asks what we're all thinking. "How do *you* know what a béchamel sauce is?"

Laughter rings out. After some good-natured grumbling, Eddie admits he has no idea how to make béchamel. He points at me. "Blame him. He made me watch cooking shows almost every night of our tour last year."

I chuckle. "I made you, huh?"

He grins. "Okay, maybe I got sucked in by how cutthroat they are with all the challenges and shit."

"Damn," says Holly with an exaggerated sigh. "I was really hoping you were dropping a hint about cooking me dinner for our anniversary next month."

Eddie gulps. "Oh shoot, I ruined the surprise."

More laughter fills the air. Over Holly's head, Eddie sends me a beseeching look. I make him sweat for a few seconds, then nod. He relaxes and slings an arm around a smugly grinning Holly.

As the merriment fades and everyone finishes eating, the back of my neck begins to tingle and tighten—the first warning sign that I'm nearing my limit on socializing. Before long, my mind will start losing clarity, my skin will grow sensitive, and the assorted sounds around me will grate.

Glancing discreetly at my watch, I'm surprised and gratified to see it's nearing ten o'clock. I made it almost four hours —a new personal record.

I push back my chair. "Who's ready for dessert?"

Soft fingertips land on my forearm. "No way," says Aubrey, her blue eyes sparkling. "You're not allowed to do anything else."

I relax back into my chair, hoping she doesn't notice that my smile is a little forced. When I told Jax that Zander and his date couldn't make it, he took it upon himself to invite

Shannon's sister. Despite suspecting ulterior motives, I didn't have a good reason to say no.

As far as Jax knows, Aubrey and I are friendly acquaintances. It's not like I could tell him we hooked up at his and Shannon's wedding last year or that I regretted it almost immediately.

"I concur," says Shannon with overly bright enthusiasm. "The chef should relax."

Jax stands. "Eddie and Holly, if you guys want to grab dessert, we'll clear the table." A second of silent but painfully obvious communication passes between the couples, then they're all moving.

I swallow a sigh. "Thanks, guys."

When Aubrey makes a weak attempt at helping, Shannon chirps, "Stay, sis. Keep Wilder company."

The moment we're alone—or as alone as we can be with the kitchen ten feet away—Aubrey whispers, "She failed out of afterschool theater club."

My lips quirk. "I think they all did."

Her laugh dances nervously. "You're probably right. I'm glad we have a second, though, so I can thank you privately for being so... not awkward with me tonight. You're a good guy, Wilder."

I shrug, smiling vaguely. "No reason for awkwardness."

Mentally, I'm chanting, *Shitshitshit.*

With a deep breath, she pivots further in her seat. Her shoulder grazes mine while her knee taps my thigh. There's no way I can pull away without being super obvious about it, and my head is already too fuzzy to think of some way to defuse the intent I see in her eyes.

I try not to grit my teeth as she leans even closer to me. "This is me shooting my shot. Any chance you're ready to reconsider the no-dating rule?"

This—*this* is why sleeping with Audrey was a giant mistake. She's kind, genuine, and charming. At the wedding last year, we talked for hours before she invited me to her hotel room. But when I woke up the next morning and saw her sleeping face, all I felt was a mix of regret and disappointment.

Through no fault of her own, the seed of connection I'd felt the night prior was gone. Shriveled before I could even consider planting it.

She sees the truth in my eyes, her hopeful expression instantly falling. I open my mouth to fumble through an *it's not you, it's me* explanation, but the chime of the doorbell cuts me off. The sound is so unexpected, I startle and recoil from Aubrey. She looks away, her face flushing.

Jax asks, "Are you expecting someone?"

Already halfway to standing, I sense rather than see Aubrey shrinking in her chair.

"No," I say quickly. I grab my phone off a nearby shelf and frown at the screen. "They're supposed to text me before letting people through the gate after dark."

"Ohhh, someone's getting fired," Eddie sings.

Holly giggles. "Stop. It's probably that weird neighbor. He saw our cars and wants to party."

Shannon chimes in, "The guy who showed up at the barbecue last summer?"

Eddie laughs loudly. "I forgot about him! Didn't he just walk right into the backyard and help himself to food?"

"Yes! Then he talked Zander's ear off for an hour about aliens until Jax finally got him to leave."

Between one moment and the next, I cross the line into overstimulation, the chorus of voices melding into an abrasive buzz. In lieu of telling everyone to shut the fuck up so I can think, I clutch my phone and walk swiftly toward the hallway.

"I can answer it, Wilder," offers Jax as I pass the kitchen.

"I've got it," I force out.

Halfway down the hallway, the chatter fades enough to no longer feel like the sensory equivalent of nails on a chalkboard. I stop beside a window and lay my palm on the glass.

Inhale. Feel the cold. Exhale. You're fine. Just tired. Breathe.

My heartbeat eventually retreats from my temples, the tightness in my lungs releasing. Leaning my shoulder on a wall, I pull up the app for my doorbell camera. If Holly's correct—and she probably is—I have no intention of opening the door. My neighbor, Herman, is a single retiree with a habit of showing up uninvited and ignoring cues to leave. He's also an absolute wacko obsessed with conspiracy theories, who occasionally forgoes pants and underwear because they *chafe*.

The video feed is slow to load. I wince in anticipation of Herman's cold-shriveled dick and balls. But when the image clears, it's not Herman.

An unfamiliar woman stands at the bottom of the porch steps, her back to the camera. Shoulder-length light brown hair, a winter coat, shapeless cargo pants, and sneakers.

Torn between curiosity and apprehension, I keep staring. Ten seconds later, she seems to pull herself straighter. Then she walks into the darkness.

On her third step, my breath stalls in my chest.

Then I'm running.

CHAPTER TWENTY-TWO

wilder

I TEAR OPEN the front door and make it across the porch before realizing I'm barefoot and wearing a T-shirt. The wind off the water doesn't care that it's technically spring, immediately diving beneath my clothes and inducing a shiver.

Not that a blizzard would stop me.

Her retreat halted when I opened the door, but she doesn't turn around as I jog down the brick path. Stopping a few feet from her back, I tuck my hands into my armpits.

"Evangeline?"

I'm aiming for calm, maybe even amusement, but I miss the mark by a mile. My chest heaves like my ten-second sprint was a triathlon. I sound angry.

I *am* angry.

It's been two months since the Grammys. Two months since she disappeared from the public eye. Eight *long as fuck* weeks in which I've wondered and worried about her, my only comfort the texts she sent Lily, Rye, and her parents before vanishing. She told them she'd left Clay, was somewhere safe with Martin Page, and needed time to think.

Evangeline slowly turns around. Her head stays lowered,

eyes on the ground between us and hands tucked in her coat pockets.

"I guess you're wondering where I've been and what I'm doing here."

I choke on a thousand replies, all of them too emotional.

She glances at the house, then at the two other cars parked in my driveway. "You have company. I'm sor—I mean, oops. I'll just... go."

I jerk forward, grabbing her arm before I even finish the thought of stopping her. "Don't."

She startles, chin and eyes lifting, her face finally visible in the ambient glow of the house lights. My brain absorbs new information so fast the steam from my breath might as well be leaving my ears.

I can hardly believe it, but she's not wearing a wig like I thought. She actually chopped off and dyed her signature white-blond locks. The color, a few shades darker than her lashes and brows, looks ridiculously sexy. She's put on some much-needed weight, too, her cheekbones not as stark and her jawline a touch softer. And she's tan—or as tan as she can get, her face and neck the light bronze, freckle-sprinkled hue I saw each summer as a kid. The final difference is the only one that bothers me: she's covered her pale gray iris with a contact lens color-matched to her hazel eye.

A gust of wind slaps me out of my stunned silence. "Are you okay? Where have you been?"

Her gaze slides off my face toward the water, visible only as winks of moonlight through the trees.

"I'm fine. I was in Baja." She sighs. "I'd still be there if a local hadn't recognized me at the market. Lazy mistake on my part—I was wearing a hat but forgot my contact lens. Honestly, I don't blame her for following me and taking photos. Hopefully she holds out for a lot of zeroes."

Given the ongoing media buzz around her disappearance, I have no doubt a few clear shots will earn the fan a life-changing payday.

I'm glad she understood the implications and left, but I still have to swallow the urge to lecture her. The mere thought of her wandering around for weeks without protection makes me feel sick. There's a reason women in her position have bodyguards. Between stalkers and obsessive fans, it's fucking dangerous.

"I've been at my parents' since I got back." She grimaces, then grumbles, "Three nights was all I could handle."

I smother a huff of laughter. Matt wouldn't have held back on telling her exactly how irresponsible it was to play tourist, and it's not hard to envision Evangeline's reaction.

"And now?"

"I'm not sure." She glances at the cars again. "I shouldn't have bothered you."

"You're not bothering me." Only when she trembles at my low tone do I realize I'm still holding her arm. My fingers loosen, but I can't bring myself to let go entirely. "Why are you here, Evangeline?"

Her tongue peeks out to curl over an incisor. Despite my balls currently impersonating ice cubes, arousal stirs in my gut. It joins lingering anger and general overwhelm, creating a mess inside me. Half of me wants to rip her pants off and fuck her against the closest tree, while the other half wishes I hadn't answered the damn door.

Wind tries to steal her next words, but I catch them.

"I didn't have anywhere else to go."

Shock forces air from my lungs in a burst of vapor.

I have no idea why she feels like she can't go to Lily and Rye, or her grandparents, or one of her aunts or uncles...

But I don't fucking care.

She came to *me*.

Mistaking my silence for confusion, she explains hurriedly, "You gave me your address that day at lunch, remember? I should have texted or called, I know, but I..." She trails off with a shake of her head. "Anyway, I'm sorry for dropping in like this."

"Try again."

She frowns for a moment, then gets it. Her lips curve. "*Oops.*"

I grin. "Much better."

Her gaze flickers between my dimples, then strokes across my mouth. When she swallows thickly, my mind cartwheels into the gutter. That elegant neck under my hand. Feeding my cock past those lips. Feeling her swallow from the inside.

"It's okay if you've changed your mind. I completely understand."

I blink away the fantasy. "I haven't changed my mind. You're always welcome here."

She sucks in a breath. "Oh."

The sight of her pursed lips sends another zap of desire down my spine. For my own sanity, I release her arm and take a half-step backward. My teeth immediately start to chatter.

"Do you have a bag? I can grab it for you."

Relief softens her features. "Yes, but I'll get it. You're obviously freezing." She turns, then pauses to grin at me over her shoulder. "Thank you, Wilder. So, so much. I won't stay longer than a few weeks."

She walks quickly toward her car, parked near the end of the drive ahead of Jax's and Eddie's. I gape after her, certain I must have misheard her final words. Because if I didn't, and she's staying a few *weeks*?

I'm seriously fucked.

Evangeline in my house, in my kitchen, on my furniture...

457

I won't survive it. More accurately, my dominant hand won't survive it.

A shiver so violent I almost bite through my tongue sends me hustling toward the house. Halfway up the porch steps, a bolt of fear halts me. I spin around and search the darkness.

Light flares at the end of the driveway, highlighting Evangeline as she leans into the back seat of her car.

I start breathing again.

A creak of wood behind me precedes Jax's soft, surprised voice. "Is that who I think it is?"

I nod and join him on the porch, sighing as the heat escaping the open front door laps against my body.

"She's on a list at the gate."

What I don't say is that the list she's on is different from the main one with approved guests. Only one person has no restrictions, can show up whenever, without notice, even if I'm not here.

Jax's sigh makes me think he can deduce as much. "Okay. I'll round everyone up and we'll get out of here. Kitchen's mostly sorted, and we already demolished the cannoli. Eddie's fault, naturally."

I chuckle. "Naturally. Thanks, man." I hesitate, then blurt, "About Aubrey, I—"

He quickly lifts a hand. "Dude, no. That was my bad. I warned Shannon it probably wouldn't go the way she wanted. I'm guessing I was right?"

Grimacing, I rub the heels of my hands into my eyes. "Pretty much. Aubrey asked me out, but the doorbell rang before I could answer. She's super cool, I'm just... I guess it was bad timing."

Lowering my hands, I see Jax's too-wide smile a second before a throat clears softly behind me.

"Hey, Jax," says Evangeline. "How's it going?"

458

evangeline

STARING at a curtained window in Wilder's guest bedroom, I rub a towel over my hair and try not to focus on how fucking nervous I am.

So far nothing has gone the way I hoped it would. Most of the drive here, I felt good. Confident and full of purpose. Both feelings drained away on the ferry from Seattle to Madrone Island, which I spent hiding in a corner with my hood pulled low.

By the time I navigated off the ferry, my stomach was in knots. I ended up driving the main loop on the south side of the island for an hour in hopes my nerves would settle. Instead, I grew more and more paranoid that I was going to be pulled over for suspicious activity.

Finally, after checking to see when the last ferry of the day was leaving, I made it to the northern tip of the island. Then I almost turned right back around when I saw the manned security booth outside of Wilder's gated community.

I stammered out my name and who I was visiting. The guard asked for my driver's license and looked between it and me so many times I half expected him to citizen's arrest me for impersonating a celebrity.

But then he smiled and gave me a small envelope with a key and a slip of paper inside. He explained that the key was for Wilder's front door and the code on the paper would disarm his security system. Before I could muster a response, the thick gate rolled open.

A minute later, I was here, crashing a dinner party with Jax and Eddie, their significant others, and a woman who glared at me like I'd shit in her cereal. Which, given what I overheard Wilder tell Jax on the porch, I kind of did.

Bad timing, like Wilder said.

Or maybe perfect timing.

Who knows what might have happened if I'd waited a few more days, or even a few more weeks? Maybe he wanted to say yes to that date—would have, if I hadn't shown up. From my ten-second glimpse of the woman, Aubrey, as everyone left, on looks alone I can't blame him.

As much as I want to slap myself for comparing myself to her, I can't help it. She was beautiful. Pacific blue eyes, bright and sparkly. Long, thick, shiny brown hair. Peaches and cream, freckle-free skin. Curvier hips. Much bigger boobs. The sweetest smile—when she aimed it at him.

She's basically animated princess material. Probably does yoga and meditates. Doesn't need therapy because she's spiritually and mentally stable. Oh, and let's not forget she's *super cool*.

"Stop it," I hiss at myself.

Giving up on my hair, I walk into the en suite to hang my damp towel on a rack.

The bathroom, like the guest bedroom and the glimpses I had of the rest of the house, is gorgeous. I feel like I'm standing in one of those architectural magazine feature homes. The ones that look so inviting, even whimsical, but also impossibly elegant. Soft white walls, rich wood floors, warm metallic accents. Tons of plants. Color and texture everywhere from rugs, throws, and art.

The style actually reminds me of the house I bought not far from my parents, which I sold before moving to Los Angeles. Or rather, it reminds me of the stylistic vision I had for that house before *someone* talked me out of finding a designer.

Before my brain decides to meander down Traumatic Memory Lane, I splash my face with cold water. Then I brush my teeth, moisturize, and finger comb my hair until I stop looking like I was drowned before being electrocuted.

Wilder still cares about me. I know he does. If he didn't, he wouldn't have run after me. Nor would he have stopped me from leaving.

That his relief manifested as anger was no surprise. Everyone who loves me is acting the same way right now. I know they're not angry *at* me—even Lily, who has every reason to be. Beneath their anger is helplessness, and beneath that is their fear for me. For my safety, my mental health, my future.

The way I unplugged and disappeared certainly didn't help. It scared the hell out of everyone. But I don't regret going. It was necessary.

Regardless of my tan, my time in Baja was anything but a vacation. With Martin's unfailing support, I started deconstructing and processing the last two years. It was fucking exhausting. A nonstop emotional spin cycle of sadness, rage, numbness, hilarity, confusion, manic hope, and sluggish depression. It took a week for me to actually break down and let it all out. I cried for three days straight.

When I woke up on the fourth day, I felt it for the first

time—the reason I'm here. Another crossroads. One that was always inside me, hidden behind the bricks I'd routinely stacked in front of it. I did my best to ignore it, but as weeks passed, it only grew clearer. Larger. *Louder.* Until I could no longer resist its call.

It doesn't matter what I interrupted tonight or what might have happened. Nor does it matter that Martin might be right and this is too much, too soon.

What matters is that time is running out.

To forgive.

To repair.

To remember.

♫

I'M PULLING BACK the covers on the bed, about to surrender myself to the lengthy process of falling asleep, when there's a soft knock on the door.

My heart yaps, adrenaline flooding my body.

"Evangeline?"

With no denial buffering me anymore, the sound of my full name on his lips weakens my knees and shortens my breath.

I glance down at myself and wince at what I'm wearing: a pair of my brother's old sweatpants and a Breaking Giants T-shirt I stole from my dad. But looking like a slob is what I get for leaving Baja for the Pacific Northwest's version of spring. Somewhere in Seattle, there's a storage unit with all my stuff, but the details are buried among the thousand other emails I've ignored for the last two months.

Running my hands through my hair one more time, I move to the door and open it. I'm still not ready for the impact of him standing right in front of me, close enough to touch in flannel pajama pants and a soft gray T-shirt. His hair is brushed back, wet from his own shower. Dark bristles shadow his jaw and neck.

A magical forest lives in his eyes.

A midnight rainstorm brews in the air around him.

My, "Hi," is embarrassingly breathy.

Wilder's gaze travels around the room, pausing on my guitar case before returning to me. He smiles, the beauty of it cranking the vise on my chest even tighter.

"Hi back. I wanted to make sure you were settling in okay. Do you have everything you need? Enough blankets? Towels?"

"Yes. I'm perfect. Super great. Your water pressure is godlike. Towels were fluffy. Ten out of ten."

His eyes flare with amusement. I mentally slap myself and pray my tan hides the heat crawling up my neck.

"Sure you're not hungry? I have leftovers I can heat up. It's no problem at all."

"Positive, thanks. And thanks again for letting me invade your space. I'll keep out of your way as much as possible."

"Not necessary." White teeth capture a corner of his lower lip, scraping gently before he clears his throat. "If you're up before me tomorrow, feel free to eat and drink whatever. Or if you want to wait, I usually make breakfast around nine."

I blink fast, my eyes burning. "Thank you."

A dimple deepens on his cheek. "Please stop saying thank you. Just treat the house like it's yours. There's a studio out back, too. Used to be a guesthouse. You can get in with the key the guard gave you. There's a piano out there and... stuff."

He shifts on his feet. Scratches his jaw. Looks down the hallway and all around me but not *at* me. And even though I can hardly believe it, it finally sinks in.

He's nervous, too.

Another surge of adrenaline lifts my heart to the base of my throat. I can hear my own breathing, steady if fast, but I'm suddenly not getting enough oxygen. My hands and feet tingle. My armpits, too.

I open my mouth.

Wilder says, "Okay. Um, good night. I'm just down the hall if you need me—*something*, I mean. If you need something."

Our eyes meet for half a second before he pivots and walks toward his room. One step, two steps, three...

"Wait!"

My plea is far too loud and high-pitched. Basically a screech.

Wilder freezes in place, then spins back around. "Holy shit, I thought I was about to fall down the stairs."

We both look at the stairs—that are at least five feet away in the opposite direction—then look at each other.

"Oops?"

He pinches the bridge of his nose, then chuckles. "Oops, she says." Lowering his hand, he squints at me. "Were you trying to give me a heart attack or did you think of something you needed?"

Butterflies thwack against my ribcage and dive-bomb my centerline. I lick my lips. Take a stuttering breath.

Fuck it.

"You."

His brows pinch. "You need..." Understanding dawns, lifting his chest on a sharp breath. His eyes darken. So does his voice. "Tell me what you mean by that."

My toes curl against hardwood. "I need—or want, I should say—what I mean is I'm offering, if *you* wanted to, you know—"

"Evangeline," he says in a pained voice. "Please stop."

My teeth click as I close them. Before I can decide whether to throw myself in the bedroom and slam the door or run down the stairs and out of the house, Wilder takes a step toward me. The intensity in his expression pins me to the floor.

"So I don't misunderstand, are you asking for my company? Like you want to talk or hang out? Or are you asking me if I want to fuck?"

I choke on my next breath but manage to force out, "Second one."

A muscle on his jawline jumps. His stare penetrates me but not in a fun way. The longer he looks at me, the tighter vines of fear wrap around my chest.

When he sighs heavily, my heart dehydrates.

I'm too late.

Whatever Wilder sees on my face makes his lips thin. "For fuck's sake, Evangeline. How are you one of the most observant people I've ever known and still so blind? If you'd so much as glanced down once in the last few minutes, you'd already know the answer."

My gaze drops right as his tattooed hand strokes across the outline of his erection. A bomb explodes at the base of my spine, instantly drenching my underwear.

"Oh," I whisper.

"I jacked off twice in the shower. *Twice.* And all you had to do was say 'hi' to me for this to happen." He grunts. "Enough. Eyes up."

My gaze lifts to his face. But instead of the anticipation I'm expecting, I find frustration.

"Me wanting to fuck you is like taxes and gravity. Immutable."

I whisper, "Why do you sound angry about it?"

Hands sinking into his hair, his head drops back. I have

465

no idea what he's looking at on the ceiling, but ten seconds pass before his shoulders and face lower.

The frustration is gone. Now he wears a patchwork mask over sadness.

"No matter how much I want to have sex with you, it wouldn't be right. Not after what you've just been through." He takes another step toward me, eyes imploring. "Let me be here for you in every other way while you heal. And I swear to God, if you still want me down the line, I'm all yours."

wilder

WHEN THE BEDROOM door closes behind her, I fold forward and release a silent scream into my fists.

I don't know if that was the best, most selfless thing I've ever done in my life, or a decision I'll regret until the day I die. Either way, it seriously fucking sucked.

Silently cursing myself and the universe at large, I retreat into my bedroom and close the door. The room is dim, only a small bedside light on. Before I'd given in to impulse and knocked on her door, I'd been reading some dry-as-hell philosophy book my dad gave me for Christmas, hoping to bore myself to sleep. And that was after back-to-back orgasms in the shower failed to exhaust me.

My body vibrates with frenetic energy as I sit on the bed and lower my head into my hands. Thumbs on my temples, I massage as I count my inhales and exhales.

It doesn't fucking help.

All I see is her endearing, stammering nervousness. Her fear and courage. The avaricious gleam in her mismatched eyes when she finally let herself look below my waist.

Mostly, though, I see the last, stricken look she gave me

before she closed the door. She thinks I rejected her. I *did* reject her.

"What have I done?" I mumble.

She's probably going to leave, might be packing right now.

The thought brings me to my feet right as my bedroom door swings open and slams against the wall. Flash frozen, I stare at Evangeline as she strides toward me.

When she's a few feet away and still moving like she's on a warpath, I open my mouth to say fuck-knows-what.

"No," she snaps, jabbing her index finger into my chest. "You said your piece, now I get to say mine. Two months ago, you told me I was powerful. A 'force to be reckoned with.' Was that a lie?"

I croak, "Of course not."

She waves a paper in my face until I take it. Angling it toward the light, I see what looks like a letter from a doctor's office. But it's in Spanish.

"What is this?" I ask, but then I turn it over and see a series of familiar-looking words, all of which have *Negativo* in bold next to them.

"That's my clean bill of health because I don't want to use a condom. As long as you can produce a similar report. Can you?"

"Yes, but—"

"Good. I'm still on birth control."

She pulls the paper out of my hand, folds it into a square, and shoves it in a pocket of her sweatpants.

Then she pulls her shirt off.

And she's not wearing a bra.

Pressure instantly engulfs my cock. I'm so hard there's a notable pulse in my shaft, and the soft flannel of my pants has turned to sandpaper.

Evangeline's breasts are every bit as perfect as I remember, teardrop-shaped and fuller on the bottom. Her nipples sit high like offerings of dusty pink hard candy. Now they're even more delicious-looking, each framed by two small, silver balls begging to be flicked, licked, and sucked.

I close my eyes. Open them.

Nope. Not dreaming.

"I want you to prove it, Wilder," she says sharply.

I have no idea what she's talking about, but thankfully she keeps going.

"Prove to me that I'm powerful. Don't treat me like everyone else right now, like I'm fragile and I'll fall apart if you tell me how angry you are with me. I can take it. I want it. Show me."

I drag my gaze from her chest and up her throat. Over her defiantly lifted chin. Along the lines of her silky, succulent, stubborn mouth. Her small, flared nostrils. The freckles on the bridge of her nose.

Finally, I study the mismatched eyes that fucking haunt me. The hazel one with its ring of green flecked with blue that blends into golden brown. And the other—her fairy eye. *My* fairy eye. Icy blue-gray with a thin border of steel, it pierces me like it always has. Cracks me in half and exposes my most feral self.

I grab the back of her neck and yank her forward. She stumbles and gasps, her hands flying to my chest to brace herself. But I already can't remember why I wasn't supposed to do this.

"I *am* fucking mad at you," I growl.

Closing my fingers around a fistful of hair, I pull her head back and bite her chin, her jaw. I scrape my teeth over her mouth but don't kiss her. Nip her lower lip, then upper. Hard enough to sting, not hard enough to hurt. *Yet.* With every bite, she jerks and produces a breathy, needy note.

Her hands climb to my shoulders, nails digging. When she tries to kiss me, I tug her hair to remind her who's in control. She surrenders with a sigh, looking up at me with lust-drunk eyes.

She's so stunning I almost wish I could be gentle. *Almost.*

Keeping her head still, I drag my mouth toward her ear. I take my time, enjoying the subtle rasp of my unshaven cheek against her smooth, warmer skin.

"Do you remember what I feel like? You told me it's close to overwhelming at first. That I stretch you so good it burns. Did you miss my cock? Did you miss all that pressure in your sweet little cunt?"

She whimpers.

"Answer me."

"Yes, I missed your cock," she whispers, writhing helplessly against my chest. "*Fuck.* Stop torturing me. I'm begging you."

I shake my head, smiling against her temple. "I've waited seven years for this. Beg all you want, Fairy. I'm taking my time."

The rhythm of her breath vanishes, then resumes even faster. Her neck tenses under my hand. A shudder runs down her body. Alarmed, I lean back to see her face.

The second our eyes meet, I realize what I said.

"Fairy," I repeat, transfixed by the lifecycle of a tear on her lower lash line. The shimmering sphere grows until it drops, splashing against her cheek.

"Again," she breathes.

"Fairy." I trail a fingertip down her nose. "You're a perfect song. Even though I know every note, I'll never be able to replicate it. It's simply too exquisite to exist outside of you."

Her lips quiver. "My God."

"Not yet, but I'm about to be."

Transferring my hands to her waist, I lift and throw her onto the bed. She squeaks when she hits, her bouncing tits an irresistible lure. A moment later, my mouth captures a nipple, and her moan slides down my throat like honey.

By the time I'm done reacquainting myself with every inch of her chest and have teased her nipples and piercings to my satisfaction, she's crying again. The kind of tears I love. *My* tears. Her head tosses, hips jerking toward my hovering body, hands fisted in the comforter.

"Such a needy mess," I whisper against her neck. "So overwhelmed, aren't you?"

She sobs my name. "Please."

My thumb sinks past her lips, capturing her lower teeth and pressing down until her jaw opens. I spit into her mouth. She makes a sound that's half lust, half outrage.

I grin.

She glares.

"You've been so good, Fairy. Keeping your hands to yourself. Letting me play with your gorgeous tits. Do you want a reward?"

She nods fast.

I push my thumb deeper into her mouth. "Suck."

Eyes flaring, her lips seal around my finger. She sucks hard, her tongue swirling. I grunt, the sensation echoing around my cock.

"Do you want more?"

Another eager nod.

I give her my first and middle fingers and she goes to town on them. Teeth and tongue, sloppy and ravenous. Then she grabs my wrist and lifts her head, sinking my fingers to the back of her throat. Eyes on mine and glittering with challenge, she sucks and swallows. When she gags a little, then moans, it's game over.

In seconds, I have her sweatpants off, her legs around my head, and my face buried in her pussy. One arm over her stomach to hold her down, I lick everywhere except her clit, reveling in the return of her taste on my tongue.

When her thighs start to shake and the tone of her cries changes from pleasure to torment, I find her hands and put them on my head. They immediately sink into my hair and clench. Her shoulders lift, upper body curving. Panting, she stares down at me like I'm more devil than god.

I wink.

She pulls my hair roughly, guiding my mouth to her clit.

"Suck," she snarls.

I happily comply.

Her grip is merciless as she rides my smothered face, too far gone to care about whether or not I can breathe. I can't, but it doesn't matter because in less than thirty seconds she comes with a gloriously profane cry.

I kiss her swollen clit, then devote myself to the task of licking up every drop of tart cum. Legs splayed and arms over her face, she's too blissed out to notice my exploration further south until my finger joins the party.

She whacks my head. "No way."

I chuckle against the crease of her thigh. But I don't move my finger. "What? I'm not even pushing."

An arm lifts off her face. Her eyes narrow, but amusement dilutes the effect of her glare. Watching her face carefully, I massage with a bit more pressure. Not breaching the ring of muscle yet, just reintroducing myself. Her breath hitches, pupils flaring.

"Mmm, that's what I thought. You remember how good it feels to take me here while I work a vibrator in your pussy, don't you?"

"Yes." She licks her lips. "Is, uh, that what you want? Tonight?"

I shake my head, almost smiling when she can't hide her relief. Then I do smile. "Maybe tomorrow."

Her eyes round in panic, but I don't give her time to think about it. Lifting onto my knees, I slide forward, forcing her legs wider with mine. With my free hand, I stroke her arms and thighs. Slow, heavy pressure that makes her eyes glaze. Then I palm each of her breasts, tapping and lightly pinching her nipples until she's panting again. All the while, I slowly increase the pressure of my other finger.

"Left foot on my shoulder. Good girl."

I kiss her ankle in thanks, then look down and bite my cheek at how she's spread open for me. How well she remembers. How naturally we still move together.

"Fucking perfect." I make her aware of my finger again, circling and pulsing it. "You're already nice and slippery. Just one finger for now. I've never hurt you before, have I?"

"No," she whispers, then nods. "I'm ready."

Her bravery, her trust, make my heart hot and my head light.

She's still better than any drug.

"That's my girl," I say, my voice gravel. "Take a deep breath, nice and slow. Now exhale and relax. *Fuck.* There you go."

Her body swallows my finger to the second knuckle before clamping down in resistance. I keep my hand still, letting her adjust at her own pace.

She winces. "I'm sorry, I—"

"Stop it. You're fucking flawless. Look at what you do to me."

I yank my pants off my hips, wincing as fabric scrapes hypersensitive skin. As intended, she immediately forgets about my finger in her ass, her eyes fixed on where I'm flushed, pierced, and leaking.

She licks her lips. When my cock jerks in response, her eyes widen in shocked delight. I take a mental snapshot so I can laugh about it later. Right now, I'm fast approaching my limit. There's edging myself, and then there's torture.

"Touch me, Fairy."

She doesn't hesitate, grabbing me in a fist and jacking her hand roughly—just how I fucking like it. I groan, battling the urge to match her rhythm with my hips. If I do, I won't stop until I come all over her stomach. And there's no fucking way I'm spilling anywhere but inside her.

Maybe she senses how close I am because she shifts tactics. One hand strokes me loosely, dipping to cup my sack on the downstroke, while the other plays over my head. She's so entranced, I don't think she realizes that my finger is all the way in or that she's been fucking my hand this whole time.

I haven't moved my arm once.

She swipes a fingertip over my slit, gathering fluid, then circles it around the balls of my piercing. Her nail grazes where I'm most sensitive, and I wince in spite of myself. Catching it, she blinks up at me with false concern.

"Oops. Did that hurt?"

I smirk. "You know one of my kinks is when your claws come out. Playtime's over, though. Can you let go of my finger? I need to fuck you and I want to look at you while I do it."

Another mental snapshot: her face as she stops using my finger as a dildo in the same instant she realizes she was. I can't stop my laugh this time.

Thankfully, before she can decide to be hurt or embarrassed, she peers up at me. Whatever she sees on my face—probably my utter joy—makes her smile sheepishly.

"You have nice fingers. Very skilled."

"Oh, do I?" I ask, chuckling anew as I gently slip out of her body.

She nods, then squeezes my cock so hard I choke. "But I want this now, please and thank you."

My laughter evaporates, single-minded intent pooling at the base of my spine. "Say it."

Her breath hitches. "I need you inside me. Fuck me. Please."

I kick off my pants and finally lower onto her. The first full contact of our naked bodies pulls moans from us both. Her hands glide down my back, legs hooking around my thighs. My cock notches right where it needs to be. Where it's supposed to be.

Home. I'm home.

Short nails dig into my ass, beckoning me closer, deeper. My body starts to shake.

"Wait. I need a second—"

"No," she says, voice firm against my jaw. "I want it. I deserve it. Make it hurt, Wilder."

I don't want to.

God, I don't want to.

But I snap anyway.

My hips work in rough thrusts, forcing her body to yield to mine one devastating inch at a time. On some level, I recognize familiar cues and sounds. Her moans and pleas. How wet she is, how she doesn't push at me but clings. But none of it is enough to change the fact I'm hurting her.

Or that I like it.

"Goddammit," I snarl, mindless and suddenly so angry I can't see. "Damn you, Evangeline. God fucking damn you."

Her arms and legs tighten around me. "I know," she whispers against my throat. "I can take it. It's okay."

I lift onto my hands, the movement forcing my cock deeper. *Not deep enough.* In a burst of unwanted clarity, I realize I'll never be as deep inside her as I want to be.

Evangeline's hands rise, framing my face tentatively. Tears leak from her eyes in continuous streams. Her thumbs stroke my clenched jaw.

"I'm sorry," she whispers. "I'm so sorry."

Not enough.

"You're not forgiven."

Her eyes close, then flutter back open. The gray one catches all the light in the room, sparkling like a star.

"Show me."

My laugh is madness as I clasp the delicate column of her throat in one hand. My other curls around her hip, fingers digging into the lush globe of her ass. I lift and tilt her hips to exactly where I want her.

Then I fucking show her.

I pound into her viciously until I bottom out, but I don't stop. There's no relief, no return of tenderness. No music, either—just a cacophony of my grunts, her whimpers, our gasps. The slap of our flesh is obscene and arrhythmic.

Sweat drips until we're slick with it. Her pussy is a molten sheath, swelling more with every thrust. But I'm still shocked when I feel the first flutters.

"You're actually going to come again. You little sl—" By some miracle, I manage to swallow the rest of the word.

"Don't hold back," she pleads, her eyes frenzied and desperate. "It's true. Only with you."

Instead of her admittance pleasing me, it only makes me angrier.

"You're such a greedy slut. Pushing me past my limits, making me fuck this cunt harder than I want to. You love this, don't you? Are you going to come all over my cock, Evangeline?"

"Yes, yes."

I bark a mirthless laugh. "Then fucking come."

Rearing back, I reach between us and pinch her clit. Once, twice, before she wails like a banshee. Her eyes roll back in her head, her body lifting like a bowstring, every muscle straining. Then her pussy clamps down and pulses so hard I know what's coming. Sure enough, her release soaks my balls and the comforter beneath us.

"I bet that felt good," I remark, slowing my pace as her contractions ease and fade. Her moans could be sobs, but it's hard to say and I'm not sure I care. She melts back onto the mattress, gasping for air, trembling all over.

Not. Fucking. Enough.

I stop moving. Anchored in her body, I lean down until my mouth hovers so close to hers that I'm swallowing the weight of our shared breath. When she tries to kiss me, I jerk my head back.

"No," I snarl. "You walked away from me like we were nothing. *Nothing.* Just like that, you wiped me out of your heart and life. And believe me, I know how messed up that sounds. How wrong it is. I'm well aware that I'm the villain in this story. But you *left me*. You fucking left me when you were supposed to forgive me."

Her chin trembles. "I know."

Unable to help myself, I grind against her. It doesn't matter that my broken heart is currently clawing its way out of my chest, or that my tears join the sweat already dripping off my chin.

My body sings for hers whether I want it to or not.

"My Fairy. My perfect song. I remade myself for you, but you still threw me away. All these years, I've been waiting for

477

my missing piece to come home. But you aren't home, are you? You're not here to love me. You're not here to keep me."

Her eyes shift between mine, sorrowful and searching. Maybe finally seeing.

I hit an angle that makes her breath hitch. Lightning zips down my spine, gathering and building.

"You *are* powerful," I bite out. "So powerful I almost killed myself for you. Because I thought if you wanted me to die, I didn't have anything to live for."

Horror slackens her mouth. "No."

Unable to look at her another second, I drop to my forearms and lower my head to the bed beside hers. My voice thickens with my cock, my hips pumping faster as release barrels toward me.

Sick, twisted release.

"I loved you so much, but you didn't feel it. How could you not feel it? How could you forget me like that? We were supposed to be more. We were supposed to be everything."

"Wilder, please. Oh God. No, no..."

She can't help it any more than I can.

Her body sings for mine.

She weeps through her third orgasm. My release slams into me between one breath and the next.

Shattering me.

When I come back together, I have even fewer pieces than before.

But it's enough.

"I know it's not your fault," I whisper, nuzzling her ear as she cries silently beneath me. "I forgive you, and I forgive myself. For all of it. And I'll be your friend always. I'll give you this, too—whatever you want for as long as you need. But please, Evangeline, please don't ask for what's left of my heart unless you plan to keep it forever."

CHAPTER TWENTY-FIVE

evangeline

I didn't mean to fall here
Bringing all my broken pieces
But I just couldn't help it—
you're the only consequence I want

WHEN WILDER TOLD me his studio used to be a guesthouse, I was expecting something small, maybe a thousand square feet. Cabin-sized. What I wasn't expecting was a whole-ass, two-story house hidden behind trees about a minute's walk down a path from the main house.

Granted, in terms of size for the neighborhood, it's a shack. But it's also twice the size of my first home, the little bungalow I still miss.

Downstairs is almost entirely studio space, a wide-open floor plan with a modest kitchen toward the back and half-bath tucked under stairs. The second story boasts two small bedrooms, a bathroom, and a closet stacked with linens.

The studio is a literal dream. Bright and airy, it has the same cozy vibe as the main house. There's a lounging area with a fireplace and inviting couches and armchairs. Rugs are strewn liberally over the hardwood floors. The walls showcase professional concert photographs, framed posters from Night Theory's tours, and floating shelves with all their awards.

It's clear the whole band spends time here. Pristine guitars hang along one wall: multiple acoustic and electric, as well as Jax's favorite Fender bass. There's a drum set for Eddie, a standing keyboard for Zander, and a massive workstation with multiple screens, extensive audio interfaces, and top-of-the-line studio monitors. Literally everything you could possibly need for recording, editing, and mixing. There's even a partially enclosed vocal booth with panels to tame sound reflections.

For me, though, the unquestionable centerpiece of the studio is the grand piano, a stunning, nine-foot-long vintage Steinway. I've been sitting at it for close to twenty minutes, my fingers ghosting over silky keys as I listen to phantom notes of memory.

I saw this exact piano nearly every weekend of my life growing up. It sat in the front room of the Ashburn home, a gift from Julian to Rose shortly after Wilder's birth. It's the piano he learned to play on. The piano I spent hours lying beneath as a child, dozing and dreaming and listening to him tinker through his first compositions. I still remember the first time he let me play it, the pride I felt when he realized how good I was.

A messy stack of sheet music sits on the shelf, the topmost page half-covered in penciled notes. I finally give in to temptation and read the first few lines. My fingers ache to descend and hear the melody aloud.

Lost in imagined music, I don't think anything of a draft of cool air against my back.

"My mom gave it to me as a housewarming gift."

I spin on the bench to find Wilder standing near the open front door. His soft smile doesn't entirely capture his eyes. In them, I easily read what he's feeling: surprise, wariness, and cautious hope.

I'm sure when he woke up, he thought I'd run. He was so exhausted last night, I doubt he even remembers falling asleep still inside me. He barely stirred when I slipped out of bed to use the bathroom or when I covered him in blankets. And he definitely doesn't know I lay awake beside him all night, watching him sleep like a total creep.

"Lucky you. I love this piano."

He nods toward it. "Go on. You know you want to."

Turning back around, I set my fingers on the keys and find the pedals. I start with scales, my pressure tentative at first, then more confident as the incredible resonance of the piano surrounds me. My eyes close in pleasure. A few seconds later, the fine hairs on my neck lift in awareness.

"Quit teasing," Wilder murmurs behind me.

Smiling, I launch into something he'll recognize, a piece he played a lot in his early teens. When I reach the final note of "In Flight" by Michael Harrison, he sighs.

"Such a show-off."

Craning my neck, I smile up at him. "Come on. I had fourth graders who could play that with their eyes closed."

He moves around the bench to sit beside me. Our arms brush, triggering a cascade of goosebumps from my shoulder to my wrist. His right hand dances over the upper register, coaxing a tinkling melody.

"Piano never came as easily to me as guitar," he says softly. "It took me months to learn that song."

I frown. "No, I vividly remember you playing it the same day you got the sheet music. It was winter, or maybe early spring. We'd just eaten grilled cheeses for lunch. You snuck out of the kitchen and I followed you to the piano room. I was nine, maybe ten? You glared at me and said you wanted to be alone, but then you let me stay."

He shakes his head, a dimple deepening on his down-turned face. "Actually, you stuck your chin out and said, 'Duh, we *are* alone,' then crawled under the piano. The last time I'd tried to pull you out of there, you'd screamed like I was sawing your leg off. I decided to spare my ears the pain."

Unduly pleased he remembers, I laugh. "That does sound more accurate."

He glances at me with teasing eyes. "You were a brat."

"Nah, I was just obsessed with you."

When his gaze narrows, I flush and look down, tapping a few keys before saying, "In any case, you told me your mom had given you the sheet music that morning."

"I lied."

My head whips up. "Shut up, you did not! Why?"

He chuckles and shrugs. "I was an adolescent boy trying to impress a girl. A few days before that was the first time I'd played the song without fucking it up."

I study his profile, struggling not to laugh. "You knew I wouldn't leave?"

"I was pretty sure, yeah." He looks up, scanning my face. "You're not mad? That I manipulated you?"

My chest tightens at the real worry in his eyes. "Wilder, I crawled under the piano, knowing you wouldn't pull me out. We were kids. I think that kind of manipulation was probably developmentally appropriate."

When he just keeps staring at me, I gently close the lid over the keys and turn toward him. My knee comes to rest against his. His eyes flicker with more wariness, but he doesn't pull back—he pushes closer instead, taking my hands and holding them over our thighs. The contact makes me forget what I was about to say, allowing him to speak first.

"I wasn't my best self last night. Cooking all day, having guests... I was already feeling dysregulated before even you got here. I said things I didn't mean. I *don't* resent you for the choice you made back then. It was absolutely the right decision. I was an addict who lied to you and betrayed your trust. And to be real with you, newly sober me didn't deserve you, either. I was a wreck and just beginning to deal with my issues. Last night, my anger... it wasn't about that. Not really."

Having spent all night thinking about and preparing for this conversation, I nod. "I know. It was super fucked up of me to push you like that. It definitely wasn't the plan, just so you know."

His brows lift. "You had a plan?"

Holding his gaze feels a bit like looking at the sun, but I manage it. "I figured that was obvious when I shoved my test results in your face."

His lips quirk. "So you did come here to get laid."

I want to tell him the whole truth about why I'm here, but the last words he spoke before falling asleep play in my head for the millionth time. I know in my gut that they were the source of his anger. His underlying fear.

We broke each other's hearts, and there's not a damn thing either of us can do to change that. Two months ago, he confessed he still had feelings for me, and last night he asked me not to take advantage of that. He's willing to be my friend, even my lover, but nothing else. Not right now. Not until I'm ready to recommit to him, to *keep him*. And while I want to be with him so fucking badly, I'm also sane enough to know I'm kind of insane at the moment. An erratic, sensitive mess—as my actions last night clearly demonstrated.

Until I can untangle the chaos inside me, the least I can do is respect his wishes.

As much as I don't want to.

"I came here foremost because I trust you, Wilder. I feel safe with you, with the man you are today. And yes, I wanted to have sex with you. But my headspace wasn't the greatest last night, either." I look down at our entwined hands. "As completely out of character as it sounds, I've been pretty emotionally volatile lately."

His fingers tickle my palms lightly. "To me, you've always been emotionally volatile."

I snort. "Yeah, well, it's kind of new to me. Generally speaking. I *was* planning on spending a few days hanging out before propositioning you, but I overreacted to, um, Aubrey."

"What the hell does... Oh, shit. Were you *jealous*?"

"Ha-ha, so funny. Laugh it up."

I try to tug my hands free, but he merely tightens his grip. The mirth on his face fades to earnestness.

"I'm not interested in Aubrey or dating anyone. Even if I was, it wouldn't have factored. Your body is my Roman Empire, Evangeline. I'd have dumped anyone for the chance to be inside you again."

Air leaves me in an unattractive *whoosh*. Wilder smirks and taps a knuckle to my chin, closing my mouth. That knuckle then grazes over my hot cheek. His eyes follow the path of his hand before he lowers it back to his lap. With a sigh, his expression turns grave.

"If you're staying, if we're doing this, we should set some boundaries. What happened last night—*how* it happened—can't happen again. I told you I'd never hurt you, and then I did. I'm so sorry."

I immediately shake my head. "I'm fine, really—"

"You're not," he growls. "The whole time we've been sitting here, you haven't been able to stay in one position for more than ten seconds. I was beyond rough with you. Fuck, I —" He shakes his head. "I can't believe you didn't leave in the middle of the night after what I did."

I stay composed with effort, rolling my eyes and shrugging. "So I'm a little sore. Have you seen your dick? It takes some getting used to. But if you think I regret coming so hard I squirted, you're out of your mind. I forgot how awesome it feels. By the way, is your washer big enough for the comforter on your bed? If not, I can soak it in a tub."

He blinks rapidly, clearly trying to juggle the pieces of his exploded brain.

"Um, yes. It'll fit in the washer."

I reach up and palm the side of his face. His eyes sharpen.

"I regret pushing you last night, but only because it caused you pain." I smile as much as I can. "Also, despite my historical difficulty with them, I promise to respect whatever boundaries you set. Can we talk about them over breakfast? I'm starving."

He scans my face, eyes full of tenderness and wonder. "Of course."

Taking my hand in his, he presses a kiss to my palm. An answering pulse in my core makes me hiss and snatch my hand back.

"Don't turn me on right now. I need another twelve hours of recovery time and at least three magnesium baths."

His smile begins in his eyes—my favorite sunrise.

Standing, he offers me a hand. "In the mood for a burned bagel?"

I want to sob.

I laugh instead.

CHAPTER TWENTY-SIX

wilder

I CAN'T BELIEVE Evangeline is finally eating my food—not the horrible first attempts she was sweet enough to pretend to like years ago, but good, seasoned food. When I set the plate down, her first words were, "This is too pretty to eat." One bite changed her mind.

I was pretty confident she'd enjoy my Eggs Benedict. What I hadn't anticipated—and probably should have—was that she'd make eating it look borderline pornographic. I've been taking distracted bites off my own plate, barely tasting them, while staring at her like a perv. She's so into the food she hasn't noticed.

In the last ten minutes, I've entertained a hundred depraved fantasies, all of them centered on stuffing something else in her mouth. Hearing what sounds she makes. Replacing the hollandaise she licks off her lips with cum.

When her plate is clean—and I mean *clean*—she seems to finally realize I'm sitting across from her. Her cheeks turn a delicious, apple red shade.

"That was really good, thank you," she mumbles from behind a napkin.

My grin has a life of its own. By the way her eyes narrow, she can glean its source.

The napkin drops. "Are you seriously hard right now?"

I bark a laugh; God, I've missed her. The *real* her. The beautiful contrasts in her personality that only those closest to her ever see. Easily embarrassed yet crass. Deeply sensual but reserved. Sensitive and compassionate, but as stubborn as a bulldozer with cut brakes. Ambitious to the point she's a workaholic, while simultaneously a homebody who'd rather take a bath and read a romance novel than endure an awards ceremony.

"I don't know why you're surprised." I stand to collect our plates, shaking my head when she starts to rise. "Don't even think about it. Do you want more coffee?"

"Yes, please."

Her ass hits the chair—padded, but she still winces. It makes *me* wince. I drop off the plates in the sink and grab the carafe of coffee, then return to the table.

"You should take a bath. We can talk later. I have magnesium salts in my bathroom—"

"Don't," she snaps. "Don't fucking do that."

The vehemence in her voice sends my heart rate into overdrive. I recover enough to refill her coffee, hoping she doesn't notice the tremble in my wrist, then return to my seat.

Feeling like my skin is suddenly two sizes too small, I study her profile as she stares blankly out a nearby window. I clearly triggered her trauma, but I'm not sure why or how to fix it.

Then Martin's words from New Year's Eve come back to me. *"Clay is really good at camouflaging control as care."*

Thinking back over what I said, my stomach sinks. I didn't give her a choice. I gave her a command.

"You absolutely don't have to take a bath if you don't want to. If you want one later, the salts are under my sink."

Evangeline draws a shaky breath. As she exhales, life returns to her eyes. She reaches for her coffee, wrapping her hands around it but not drinking.

"You didn't deserve that. I know you're not... that you don't—" She cuts herself off, lips pressing tightly together.

"It's okay," I say, firm enough that her eyes lift to mine. "You never have to dilute yourself with me. Ever. If you're not ready to talk about what you've gone through, that's okay too. But I also won't tiptoe around it. You reacted that way because I didn't ask what *you* wanted, right?"

She blinks fast, fingers whitening around her mug. "I don't know. Probably. It's like my brain just shuts off. I'm suddenly so angry I could scream and have zero control of what comes out of my mouth." Her eyes redden even as she smiles weakly. "Things got pretty tense with my dad because of me freaking out on him for no reason."

"It's not for no reason, Evangeline. You know that, and I'm sure he does too."

She nods distractedly, gaze roaming over the living room. "Between my mom and Martin, I've had a crash course in PTSD. But even that's hard to wrap my head around. Intellectually, I know what I experienced is affecting me, but processing it in real time feels like trying to shape water."

"Give yourself a break," I murmur. "It's only been two months."

In a clear bid to change the subject, she points into the living room. "Why haven't you hung anything there? It's the main focal point of the space."

I study her for another moment, then follow the line of her finger to the glaringly empty spot above the fireplace.

My long-held commitment to not looking at the painting

there broke last month. For days afterward, I stared at it obsessively and even slept on the couch one night so I could see it right upon waking. I finally confessed the unhealthy habit to Frank. He stayed on the phone with me as I pulled it off the wall and stored it in a closet.

As hard as it was to remove the art, I'm glad I did. Otherwise I'd have to explain to Evangeline why I have a painting hanging in my living room of two kids—obviously us—sitting with guitars under a sycamore tree.

"I've been meaning to," I hedge. "Maybe you can pick something out. I have a few of River's paintings that I haven't decided where to hang."

She looks startled. "No way. I mean, I'd love to check out River's stuff, but you should choose what goes there. It's your house."

I capitulate with a nod, ignoring the rebellious urge to tell her that when I built this house, it wasn't just for me. A bad idea on several levels, not the least being she's not mentally or emotionally ready to hear it.

Her wandering gaze returns to me. "This place is amazing, by the way. The design, the flow, the window placements —everything. I love that it feels spacious, but it's not giant, if that makes sense."

"It does, yes. And thank you. I'm proud of it."

"Did you and your dad really tear down the old house and build this by yourselves?"

I chuckle, shaking my head. "My dad loves spreading that rumor, but no. I partnered with an architect for the design, then worked with a general contractor and subcontractors for the actual demo and remodel. I wasn't about to let my dad touch electric or plumbing, no matter how confident he was in his YouTube education."

She laughs. "So you didn't hammer in every nail?"

"Only a few thousand of them. But I did lay all the flooring and tile and installed most of the drywall." Far too pleased by the impressed look on her face, I grin. "I don't know why you're surprised. According to you, I have skilled fingers."

I love that she doesn't hide her blush.

"Stop it."

I feign innocence with raised brows. "Stop what?"

Evangeline rolls her eyes and stands, taking her coffee with her into the living room. "Let's go, Mr. Fancy Fingers. Time to tackle the hard stuff."

At my laugh, she throws a disapproving look over her shoulder.

"What did you expect? I know I've changed a lot, but some things never will. Especially around you."

Adorably flustered, she sits on the couch facing the water and pulls a nearby blanket over her legs. When I approach her, she points to the other couch.

"For my vagina's peace of mind, you're sitting over there."

I veer around the coffee table and sit. "If you're trying to make me stop thinking about sex, it's not working."

She hides a smile behind her mug. "Given the conversation we're about to have, it would be pointless to try."

"I'll show you something *not* pointless."

She groans. "Horrible. Really horrible."

Smirking, I toss my legs onto the coffee table and cross my ankles. To my satisfaction, Evangeline's gaze drops to my groin—namely, the tent in my sweats.

"Yep, still hard over here."

Her eyes flash up. "Since we're all about honesty these days, why did you never let me give you a blowjob when we were together? Was it because you thought I'd suck at it?"

My lips twitch and she glowers.

"I wasn't trying to be punny."

I sigh, allowing the gravity of her question to settle inside me. "There isn't a simple answer."

"Then give me the complicated one."

Despite literal years of wanting to have this conversation with her, now that the door is open, I can't decide where to start. There's too much I want to say all at once.

When the curiosity in Evangeline's eyes shifts to apprehension, I give up and pick a random thought.

"Do you remember the day I sat in on the music lesson with one of your students?"

"Yes," she answers, her blush conveying that she remembers what happened after the lesson. How she was so turned on she forgot where she was and almost went down on me in the classroom.

"I had every intention of letting you... you know, later that night. But then we had dinner with the guys."

As the words pass my lips, a wave of anxiety crashes over me. My throat closes. Imaginary fire ants march down my arms.

"Shit," I mumble. "Give me a sec." Closing my eyes, I focus on my breath.

"If you don't want to talk about this..."

"No. I'm okay." I force myself to look at her—at the woman I hurt. "I do need to back up a bit, though. Or a lot. I'd like to explain from the beginning."

She nods hesitantly. "Okay."

Dropping my feet to the floor, I rub my face roughly. *Just do it. Tell her.* I take one more deep breath, then prop my elbows on my thighs and begin.

"I learned really young that being around you was like

taking medicine for my anxiety. From thirteen on, I lived for the weekends. Making music with you was the only time I felt relief."

"Really?" she whispers.

I nod. "I know now it was because I felt safe to be myself around you, but back then..." I shake my head. "I think I was fifteen when I wanted to kiss you for the first time. By seventeen, I fantasized about you constantly. I didn't know how to handle it, so I made all these rules for myself. For us. But at the same time, I was doing weird shit like deleting texts from boys on your phone."

Her jaw drops. "That was you?"

I offer a wincing smile. "I might have also pretended to accidentally touch you in the pool more than once."

Her eyes flare with laughter. "I was guilty of that too."

"Did you also sneak out of the pool, find my clothes, and steal my boxers to masturbate with?"

Evangeline gapes. "Oh my God, I remember freaking out when I couldn't find my underwear. That's nasty, Wilder!"

I roll my eyes. "It's like you've never met me."

She considers me for a moment, then nods. "Fair point."

Our shared smile fades from my face first.

"By the time you left the band, my feelings for you had become synonymous with my fear of losing you—or more accurately, my fear of your rejection and this perceived control you had over me. It was a self-fulfilling prophecy. I was abusing substances by then, too, so my self-loathing and denial journeys were well underway."

She frowns, her gaze falling to her lap. "When we started dating, you told me that you'd pushed me away because you were afraid." I'm not sure what she means until she adds, "You were telling the truth. Or as much of it as you could articulate at the time."

I swallow so hard I almost choke. "Yes. The only thing I lied to you about was my using."

She nods to herself. "Go on."

"Fast forward a few years—I met Kendra, who was already strung out on pills. With access to a steady supply through her, I started using Oxy consistently. There were immediate benefits. My drinking slowed down, I finally wrote our sophomore album, and my anxiety was managed for the most part. For the first time in years, I felt like I was in control of my life. I even developed rituals to support the narrative that I wasn't an addict."

Her eyes widen. "Really? Like what?"

"I was obsessed with finding the right dosage to not look high while also shutting off my disorder. I was militant about controlling how much I took and when—even had a hidden calendar on my phone to track everything. And every few months, I'd detox myself. I convinced myself that if I cleared the drugs out of my system periodically, it meant I wasn't addicted."

Evangeline shakes her head in disbelief. "That sounds like a nightmare."

"It absolutely was. But I was so locked in, I couldn't imagine living a different way. When I showed up at your Cathedral show, I was coming off a really rough detox. I'd been sober for ten days. Jax had figured out what was happening, and earlier that night he'd offered to do a dry month with me. For the first time in a long time, I felt hopeful. I didn't agree to it for you, exactly, but I'd be lying if I said you weren't part of the reason. After all, you were my first addiction. My favorite high."

She makes a soft, distressed sound, but my gaze has dropped to the floor and I can't bring myself to look up.

"I made it another four days. Until dinner that night with

the guys. When I left the room, I had the worst panic attack I'd had in years. Completely debilitating. And I cracked. I found two pills that I'd hidden in my bathroom and took them. I didn't want to, but the compulsion was overwhelming."

I glance up, catching the tail-end of her pained expression, and add quickly, "My relapse had nothing to do with you. It had to do with me not addressing any of the underlying causes of my addiction. Any substantial stressor would have yielded the same result. It was going to happen sooner or later no matter what."

She blinks a few times, then nods. "Thanks for saying that. So from that point on you were using daily again?"

"Yes," I admit hoarsely. "In the following weeks, I learned what true self-loathing was. I'd finally admitted to myself that I was an addict, but I didn't know how to stop or ask for help. I couldn't see a future where I had what I wanted: freedom from anxiety and you. All I knew was that I couldn't lose you. So I lied."

Her mug clanks on the coffee table. Wiping her tearing eyes, she whispers, "I hate that you went through that just as much as I hated you back then for lying to me."

"Losing you was my rock bottom, Evangeline. It's what made me ask for help. You saved my life."

The glassiness in her eyes doubles. "But then I told you I wished you were dead."

I grimace, my entire body clenching with regret for what I said—*how* I said it—last night.

"Just like my relapse, what I did was *not* your fault. I'll put you on the phone with my sponsor right now and he'll tell you the same thing. I was newly sober and barely coherent. I knew fuck-all about how to handle my emotions and was too self-centered to see the situation from your perspective."

She sniffs loudly, then uses her sleeve to wipe her nose. "Tell me. Please?"

Breathe in.

Breathe out.

"I found an old stash, a half-full bottle my parents had missed when they searched my bedroom. I took..." I swallow a few times to coax the words past the resistance in my throat. "I took all of them."

"What the fuck?" she whispers, a hand lifting to her mouth.

"It was almost one a.m., but my parents showed up not five minutes later. An ambulance arrived a few minutes after that."

"What? How?"

Blinking back tears, I smile slightly. "It doesn't make sense, does it? It's almost like someone knew what I was going to do before I did it."

She gasps, understanding instantly. "Katherine."

I release a strangled laugh. "Yep. She called my mom, waking her up, and told her I was going to die if she didn't get an ambulance to me. And my mom believed her. My dad, too."

Evangeline's face crumples. She folds over her knees and makes the worst sound I've ever heard, a jagged wail like I just ripped her heart out. In seconds, I'm around the coffee table and pulling her into my arms.

"I'm sorry," I say into her hair. "I'm so sorry. It wasn't your fault. You've never once been responsible for my choices."

She fists my shirt, her forehead rolling against my chest.

"I can't believe you almost *died*. I can't—it's too much."

Closing my burning eyes, I allow myself to feel and accept her shock, anger, and pain.

"I'm never going back there, Fairy. I won't make you any

promises, but only because actions speak louder than words. I'm going to show you the same way I show myself. One day at a time."

CHAPTER TWENTY-SEVEN

evangeline

I DIG my fingers into Wilder's waist, flooded with a confusing mess of anger and imagined grief. I want to punch him repeatedly, then handcuff him to me for the rest of his life.

"How do you know?" I whisper against his chest. It's not a fair question, but I can't help my need to hear his answer.

A warm palm cups the back of my neck. "A lot of reasons, but mostly because I'm selfish. I'm not willing to give up the life I've built or the person I am today. Shockingly enough, I kind of like the guy."

Sitting up, I wipe my wet cheeks. "I get it. He's pretty cool. Makes great music and a mean Eggs Benedict. He does have a weird obsession with sexual puns, though."

Wilder grins. One dimple deeper than the other. Eyes a bright forest, with those unbelievably charming crinkles at the corners.

Although I'm well aware of how much he's matured in the last seven years, it suddenly hits me how different he *feels*. He's still himself—unquestionably the boy I grew up with—

but gone is the undercurrent of volatility I remember. Missing, too, is that old feeling that I'll never really know him. Because he's not hiding parts of himself anymore. He faced his demons. Drew all those disparate, dark elements of himself inward and used them to repair his cracks.

"What's that look for?" he murmurs, eyes scanning mine.

"You're like Kintsugi," I blurt.

His brows jump. "The Japanese art?" When I nod, he gives me a questioning smile. "What made you think of that?"

My face warms. "I don't know. You seem so different. Grounded, I guess. At peace with the past and yourself."

He squints doubtfully at me. "I wasn't very peaceful last night."

I shrug, scooting back on the couch and drawing my knees to my chest. "I think what happened last night was a long time coming." I tilt my head. "Speaking of coming... you never answered my question."

Wilder laughs. "Look who's the conductor of the Pun Train now."

I roll my eyes but can't resist a laugh. "Whatever. Are you going to tell me why you never let me give you a blowjob? No joke, your refusal gave me a complex."

His eyes widen. "It did?"

Ignoring the prickling heat crawling up my neck, I mumble into my knees, "I've never given one because of you. I was too afraid I'd be bad at it."

Wilder stares at me unblinking for an extended moment, then jerks halfway to his feet before collapsing back to the couch. He covers his face with his hands.

"I can't believe this."

My embarrassment spikes even higher. "What did you expect? You went down on me all the time, but every single time I tried to return the favor, you rejected me."

His hands drop, revealing a stricken expression. "No, Fairy. No, no. My refusal... that was a combination of some weird mental shit and being on opiates."

I frown. "Explain."

"Once I started using again, it wasn't easy for me to come. I didn't want you to think you weren't able to get me there with your mouth. The main reason, though, was that I constantly felt like a piece of shit for lying to you. The idea of you doing that for me, with how vulnerable and selfless the act is... I couldn't stomach putting you in that position."

My left eyelid twitches. I press a finger to it, then glare at him through my other eye.

"Let me get this straight. You thought you were being *noble*?"

He grimaces. "Yes?"

A laugh bubbles out of me. "What the hell, Wilder!"

The glint in his eyes ruins his attempt to hide amusement. "You've seriously never given a blowjob?"

"We can stop talking about this now. Thanks for answering my question, and also, screw you."

His rich laughter fills the room. "This is so twisted. I should feel bad—I know I should—but I can't. It's like I accidentally gave myself a gift."

"You're such an asshole."

Sparkling eyes slant my way. "I volunteer as tribute. Anywhere, anytime you want to practice, whether I'm awake, asleep, driving, cooking, doing laundry..."

Fighting a smile, I kick his thigh. "What makes you think I want to give you a blowjob anymore? Maybe I'm perfectly happy with my virgin mouth."

"Liar," he murmurs huskily.

Ignoring the blush that gives me away, I fake a yawn that turns into a real yawn. "I need a nap and a bath." He frowns and I quickly add, "We're not discussing my sleep issues, but if you want to talk about boundaries, now's the time."

He bites his lip. "Have I ever told you how hot it is that you're a boss in the streets but a total slut in the sheets?"

I kick him again. "Focus!"

"Fine, fine." His grin fades as he sits up and drags fingers across his scalp. The action makes *me* sit straighter since it's his nervous tell—that and the fact he's not looking at me but staring out the windows lining the back of the house.

"Wilder?"

"I'm getting there. Just fighting with myself." He glances at me, smiling slightly. "I'm not sure how you'll respond to this."

I hug my knees tighter as my stomach flutters. "If you don't want to do this..."

"Nope. Definitely want to." He sighs heavily and faces me. "I want you here, Evangeline. I always have. But I'm also too old and too sober to pretend a friends-with-benefits situation with you is the healthiest choice for me."

I swallow back denials. "I understand. What do you need?"

"If at any point I feel like I can't do this anymore, I'll tell you. I need your commitment that you'll do the same."

"Agreed," I whisper.

He nods and looks away again. "No holding hands, kissing on the mouth, or sleeping in the same bed."

Pain flares in my chest—sharp, pinpointed like a bullet—and spreads down my arms. I want to cry. Applaud him. Slap him. So many feelings flood me all at once that I can't speak or blink or even breathe.

I finally manage enough air to ask, "Really?"

Wilder looks at me and nods. Eyes wary but resolute. The soft lips I suddenly can't imagine not kissing open on a swift inhale.

"Are you okay with those stipulations?" he asks tentatively.

"Sure." The word feels like broken glass on my tongue.

"Is there anything you need? A boundary that will make you feel more safe?" He hesitates. "I could try not to call you Fairy."

I'm the one who looks away this time. A storm is rolling in, darkening the sky and water, but a few stubborn rays of sunlight cling to a sycamore. The branches are still bare, ghostly and glowing against a shadowed backdrop. As the clouds thicken and the branches dim, something inside me dims too.

I would give anything to be able to trust what my heart is telling me—that I love Wilder more in this moment than I ever have before. But I don't know how to trust myself when I feel so tainted. So unworthy.

So small and violent and broken.

I finally turn back to him, meeting his worried eyes. A smile comes with surprising ease.

"Don't you dare stop calling me Fairy. As for boundaries, I can't think of anything right now, but I'll let you know if I do." I stand up, grabbing my mug. "I'm going to pass out for a bit, then I'm commandeering your bathroom. That soaker tub is calling my name."

He stands with me. "Of course. I'll be around—if I'm not in the house, I'm in the studio."

"'Kay."

I rinse the mug, pop it in the dishwasher, and head toward the hallway. As soon as I know he can't see me anymore, my eyes flood with tears.

I'm almost to the stairs when his voice stops me.

"Evangeline?"

I pause but don't turn around. "Yeah?"

"I'm really glad you're here."

"Me too."

I duck around the corner and haul ass upstairs.

CHAPTER TWENTY-EIGHT

wilder

WE WERE WASTING TIME
RACING TO HOLD STEADY
SO EITHER LEAVE ME HERE
OR KISS ME ALREADY

I PLAY A SMALL, morose melody on the piano, then sigh and look at my phone. It's propped on the shelf against sheet music, my mom's face visible on the screen.

"I'm almost positive she was crying when she left the room. What if I royally fucked up?"

She shakes her head, curls swaying around her shoulders. "You did the right thing, Wild. For both of you."

"I don't know. I can't stop thinking about the look on her face when I told her my limits. She was hurt. What if she actually does want..." I finish the sentence silently.

Me.

Maybe she wants *me.*

503

The possibility is too big to hold, too close to my longest-held dream to consider as a real possibility.

Gleaning where my head went, my mom says gently, "Maybe she does want more, but you need to remember what she's been through and her mental state right now. I love Eva, and my heart breaks for her, but I won't tell you not to protect yourself."

I nod for her comfort, knowing that my so-called boundaries are performative bullshit. I'm trying to bulletproof myself with Styrofoam.

There's no way to protect myself from this, from Evangeline. I'm in love with her. I always have been and always will be. The only thing I'm really doing is preparing for the pain when she leaves.

My mom continues, "I haven't been exactly where she is, but I do know what it's like to have your foundation cracked and your sense of self turned upside down. She doesn't trust her own feelings right now. Even if she wants to."

Wind lashes rain against the nearby windows. The lights in the studio flicker.

"Shit. I forgot to call someone to fix the generator last week."

"I thought your dad looked at it," she says with a knowing smile.

I roll my eyes. "I stopped him before he took the whole thing apart and started Googling."

From somewhere behind my mom, my dad says, "I totally could have fixed it!"

She laughs. "Sure you could have."

His face appears beside hers, whiskey-colored eyes locking on mine. "For what it's worth, I agree with your mom. I know it wasn't easy setting boundaries with Eva, but it was the right choice. It's the selfishness paradox of recovery—we

504

stay clean and sober by learning how to be of service to others, but we can't show up for anyone unless we're first selfish about our recovery. Unfortunately, sometimes that means going against our own hearts."

He gives my mom a weighted look. She smiles softly, and he kisses her forehead.

"You did something like this?" I ask, stupefied.

His eyes return to me. "In the same wheelhouse."

My mom laughs lightly. "We weren't even technically together, but he preemptively dumped me because I was in the way of his sobriety."

I gape as my dad grimaces. "Keep in mind I'd just been hit by a car, broken most of my bones, and was on a steady drip of painkillers. And before that, I'd been on the verge of relapsing. I loved your mom, but I knew I couldn't give her what she needed. I had to fix my shit—physically and mentally—before I felt worthy of her."

She strokes his cheek, then turns to me. "He did what he had to do to protect us both, which is what you're doing now. Sometimes you and Eva remind me a lot of your dad and me —it took a while for us to be on the same page."

"At least it wasn't seven years," I mutter, and she winces in sympathy.

The lights flicker again, this time staying off for several seconds. I grab my phone and stand. "I have to go."

"Be careful walking back to the house," she says, big eyes filled with worry. "Love you."

My dad squeezes her shoulder. "We trimmed all the trees around the paths last fall. He'll be fine. Love you, son."

"Love you guys."

After I make sure the computer and lights are all off, I slip my feet into the dirt-speckled rain boots I left by the door and shrug into a raincoat.

Neither matter much the second I step outside, as nothing short of a hazmat suit will keep me dry in these conditions. We're at the tip of the island and the winds are merciless, driving the heavy rains in gravity-defying directions. I'm forced to hold a hand over my eyes to keep it from blinding me.

Despite it being the middle of the day, the sky is so dark the solar lights along the main path have come on. They're dimmer than usual given the lack of sunlight today, but their glow guides me as I jog toward the house.

Right as I reach the back door, the single light I left on in the kitchen goes out. I let myself into the mudroom and shuck off my jacket and boots. It's almost as loud inside as it is outside, the rain pounding on the glass over the dining area. But there's a stillness, too. A quietude that unnerves me.

My hair drips onto my shoulders and my pants are wet and heavy, but neither sensory irritation registers as I walk quickly toward the stairs and take them two at a time.

Evangeline's bedroom door is open, enough light coming through the windows for me to see it's empty. The sight of her duffel and guitar case at the foot of the unmade bed should reassure me. Instead, my heart rate triples. I was in the studio for a couple of hours. She said she was going to nap, then take a bath. Did she already wake up, or did she decide on a bath first?

Dear God, please don't let her have fallen asleep in the water.

I tear into my bedroom, the space notably darker due to the thicker tree line on this side of the house. When I see the closed bathroom door, panic destroys any semblance of propriety. I pound on it once before swinging it open, my eyes snapping to the extra-large soaker tub.

Water sloshes as Evangeline jerks upright, a hand slamming against her chest. "Mother of pearl!"

My relief is so heady my knees almost buckle. "Sorry. The power went out, and I wanted to check on you. When you weren't in your room, I freaked out."

Thanks to the abundance of white tile and the massive skylight over the tub, I can clearly see her confused expression—and the moment it clears.

"You thought I fell asleep and drowned."

It's not a question, but I nod anyway. She doesn't sound angry, at least.

"My brain is hardwired to jump to worst-case scenarios," I admit, my voice still shaky from the offload of adrenaline. "You should have seen me the first few times I babysat Emma. I was an absolute wreck. I'm not much better now, honestly."

Her lips tug upward. "Helicopter parent, huh?"

"Probably worse than your dad," I say wryly.

Smiling wider, she sinks back into the water. "Well, as you can see, I'm fine. I had a lovely nap, and now I'm soaking up the ambiance of the storm. Water's still hot if you want to join."

My system resets from anxious to aroused in a second flat. Evangeline giggles as I rip off my clothes.

"Damn," I hiss as I lower into the water. "Are you trying to burn your skin off?"

"Scalding is the only acceptable temperature for a bath," she says primly. "Besides, it's not as hot as you think. You're just cold."

The stinging fades in a matter of moments, encompassing warmth melting tension from my muscles.

"As usual, you're right."

She gives me a smug smile and leans her knees to one side. "There, now you can stretch out."

I take advantage, extending my legs and sliding down to

507

dunk my head under. When I come back up, I make a face. "How much salt did you put in here?"

"Um, the whole bag?"

I laugh, wiping my stinging eyes. "No wonder your hair is dry. By the way, did you actually say 'mother of pearl' when I came in or did I hallucinate that?"

"Sure did," she says with a smile. "It's a Lily-approved cuss word. I'm actually kind of impressed with myself for using it spur of the moment like that."

"Very impressive," I say drolly.

She whips a foot out, presumably to kick me, but I grab it and start massaging. Revenge instantly forgotten, she offers me the other one as well. Humming happily, she closes her eyes and drops her head back. I'm extra grateful for the extended length of the tub when the position elevates her off the bottom, giving me a mouthwatering view.

"How are you feeling?"

"Right now? Amazing. Don't stop. Oh, right there."

"Are you *trying* to torture me?"

She smirks. "Maybe."

"Brat."

The foot I'm not massaging slips up my thigh. I think the movement is unintentional until her toes brush purposefully along my stiff cock. When it jerks, her smile widens.

"I hope that's not left over from breakfast."

"A brat *and* a menace." I release a slow breath, my hand tightening reflexively on her foot. "How sore are you?"

Even in the low light, I see her breath quicken and her already flushed skin turn a darker red. Her eyes open, the gray one so dilated it's almost as dark as the other.

"Turns out I'm not nearly as sore as I thought."

CHAPTER TWENTY-NINE

wilder

I FORGET how to speak for a few seconds. When my voice returns, it's sandpaper.

"You touched yourself? Put fingers inside that pretty pussy?"

Evangeline bites her lip and nods. I reach over and flip the drain, then toss her feet off my lap and stand.

She laughs. "We need to wash the salt off first."

I'm already halfway out of the tub. "Way ahead of you."

I crank on the dial in the walk-in shower. Water cascades from the oversized showerhead, steam billowing almost instantly. I say a silent thank you to my dad for convincing me to install a gas water heater with a standing pilot light.

When I turn to help Evangeline out of the tub, she's already walking toward me. Glistening like Venus from the sea, loose tendrils of hair curling around her determined face, she steps into the shower and points.

"Rinse, please."

I don't bother pretending ignorance—or hesitance. Ducking beneath the water, I rinse as quickly as possible. When I'm done, Evangeline nods at the tiled bench beneath a high window, close enough to be within reach of the steam and mist.

"Sit."

I'm so fucking turned on I don't even make a quip about her bossiness. Nor do I feel the cold tile as it meets my ass. I do, however, have enough functioning brain cells to say, "Please get a towel for your knees."

Her eyes narrow like she's considering arguing for the sake of it, but then she looks down at the tile and sees the wisdom in my statement. After a quick detour to the towel rack, she drops the twice-folded material between my spread feet. Delicate hands grip my knees, and then she's lowering to hers.

My breathing turns harsh as her eyes meet mine, then meander down my tense body. Chest. Arms. Abs and thighs. When they land and narrow on my cock, she licks her lips. It's too fucking much. I hiss and grab myself to keep from erupting.

Evangeline's head tilts, a tiny, devious smile on her face. "But I haven't even touched it."

As soon as I'm under control, I croon, "You're so beautiful on your knees for me. I can't wait to see my cum dripping off those lips."

Her composure cracks, then shatters. She pulls my hand away and replaces it with both of hers, then bends forward and licks my tip like a lollipop, humming at the taste of me.

Every nerve ending in my body singing, I hang on to the bench and let her explore. Her tongue swirls all over my shaft and piercing before she takes me slowly into her mouth. Shallow the first time, then a little deeper. When she draws back completely, a thin ribbon of saliva follows. Her tongue flicks out, capturing it, and I make the world's most pathetic sound.

Evangeline pauses, her eyes jerking up to mine. The haze of lust in them falters, hesitance and self-consciousness taking its place.

Oh, fuck no.

I sink my fingers beneath the loose bun at the back of her head. "You're perfect. I guarantee I'm going to come really hard and really soon. I also don't care where. Neck, chest, face, mouth, tile—it's all the same to me, all perfect because it's you. Do absolutely whatever the fuck you want."

She chews her lips, frowning. "I want to make you lose it. Tell me how?"

I gaze reverently down at her, my heart on fire. "Stop thinking so hard and eat my cock like you've always wanted to. I'm not an appetizer, baby. I'm your favorite main course."

Her eyes glaze again, thick lashes fluttering as her breath quickens. Knowing she's close to letting go, I give her hair a little tug.

"And rub that needy clit for me while you're at it."

With an eager whimper, she sneaks a hand between her thighs as she lowers her head.

This time she doesn't hold back. And now that I know what she needs, I don't hold back either. I give her my unrestricted moans and praise. My hand stays on the back of her head, my fingers tight in her hair, but I don't guide her. She doesn't need me to.

Evangeline devours my cock like she's starving for it. Zero finesse. Sloppy as hell.

Abso-fucking-lutely perfect.

It's beyond a doubt the best blowjob of my life, and my body knows it. Telling pressure builds fast in my spine. My fingers and toes tingle in warning.

"Fuuuck," I grit out. "Make a choice, baby."

Her eyes roll up to mine, fierce despite the tears leaking

from the corners. She squeezes her hand around my base and takes me to the back of her throat. When she swallows around me, I'm *done*.

The first pulse of euphoria is followed closely by a second, third, forth. I come so hard, for so long, that my soul leaves my fucking body. My head snaps back, hitting the wall with enough force I see stars. The pain compounds the pleasure, making it unbearable, and my vision spirals into blissful white.

"Wilder? Wilder! Are you okay?"

I blink at Evangeline. Her worried face is sideways and right in front of mine, which makes zero sense until I realize I'm lying on the bench. Mist from the shower tickles my forehead and nose.

"Yeah," I croak. "You have a little something..." My thumb swipes her chin, then her cheek.

As more brain function returns, I realize how pointless my efforts are. There's cum in her hair. On the tip of her nose. In her eyebrows.

My stomach contracts. My cheeks tighten. I try—I really, really try—not to laugh. But it's another wasted effort.

Evangeline's worry makes way for rage. She punches my shoulder. "Goddammit! You cracked your skull on the wall and keeled over. I was about to call a fucking ambulance."

I can barely breathe I'm laughing so hard. "I can't... your eyebrows—it's all over you."

"Obviously," she hisses. "You convulsed right out of my mouth and Jackson Pollack'd me as I was trying to grab you. Ugh. Whatever. I'm done playing nurse."

She stands and turns toward the water. I sit up fast and grab her arm before she can escape.

"Fairy," I cajole, tugging her between my knees. She sighs as I draw a pert nipple into my smiling mouth, flicking it with

512

my tongue until it hardens before giving the same treatment to the other.

Her hands come to rest on my shoulders. "You scared me," she whispers.

"I'm sorry." Sliding my hands to her ass, I squeeze. Her back arches, fingers clenching. "I have a hard head—I'm perfectly fine. That was the best blowjob of my life."

"Liar," she says breathily.

My mouth is full, so I shake my head as I slip a hand between her legs. I tease with my tongue and fingers until she's panting and circling her hips.

"Wilder," she whines.

I release her nipple with a pop and look up at her flushed, beautiful, cum-speckled face. "You did so good," I purr as I sink a finger inside her. Her body clenches around me, her breath hitching. "How much did you swallow?"

Her eyes flash. "Quite a fucking lot, thank you very much."

I grin and give her another finger, curling both toward me and pulsing them against her G-spot. Her head cants back, a low moan saturating the air.

"Give me those fairy eyes." I wait until she complies, her gaze focusing when she registers my serious expression. "I'm so proud of you. Thank you for trusting yourself and letting go for me. You were an absolute savage, and I fucking loved watching you swallow my cock. That *was* the best blowjob of my life."

My praise princess melts in my arms, her entire body shuddering.

I swirl my tongue around a nipple piercing. "Do you want to get off on my fingers, my mouth, or my cock?"

Her eyes flicker downward. Swollen lips part in surprise, and a small, pleased smile follows.

"Always hard for you, Evangeline," I murmur.

When she sways toward me, I immediately read her intent and lift her by the thighs, spreading them over mine. Her arms come around my shoulders, breasts mashing against my chest. She wiggles around until she finds what she wants, then rocks her way slowly down my cock. By the time she's seated on my thighs, we're both panting.

Her wide, awed eyes roam my face and she whispers, "Nothing feels as good as this."

I manage to nod before my thoughts scatter as she starts to grind. Her heavy-lidded gaze falls to my mouth, and it takes every last drop of my willpower to resist the lure. Tightening my arms around her, I tuck my face against her neck and mirror the rhythm of her hips with mine.

The prettiest whimpers fill my ears.

"More," she says on a gasp. "I want you everywhere."

Her admission triggers another wave of building pressure inside me. "Fuck. Just like that, you're gonna make me come again."

I draw back enough to feed two fingers into her mouth. She moans, sucking and coating them with saliva, then bites down when I try to pull them out.

I slap her ass. "Bad toy."

Her teeth sink deeper into my knuckles, so I slap her ass harder. A gasp frees my fingers to find her ass. The second I start applying pressure, she pushes back and swallows them both. With a guttural cry, she picks up the pace, fucking my cock and fingers with abandon. Hell-bent on taking what she needs from me.

I've never seen anything more beautiful.

"Yes, yes, ah—"

Her breath stalls, body arching. I bite the juncture of her shoulder and neck as she falls over the edge, pussy and ass clamping down and throbbing, her cries echoing around us. Free and safe in her pleasure, without thought or reservation. Messy, loud, and mine.

Exactly as she should be.

As my own release races toward me, I take over from below, bucking my hips hard and fast. And when I go rigid, she bites me in the exact same spot I bit her.

Because we're a perfect song.

Matched note for note.

CHAPTER THIRTY

evangeline

WILDER BUILDS a fire in the living room fireplace as I light candles on the mantel and make a nest on the floor out of pillows and blankets. He digs out a deck of cards. We play Go Fish, Hearts, and Crazy Eights.

I win every round for twenty straight minutes, and I'm smug about it until I remember I always won whenever we played card games as kids too. Annoyed, I tell him to stop losing on purpose. He complies and wipes the floor with me until I throw the cards at him.

When my stomach growls, he puts together a massive charcuterie board that looks like it belongs on a food blogger's Instagram. I eat like I'm feral, moaning and licking my fingers, which has the intended effect of him tackling me to the ground and yanking off my sweatpants. After, we doze on the blankets, my head on his chest and his fingers twirling in my hair. With the soft snap and crackle of logs and the steady patter of rain on the roof, I float in sensory heaven.

The power comes back on midafternoon, but we don't bother turning on any lights. Wilder makes us tea and disappears upstairs, then reappears with my guitar. When he asks me to play some of my new material for him, I do. He listens the same way he always has, with a rapt expression that makes me feel like the center of the universe. Like I'm precious and worthy and magical.

I have to stop to wipe away tears. He doesn't ask me what's wrong, simply holds me until I'm calm again. I reward him with another blowjob, thankfully less traumatic than the first. Then I make the mistake of confessing that I thought swallowing cum would be grosser.

He laughs so hard, for so long, that I attempt to smother him with a pillow. My punishment is his mouth on my pussy, two fingers in my ass, and a husky warning that soon it'll be something a lot bigger than his fingers inside me. The so-called threat triggers an immediate, shattering orgasm.

I'm still buzzing and relearning how to breathe when he whispers in my ear, "The reason my cum tastes good is because I'm made for you." He leaves right after to wash his face and hands, sparing me the embarrassment of a witness as I dazedly wonder if he's right.

When he returns, he has his own acoustic, a custom Gibson slightly larger than mine. I cozy up in blankets, grinning like a fangirl because I haven't heard him play in far too long.

He stands dramatically before the fire. Makes a show of tuning the guitar with a frown of concentration and nervous glances. Right when I'm convinced he's about to break my heart, he launches into a ridiculous, ad hoc song about a storm cloud that contains no less than five sexual puns.

We spend the rest of the afternoon playing an old game where we give the other person a color, emotion, and a setting, and five minutes to come up with a jingle.

Just before sunset, the rain lets up and the sky partly clears. We bundle up and go outside, presumably to see if any tree branches have fallen, but end up walking down to the water on a path clogged by yellow and white daffodils. The blooms are a little beat up from the storm but glow like fallen stars in the fading sunlight.

I crouch beside a section of flowers near the small beach and gently lift bent stalks. "I planted these same colors once. Did you ever see them? At my first place?"

Wilder's gaze lifts from the flowers. "I saw them."

I almost ask whether these were here when he bought the property or if he planted them, but something stops me. Maybe how presumptuous the question is, but more likely his lack of smile.

A cloud covers the sun, the temperature instantly dropping, and a gust off the water makes me shiver.

"Let's head in," he says softly. "I'll get started on dinner."

He pulls me up, warm fingers around mine for two seconds before he releases me and tucks his hand in a pocket.

Those two seconds—and the loss of them—stay with me as he reheats leftover pastitsio. As I fold the blankets and clean up the mess we left on the coffee table.

Lights are turned back on. Candles are blown out. The fire is covered by a grate and left to die.

Over dinner, we try to get it back—the peaceful, joyful bubble we floated in most of the day—and we almost do a few times. But as we finish eating, Wilder's phone starts vibrating on the mantel and doesn't stop. He ignores the first two calls, but on the third, he leaves the table to grab it.

He frowns down at the screen.

"Everything okay?" I ask.

His eyes meet mine for a moment. "Fine, but I need to return a call. Be back in a sec."

He walks from the room before I can decide whether or not I have the right to ask who's calling.

By the time he comes back, the kitchen is clean and the dishwasher is running.

"Don't tell me I didn't have to," I say as he opens his mouth. "I might throw a chair at your face."

He chuckles. "I was going to say 'thank you,' you maniac. Want to watch a movie?"

I stare at him, waiting for more before realizing he's setting another boundary. He's not going to tell me who was on the phone, and he doesn't want me to ask.

Because he's not mine.

The silence vibrates, a rubber band stretched to snap. I can already feel the impending sting.

I summon a weak smile. "I'm actually pretty tired."

Concern, regret, acceptance—they cross his face like fast moving clouds before he nods. "Absolutely, sure. Sleep well, okay? I'll see you in the morning."

I'm smiling as I thank him for dinner and say good night. Smiling as I grab the two blankets I brought down from the guest room. *Smiling, smiling* as I say good night again and leave him standing in the kitchen with a lost expression on his face.

Upstairs in my room, I close the door, flip on the light, and faceplant on the bed. The sting in my chest intensifies. When it migrates to the backs of my eyes, I growl and haul myself into the bathroom.

Wilder's doing what's right for him, and the only thing I can do is respect that and hope that within the next few weeks, I'll find the fortitude to lay it all out for him. How I'm scared of the future but equally certain I want to spend it with him. How I want to keep him, keep *us*.

I just need a little more time to get a handle on myself. To remember who I am and resuscitate my confidence. To learn how to tune out the voice in the back of my mind that's so intent on undermining every moment of peace with parroted, poisonous words.

Helpless.

Lazy.

Crazy.

Too much, too much, too much...

Showering brings me back to the present via the unavoidable evidence of the last twenty-four hours. I relive every touch. Find and press every tender spot. Stretch to feel the burn of muscles and sigh into the phantom warmth and fullness.

Wilder and I may be in another limbo—this one a strange inversion of our vow as teens—but I take comfort in what my body tells me. What *he* told me. What my soul has always known.

We're made for each other.

Somehow, someway, I'm going to fix what's wrong with me. Course correct our past. Because I'm not letting him go.

Not ever again.

♪

A FEW HOURS LATER, the soft creak of the door opening wakes me from a light sleep. Footsteps cross the room. I hold my breath as the covers lift, as the mattress dips and the sheets whisper. His arm slides over my waist. He fits himself against my back, tucking his knees beneath mine.

Relief pours from my lungs in a sigh. I find his hand and draw it to my face, pressing a kiss to his warm palm.

"I can't do it," he whispers. My stomach drops, but then he continues, "I can't sleep knowing you're right across the hall and I could have you in my arms."

Guilt and elation war inside me. "I'm sorry."

His exhale is thick with humor. "Liar."

I kiss his palm again before cradling it to my chest. Looking over my shoulder, I find his eyes in the shadows. "You're right, I'm not sorry. Sleeping beside you was at least twenty percent of why I came."

His brows lift. "That so?"

I nod. "You're the only nightlight that's ever worked. I haven't slept for seven years. Not really. Not like I did with you."

He exhales my name, eyes dropping to my mouth. My lips tingle. His features tighten, head tilting slightly with intent.

I don't know where I get the strength, but I turn away before he can break another one of his rules. His forehead drops to the back of my head, a long sigh warming my neck.

"I suck at this," he murmurs.

I hug his arm tighter. "I think we both do."

"The phone call—that was stupid, not telling you. It was just band shit I forgot about. Our manager needed a confirmation for a festival headliner slot next summer. Eddie took it upon himself to call me over and over until I picked up."

"Are you taking the slot?"

He rubs his face against my hair. "Mmhm. The booking agent has hounded us for years, but our schedule never lined up before now."

"Bullshit. You hate festivals."

He chuckles. "Truth. They're chaotic as fuck and hell on my nerves. At least this one is local, and the lineup is pretty killer. Horizon Fest at the Gorge. Heard of it?"

I gasp and slap his arm, then twist to see his grin. "Glow is headlining Saturday night. Lily and I just confirmed last week. Are you Friday?"

Wilder nods, chewing his lip. "We could write a song. You and me, I mean. No pressure or anything, obviously." He pauses, taking in my shocked expression. "Sorry. *Shit.* I shouldn't have—mmfph."

His eyes widen above the hand I've pressed to his mouth.

"Yes," I say emphatically. "I'd love to write a song with you."

bridge

bridge : *a section of a song that provides
contrast, variety, or tension.*

CHAPTER THIRTY-ONE

wilder

YOUR FINGERTIPS LEFT MARKS
LIVING BRUISES I DIDN'T FEEL
UNTIL I HEARD THEM LIKE A HEARTBEAT
REMINDING ME YOU WERE REAL

I OPEN MY PARENTS' front door and wave Evangeline inside ahead of me. The hallway is empty, but the sound of a large gathering floats to our ears from the back of the house.

"I'm starting to think this is a bad idea," she mutters.

"A little late for second thoughts, Fairy. Besides, we've been cooped up for almost two weeks. It was either this or an ambush—trust me, one was coming. This way, we can leave whenever we want. And it's a party. There will be cake. You love cake."

"Ugh, stop it. I'm fine. This is fine. Everything's fine."

When she still doesn't move, I give her a nudge between

the shoulder blades. She snarls at me. I smile back until she sighs and trudges inside.

Hiding my relief, I follow.

The last two weeks have been incredible. They've also been super fucking intense. We haven't written one song—we've written an album's worth. We've talked and laughed and fought and fucked until our bodies literally stopped working. There have been countless moments of solace, softness, and peace.

But despite the intimacy of our renewed *friendship*, she still won't talk about Clay or her trauma. Not when she wakes me up thrashing in her sleep in the throes of a nightmare. Not when she comes back from what I call her Empty Place, where she shuts down and withdraws with a thousand-yard stare.

Even worse than the Empty Place, and happening with increasing frequency, are the times she erupts out of nowhere. Her tears, guilt, and negative self-talk afterward are slowly killing me, as is the fact nothing I say seems to make it any better.

I've never felt so close to her before. Or so far.

The emotional strain is affecting me. Not kissing her. Not telling her I love her. Not knowing whether I'm a stop on her journey or the destination. Not knowing what she needs but suspecting more and more that it isn't me...

We both need a distraction.

Halfway down the hallway, Evangeline glances aside at a mirror. She makes a face and halts, pulling the tie from her hair and fussing with the strands.

"You look beautiful."

I brace for an angry denial, but when she meets my stare in the mirror, her eyes are soft and sad. "I should have washed it again this morning."

I slip my hand up her back and curl my fingers around the nape of her neck. Her hair is soft on my skin—and a lot lighter than it was two weeks ago. It's now more of a dark blonde than brown. She hates it. If it weren't for me, she'd be in the shower twice or more a day, trying to speed along the fading process of something called *toner*.

"I washed it for you yesterday," I murmur, dragging my lips over the back of her head and inhaling. "And I have hair-washing rights for the rest of the week."

Her lips shift into an almost smile. "I still think you cheated."

"Nope. You just suck at Gin Rummy."

She snorts.

"There you two are!"

We turn to see our moms walking toward us, both of them beaming. I gently squeeze the back of Evangeline's neck, bending to whisper, "If you get overwhelmed, hide in my bedroom."

She nods subtly. The moment my touch leaves her neck, a practiced smile slides over her face, her eyes lighting up. She rushes forward to hug both women, then she and Sophie walk arm in arm down the hallway and vanish around the corner.

A pointed throat clearing brings my attention to my mom. Before she can voice the concern I see brewing in her eyes, I pull her into my side.

"I'm okay, Mom. I've honestly never been this happy."

She makes a soft, sympathetic sound. "Or this sad."

I grunt as the words land. "That too." I give her a squeeze, then let her go. "Thanks for putting this together."

She smiles. "Of course. We're missing a lot of the crew, but that's what you get with a bunch of twenty-somethings in the mix. All the old folks are here, though."

Emma's distinctive screech carries down the hall before tapering into a high-pitched giggle. A chorus of adult laughter follows, including Evangeline's. A knot inside me releases.

My mom adds with a grin, "And the star of the show. Come on, let's go see everyone."

My phone vibrates. Glad for the excuse to have a few seconds alone, I pull it from my pocket. "Go ahead. I'll be right behind you."

With a squeeze of my arm and a soft smile, she walks away. I lift my phone to my ear as I turn and veer into what used to be the piano room.

"Shelley? What's up?"

My publicist's voice is sharp as ice and freezes me mid-step.

"I just got off the phone with one of my media contacts. You were right."

I sag against a bookshelf. "Fuck. How much time do I have?"

"Monday morning." She pauses. "Most major entertainment outlets."

Frissons of anxiety skitter up my legs, wrapping spiked tendrils around my chest.

Two days.

Since that lunch in Los Angeles four months ago, I've known this was coming. Clay was never going to go down without a fight. His ego is too big, his pockets too deep, and he hates me almost as much as I hate him.

But I thought I'd have more warning. More time to prepare.

As panic roars in my ears, I realize he must have found out Evangeline was with me. There's no way the leak came from the security guard who let her through the gate, so she must have picked up a tail somewhere in Seattle. Maybe when she landed or at her parents' house. Hell, for all I know, there was a telephoto lens on the speedboat we saw when we were on the beach last week. I remember thinking it was strange when it slowed as it passed.

Chances are I'll never know. This is Clay's hometown. Between his shady contacts and his father's, it was only a matter of time.

It doesn't matter, anyway. He's calling my bluff.

The reckoning is here.

"Wilder?" Shelley's tone tells me it's not the first time she's said my name.

"I'm here. What's the angle?"

"What you thought it would be." For the first time since meeting Shelley eight years ago, I hear a tremble in her voice.

The first zings of anger heat my blood. "Is fact-checking not a thing anymore? Everyone's willing to publish whatever stupid rumor will sell more ad space?"

She hesitates. "He went to the press himself. It's an interview. My source is trying to get her hands on it, but I'm not hopeful."

I clench my teeth so hard pain blooms in my temples. "Fucking figures. He's made a career off convincing people of lies."

"I promise you, Wilder, we'll fight this with everything we have. The second we get off the phone, I'm sounding the alarm. Cease and desist letters will be sent within the hour. It might stop them."

We both know it won't stop them all, or even most. Especially if the story was juicy enough to be grabbed by multiple outlets. That means whatever is coming was deemed as having enough merit to risk defamation suits. It means he's already convinced people.

Shelley knows as well as I do that no matter what she does, no matter how good my lawyers are or how aggressive our defense is, I won't escape unscathed. And that means Evangeline won't, either.

I look across the room at where the Steinway used to sit, now occupied by cozy armchairs. My vision blurs. In the distortion, I see two kids huddled on the piano bench arguing about a song bridge.

The fire in my blood flares hotter.

"Call Anita Allman and make sure she knows what's coming. Tell her what I told you last month."

"Wilder—"

"No," I interject firmly. "Her job is to protect her client, not me."

She huffs in frustration. "Fine, but we both know it won't be up to her. And from everything you've told me about Eva, she's not going to let you take a fall to save her own face. Neither will Lily Aoki—you're her kid's godfather, for Christ's sake."

"I know," I assure her. "All I need Anita to do is stall them from making any statements for a few days."

In the following pause, I imagine her eyes narrowing to slits behind her glasses. "Is this about the hint you dropped last month? If you have ammunition up your sleeve, now's the fucking time to share it!"

I pinch the bridge of my nose. "It's not my information to share. I'll be asking someone else to put their neck on the line. I'll talk to them today, but I need you to proceed like we don't have a smoking gun."

Shelley's exhale crackles in my ear. "Fine. Sorry for snapping. Keep your head up, okay? A lot of people have your back. In fact, I think you're going to realize just how loved you are."

My throat thick, I say, "Thanks, Shelley. I'll get back to you soon."

As I end the call, movement snaps my head toward the hallway. My dad's eyes lift from the phone to my face. He frowns in concern.

"I only heard the end. Is it happening?"

I nod. The tiny movement is an earthquake, cracking my control. My next breath is a strangled gasp. He rushes forward right as my legs give out, catching me and lowering me to my knees. He guides my head down, a warm hand on my back.

"Breathe, Wild."

He counts for me, breathes with me, until the worst of the dizziness passes. I lift my head, still shaky and slightly nauseous.

"It's over for me, Dad."

"You don't know that," he says gruffly.

"What I know is to not underestimate Clay Eaton." I shake my head with a resigned sigh. "As fucked up as it sounds, I don't even care about losing my career. Not for my sake, at least. And as hard as it will be for all of us, the guys will recover. They'll move on. All I really care about is how it will affect Evangeline. Whatever Clay is about to throw at me will follow me no matter what. I can't protect her from it— from me. Once again, I'm going to fuck up her life."

My dad's eyes burn with intensity. "I had a similar mindset once. Martyrdom with a side of victimhood. You know what it got me? Almost dying in a car accident and losing your mother."

I stare at him in shock; he smiles grimly. "Trust me, Wilder, women don't want our protection—at least not the kind where we decide what they can and can't handle. What they want is to be invited to fight our battles beside us." He clasps my shoulder, placing his other hand over my heart. "Who you shouldn't be underestimating is *Evangeline*. Stop treating her like she's fragile when she's always been your greatest source of strength."

The words resonate, sending chills down my body. Whatever expression I'm wearing lifts my dad's eyebrows.

"What? Did I say something profound?"

My laugh is closer to a wheeze. "Something like that."

"Good. Oh, one more thing." He reaches into his pocket and pulls out what I call his talisman: a vintage pocket watch that was a gift from his first sponsor before he died. He grabs my hand and puts it in my palm. "I want you to have this."

I look down at the watch, my fingers tingling. I've never seen him without it, and holding it feels surreal. Like I'm staring at a vital piece of who he is.

"I can't take this. No way."

"Then consider it a loan. You can return it when you don't need it anymore."

My thumb grazes the surface his own has worn smooth over time. A painful memory floats forward of him sitting beside my hospital bed, head down, thumb moving in circles over the metal.

"How am I supposed to know when I don't need it anymore?"

He smiles serenely. "Sounds like a you problem."

With a rough laugh, I press the catch at the base near the silver chain. The case pops open, revealing the familiar off-white face with thin, black Roman numerals, the hour and minute hands forever stuck.

"Thanks for the broken watch." The emotion in my voice outweighs the sarcasm.

"That's the point," he says with a squeeze of my shoulder. "Nothing's perfect, Wild. All of us are a little broken. If we let go of trying so hard to make everything work the way we want it to, we get to see how beautiful that brokenness is."

I smirk. "Twice a day, at least."

"Smart-ass."

He stands and offers me a hand. I let him pull me to my feet, then close the watch and tuck it in my pocket.

"I'm going to find somewhere more private to call Kendra."

He nods, pulling me in for another tight hug. "We're with you, son. Don't forget that."

"Thanks, Dad."

CHAPTER THIRTY-TWO

evangeline

Find her tomorrow
where the river begins
Listen for mayhem
A storm in the wind

THERE'S a protrusion of bark digging into my spine and a sharp rock under my thigh, but I can't muster the energy to remedy either discomfort. Full-body goosebumps periodically burst along my skin beneath my jeans and sweater—not from the cold, but from the woman I'm watching walk toward the glow of the Ashburn's house.

Katherine moves slowly and gracefully. Long hair, mostly gray now, spirals down her back. A green velvet and lace duster whispers lightly over dirt and grass behind her.

"It was never the darkness outside of you that needed to be embraced, but the darkness within."

Her voice stays long after she's gone, twirling on the breeze, airy and ageless. As does the challenge that lay within her eyes alongside a kind of detached compassion. Like she expected I already knew what she was telling me. Like the words themselves weren't all that important.

I tilt my head back against the tree. A peel of bark snags my hair, but the tug and tiny flare of pain don't register. Overhead, stripes of shadow paint the giant sycamore. Its curves are sensual, distinctly feminine, the lowest branches resembling arms reaching for what they crave most. Space, oxygen, sunlight. The promise of life. Of love.

"The dam was always meant to break, Evangeline. Let the last barriers fall away. Trust the current and the light you see ahead. He's waiting for you. He will not falter—he will not dim. But hurry. A storm approaches, and only together can you keep the light safe."

The shadows around me have deepened by the time I hear footsteps approaching. Awareness curls through me, opening my eyes as Wilder crouches before me. A warm palm cups my cheek. I turn my face to kiss his palm.

The air stills and thickens with unspoken words. I don't ask him why he disappeared for an hour right after we got here or why he seemed so distracted when he returned. He doesn't ask why I'm here instead of in his room or what Katherine said to me when she followed me outside.

He glances up at the tree, inhales shortly, then rocks back to his feet and extends a hand.

"Let's go home."

Home.

My smile hurts, but it's a stretching pain, like blood circulating to sleeping muscles. Weightless like imaginary barriers falling one by one. Freeing like water rushing forth, finally on its destined path.

I follow the light.

♫

AN HOUR LATER, curled against Wilder on a couch with his fingers in my hair, the final barrier inside me silently crashes down.

My words are fumbling at first. Serrated sentences and stutters. Like spitting rocks from my lungs. But as I go on, they begin to flow. Not easily or smoothly, but unstoppable. Downhill river rapids.

I purge it all. How I buried my pain seven years ago instead of facing it, numbed myself from the inside out until I forgot who I was. How much of my mid-twenties is a blur of brittle effort and flagging self-esteem. Planes, buses, hotels. Stadiums and stages. Roars and flashing lights. The voices of the many becoming louder and louder as I closed myself off to the voice of my own heart.

My pride, turning ever more toxic. My growing fears and personal failures. My insides and outsides becoming as mismatched as my eyes. How my music—the only pure thing left inside me—faded away and took my last whisper of identity with it.

The numbness. Emptiness. The silence and the dark.

I can't look at him when I tell him about Clay, but I feel his subtle flinch when I admit what a relief it was at first. How I was in a downward spiral and Clay's control felt like landing on solid ground.

"Maybe that's where my anger comes from."

Wilder brushes my hair back from the side of my face. "What do you mean?"

"I did this to myself," I murmur. "I ignored all the warning signs, dismissed the concerns of my closest friends, my parents... As angry as I am at Clay, I'm ten times angrier at myself. So maybe when I lash out, I'm really lashing out at myself for being so fucking weak."

He tugs my chin until I lift my eyes to his. "I'm no expert, but I think those are probably normal feelings given what you've been through. But you're not weak—far from it. It's not your fault Clay took advantage of you. He's an experienced manipulator. How the hell were you supposed to know?"

"Logically, I know that. But I can't help feeling like it's my fault."

He nods, sighing. "I'm intimately familiar with guilt, so I get it. Imagine how many times I've wondered if you ending up with Clay is *my* fault."

I stiffen. "What? How can you even say that?"

His eyes squeeze shut. "The night you first met him, at your showcase, I should have told you what he did to Kendra. If I had, maybe—"

I palm his face, silencing him. He opens agonized eyes. "No. I prohibit you from feeling guilty."

Some of his misery fades, a smile lifting one corner of his mouth. "You *prohibit* me?"

"Yes. Besides, you did warn me about Clay. I was the one who didn't listen—or didn't let myself remember." I blink against the sting of tears, my voice dropping to a whisper. "Deep down, I knew he was a bad person. Maybe I felt like I deserved him. Or I was punishing myself. I don't know."

He makes a soft, sad sound and draws me against his chest. I listen to his heartbeat, slow and steady beneath my ear, and pull his scent into my lungs. Glowing warmth spreads through me, burning away the taint of my memories.

In their absence, the truth resonates. Katherine's words, my salvation.

He will not falter—he will not dim.

"You saved me, Wilder. Even though I turned my back on you, you still came for me when I needed you most. I couldn't hear music anymore, but I heard you. Your voice led me out of the darkness, just like it did when I got lost on that camping trip. So yes, you're prohibited from feeling guilty about the choices I made in the past."

A tremble moves through his arms. He sighs into my hair, and there's a smile in his next words. "Maybe we should stick together from now on. Seems safer."

"I think that's a good idea," I whisper, gratitude and hope shining painfully bright inside me. "I talked to my mom today, by the way. She's going to help me find a therapist. I... I'm sorry for what I've put you through the last two weeks. All my mood swings. I know I've been a lot."

He shifts against me, lifting me off his chest so we're face-to-face. Warm hands cup my cheeks. His eyes are almost unnaturally radiant in the dimly lit room, shimmering brown and gold flecks on a rich emerald canvas.

"I'm so proud of you for asking for help." His tongue runs subtly along his teeth. "But I want to redden your ass for that bullshit about mood swings."

My face heats beneath his hands. Fighting the flames of arousal, I shake my head. "It's not bullshit. I literally screamed at you yesterday for putting my underwear in the dryer, then locked myself in the bathroom and cried for an hour."

His brows jump. "So what? Shit, you should have seen me in my first year of sobriety—actually, I'm glad you didn't." The brief flash of humor in his eyes fades. "With what you're processing right now, emotional anarchy is a given. You think

I care that you pop off on me sometimes? You think I can't take it? Fairy, I'd face a thousand times worse for the privilege of sharing the same air as you."

That air thins, leaving me breathless. "Then maybe you're as crazy as I am."

A thumb slides across my hot cheek. "Call yourself crazy again and I'll punish your ass with more than my hand."

The throb between my legs intensifies so suddenly I squirm. "Is that a promise?"

A slow, wicked grin spreads on his face. "How pissed are you that I haven't taken that beautiful ass?"

I bare my teeth, more challenge than smile. "The toys and lube you ordered came over a week ago. You haven't even opened the box. I'm starting to think you're trying to give me another complex."

His grin sharpens for a moment before falling. Eyes darkening, he wraps hot fingers around my throat. I swallow against his palm and his gaze drops to my mouth. Parting my lips, I drag the tip of my tongue between them. Wilder grunts, his eyes narrowing in censure.

Being denied his lips on mine has been torture. I hate that he's been strong enough to resist temptation, but I'd be lying if I said I didn't also love him for that strength. For his unfailing commitment to what he feels is right. His never-faltering light.

"Sweet Fairy," he murmurs. "Never doubt that I want all of you all the time. Every inch of your body. Every mood, every scream, every tear and laugh. Thank you for opening up to me tonight. You're so brave, and I'm so fucking proud of you." He pauses, regret flashing in his eyes. "As much as it pains me to say this, tonight probably isn't the time to open that box. It's been a long day. We should get some sleep. Unless you want me to run you a bath first?"

His fingers loosen on my throat. Before he can fully release me, I grab his hand with both of mine and hold it to my skin. I almost smile at the surprise in his eyes, but the moment is too massive, ringing in my body and soul like a mighty bell.

"I'm not using you as a distraction, Wilder. Not right now, and not once since I got here."

I know I've hit the mark when his expression shutters. An ache spreads through my chest as the full scope of our lives unfolds in my mind's eye. Who we are and have been. How we match and mirror each other now and across the pages of the past.

My first steps as a child were to follow him. The first time I sang was to sing with him. The first poem I wrote and every song I've written since—every single one—all belong to him.

We've been each other's light and darkness. We've broken each other. Saved each other. We've stretched our souls' tether to the point of fraying. But it will never snap. Nothing can destroy the bond between us.

He was right all those years ago, the day we sat beneath the sycamore and promised each other forever.

We *are* more.

We're everything.

My heart flutters, heavy and impossibly light.

"I've been trying to be the girl you loved before, to get back to that version of myself. I thought that was who you wanted, who you deserved."

Frowning, he opens his mouth, but I press a finger to his lips.

"I've realized it wasn't about you at all. *I* wanted to be that person again because I've been struggling to accept who I've become. How my choices have changed me." I trace a fingertip along his lower lip. "But you don't see any of that, do you? You just see me."

He nods. "All I ever see when I look at you is my Fairy—my muse, my reason, my everything. You're the only addiction I'll never give up. My obsession forever."

I blink away a veil of tears. "I see you too. You're *my* perfect song. If the offer is still on the table, I'd like to return your missing piece and come home. Can I keep you forever? Will you keep me?"

His chest convulses and his beautiful eyes shine with tears. "Yes. More yeses than stars in the sky. Always yes."

Shadows swirl around us, the ripples of Katherine's warning: *A storm approaches.* But they can't touch or dim this light.

Wilder's forehead drops to mine. "I love you, Evangeline. So much I burn with it."

"I love you, too." I grip his wrist, straining my face toward his. "But if you don't kiss me right now, I'm going to smother you in your sleep."

A dimple flashes, then his face lowers. Parted lips meet mine, soft and warm and achingly sweet.

Time stops.

Everything fades away.

And it's just us.

Like it's always been and always will be.

CHAPTER THIRTY-THREE

evangeline

I SLIP out of bed as dawn brightens the crack between curtains. Wilder's arm curls over my absence, a small frown flickering across his brow before smoothing as dreams reclaim him.

Drawing a blanket over his shoulder, I study his peaceful face. Dark lashes twitching against golden skin, chaotic waves of hair fanning his forehead and cheek, lips a little swollen and chapped. My fingers lift to my own lips, still tender from last night, and trace the edges of my smile.

We made out like teenagers until we couldn't keep our eyes open anymore, then stumbled upstairs and fell into bed. I can still hear his whispered, "Love you always," right as we drifted to sleep.

Leaving him to rest, I retreat to the guest bedroom to dress and brush my teeth, then head downstairs to make a cup of tea. As it steeps, I pull my phone from the charger on the counter and call Lily.

She answers on the second ring, grumbling, "I can't wait for the day I can sleep past six again."

"Aww, you won't miss our morning chats?"

"We'll move to a decent time. Like ten or eleven."

I laugh. "I hate to break it to you, but you have another eighteen years before you can sleep in again."

"More like twenty," she mutters.

Grinning at the reminder of what she whispered to me at the party yesterday, I ask, "Have you told Rye yet?"

"Hold on." A door closes in the background and her voice lowers. "No. I'm going to take another test today. Maybe it was a fluke."

I take my steaming mug to a couch and sit, tucking my legs beneath me.

"Do you want it to be?"

"Not really, but... kind of?" She sighs. "I know it's lame, but I wanted to get married before we had another baby."

Inspiration strikes and I straighten eagerly. "You've seen Wilder's property. The gazebo on the water? And there's a beautiful clearing that would be perfect for a reception. We could plan a wedding in no time at all."

There's a small, shocked pause. "Are you serious?"

"Totally serious. Except for the doing it ourselves part. We'd definitely hire someone."

She laughs shrilly. "And Wilder would be okay with this? You're sure?"

"I'll ask him today, but I'm sure he will be." I smile to myself. "I have ways of sweetening the deal."

Lily squeals, the sound muffled like she's covering her mouth.

"Is that a yes?"

Another squeal. "Yes! Let's do it. Oh my gosh, this is amazing. Can I call you later? I have to tell Rye we might be pregnant again and that we're finally getting married."

"Of course. Say hi to—" I laugh when I realize she's already hung up.

"I love that sound."

I whip my head around, a different smile blooming at the sight of Wilder turning the corner into the living room.

"What are you doing up? It's barely seven."

He shrugs, not answering. I'm not sure I'd hear a reply anyway, my brain fogging as I take in his bare chest and the pajama pants riding low on his hips. My eyes wander greedily, lingering on the dips of muscle cradling his ink-littered abs before dropping lower.

Pajamas beat gray sweatpants any day of the week.

"And I love it when you look at me like that," he purrs.

I hide my smile behind my mug. "Are you flirting with me?"

He pauses to yawn and stretch, the movements slow and intentional, arms lifting, muscles bunching and extending as he rotates and bends from side to side. I ogle him shamelessly until a chuckle lifts my gaze from the music notes wrapping around his hip.

Even his dimples look smug as he sits and pats his lap. I dutifully unfold my legs and give him my feet.

As his thumbs work magic on my soles, he says idly, "Everything, and I mean *everything* I do, is me flirting with you. Case in point—the tattoo you were just staring at." He lifts my feet so I can see it. "Do you recognize the song?"

Leaning forward, I study the notes and my mouth drops open in shock. Not only is it the Night Theory song that put us on the map, it's *my* handwriting.

Wilder snorts. "I don't know whether to be offended or proud that the thought of my dick is so distracting you've never actually read the music."

I trail a finger over the notes, gratified when he shivers. He lowers my feet back to his lap and resumes massaging them.

I can't seem to stop smiling. "What about when we argue? Are you still flirting then?"

"Definitely." He slants a knowing smile my way. "I knew that comment I made on New Year's would piss you off."

I laugh, then lower my voice in a comic impersonation of his. "'You've never even seen me flirt. In any case, I think we can agree that ship has sailed.'" I punch his shoulder playfully. "Asshole."

He grins, lifting my foot to kiss my ankle. "Undeniably *your* asshole."

I arch a brow. "Speaking of..."

Wilder throws his head back and laughs, the sound rich and lovely, his stomach shaking under my feet. I watch him in a lovestruck daze, my ears and heart full. He's still grinning when he plucks my mug from my hands and puts in on the coffee table, then pulls me into his lap. Grabbing his shoulders, I roll my hips and grin as his eyes darken.

Just when I think he's going to crack, his hands tighten on my waist to stop my movements.

"Fairy, wait."

The regret on his face protects me from the sting of rejection, but I still frown. "What's wrong?"

He hesitates, fear flashing in his eyes. And I *know*.

"Already?" I whisper.

Confusion draws his eyebrows together. "Already what?"

I move off his lap and settle beside him, then reach for my tea. A long sip fortifies me.

"Katherine warned me something bad was coming." I glance at him, catching his shocked expression before resignation replaces it.

He leans forward on his elbows, fingers tangling in his hair. "What did she say exactly?"

"'A storm approaches, and only together can you keep the light safe.' She made it clear that you're the light."

Head jerking up, he twists to face me. Reading the wary hope on his face, I belatedly realize his fear wasn't about whatever news he's received but about my reaction to it. He was worried I was going to leave him.

Taking his closest hand, I thread our fingers together. "She basically told me to pull my head out of my ass and trust you. And I do, Wilder. I trust you—and us—implicitly. Whatever it is you need to tell me, I'm not going to run. I'm not leaving you. We're going to face it together."

A moment later his mouth is on mine, the kiss deep, fierce, and all too brief. Cradling my face, he whispers, "You're amazing. I love you. I'm sorry I didn't say anything yesterday."

I nip at his lower lip. "It's okay. I'm used to you withholding crucial information due to misplaced protective instincts."

He huffs a laugh. "I take it I have Katherine to thank for last night?"

I wince. "Pretty much."

"So stubborn," he murmurs, his eyes alight with humor.

"I would have gotten around to confessing my love eventually," I mutter.

He gives me a quick, smiling kiss. "You need to eat before this conversation. Veggie omelet and a smoothie okay?"

I almost protest, but his knowing look stops me. With a sigh, I concede that he's right. My stomach is already grumbling at the mention of food, and it won't be long before I'm officially hangry.

"That sounds good."

Hearing the undertone of irritation, he smirks. "Proud of you, baby."

I grab a throw pillow and chuck it at his head.

CHAPTER THIRTY-FOUR

WITH A SCREAM OF RAGE, Evangeline swings the axe at the giant tree stump I use to chop firewood. She misses the standing log by at least four inches. It topples over as she wrestles the heel of the blade from the stump.

As she heaves and pants, she mutters under her breath. I can't hear every word, but catch "motherfucker" and "fucking kill him."

I'm not sure what it says about me that I'm hard as fuck right now, but I blame it on the sweat glistening on her face, chest, and arms. Then again, I was hard on her first swing, long before she pulled off her sweatshirt to reveal a black sports bra.

I shift against the tree I'm leaning on, adjusting myself discreetly. Evangeline catches the movement, sending a searing glance my way before righting the log and lining up for another swing.

Arms shaking, she lifts the heavy axe. Her form is shit, but I learned my lesson twenty minutes ago and keep my mouth shut.

I can't help a small smile as she bellows her rage into the forest and swings again. I'm not happy about her pain, obviously, but I'm ecstatic that she's expressing it. It means she feels safe to show me the full, messy range of her emotions.

"Wipe that smile off your face," she snaps, hefting the axe and stumbling a little. "There's nothing funny about this."

My smile instantly dies. She's right. There's nothing funny about any of this, especially since Shelley got her hands on a few of the headlines publishing in less than forty-eight hours. Her phone call is what woke me up so early, and I spent five minutes dry heaving over the toilet before I came downstairs.

I knew Clay was going to go for my jugular, but I thought —naively, I guess—that he'd leave Evangeline out of it.

He didn't.

There are the expected, shock-value headlines like, **Sex, Drugs, and Rock 'n' Roll: Wilder Ashburn Exposed,** and an assortment of others all implying I'm back on drugs and a literal monster. Clay apparently found a handful of random industry people to support the narrative, no doubt individuals I've either pissed off or were all too happy to sacrifice morals for money. Shelley even said there are a few publications touting so-called photo evidence. I can only assume they're passing off pictures of me mid-yawn as proof I'm loaded. Either that, or they went straight AI and are hoping the public doesn't notice.

But my literal worst nightmare is the main headline attached to Clay's exclusive interview: **Eva Marie: Mentally Unstable and Back with Abusive Ex-Lover. Estranged Fiancé Asks Public for Help.**

Every word is bullshit, but it's the kind of headline that plays to empathy and will trigger pitchforks. And Clay knows it. He's preemptively pinning his sins on me, attempting to turn me into a straw man the world will light on fire while he stays safe in the smoke.

In his twisted head, I'm sure he believes Evangeline will eventually turn against me and come crawling back to him.

He really doesn't know her at all.

"I'll show him mentally unstable," she snarls.

She swings the axe again and again, each progressively sloppier arc punctuated by insults.

"Saggy-balled—tiny-dicked—hair-plugged—fake-tanned —*psychopath*."

She finally clips the edge of the standing log, sending it flying off the stump. The axe almost flies, too. I push off the tree, but she throws me a look that makes me freeze and lift my hands.

"Just here to make sure you don't lose a hand."

She bares her teeth. "Suck my dick, Wilder."

Maybe I'm experiencing some weirdly euphoric version of shock, but I've never wanted her so badly in my life. "If you had one, baby, I'd drop to my knees right now."

With a groan more amused than annoyed, she lets the axe fall to the ground and sits heavily on the stump.

Panting, she wipes damp hair off her forehead. "There's something seriously wrong with you."

I grin. "You love it."

Sunlight cuts through the clearing, bisecting her flushed face and making her gray eye glow with predatory light. My mouth drops as she spreads her legs and arches an eyebrow.

"Well? What are you waiting for?"

Four strides and I'm dropping, my knees slamming into dirt as I rip my T-shirt over my head. Evangeline's pupils dilate, her breath stuttering, but she still manages a haughty sniff.

"I didn't say anything about returning the favor."

My chuckle is so full of dark promise that goosebumps lift on her chest and arms. "It's to keep splinters from your ass, you brat. Stand up."

She stands fast, betraying her eagerness. My nose brushes her bare stomach, and I suck in the delicious fragrance of her sweat as I spread my T-shirt over the stump. Then I grab her hips and lick from the waistband of her sweatpants to the edge of her sports bra. She gasps, grabbing my shoulders to stay upright.

Finding a hard nipple through cotton, I flick it with my tongue before closing my mouth around it and sucking hard. She whimpers, rocking toward me. I take advantage, seizing the fabric under my fingers and yanking her pants down, baring her to the sunlight and fresh air.

"Oh, fuck, we're really doing this?" she asks in a high voice. "Are you sure no one can see us?"

I gaze up at her. "I'd never do this if I wasn't one hundred percent sure it was private. This is the densest part of the property, the farthest from neighbors and the water. I'm also not even close to the most famous person in the neighborhood, hence the giant walls and armed security. But if you feel unsafe at all, we can absolutely go inside."

A smile teases her lips. "Get back to work."

I bite the closest nipple, grinning around her flesh when she smacks my head. There's no power in the blow, probably because her arms are limp noodles from rage-chopping a stump that's so old and hard it barely noticed.

"God, I love you," I murmur, pulling up the band of her sports bra to expose her breasts. I tongue her nipples until she's panting again—for a different, better reason this time. When her hips start moving in needy circles, I guide her down to the stump until she's on her back, splayed out like a wicked offering.

"Fucking look at you." Shadows play over her body, cool air dancing with warm beams of light. I pull her sweats over her sneakers and toss them to her. "For your head."

As she tucks the fabric behind her neck, I shift forward until my knees hit the trunk before lowering to my heels. Sliding my hands up her silky thighs, I spread them up and to the sides. My cock jumps at the beautifully indecent way she's bared to me. Arousal shimmers on her pussy, gravity carrying lubricant exactly where I need it. With a groan of appreciation, I kiss my way up one thigh before blowing over her center.

Her legs stiffen under my hands and I glance up, stilling when I register her closed-off expression. "What's wrong?"

She hesitates, then blurts, "How many women have been on this stump?"

I'm powerless over my slow, satisfied grin. "Why?"

She scowls. "Just answer."

I bite the nearest skin, earning another feeble slap to my head. "You first. Why, Fairy?"

Her chin lifts, jaw set with defiance. "Because it's suspiciously the perfect size and height for this."

The effort of holding back a laugh makes my eyes water and my voice strangled. "You think I had a tree cut down in order to make a sex stump?"

Her face turns red, thighs tensing as she pushes against my hold. "Let me up. I'm not in the mood anymore."

Twenty-four hours ago, I would have obeyed without question. Now, I shake my head. "Too late. You're a sacrifice to the sex stump." Holding her straining thighs, I press a kiss to her clit.

"Wilder," she hisses.

Tracing the tip of my tongue around the flushed, swollen bud, I roll my eyes up to see her livid expression war with equally potent lust. "No one's been on the sex stump but you. No one's been in my bed or shower, bent over furniture or splayed out on my kitchen counter but you. Just you. Only you."

Expression softening, she sighs out her relief. "Suck me," she whispers.

I cover her clit with my mouth. She groans, spine arching. I alternate deep, pulsing suction with taps of my tongue. Her fingers dig into my hair, fisting and yanking me closer so she can grind against my face. Her gasps and moans fill the clearing, making my hips rock and my cock throb and leak.

Content to let her use me for a minute, I pull out the items I stowed in my pocket before we left the house. Focusing isn't easy, especially when her thighs are strangling me and I'm close to coming in my pants, but I manage to squirt lube on the silicone plug and turn on the vibration.

Evangeline's head lifts at the sound, her thighs releasing my neck. I take advantage of the freedom, straightening to show her the toy. Her already blown pupils flare wider, belying her next, irate words.

"You're not fucking my ass in the forest!"

My smile makes her shiver. "We both know you'd let me and love it, but I'm not going to—today. You *are* going to take this plug and wear it as you walk to the studio and find a soft surface."

"But I'm so close," she whines.

"Oh, I know." I drag the slick, vibrating toy over her clit, enjoying the way her hips jerk. "Do you feel empty, baby?"

She nods and cups her breasts, teasing her nipple piercings. "Please make me come first?"

My smile sharpens. "Nice try. You'll come when I let you. If you're a good little slut for me, I'll put another toy in your cunt while I'm in your ass."

Evangeline's eyes glaze, her body shuddering. "Yes, Wilder," she whispers.

Her submission is an axe to my patience. I drop the toy to her ass and apply pressure. "Let me in. Good girl. Fuck, so pretty. Does it hurt?"

"No. Feels good."

Releasing the base of the toy, I trail two fingers through her folds and tease the hot, silky entrance of her body. She whimpers and undulates in search of penetration.

"Ah-ah." I slap her clit, making her arch with a cry. Her eyes close, breath stalling. "Don't you dare come, Evangeline."

She fights her body's demand for several taut seconds, then relaxes, her chest heaving with the effort.

"Good job, baby. Ready to go?"

She nods, her soft, guileless smile almost undoing me. Before I lose the ability to resist her, I push to my feet and offer a hand. She stands up and gasps, swaying into me.

"You okay?"

"Yes," she says with a soft giggle. "Just feels weird. Kinda heavy."

I smack her ass. She yelps, then groans. Tilting her chin, I give her a soft kiss and a parting nibble.

"I'm going to grab something from the house, then I'm coming for you."

"Ladies first." As soon as the words are out, she cringes.

My delighted laugh startles a pair of squirrels, sending them scampering up a nearby tree.

She glowers at me. "I'm deeply disappointed in myself."

I reach out and gently tweak her nipple. "Get moving, Pun Queen."

She unfurls a middle finger, then turns on a heel and

takes a step, only to jerk to a stop. A soft, strained sound rides her heavy exhale.

"You can do it," I say through my grin.

Both middle fingers float up as she begins walking carefully and *very awkwardly* toward the path leading to the studio. Once I'm confident she has the hang of it, I sprint to the house, barely making it inside before I fold over laughing.

CHAPTER THIRTY-FIVE

evangeline

HOBBLING FURTIVELY through the woods wearing only sneakers and a sports bra hiked to my armpits is... weird. Almost as weird as the heavy, vibrating plug in my ass.

The latter is a perfect distraction, not allowing for much coherent thought. Every step sends a wave of daunting sensation through my lower half. My thighs are embarrassingly wet, my labia uncomfortably swollen. I focus on putting one foot in front of the other, doing my best to ignore the feeling that something is going to slip out of me any second. From the size of the plug and the initial burn, it's not going anywhere. I still find myself clenching, which only makes the sensations more intense and my steps more wobbly.

Wilder knew exactly what he was doing when he put the axe in my hands, just like he knew what I'd need after. Sneaky man had the plug and lube in his pocket before we even left the house. If I wasn't so uncomfortably aroused, I might have pretended to be more annoyed by his presumption. In reality, I'm amused. And grateful.

I'm so fucking grateful for him.

When I reach the studio, I waste no time rushing inside.

The air is cooler indoors, hushed and still. Without the ever-present breeze, my skin itches with a reminder that I'm coated in drying sweat and a fine layer of dirt from my failed attempt at chopping wood.

Glancing toward the stairs, I briefly consider a quick shower before discarding the idea. Not only does it sound too challenging at the moment, Wilder has a kink for me being sweaty. Biting my lip, I look around the room in search of a soft surface.

My gaze catches on the Steinway. Namely, on the piano's long, padded bench.

I've just made it to the bench when the door opens behind me. My body recognizes his presence with a tingle of familiar energy, so I don't look back as I toe off my shoes and socks and pull off my sports bra. Then I tug the bench out a few more inches and carefully climb on.

His soft groan and rapidly approaching steps are music to my ears, as are his crooning words, "Better than any fantasy."

Strong, hot hands stroke down my spine and over my hips. I gasp, my skin shockingly sensitive, all my nerves afire so that I feel his touch everywhere. He seems to know it, his strokes exceedingly gentle. When he begins dropping soft kisses down my spine, the pleasure is so consuming I almost fall off the bench. My arms and legs quiver, muscles burning, as I try to stay balanced.

"Wilder—"

"I know, baby, it's okay." He scoops me into his arms and smiles down at me. "We'll try that on a day you didn't spend forty minutes trying to murder a dead tree."

I laugh, then choke on a moan at the unexpected result.

Wilder chuckles. "Hang on for just a few more minutes."

He carries me across the studio, then lays me gently on my back atop an oversized ottoman. A hand clasps my neck possessively, then slides heavily down my chest to my stomach. Eyes bright with love and dark with need meet mine. I squirm, then whimper at the assault on my nerves.

"I need you," I whisper.

"You have me."

He slips out of his shoes and pulls off his track pants. My mouth waters at the sight of his cock, hard and flushed, and I open my mouth in silent demand. With a muffled curse, he kneels beside my head and feeds me what I want.

I lick the salty offering at his slit, then take him into my mouth. He watches with glittering, slitted eyes as I work up and down his length. Between his taste, the rough sounds he makes, and the vibration in my ass, it doesn't take long for me to return to the precipice of orgasm. But when I try to sneak a hand to my clit, he grabs my fingers.

"Not yet," he rumbles as he pulls himself from my mouth.

Thankfully, he's just as worked up as I am and moves quickly, positioning himself between my legs. Lifting and spreading my knees, he guides them toward my chest.

"Hold them right here for me, baby."

I do as he says, my reward his immediate groan. His eyes flash up to mine, jaw clenching and unclenching.

"You ready?"

"Is that a joke? Please, please get on with it."

A small, impish smile flashes before his features tighten with focus. He grabs something from his pants. There's a *snick* as a bottle top opens, then the sound of lube squirting into his hand. As he rubs the liquid over himself, I feel a tug at my ass. The vibration in the plug turns off.

"Deep breath in, Fairy. Relax and exhale."

The toy slips out of me with a faint sting. Before I can process the mingled relief and loss, he presses himself inside me. I tense on instinct, waiting for pain that doesn't come. All

I feel is pressure and fullness and a surreal sense of being both inside my body and outside of it.

Wilder moans, low and breathy, his head bowing and hands clenching on my inner thighs. "Don't move for a sec." I stay still and a few deep breaths later, his eyes find mine. "Good?"

"So good." My voice wavers, tears spilling from the corners of my eyes. "I don't know why I'm crying. I'm totally fine. It doesn't hurt at all."

The intensity in his face softens. Leaning forward, he gives me a tender, consuming kiss. "I've edged you super hard. Almost there. Trust me?"

I nod and he grabs something else from the floor. More lube squirts, and then something blunt presses to my pussy. It feels... way too big. I lift my head, focusing with effort. When my eyes finally compute what he's holding, I gape in horror.

"No way is that fitting inside me. It's bigger than you."

He smirks. "Oh ye of little faith."

The toy comes down on my clit. Sensation explodes, bowing my back. When I fall back to the ottoman, my body is lax with surrender.

"Yes, Wilder."

"Good girl. Relax for me."

He presses the dildo back to my pussy. It starts to vibrate, sending rippling shocks through my body. As he pushes it inside me, my eyes roll back in my head and all hesitance falls away. The stretch of the toy magnifies the fullness of him in my ass a thousandfold. Vibrations roll against my G-spot, radiating through my clit and outward. Every inch of my body pulsates, poised on some unfathomable breaking point.

I'm dimly aware of warm, calloused hands stroking me—breasts, stomach, arms, thighs—and of his whispered words,

"So perfect. I knew you could take it. Thank you, baby. You can let go now. I've got you."

He draws back slowly, then snaps his hips.

That's all it takes.

I fracture with a sob.

Waves of ecstasy hit one after the other, each bigger than the last. With a guttural groan, Wilder begins fucking me in earnest. Just when I think it's too much, that I need it to stop, I'm carried to another, higher peak. And as I drop off the ledge, he follows me with a deep, delicious moan.

Floating weightlessly in bliss, I sigh as his body curls over mine. His eyes are all I see. His breath is my breath.

A pure note of rapture sings in my body and soul.

"Forever," he whispers.

Tasting his tears and mine, I whisper back, "Forever."

CHAPTER THIRTY-SIX

evangeline

AS WILDER ASSEMBLES and plates the salad we're having for dinner, I muse that watching him make food is to my eyes what his music is to my ears. His artistry looks effortless, but purpose and passion drive every movement.

Just a few weeks ago, I believed I'd never enjoy salads again. But that was before I watched Wilder make a salad and tasted the result. This one is no exception. Homemade balsamic dressing is tossed with arugula, cucumbers, avocado, and cherry tomatoes, then topped with slices of perfectly grilled steak and a sprinkle of blue cheese. It's nowhere near the most complex meal I've seen him make, but I'm nevertheless awed by the process.

On any other day, I'd be asking for seconds, but today I can barely taste the incredible flavors. I manage six bites before setting down my fork. Wilder is likewise affected and looks relieved to stop picking at his own meal.

"I know it sucks," he says softly. "But there's nothing we can do right now except wait."

I breathe past the urge to snap at him. "Even if this goes

like you hope it does, there's no guarantee it'll stop the articles from being published."

He shrugs a shoulder. "Then we'll deal with the fallout."

My teeth clench. "How can you be so calm about this? He's about to tell the world you're an abusive drug addict and I'm your emotionally unstable victim."

Wilder drags a hand over his face and through his hair. "I'm not calm. My anxiety is through the roof." His eyes meet mine, raw and pleading. "You watched me chop wood for an hour this afternoon when there's already enough for next winter. Was it not obvious I was imagining every log was Clay's face?"

Watching Wilder swing the axe, I hadn't been thinking about anything beyond the beauty and power of his body. While he was processing his anger, I was salivating over the glistening muscles in his back.

I wilt, duly chastised and chagrined. "I don't understand why you don't want me to help. I could be on television tomorrow refuting everything. Why aren't we planning with Anita and Shelley?"

The look in his eyes shatters me—fear and helplessness and stubborn conviction. "Kendra's going to come through."

That now-familiar switch inside me flips again. I shove to my feet and grab both our plates. "Excuse me for not having the same faith in your ex-girlfriend."

I stomp into the kitchen and aggressively rinse our dishes. My arms tremble uncontrollably, sore and weak from the axe. The fear and adrenaline coursing through me aren't helping matters. When the glass container he used to make the salad dressing slips from my hands and shatters against the sink, I scream, "Fuck!"

A second later, my spine warms as Wilder presses against

me. Arms cradling my body, he takes my hands and rinses them, making sure I didn't cut myself.

"I'm sorry," I whisper. "I'm just scared. And I'm so angry. I hate this. I hate him."

"Me too, Fairy. All of the above." He shuts off the water and grabs a dishtowel to dry my hands, then turns me around. "Come on, I want to show you something."

He leads me down the hallway and into the office opposite the stairs. Built-in bookshelves cover the wall behind a desk holding a laptop. The rest of the space is devoted to babysitting and entertaining our goddaughter. There's a portable crib, sensory play mats, and a wooden storage unit stuffed with books and baskets of supplies and toys.

Wilder stops at a closet, toeing aside the giant bag of diapers blocking it. He flashes me a small smile as he opens the door. "That was to deter you from looking in here."

Curiosity piqued, I peer around his shoulder as he retrieves something leaning against the wall behind coats. It's obviously a painting. A big one. I shuffle backward, giving him space to turn the canvas around. I'm expecting River's bold, graffiti-inspired style, but although I can immediately tell he's the artist, the subject is nothing like what he's known for.

I stare at the painting so long that Wilder says nervously, "This is what was hanging over the fireplace until about a month ago. Is it too much? We can hang something else."

"No, I love it," I whisper, looking up at him through tears. "How?"

His smile is giant, so radiant it burns away everything but my love for him.

"My mom snapped this photo of us years ago, and River owed me a favor. Should we put it back up?"

"Absolutely."

562

I step aside as he hefts the canvas and turns for the hall-way, then almost collide with his back when he stops suddenly. He looks over his shoulder at me.

"I have to confess something. When I told you I'm obsessed with you, I wasn't kidding."

I arch my brows. "I think the painting is proof of that."

He shakes his head, gaze falling to the canvas between us. "It's way more than the painting. I..." He blows out a breath, then says in a rush, "I bought this property because of the sycamore out back and because of all the trees and water. You always said you wanted to live by both. I planted the daffodils for you. Fuck, I designed and built this house and the studio with you in mind. It's all for you—for us. Even though I didn't know if you'd ever see it."

Warmth blossoms in my chest, a crackling expansion that takes my breath away.

He continues before I can speak, "Also, that journalist was right about me. Every one of my songs is a love letter to you. I've never written anything that's not in some way inspired by you. I've never loved anyone but you, never dated anyone seriously in the last seven years. I guess what I'm trying to say is if all that doesn't freak you out, I want you to live here. With me."

"Okay."

His head whips up, eyes wide and shocked. "What?"

I swallow laughter, shrugging. "My master plan showing up here was to never leave, so that works."

Sparkling eyes narrow. "It was?"

I nod. Wilder leans forward to kiss me, but I dance out of reach and dart into the hallway. As I walk away, I throw over my shoulder, "This is perfect timing, actually, because I'm about to be billed for another month of storage. I'll call them right now and arrange delivery. We'll need to pull our cars out of the garage so they can unload all the boxes. Oh, and fair warning, I have a lot of clothes. You should probably just give me the whole walk-in."

The painting thuds on the floor.

"Evangeline," he growls.

Grinning so hard my face hurts, I walk faster. "You're going to need more shelves in the studio, too. Glow has *a lot* of awards. And before I forget—Lily and Rye want to get married on the property. Since I live here now, I'll go ahead and say yes."

His footsteps break into a run.

With a breathless squeal, I sprint for the back door. I don't make it, but I can't say I'm disappointed by the result.

outro

outro : *the ending of a song*

CHAPTER THIRTY-SEVEN

evangeline

THE CALL COMES at a few minutes past seven that evening. Wilder and I are on the couch, where we've been trying to distract ourselves with a cooking show. The second his phone starts vibrating on the coffee table, I fumble for the remote and mute the television. He sits up, takes a deep breath, and answers.

"Hey, Kendra." He listens for an excruciating thirty seconds, his impassive expression never changing. Then he says, "Yep," and offers me the phone.

My heart skips a beat, my thoughts freezing. I stare blankly at his lifted hand until he lowers it and mutes the call.

"She wants to talk to you, but if you don't want to..."

His gentle tone restarts my brain. "No, no. It's okay." I take the phone and unmute it. "Hello?"

"Hi, Eva. Thanks for speaking with me. I won't keep you long."

Kendra sounds shockingly different, her voice mellow and mature. Thrown, I stammer out, "H-hi. How's it going? I mean, how are you? Besides… everything." I grimace, embarrassment flooding my body. Wilder grunts in amusement, his hand squeezing my knee but retreating before I can slap it.

Kendra's laugh is breathy with relief. "Oh, good. I thought I was the only one with sweaty armpits right now."

My shoulders relax a fraction, a smile twitching my lips. "Definitely not."

"I'll get right to it, then. I know you've been through hell, and this weekend was probably torture because Wilder hasn't told you what my role is in all this. I didn't want him to give you false hope. But now that it's happening, I wanted you to hear it from me first."

I glance at Wilder, confused, but he merely nods encouragingly.

"I'm listening."

"Wilder told you some of what I went through as a teenager, but what he didn't tell you was what happened right before I left Seattle. That day you found me screaming at him in his bedroom? It ended up being rock bottom for me, too. I went straight to my parents' house afterward. I was out of my mind, out of money, and was planning on stealing some of my mom's jewelry. But when I snuck past my stepfather's office, I heard him and Clay talking inside."

She takes a deep breath, and I hear a woman's soft murmur on the other side of the line. Her voice firms. "My stepfather has always had a short fuse. He once threw a paperweight at a wall in his office and put a hole right through the plaster. He never fixed it, just hung a photo of himself and some politician over it. On the other side of that wall, there's a small closet. I don't honestly know what possessed me, but I remembered that hole and hid in the closet to listen to them.

"I'd always known they were shady, but the things they were talking about... it was another level. Blackmail and extortion, exploiting witnesses and minors, the list goes on. They dropped names. Talked about a 'black book.' Basically incriminated the fuck out of themselves and their buddies."

I gasp in understanding. "You recorded them."

"Sure did," she says with grim amusement. "I stayed in that tiny closet for over an hour, listening to them jack each other off over how smart they were. They eventually left to go golfing. When I was positive they were gone, I went into the office and straight to the wall safe. My mom had let the code slip once when she was drunk off her ass. I opened the safe and stole everything in it. Jewelry, a few watches, some serious stacks of cash, and that black book."

Chills drip over my scalp and down my body.

"I went straight to a seedy pawn shop and sold what I could. A few hours later, it finally occurred to me how much shit I was in. But I also felt this sense of freedom and... rightness, I guess. I packed a bag, ditched my car, and caught a bus out of town. By the time I reached Idaho, I was dopesick as hell. I also knew it was only a matter of time before those assholes started looking for me, and I wasn't about to be outsmarted by them. So I holed up in a motel and detoxed, and I've been clean ever since."

She pauses, then continues mutedly, "You're probably wondering why I've kept everything to myself all these years. Honestly, I wouldn't blame you if you hated me for it. If I'd handed the book over to the police, you never would have gone through what you did with my stepbrother. He'd be behind bars where he should be."

My throat tightens, cutting off a protest before I can voice it. Because she's right. Even now, resentment prickles over my skin. But it's also not black and white, my emotions complex. I feel sympathy and sadness for her, too.

When I don't say anything, Kendra adds, "I know it's a weak excuse, but the simple reason I never came forward is fear."

Compassion for her drowns out everything else. "Of course you were afraid. You'd been abused and traumatized by them for a decade!"

There's a small, teary laugh. "Yeah, that played a role for sure. Plus, their goons almost caught me twice. After the second near miss, it was obvious they just wanted their dirty secrets back. When I realized my actual life was in danger, I stopped making amateur mistakes. After running for close to six months, I landed in a tiny town on the other side of the country. I met my wife, Kelly, at my first job here. We have two kids now, twin four-year-old girls."

She pauses, and the woman in the background murmurs something I can't hear, her tone comforting. Kendra takes another deep breath.

"I guess as time went on, it became easier to convince myself the past was just the past. I had a new life—I just wanted to forget it all, you know? Then I saw a photo of you and Clay online, and I've been wracked with guilt ever since. I wanted to reach out to you, but all that fear came right back and paralyzed me. I'm sorry, Eva. I'm so sorry I didn't stop him. I'm sorry for putting you in his path in the first place and for how I treated you back then." Her following sob is barely muffled by her hand.

Sympathetic tears prick my eyes. "Kendra, listen to me." I wait for her to sniff and go silent, then soften my voice. "As far as I'm concerned, you don't owe me an apology. Not to compare trauma here, but Clay never threatened my life. I'm sickened by what you went through and don't blame you for wanting to keep yourself and your family safe."

"I'm not sure I deserve that, but thank you," she says tremulously. "When Wilder called me on Friday, I knew I couldn't live with myself if I didn't do something. I already had a basic plan—a failsafe I put together when I was on the run in case something happened to me. Kelly helped me fine-tune and execute it."

Hope soars. I instinctively reach for Wilder's hand, letting the strong grip of his fingers anchor me. I stare into his eyes as I ask, "What does that mean exactly?"

Kendra's voice steadies and sharpens. "In the black book, there was a name—a Seattle detective my stepfather tried and failed to bribe. The detective was pissed, arrested him and everything, but Conrad had a judge in his pocket and made it disappear.

"Suffice to say, that detective held a grudge, and I made his day when I sent him everything. Some of the potential charges, like extortion and wire fraud, have passed the statute of limitations, but a judge has issued warrants for the rest. There's also more than enough to open investigations into the last six years of their practices. He's going to tear them both apart."

My eyes widen more on every word, and Wilder's smile grows.

"He made four arrests today, including my stepfather, and the LAPD should be surprising Clay any minute. Thanks to all their hard work making themselves famous, tomorrow every major news network on the West Coast will be covering the story."

There's vicious satisfaction in her voice as she finishes, "A bunch of assholes are about to have the day they deserve."

I slump into Wilder's chest, boneless with relief.

"Thank you, Kendra. *Thank you.*"

She says thickly, "I can't change what either of us went through, but at least the world will be a tiny bit safer for my daughters. Maybe... maybe someday you guys can meet them?"

Wilder's thumb catches a tear on my cheek as I choke out, "I'd like that."

CHAPTER THIRTY-EIGHT

wilder

THE FOLLOWING MORNING, after arguably the best night's sleep of my life, my own moan transports me from an X-rated dream into an X-rated reality.

"Fuucck."

Evangeline's mouth pops off my cock. She swirls her tongue around my piercing before giving me a wicked smile. Her hands, slick with saliva, keep pumping me at a torturously slow pace.

"Good morning," she says huskily. "Is this okay? You said I could practice while you were asleep."

"Yes. Absolutely. Zero complaints."

She smirks, teasing me with barely there swipes of her tongue. I sink my hands into her sleep-tousled hair, my hips straining off the bed.

"Put me back in your mouth, brat."

Her naked chest flushes, eyelids falling to half-mast. With a small moan, she lowers her head and—shocking the fuck out of me—spits on my dick. The visual makes me jerk in her hands and leak pre-cum right onto her tongue. She hums happily as she laps it up, then takes me into her mouth again.

My fingers tighten in her hair as she returns to a rhythm guaranteed to destroy me. I'm already on the edge, and it takes mere seconds for me to lose it. My fingers and toes tingle, pressure gathering.

"You want my cum, baby?" She whimpers and nods. "Relax your throat. Yessss. *Fuck*, just like that. Swallow every drop."

I groan mindlessly, my climax all the more intense as I keep my eyes open to watch her struggle to swallow it all. She finally rears back, panting, red-cheeked, and glowing with accomplishment.

Fucking immaculate.

She squeaks in surprise as I grab her under the arms and flip us. I drop between her legs, throwing her heels over my shoulders.

"My turn."

♪

A FEW HOURS and orgasms later, we greet Lily, Rye, and Emma at the front door. It takes less than ten minutes for the women to disappear outside, chatting animatedly about weddings and some famous coordinator who agreed to meet with them next week.

I have a feeling we won't see them for a while; if they end up in the studio, I doubt they'll return before dinner.

"Who's my favorite small human?" I ask the giggling toddler standing on my thighs.

"Me, Whyder! Me!"

I gasp and glare at Rye, who's slouched on the opposite couch scrolling on his phone.

"How dare you teach her how to pronounce my name."

He rolls his eyes, not bothering with a reply. Emma

throws her bowl of tiny kid crackers onto the cushion next to us, then squirms off my lap and starts hunting the scattered snacks with her mouth.

"Just like her dad," I note, shifting so I can catch her when she invariably loses balance and tumbles toward the coffee table.

Rye chuckles. "Want to be my best man?"

My head whips toward him at the same time my arm flies out to stop Emma from rolling off the couch. She course corrects, dismissing the crackers in favor of using my arm as a railing to drag herself onto my hunched back.

"Are you serious?" I finally ask.

Rye looks up from his phone with a speculative frown. "You *do* know you're my best friend, right?"

I grin, then let out a grunt as Emma's feet slam into my kidneys. "Hell yes, I'll be your best man." I pause. "Did Evangeline tell you I asked her to move in and she said yes?"

His brows lift in dry amusement. "She did. So did my mom, who heard it from Rose, who heard it from Sophie. At this point, we can assume at least a hundred people know."

"Seriously?" I groan. "Damn, I wanted to surprise my parents."

Rye shakes his head in disbelief. "How have you not learned this lesson? The second Lily finished telling me we were getting married here, I texted my mom, beating Sophie's text by five minutes. Just wait until you have a kid. My mom knew Emma had taken her first steps before I did."

My sympathetic grimace becomes one of pain as Emma yanks my hair. I gently peel her fingers away and swing her around to tickle her. She cackles, swatting at my hands, then abruptly dives off my lap to fish for more crackers.

"How are you feeling about tomorrow?" asks Rye.

My eyes on Emma, I murmur, "Not as nervous as I was.

Shelley told me this morning that only two publications have yet to confirm that they're pulling their articles."

"That's amazing, man. You must be so relieved."

Emma loses interest in the crackers again. Before she can launch onto my back, I hand her a sensory toy with a bunch of colorful domes to pop. She thumps down beside me and starts jabbing the toy like it's personally offended her.

"I don't think it's fully hit me yet. It's been an intense weekend. A lot of emotional extremes."

Rye nods in understanding, then asks hesitantly, "How's Eva handling everything? Not gonna lie, Lily and I were prepared to unplug the TV and hide her phone, but she seems... fine."

"I've been distracting her since we woke up. We only put clothes on ten minutes before you got here."

He makes a face. "Bleh."

My chuckle tapers into a sigh. "She's going to find out all the details soon enough. I wanted her to have a few hours of peace."

"Understandable. The news is awful."

I nod, having skimmed some of it while Evangeline was showering this morning. A lot of what I read wasn't surprising, but there was a summary of a joint LAPD and FBI press conference that I could barely stomach.

In a twisted coincidence, Clay was already on law enforcement radar in a big way, the added evidence from Seattle merely accelerating his arrest. The bulk of the charges are for white-collar crimes: fraud, tax evasion, money laundering, witness tampering, and the like. As with Conrad, Clay is taking others down with him, among them a well-known music producer, a local politician, a judge, and two other lawyers.

But there are other charges against Clay, ones for far more

egregious crimes: multiple counts of sexual assault of a minor and production and distribution of child pornography.

That, I know, is what will fuck Evangeline up the most, not to mention Kendra.

Clay's victim was sixteen when he targeted and coerced her with promises of fame. He also recorded her without her knowing, then threatened to release the videos if she ever told anyone about him. Not only was the footage found on Clay's home computer, there was evidence of it being sent to multiple people.

Now twenty and famous, the victim allowed herself to be named in connection to the case, which is why the story is breaking nationally.

Poppy Cole, Grammy-winning pop star, has vowed to use her platform to spread awareness to her young fanbase about how to recognize and defend against predators.

"I hope he gets prison justice," Rye murmurs.

I nod somberly. "Same."

Emma squirms, huffs in annoyance, and promptly chucks the sensory toy across the room. Rye and I share a knowing smile.

Facing Emma, I widen my eyes. "Who wants to go for a walk and collect flowers for their mommy and Aunt Eva before lunch?"

"Me!" she screeches, jumping up and down. I catch her as she nosedives off the couch.

CHAPTER THIRTY-NINE

evangeline

THREE WEEKS LATER

MY PEN SCRATCHES over a page in my journal, the words sloppy, almost illegible. But I don't suppose it matters. I already know I'll never read this one again.

I'm barely cognizant of what I'm writing, only the effort and necessity of it. My aching fingers. Shallow breaths. Sweaty palms. The unknown force that wakes me each morning and propels me into the office downstairs, where I spend an hour or more metaphorically bleeding onto a blank page.

Pausing to stretch a cramp from my hand, I look at the sticky notes lining the top of the desk. A new one appears every day, all of them various quotes in Wilder's handwriting.

The newest reads:

> FORGIVE YOURSELF FOR
> NOT KNOWING WHAT YOU
> DIDN'T KNOW BEFORE
> YOU LEARNED IT.
>
> ~MAYA ANGELOU

I'm trying.

Fuck, I'm really trying.

Talking to Kendra has helped, as have conversations with my mom, Rose, and Wilder. Each of them has experience with where I find myself—at the intersection between anger, guilt, and self-forgiveness. Between them and twice-weekly video calls with my new therapist, I'm learning how to navigate my jagged internal landscape.

I do my best to stay focused on the present and grounded in gratitude for my life. For the opportunity to learn and heal and *feel*. For Wilder, for the love and forgiveness of my family and friends. For the Glow album Lily and I are recording, and for the magnanimity of Cory Donovan at Indigo Records, who accepted my stumbling, heartfelt apologies and didn't hesitate to offer us a new contract.

And I'm deeply grateful for Poppy Cole, who reached out to me after a video I posted on social media went viral. In it, I spoke candidly about Clay's emotional abuse, my shame and struggles to recover from it, and my disgust for his actions. I also said I hope his dick falls off and he never sees the sun again, but Anita made me cut that part out.

Poppy's and my first conversation started off painfully awkward and ended with tears. She shared that a week or so after I left Clay and disappeared, their paths crossed at a charity luncheon. Over the years, she'd grown numb to seeing him at events, but this time he was baldly attempting to charm a seventeen-year-old singer just starting out in the industry. Overcome with rage, she intervened. He later pulled her aside and threatened to release the videos of her at sixteen if she stepped out of line again.

The interaction sent her into a week-long depressive episode that ended with what she called, "the mother of all 'fuck it' moments."

Turns out that Poppy, like Kendra, kept receipts. Emails. Text messages. Voicemails. Photos. All damning, all proving that not only did Clay manipulate her into thinking he was the ticket to success in the music industry, he coerced her into having sex not only with him but several others. All when she was barely sixteen, newly emancipated from her parents and fresh off the bus from a small town in Colorado.

Through untamed sobs, I told her how sorry I was, that I was in awe of her, and that I hoped she knew how unbelievably brave she was. She broke down too, then said something that cemented her a place in my heart forever.

"In one way or another, I've been a victim my whole life. Of people like my parents, of men like Clay, of a world that taught me that my worth was measured by how pleasing I was to others. I'm done with all of it. No more contorting myself to fit into the tiny box they forced me into. I want to be free."

We've talked almost daily since, and I've basically adopted her as my little sister. She's visiting Seattle soon; I'm flying down to support her when she's called to testify. Lily and I have also committed to partnering with her on her campaign aimed at empowering young women.

None of this has been easy, but every day I find a little

more space in my heart for acceptance of the past and of myself.

Closing my journal, I scan the collection of sticky notes. My lips quirk at the randomness of Wilder's small, daily gifts.

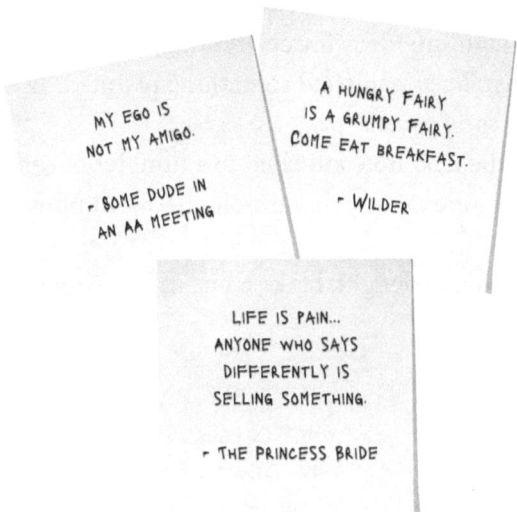

MY EGO IS
NOT MY AMIGO.

⌐ SOME DUDE IN
AN AA MEETING

A HUNGRY FAIRY
IS A GRUMPY FAIRY.
COME EAT BREAKFAST.

⌐ WILDER

LIFE IS PAIN...
ANYONE WHO SAYS
DIFFERENTLY IS
SELLING SOMETHING.

⌐ THE PRINCESS BRIDE

When I read the last one, my stomach growls. A glance at the clock startles me—it's almost ten. Usually by now, I'd have heard Wilder singing in the kitchen, as he does whenever I lose track of time writing and breakfast is getting cold.

I tuck my journal and pen into their dedicated drawer, then poke my head into the hallway. Silence greets me, and a sniff confirms the absence of the French toast he promised to make for my birthday.

Rather than disappointment, giddiness fills me at the possibility he might still be asleep. He doesn't sleep in often, and since my own sleep has drastically improved, I haven't had as many opportunities for my favorite challenge: seeing if I can make him orgasm before he wakes up.

581

I take an eager step toward the stairs, then stop abruptly when a flash of bright yellow catches my eye. A few feet down the hallway, a sticky note is attached to the wall. There are no words, just an arrow pointing toward the kitchen.

With a rueful smile for the lost opportunity, I follow Wilder's prompt. Given his caginess over the last week whenever I brought up ideas for celebrating my thirtieth, I should have known he already had something planned.

Sweet, sneaky man.

I find the next note attached to a tumbler of coffee, beside which sits one of the lemon-blueberry muffins we made yesterday.

Humming in delight, I take a bite as I peel off the note.

WHAT IS ROUGH
BUT SMOOTH
AND ALSO
SUSPICIOUS

Laughing softly, I grab the tumbler and head out the back door into the morning sunshine.

Despite my rising excitement, I walk slowly, enjoying the fresh air as I nibble on the muffin and sip delicious coffee. Each deep inhale brings a bouquet of scents I've come to associate with peace and happiness: salty air, pine, and petrichor mingling with the faint sweetness of lilacs and lilies.

I'm mid-swallow when I reach the small clearing and see who's sitting on the sex stump. I promptly gasp, then choke, and end up bent over and coughing uncontrollably. Footsteps rush toward me and a broad hand pounds my back—a completely unhelpful and yet utterly reassuring gesture.

"Dad?" I wheeze, straightening and wiping my tearing eyes with the back of my hand. "What—what are you doing here? How did you get here?"

Pale eyes sparkling warmly, he hands me three bright red tulips. "Wilder opened the side gate for me. Happy birthday, pipsqueak."

I snort at the ancient nickname. "Thanks. Is Mom here? Where's Wilder? I'm so confused."

He grins. "It'll make sense eventually. Will you sit with me for a minute?"

Smiling uncertainly, I nod. He returns to the stump and I settle beside him, hoping my coughing fit is a sufficient explanation for my red cheeks. Privately, I vow to punish Wilder, as I have zero doubts he suggested this location to my dad just to mess with me.

Especially since the last time I was naked here was *yesterday*.

Oblivious to my inner freak-out, my dad says, "There's something I wanted to talk to you about."

At his serious tone, my tumbler stalls halfway to my mouth. I lower it back to my knee, belatedly registering his tense shoulders, fidgeting fingers, and tapping feet. All rare signs of nervousness from a man who normally drips easy confidence.

I clear my throat weakly. "Sure, Dad. I'm all ears."

"This may sound random at first, but bear with me." He takes a deep breath, his gaze lowering to the forest floor. "I had a pretty great childhood. Lived in a good neighborhood. No abuse, no financial or food insecurity. No major trauma besides my dad splitting when I was eleven, which was honestly a good thing for all of us. Plus, your grandpa Bill came along a few years later and he was an amazing stepdad. And I'm sure this next information will come as a surprise, but I was also popular in high school."

I gasp dramatically. "No way!"

He chuckles. "I had a ton of friends, and don't tell your mom, but I've always been a hit with the ladies."

My laugh is mostly a groan. Growing up with a sex symbol for a father was both aggravating and hilarious. It wasn't uncommon for my friends to blush and stammer in his presence, thanks to easily accessible old photoshoots of him in his underwear. Their moms weren't much better and in a few cases, they were a lot worse. Talk about awkward.

My mom truly is a saint, though my dad does deserve some credit for making her feel secure. He's never been shy— in fact, he can be downright obnoxious—about expressing his devotion to her in public.

"I met Julian and the guys right after graduation, and within two years, we were famous." He pauses, the vestiges of humor fading from his face. "Nothing was ever really *hard* for me. I wouldn't say I was oblivious to pain or struggle—I had my fair share of disappointment, heartache, and the like. But I was seriously lucky on a lot of levels. And for the most part, I stayed that charmed, clueless kid until my early thirties."

He looks up at me, his expression anguished. Fine hairs lift on my arms, my awareness narrowing to the pain in his eyes. Though a breeze teases strands of my hair against my cheek, I can't feel the tickle. Nor do I register the wood beneath me, the white-knuckled grip I have on the tumbler and flower stems, or the air trapped in my lungs as I hold my breath.

"The thing is, Eva, I'd never experienced true grief until your mom and I lost your older sister to a miscarriage. And I'd never felt real fear until the day I found out Sophie was pregnant with you. From the moment you were born, I've been terrified of something happening to you. When you were a baby, I'd watch you sleep to make sure you didn't stop breathing, then pass out in the morning when your mom woke up. As you grew up, the fear ebbed and flowed. Some ages were easier than others."

I stare at him, completely blindsided but also... not. He's always been protective of Hunter and me, but especially me —to the point it became a running joke among my friends. At varying times, I've appreciated and resented him for it. But while I've always suspected the loss of my older sister had something to do with his status as a worrier, I had no idea the underlying fear was so extreme.

He continues hoarsely, "It got really bad after you moved out at eighteen. I'd wake up in the middle of the night freaking out that something was wrong. More than once, your mom had to stop me from calling you or driving to your place to make sure you were okay. She eventually bullied me into talking to a professional."

Despite the gravity of the moment, my lips quirk. "You mean she casually suggested it?"

His eyes crinkle as he nods in concession, but his expression swiftly sobers.

"I started seeing someone again a couple of years ago. They've helped a lot. I'm not perfect yet, but I'm working on it. All that is to say, I'm sorry for being a controlling, overbearing ass of a father. I'm sorry for not being strong enough to fight the fear that told me I had to shelter you from a world that could hurt you, even if it cost me your trust. All you ever needed was my compassion and love, and I..." His eyes redden, tears welling. "I failed to give you what could have actually protected you."

The words drop inside me like boulders, the ensuing

ripples spreading and illuminating my father in a new and profound way. Moreover, I see myself and so many others inside him, our experiences different reflections on the same water. And for an instant, I also glimpse something bigger than all of us.

I see *love*—the complexity and potency of it. The brilliant light it casts and the shadows that light naturally creates.

Trust. Tenderness. Peace.

Guilt. Worry. Fear.

I set down the tulips and my coffee, then grab my dad's hands.

"You know what I remember about growing up with you as my dad? Nature walks, making forts, and epic scavenger hunts. The countless times you read me another book when I asked, even though it was past my bedtime, and all the funny voices you did for different characters. I remember your endless patience when teaching me how to swim, how to play guitar, how to drive. I remember how much we laughed—you made me laugh so, so much. Mostly, though, I remember feeling safe."

Tears spill down his cheeks. Down mine, too. I squeeze his hands harder.

"You are and have always been exactly the father I need. I've never once doubted that you loved me. Don't you see? You did protect me, Dad. I'm here. I'm okay—more than okay, actually. I'm *happy*. And a huge part of why is that I finally found my way to something you taught me was possible. The ultimate prize on your greatest scavenger hunt."

"What's that, pipsqueak?" he whispers.

Emotion overwhelms me. I don't fight it, instead letting it emerge as a tear-soaked laugh.

"Joy, Dad. You showed me the way to joy."

CHAPTER FORTY

wilder

THE PIANO BENCH creaks as I sit with a huff and check my watch for the tenth time in the last five minutes. Unfortunately, I'm once again shown that my racing thoughts haven't affected the rotation of the planet, which continues at a snail's pace.

What the hell is taking so long?

Before leading the people I roped into Evangeline's first birthday surprise to five different, memorable-to-us areas on the property, I made sure they knew to keep each visit to ten minutes or less. Matt texted me over two hours ago when he saw her approaching him from the house, but I haven't heard from anyone else. Has she seen Martin yet? Rye and Lily? Her mom and Hunter? My parents?

Unable to stay still, I spring to my feet and start pacing again.

If all she had to eat was the muffin I left for her, she's likely starving by now. I should have had everyone give her little snacks instead of flowers. Or flowers first, then a snack when they gave her the next clue.

Pausing near a couch, I press the heels of my hands into

my eyes and groan. Maybe this was a bad idea. Just because she used to never shut up about her dad's scavenger hunts as a kid doesn't mean they're still important to her.

I should have stuck with French toast and orgasms for her birthday morning and kept with my original plan of a surprise dinner party tonight. The party is still happening, but at this point I won't have enough time to make the focaccia from scratch.

Five minutes later, I've walked around the studio another few times, reworked the grocery order in my head, and am halfway through scripting an apology for fucking up her birthday when the door of the studio swings open.

My stomach does a backflip.

I spin around.

The first thing I notice are the flowers I cut this morning, now an impressive bouquet. Then I see her teary, mismatched eyes. Finally, I take in her bright, gorgeous smile.

Air rushes from my lungs. Relief turns my legs viscous, gluing me to the floor.

"Happy birthday, Fairy," I croak.

Evangeline closes the door, then sets down the bouquet and a small stack of yellow sticky notes. As she walks toward me, her smile softens, changes, until it's *my smile*.

She's every sunset and sunrise.

Moonlight on a moving river.

Wind in a desert canyon.

Music on the precipice of sleep.

When she jumps into my arms koala-style, I catch her with an "ooof" that makes her giggle. She peppers kisses all over my face, then hugs the shit out of me.

"Thank you, Wilder. It was perfect. I love you so much. You did so, so good."

Warm, fuzzy bliss spreads through me. Melts my anxiety. Relaxes my muscles.

Huh. Guess I'm a praise princess, too.

"Isn't that my line?" I rumble.

Her smile curves against my ear. "Not this time. Carry me to the couch, please."

There's a rasp in her tone that my body hears before my ears, sending a rush of blood south. I do as I'm told, dropping onto the cushions with her in my lap. She makes soft, happy sounds as she trails hot kisses over my throat.

When her hips start to move, I groan and grab her waist. "While I'm completely on board with this, I want to make sure you—"

"Yes, Wilder." Her kisses move over my jaw toward my mouth. "I know there are eight people waiting for us at the house. Our dads are making lunch for everyone, but we should probably hurry."

"Say no more."

Our lips brush, smiles meeting. Despite our words, our kiss begins softly, slowly. A tender exploration sprinkled with sighs. But when our tongues touch, fire meets oxygen.

We ignite.

My jeans are unzipped, my cock seized by strong, delicate fingers. I pull off her baggy shirt, then tug the cups of her bra down to expose her breasts. The decision backfires, immediately distracting me from my primary purpose. I twist us to the side and lower her to the couch, then shimmy down to feast on her nipples.

I barely get a taste before she tugs my head up. Blinking in confusion, I take in her glazed eyes, flushed cheeks, and swollen lips that curve into a knowing smile as I watch.

"Inside me. Now. Kiss me as you fuck me hard and fast."

I surge upward, claiming her lips. She opens to give me

her tongue. I suck on it, swallowing her thready moan as I fumble for the waist of her cotton bike shorts. She tries to help, lifting her hips so I can pull them down, but ends up almost kneeing me in the balls. Her gasp and my chuckle are joined by the sound of cotton tearing.

"Oops," I mumble, tugging the now-loose fabric away from her body.

She fists my hair. Kisses me harder. Writhes beneath me, soft and warm and silky. Her legs frame my hips.

We move like music. We *are* music. Mesmerizing and melodic, electric and haunting. Transcendent.

As I sink inside her, I surrender myself to our song. To her. Only now when I give her all of me, she gives me all of her in return.

Every note, breath, and word.

Intro to outro.

First verse to last chorus.

EVANGELINE

ONE YEAR LATER

"DID EVERYONE HAVE FUN TONIGHT?"

The roar that answers me raises the hairs on my body and buzzes beneath my skin. I look across the stage at Lily, who grins back from behind her DJ deck.

"I think that's a yes," I tell her.

She leans toward her mic and says with mock serious-ness, "I'm not convinced. Let's try that again. *Horizon Fest, did you have fun tonight?*"

The volume of sound almost doubles, drowning out my laughter and filling me with effervescent joy. The stage lights flash, purple and blue beams obscuring the stars overhead and strobing across a sea of twenty-five thousand screaming faces.

A subtle, atmospheric beat begins courtesy of Lily.

"You've been amazing," I tell the crowd. "We have one last song for you. It's a new one you might have heard recently."

I pluck a series of chords on my guitar, and the crowd responds immediately to the melody of our newest single's chorus.

Lily's beat silences abruptly, the light display freezing.

"Wait a sec," she says. "Aren't we missing something?"

I look offstage, my heart skipping when I see Wilder already watching me.

"You're absolutely right. Hey, Night Theory, are you guys too tired from your set last night or can you help us out?"

The crowd goes berserk as the men walk onstage. Wilder angles for me, Zander beelines for the baby grand piano, and Jax takes a seat behind my cello. Eddie walks out last and wanders in exaggerated circles until Lily offers him a set of maracas.

"I handle the beats on this stage," she says sweetly.

As the crowd laughs and screams, Wilder's hand slides across the bare, sweaty skin of my lower back. When his fingers clench on my hip with dark promise, my small, involuntary gasp is amplified. Which, naturally, the crowd loves.

Wilder's soft chuckle floats around the amphitheater, followed by low words that drip suggestion.

"I'm always available to help you, Evangeline."

Catcalls fill our ears as I roll my eyes. "Flirt with me later. We have a song to sing."

"Actually, there's something I have to do first. It'll just take a minute."

My lips part in shock as he steps back. He looks offstage and nods at someone I can't see.

"What's going on?" My question falls flat, the mic in front of me having been turned off remotely.

Lily's mic, however, is still on. She says lightly, "No problem, Wilder. Take all the time you need."

I whip around to see her grinning at me. Quick glances

confirm that Jax, Eddie, and Zander wear similar expressions of conspiratorial glee.

My heart stampedes.

My breaths turn shallow.

I spin back toward Wilder right as the stage lights go out completely. Momentarily disoriented, I seek the ever present glow of phones in the crowd.

But what I see isn't an ocean of bobbing, tiny white dots anymore. Floating on the surface are hundreds, possibly thousands of bright blue LED lights. They're organized into wavy, imperfect lines. Creating letters. Forming two words.

MARRY

ME

The crowd begins to chant.

"Say. Yes. Say. Yes."

Sparkles line the edges of my vision, then grow brighter. It takes me a second to realize the stage lights are slowly rising. My body feels heavy, unusually clumsy as I turn fast, almost taking out the mic stand with the headstock of my guitar.

Wilder is down on one knee.

I absorb him in sequence, like dramatic notes of an incomparable song. Messy dark hair, strands dancing in the wind from a nearby fan. Golden, inked skin. My sunrise smile, one dimple deeper than the other. Enchanted forest eyes radiating hope and love.

My gaze finally falls to his uplifted hand and the glittering ring pinched between two fingers.

The chanting is so loud he has to shout. "Evangeline

Marie Sullivan, my Fairy and muse forever, will you marry me?"

I'm already nodding—laughing and crying—as I fumble to unfasten the strap of my guitar from its pins. Thankfully, Eddie steps forward to help and in seconds I'm free.

I launch at Wilder, catching him as he starts to rise and propelling us both to the ground. He shakes with laughter beneath me. Squeezes me tightly. Lifts my hand, slips the perfectly sized ring on my finger, then grabs my face for a kiss.

"Aww," coos Lily. "I think that's a yes!"

A mighty wave of sound crests and crashes atop us. Swirls and cocoons us. I savor the remains of Wilder's smile. Drink our mingled tears. Revel in the harmony of the small, perfect space we create in the universe.

"I love you," I mumble against his lips.

I feel rather than hear his hum of satisfaction. His hold shifts, hands lowering to my hips as his tongue dips inside my mouth.

"Hey, now!" hollers Zander. "This isn't that kind of show."

Wilder chuckles and gives me one last kiss. Then he sits up, bringing me with him. I'm grateful when he does most of the work getting us back to our feet.

Hands cupping my shoulders, his eyes twinkle down at me.

He asks, "Will you sing with me?"

The nearby mic is back on, projecting his question and my answer: "Always."

He retrieves my guitar from Eddie, and I cradle the comforting weight as he reattaches the strap. When the instrument is secure, I quickly wipe my eyes, then step back into position with a small, ecstatic laugh.

Over deafening cheers, I say, "I think it's safe to assume I'll never forget tonight. Thank you all for being a part of it."

The audible strain in my voice sends my barely recovered pulse racing anew. Swallowing heavily, I look imploringly at Wilder. I'm supposed to introduce the song, but I need a minute if I have any hopes of doing it justice. And my emotional overwhelm is his fault, anyway.

Wilder reads the request in my eyes and doesn't hesitate, grabbing my reaching hand and stepping up to the mic.

As he speaks, I slow my breathing and stretch out my neck and shoulders. The last few minutes go into a box in my head—a temporary one that I'll gladly revisit when we're alone. When I can break down in the privacy of our trailer. Actually look at the ring he put on me. Let him hold me while I cry through the endorphin crash. *And* maybe yell at him a little for blindsiding me before tearing off his clothes.

"Horizon Fest, your energy is fucking nuts. I love it. I want to say a quick thank you to my blue-light volunteers. You guys came through for me in a big way. I'll be forever grateful. Unfortunately, you're still not invited to the wedding."

Laughter and whistles float toward the stars. The joyous sounds are a magic spell on my nervous system, leveling out my energy and relaxing my throat. With a sigh of relief, I squeeze Wilder's fingers to let him know I'm good to go. He squeezes me back, and another shot of calm hits my bloodstream.

"Eva and I wrote this next song together. It's dedicated to two amazing, brave women who happen to be here with us tonight. Everyone say hello to Poppy Cole and Kendra Monroe!"

The screens around the stage switch to a crowd view, zooming in on the VIP section where Kendra, her wife, and their twins are screaming and jumping. Next to them stands

Poppy, casually dressed and makeup-free. Her response is genuine but more subdued, a smile and a small wave.

Wilder winks at me, then releases my hand and shifts into position for backup vocals. The stage lights dim, and the multi-tonal roar of the crowd tapers to an expectant thrum.

As I make a final adjustment to the pedals at my feet, Jax plays a few spine-tingling scales on the cello, and Zander teases the song's piano intro. Not to be excluded, Eddie shakes a maraca near his brother's microphone.

I glance over at Lily. We share a giddy smile. As I turn back around, a deep breath creates space in my lungs, in my heart. I gaze out at the crowd, a writhing sea of light and shadow.

Wilder's fingers graze my back.

"Thanks again, Horizon Fest. We're Glow, these guys are Night Theory, and this song is 'Accidental Grace.'"

"Accidental Grace" ♡

SHE RESTS BETWEEN STARS
DREAMS OF WATER AND WIND
UNTIL HER PATIENCE THINS
AND SHE WAKES

THE WORLD WILL SHAKE
THE CHAINS WILL BREAK

Find her tomorrow
where the river begins
Listen for mayhem
A storm in the wind

Her tears, they'll carve canyons
Bring life to our wastelands

So find her tomorrow
where the river begins
Listen for mayhem
A storm in the wind

SHE'S COMING
OH LISTEN, SHE'S COMING
ACCIDENTAL GRACE
CLAIMING HER PLACE

six months later

BONUS EPILOGUE

MUSIC TALKS

WITH ALEX ILOKA

ALEX: Welcome back to Music Talks. We just heard "Parade of Stars," the newest single from Night Theory's forthcoming album, *Vespertine*. If you're just tuning in, I'm here with frontman Wilder Ashburn. Wilder, I really love this song. Is it true this was the first time in a decade you cowrote lyrics with someone?

WILDER: You look entirely too thrilled, Alex.

ALEX: (laughs) Sorry. You know how much I love Night Theory's first album.

WILDER: In case any listeners are as annoyed with Alex's vagueness as I am, the track was cowritten with my fiancé, Eva Marie. She was a founding member of Night Theory, and she also happens to be the only musician— besides Lily Aoki—who Alex hasn't roasted the fuck out of at least once.

ALEX: (laughs) What can I say? The dynamic duo of Glow has proven to me time and time again that musical genius survives in this world.

WILDER: I'd have to agree.

ALEX: These days Glow and Night Theory have drastically different sounds—I can't be the only one curious as to whether your individual songwriting processes have changed over time, perhaps making it more challenging to work together.

WILDER: Was there a question in there?

ALEX: This is exactly why my colleagues have stopped trying to interview you, Wilder.

WILDER: (laughs)

ALEX: Talk to me about what it was like to cowrite with Eva again. Was it more challenging than when you were in Night Theory together?

WILDER: Not really. In a lot of ways, writing music with Eva again was like coming home. Nostalgic. Did you know we wrote our first song together when she was eleven and I was thirteen?

ALEX: No, but I'd pay money to listen to it.

WILDER: We'd both pay you not to.

ALEX: (laughs) So was cowriting now a conflict-free process for you guys?

WILDER: Fuck no, but I do think that when we were younger we argued a lot more. Probably because of unaddressed tensions in our friendship.

ALEX: Ahh.

WILDER: Stop winking at me.

ALEX: (laughs) Sorry, continue.

WILDER: You're right about our individual processes changing over time, so yeah, it took us a few hours to merge back together creatively.

ALEX: A few *hours?* That's impressive.

WILDER: I guess. But we had a solid foundation, so it felt natural. Kind of like, I don't know... putting together an old puzzle for the millionth time. We could do it blindfolded. Only now, there's a clearer, bigger picture on the surface. Basically no matter how much time passes, our pieces will always click.

ALEX: (blows nose) Shit. That made me emotional.

WILDER: You should talk to a therapist about that.

ALEX: Let an old man have his feelings, Wilder. I have to ask—are we going to hear Eva singing on the *Vespertine* album?

WILDER: I can neither confirm nor deny.

ALEX: That's a yes.

WILDER: Have I told you how much you annoy me?

ALEX: Many times.
    Speaking of time, we don't have much left. I'd like to veer briefly into more serious territory, if that's okay with you?

WILDER: Yeah, okay.

ALEX: In the last few months, you and Eva—among a slew of other famous faces—have been vocal supporters of Poppy Cole's new organization, GirlJoy.

WILDER: That's right. We believe wholeheartedly in what she's doing.

ALEX: I do as well. I'll be dropping more information on GirlJoy in the show notes so our listeners can check it out. It's a great organization that's already accomplishing a lot.
    (clears throat)

WILDER: Unless the constipated look on your face means you're having another heart attack, find your balls and get to the point.

ALEX: Funny. (pause) Clay Eaton's final sentencing hearing was all over the news last week. How are you feeling about the judge's decision?

WILDER: How I'm feeling about it doesn't matter.

ALEX: Right, of course.

WILDER: Don't be a chickenshit, Alex. What you really want to ask is how Eva's feeling about it.

ALEX: I can't tell if you're about to punch me or not.

WILDER: Relax, this is my resting expression. I actually had a feeling this topic would come up, so I already discussed it with Eva. Lucky for you, she has a soft spot for your crotchety old ass. The simple answer is that she's relieved—obviously, since the chances of Clay breathing free air in the next eighty years years is slim. But like Poppy said publicly last week, trauma doesn't magically disappear when your abuser is held accountable. And that's all I'm going to say.

ALEX: I'm really glad Eva has you for support, and that Poppy has the two of you in her corner. The whole situation is vile, especially the backlash online against Poppy. I can't believe some of the shit I've read. It's like it didn't matter that there was irrefutable evidence of Eaton's crimes. Somehow, because a woman was at the forefront of the media coverage of the trial, it must have been some elaborate frame-job? Fucking absurd.

WILDER: Preaching to the choir, Alex. We could talk all day about how fucked up society is, but what's the point? All we can really do is speak up for what's right when the opportunity presents itself. That, and remind the people we care about that no matter how loud the bullies are, they're still bullshit background noise. Meaningless static. Eva and Poppy know this, which is why one of the objectives of GirlJoy is to help women everywhere learn how to protect their peace both online and offline. The bottom line is that Clay Eaton was found guilty on all counts in both federal and municipal courts. Case fucking closed.

ALEX: Amen. Thanks for answering.

WILDER: Thank Eva.

ALEX: Ha, will do. Back to a lighter topic before we wrap things up—I want you to know how much it warms my pacemaker that two of my favorite musicians are making music and memories together again.

WILDER: Nice try, but you're not invited to the wedding.

ALEX: Joke's on you, buddy. Got the invite in the mail yesterday.

WILDER: (groans)

ALEX: Shit, I almost forgot to ask—what did you think of my article?

WILDER: What article?

ALEX: I'll give you a hint—two years ago, it was a happy new year.

WILDER: No idea what you're talking about.

ALEX: Come on! Okay, here's another one: I used my initials for the pseudonym.

WILDER: A... I... (pause) Hold up, are you seriously telling me that *you're* Angie Irving? You wrote that long as fuck 'star-crossed lovers' article?

ALEX: In the flesh.

WILDER: - - -

ALEX: Do I get to come to the wedding now?

WILDER: Fine.

ALEX: (laughs) Thanks for coming on the show today, Wilder. I can't wait to hear the entirety of *Vespertine*. If the rest of the album is as good as "Parade of Stars," I predict you'll be taking home another gramophone next year.

WILDER: Thanks, Alex. Always a tolerable experience talking with you.

ALEX: (laughs) This is Alex Iloka with *Music Talks.* Thanks for joining us, everyone. Until the next song.

Want more bonus material?

afterword

Thank you so much for reading Wilder and Evangeline's love story. I know it was hard at times, but I hope the landing was soft.

I'd like to briefly address the two heaviest themes in the duet: addiction and emotional abuse. If Wilder's struggles or Evangeline's experience resonate with you, **you are not alone.**

Asking for help can be daunting, but I promise—*I promise* —there are hands outstretched to catch you. All you have to do is keep your eyes on the horizon and reach. And you'll fly.

If you or someone you love is suffering, here are some resources to be used when it's safe to make a phone call:

National Drug Helpline
1-844-289-0879

National Domestic Violence Hotline
1-800-799-7233

Suicide & Crisis Lifeline
Dial 988

Substance Abuse and Mental Health Services
Administration (SAMHSA)
1-800-662-HELP

All my love,
Laura

stay connected

www.lmhalloran.com
lm@lmhalloran.com

playlist

"Can't Get You Out of My Head"—Johnny Goth
"You Broke Me First"—Tate McRae
"buzzkill"—MOTHICA
"Girls Like You"—The Naked And Famous
"Wasted Youth"—goddard, Cat Burns
"War"—Chance Peña
"Darkside"—grandson
"Oxytocin"—Chandler Leighton
"Your Touch"—Foreign Air
"My Perfection"—Tokyo Project
"Toxic"—Omido, Rich Jansen
and more...

also by c.m. halloran

about the author

When not writing or reading, the author can be found daydreaming or trying to keep up with her daughter (and laundry). Some of her favorite things are walking barefoot, moon gazing, and small dogs that resemble Ewoks.

Home is the Pacific Northwest.

lmhalloran.com